I0638967

Sundry Short Stories
by
Richard R. Kennedy

Publisher
Author
Boynton Beach, FL

(© 2002, Unpublished. Revised for publication: © 2006)

Second printing

ISBN: 978-0-6151-6823-4

Published by
Richard R. Kennedy
Boynton Beach, FL 33426-8331

Printed by Lulu in the United States of America

Contents   Page #

 The author was born at the family home in the Bronx, Throgs Neck, long before the bridge was built and grew up during the Depression. In early '44, he joined the Marine Corps. He was in the first wave at Okinawa. After the war, thanks to the GI Bill, he went to college and later became a high school English teacher, and is now retired. Richard fell back on his experiences to write a war novel, including his observations on difficult times in the 30s.

These short stories are a result of his long experiences as a teacher, husband and father who was never distant from sensitivity toward the human condition.

Asides

A new driver walked up to the counter at her office to drop off supplies; he was struck by the young woman whose eyes flashed up from the terminal screen. She jumped from behind the desk to receive the order. The simple transaction was invaded by curious glances and flirtatious remarks. He left with her phone number, confident she was a descendant of Helen of Troy. She returned to data-entry all thumbs, forgetting her lighted cigarette, so taken by this new dimension. Sated by the singles scene and thus vulnerable to the vagaries of romantic perceptions, both tagged karma to this chance meeting.

Several enchantingly romantic weekends led to decisive marriage rather than to an insulting arrangement, hedging the purity of their feelings. Both were reasonably ambitious, going to night school together, twice a week; still they sustained uninterrupted time for each other going into the fourth month of their blissful relationship.

From the outset of their marriage, and despite her feminist leaning, on the way home from work—when free of night school—an unlit cigarette in her mouth, and filled with the expectation of a lovely evening, she would stop at the neighborhood supermarket. Shopping was dominated by what she thought— more accurately what his mother knew—would please him. Before reaching the apartment she would slide the unsmoked cigarette back into its rumpled pack. Recently, however, work and school, caught up to her, and she had to skip the ritual; they settled for frozen dinners. Today she would shop for him.

His custom was to arrive home before her, tidy up a little and shower. Every week, he would first stop at a florist. He had been indifferent to flowers—they belonged in a yard. Since the advent of love he perceived their soft gracefulness as symbolic of his beloved. In the beginning he would come home with a dozen. The second month was reduced to a half dozen every other week. Today he arrived at the modest apartment and replaced last week's desiccative single rose on the snack bar with today's gardenia. He pushed aside yesterday's newspaper and sat down on the sofa to watch a talk show.

He heard her coughing at the door and rushed down to the entry. She had elbowed her way through the downstairs door and placed the bags on a bench so she could remove the over-puffed cigarette before it burned her mouth. He carried up the parcels for the night's dinner.

He praised her for the choice of menu; for she was steadfast in keeping within the stricture of what his mother advised. She had prepared chicken fricassee, which she detested. Nevertheless, to her it was not a sacrifice; she held fast to the belief that it was a deserving service to the goddess of love. When she was finished with the cooking, the kitchenette looked to him as though she had serviced the god of war.

After his second helping he smiled, leaned over and kissed her. Considerately she concealed from him the awful aftertaste of slimy chicken on her lips; nor did he evidence repulsion from her cigarette breath. As always he bounced up to clear the table and wash the dishes, nobly insisting that she relax and watch the VCR's recording of the day's "soaps."

The soaps habit was simply a carry-over from her early single days when she would squeeze the recorded shows in between her business course assignments. At first, little attention was paid to them: she preferred to look admiringly over her shoulder at his busying about and whistling behind the bar. When he would return to the couch, their intense interest in each other took precedence over the TV. After the third month she would occasionally take her eyes from the screen and look over her shoulder with mild humor at the many different expressions on his face. Tonight, she cast a scowl over her shoulder at his rough handling of pots and dishes—punctuating his mumbles and growls concerning her disorderly kitchen style.

He sat down beside her, and she kissed him on the cheek in gratitude that he had finally ended his clanging session in the kitchenette. Weary and restless from staring at the same old faces and hearing the same old cliches from the TV, he picked up *Sport's Illustrated* and noisily thumbed the pages. She placed a delicate hand over the magazine and shushed him. He tightened his lips, wobbled his head and resumed browsing through the swimsuit edition unobtrusively under the drone of soapy chitchat.

Without taking her eyes from the tube, she reached across him, her hand fumbling for the cigarettes on the end table. He grumbled and put the matches and pack in her hand and followed up by placing a shiny ashtray on her lap. Again he rustled the pages noisily until pausing at the swimsuit section. He gazed into the breasts of one of the healthy models; he was sure the curvaceous model never smoked. She struck a match. He hated the rude spike of sulphur. "I must buy her a lighter," he thought. He coughed and rubbed his eyes to gain attention. Oblivious to him, she just gazed at the smoky screen of daily icons. When she crushed out her cigarette, he immediately reached for the ashtray, jumped up, emptied it behind the bar and scrubbed it under the faucet and left it to dry. He reached into the sink cabinet for deodorant and sprayed the room.

When he sat down again to resume ogling the magazine, she tugged his arm, wrapped it round her shoulder and snuggled up to him, but sniffed his uniform shirt and jerked her head away. He forgot the magazine, contented for a while just to watch the cast of dozens dodging in out of fleeting scenes. In a few minutes he was bored; he rested his cheek on her pate to luxuriate in the silky softness, but he recoiled from the reek of dead smoke in her hair. He opted for the screen's display of beautiful people leading ugly lives.

She slid from under his arm, exhaled short spurts from her nostrils and lit another cigarette. She looked at him quizzically, not knowing where to put the match. He jumped up to retrieve the ashtray. With a smirk he handed it to her, then returned to sulk in the swimsuit world. He was certain that the long flowing dark hair of the bathing beauty was smoke free. Putting down her cigarette she picked up the remote and fast-forwarded through commercials.

She moaned, "Oh, darling, my cigarette is all wet!" She crushed it out, and lit another, then whined, "Why can't you simply empty trays like normal people?"

He countered, "Why can't you give up smoking? It's the normal thing to do nowadays." She glowered at him and puffed away. He rose up sharply, magazine tightly rolled in his fist, and stormed the bathroom. Undisturbed, she lay back, stretched her legs on the sofa and lost herself in the eternal twining of pseudo plots.

Still clothed, he emerged from the bathroom after a half hour. She rolled her head in the pillow grimacing, having hoped he would appear—commensurate with her Adonic impression—wrapped sexily in a towel, his body and hair refreshed as had been his custom in the beginning. He announced he was going to bed. She looked up askance, nodded absently and before re-engaging the electronic world of enviable lives, she sighed in relief that he would be sound asleep by the time she was ready for bed. She picked up the remote to fast forward, but hesitated when a handsome model was sudsing his powerful chest under the spray. She glanced at the bedroom door and mumbled to herself, "Humph,…and *he* washes ashtrays!…Hmm, maybe this brand.…" She went back to the unending cast of budding and has-been stars.

After an hour and three more cigarettes, she called it a night and headed for the bathroom. Entering, she noticed the shower had not been freshly used. She looked down at the basin; it was bone dry. Glaring at herself in the mirror, then lowering her eyes, murmuring, "God! Why doesn't he ever put away the shampoo and mouthwash!— it's not like he uses them every day!"

Journey to Athens

A copy of Plato's Dialogues patched with duct tape was endearingly pressed to his tweed. A wrinkled folder containing copies of a course outline and a reading list was in his other hand as the old professor hurriedly left his office and headed for his class to launch the new semester. He hoped, though forty years of experience dictated otherwise, this would be a banner year. He wanted to retire with a flourish—recover some of the glory years when he began teaching after the noble war. The campus then was filled with vibrantly searching WWII veterans who had not so much as dreamt before and during the war that they would ever be so honored as to be granted a college education through the G.I. Bill.

Not only veterans were gripped by the thirst for knowledge. The nation was on a high: knowledge was in demand because of the euphorically expanding nation in which anything was possible. Teenage males fresh out of high school and through some means escaped Universal Military Training; the females lucky enough to have parents willing or substantially well off to invest in forward-thinking daughters—came to the campus already mature and responsible to prepare to take on the adult task of higher learning. However, over the years a glut prevailed, glazing over the reverence of college for its own sake in favor of but another step in the syndromic path to material gain.

As he entered the building to the classroom, he paused in the entry, switching the folder to join the book, He unbuttoned his elbow-patched tweed jacket to extract from the vest-pocket of his cardigan his father's old Elgin watch, tethered to a silver chain his wife had given him years ago. He was on time. He remembered how years ago, no matter how late he arrived, the students then would always wait beyond the mandated twenty minutes grace. Today, God forbid, he should be five minutes late with a punctual class, for the room would be emptied out in a flash. As a rule, however, students arrived later than he. He wondered if compulsory attendance in the old days helped sustain the respectful attitude. Nevertheless, he thought it ironic that attendance-taking was least needed then and more accurately superfluous. As he passed by a few smokers in the corridor, he recalled how in the old days the corridors were smoke-leaden. In this respect at least, he reflected, great advances have been made.

He turned into his room; at his desk he drew the class list print-out from his folder: there were some thirty names at minimum. He looked up as a host of tank shirts of both sexes and other motley vogue drifted into the room. For a couple of decades now he bemoaned the lost styles of dress shirts, creased trousers, and blazers of the youth and the crisp lace blouses and plaid or pleated skirts of the young ladies. He glanced round and estimated there were still some twenty students still to enter. He called for the registration cards. He asked one young lady, whose heavy strands of long hair cob-webbed her tan shoulders and curving descent of her loose bosoms, to hand out the required and reserved reading lists while he matched the cards to the class list—there were still eighteen short. He could hear their moaning and groaning as the reading list was being distributed.

One young man blurted out, "I don't have the time for this Shii…!" as he waved the paper in front of him. "Professor Garret, I'm a business major. This required list is bad enough without the hogwash of library time for the reserve readings!"

Garret peered over the rims of his glasses and stared momentarily at the troubled youth with an olive tank shirt accentuating his muscular arms and shoulders. In a placid tone the professor said, "Business, you say? My, that's splendid—I wish we had more of your kind taking philosophy."

The youth shook his head and compressed a smirk, replying, "You can be sure, I didn't want to…only course available for my schedule."

A youth in a Mets t-shirt, sitting next to him spaced by several desks grunted to confirm, "Seems like the registrar rigged it so there would be little choice!"

The professor smiled, turning attention to him. "I too am entitled to make a living, young man. I think you might be right, the administration feels sorry for me. After all, I'm not exactly popularity timber, you know." He heard light twitter among the other sex. "Of course,…uh, what is your name, young man?"

The youth in the Mets garb answered, Jimmy…Jimmy Collins."

"Well, Mr. Collins, it seems your plight is not as dire as…" interrupting himself to glance at the one in the muscle shirt. "And your name, sir?"

"Oh, just call me Rocky," he rumbled. The ladies in the class giggled.

Garret looked down his class list. "Hmm, perhaps you don't have a problem, after all, Mr. Rocky, as I don't see anyone by that name on the list." There were a few chuckles and giggles.

"Oh, …the joker card, eh?…Tony DiAngelo."

"Oh, yes, I see it here now." He looked up from the list and aimed his eyes at Jimmy. "At any rate, Mr. Collins, you say you *do* have other choices; whereas Mr. DiAngelo does not."

Jimmy jumped, "Oh, sure, if I want to take drudgery like Statistics in sociology or the history of television!"

"So, there is hope, after all, Mr. Collins: at least, you value philosophy over the others. You should feel at home here....Apparently there is no such satisfying compromise for Mr. DiAngelo." He glanced over at the youth unconsciously flexing his biceps. "Poor Rocky has no options and is unhappy with his new home here."

"Well, I wouldn't call Indian Theatre an option." He laughed and turned his head side to side glancing at his peers apparently to urge them to pick up his laugh. He had few takers.

"Why that's simply marvelous, Mr. DiAngelo, that you indeed had a choice and as a result you have not chosen this one under duress; consequently time in the library cannot logically breed a feeling of tyranny and subsequent contempt since it follows that you have voluntarily accepted this course." He grinned at the young man who seemed flustered, and went on in a conciliatory tone, "Lest I be accused of devaluating Theatre, let me assure you that the history of theatre in India is a marvelously interesting and culturally enriching course."

DiAngelo slapped his forehead. "Not the American Indian?" The class laughed.

"If you read the entries in the catalogue, you would not be surprised, Mr. DiAngelo."

"Well, I'll be...." DiAngelo slouched down in his desk-chair, then popped up again. "Maybe...na,...what good would that do me in business!"

The professor chuckled. "Oh, one never knows, Mr. DiAngelo,...just as you don't know yet what philosophy has to do with business."

A young dark-complexioned lady in hip-high cut jeans and breasts wrapped in a bandanna, got up out of her seat. "Well, I still have an option," she announced, and slinked to the professor's desk. "No problem for me is Theatre—in fact, sounds cool." She thrust out her hand to him, while with the other hand flipping the reading list on the desk. "I'd like my card back."

Calmly, Garret looked up and asked pointing to his class list, "Would you point out your name for me, please?" She complied, and he then shuffled through the cards. As he was about to hand it to her, he briefly flicked back his wrist, withholding it from her while he said, "You, know young lady, it grieves me to do this—what with your Greek name it seems a shame that you would abandon the great Greek philosophers, the founders, as it were, of civilization."

She wrested the card from him as she grated. "Couldn't care less, prof,..." She abruptly headed for the door as his and others' eyes followed. She turned, "In case, you haven't heard, Dr. Garret, there's a different civilization today that your darling ancient friends never dreamed of." She left, and his jaw dropped.   He cleared his throat and composed himself. He stood up and paced awhile before turning to the class. He cleared his throat again. "Well, class, it behooves me to begin—it appears the others on the list have chosen *a priori* not to attend and are at this moment obviously beating down the doors to Theatre, Statistics or, God have mercy, the History of Television." The class laughed—even DiAngelo and Collins. He continued, "I promise not to bore you this first day for too long. I shall keep it short so that hopefully you will be motivated to head for the bookstore. I think you will be pleased when requesting the texts, though there are several—and very fat— they are paper back and shouldn't cost you more than sixteen dollars in total." The class cheered. "Ah, yes, you have reason in this day and age to rejoice—the poor girl who just left will have tantrums when she finds out the price of the drama text!— the hand-me-downs alone are going for forty dollars." The class whistled. With a twinkle in his eyes, he said, "Perhaps, then, out of gratitude you will find it in your hearts to humor me in my final year."

He spent most of the period talking to each, one on one, to get to know them as living individuals in lieu of mere names in the register and faceless physical space in class. Other than for their names, grade levels and majors, he would seldom ask a member the same questions. He was careful to frame them so that the students would be required to explain beyond yes and no. For instance, when it came to Collins' turn, Garret asked him why he felt that there was, however little and reluctantly, some value in choosing philosophy.

Collins scratched his head for a while, nervously grinned and replied, "I guess there's always some hope."

In waiting a moment, it became obvious that nothing more was forthcoming, so Garret asked, "Could it be, Mr. Collins, that by choosing the least of three evils one could salvage some value through the mere satisfaction of making a judgment call?" The professor went on, "Tell me why judgment calls and not simplified, clear-cut objectives and decisions are made more often than not—surely, Mr. Collins, you have had to make other such choices."

"Oh, yeah, Dr. Garret, many times things don't work out like they should and I guess you sort of have to compromise and hope you get by."

"For instance?— aside from having to choose this course—what choice did you make that was compromising to a more resolute decision?" the professor pursued.

"Well, just this summer, I almost made one—I guess, depending on how you look at it. I was making good money as a roofer. It's tough work, but it ends your budget problems. My boss tried to persuade me to stay on as a union-paid full time employee...." He smiled at Garret. "I gotta tell you, doc, I was really tempted. I figured I could keep the job and go for my degree at nights—and never have any student loan problems again....But then I figured, Jeez, if I did opt for it, I'd be an old man by the time I got a degree in engineering."

"Are you sure that was the reason, Jim?" Garret asked with a glint of skepticism in his eye.

A girl, who was fresh out of high school, chimed in, "I'll bet, Dr. Garret, that Jimmy was afraid he would *never* pursue that degree."

Jimmy looked over at her. "Yeah, you might be right there. After a day's work on a roof you don't much care to crack the books."

The professor rubbed his chin and then inserted, "I noticed you said at the outset that you *almost* made the compromising decision. I take it then you made an absolute decision that by coming back here you made the only purely logical decision because you perceive yourself primarily as a student and not a roofer."

"Check, doc," he agreed, shaking his fist. "I would have made a mess of my life if I had let the convenience of big bucks decide for me."

"You are a very perceptive lad; there's no wonder that you chose philosophy, then, is there, Jim?"

The young girl who Garret learned in the class interview was an eager freshman already bent on a writing career. In questioning her, Garret was intrigued when she reverted back to Jim's situation and reminded him that Jim's decision was in fact uncompromising and therefore had never really answered his question. She proceeded to cite the following case: "When my closest girl friend graduated with me last June, she made one of the worst decisions in her life. Of course, I blame her father because it never should have been her privilege to make the decision."

"Oh?...And just why was that, Yvonne?" Garret was already beginning to feel that his final year might indeed turn out to be a rather successful one.

"Well, she and I had planned for years to come here together as English majors. But she also wanted her cake and to eat it too. Her father promised her a new car as a graduation present. Instead of just buying her any new car, he made the mistake of letting her pick it out—without any restrictions. Of all things she fell in love with a Porsche! Her father, of course, objected....Well, being the spoiled brat that she always was, she stormed up a fit of passion to the extent that neither would talk to each other. Her mother interceded by trying to convince her daughter that a modest little Civic or Escort was more than enough to expect from them. My friend, having lost all sense of values, would not even follow up with pre-registration and announced to her father that since she was not going to college, she was entitled to the Porsche and in actuality was saving them money! Her father was so infuriated that he bought her the Porsche and then promptly threw her out of the house!" The class burst into laughter. DiAngelo blurted, "The father should've thrown her out to begin with! To buy her the car and then do it is ridiculous!"

"I agree," Yvonne said. "That's like throwing the baby out with the bath water. But as I said, she was spoiled all her life and knew that the father would relent which he did. He was so gratified to have her back home after staying with me for three weeks, he completely ignored his primary wish to have her go to college. And as Zeus is my witness, by this time next year she will have her cake and eat it too!"

Professor Garret arched his gray brows. "Are you serious, Yvonne? You really think the father will relent after all that?"

"Absolutely."

Jim piped, "Then where's the compromise?"

The young girl quickly responded, "Only that she loses a year for being a wretched daughter! But more so in that she has lost her self-respect."

The blonde with the tan shoulders interjected, "Seems to me that little bitch never had it to lose."

Yvonne's bright eyes popped innocently and she cried, "Oh, no, all of us have it by nature, though we may not realize it at any given time. Someday she'll look in the mirror and notice it missing."

Jim shook his head and said, "I don't know, Yvonne; I still don't get how that ties in with it." He then glanced over at his professor.

"Well," Garret began, then rubbed his chin, "at first, this girl had the option of choosing a car within reasonable means as any of you would have done. Perhaps the father in leaving it to her was testing her character. Some of us might have said right off that since there was the expense of a four year college, basic transportation is more than enough—perhaps even gratefully settling for a used car or perhaps even none at all. But this young lady worked herself into a corner by displacing her values in education and seeing only the glamour value of an automobile. Having graduated from high school, and evidently being well-off, she had a zest for immediate adult life of high society. Therefore she chose, without even realizing the compromise, the lesser value. By this time next year, even if her parents do not send her to college, the Porsche will no longer possess the value in more ways than one as she values it today. Furthermore, and ironically, if she does win and her parents relent by sending her to college, she will feel more cheated because of an invaluable year that she lost. I would go so far as to say that when Yvonne returns home for the Thanksgiving break this girl will have realized that she disastrously compromised her values because she will be forced to look into that mirror and compare herself with the progress of her friend."

As was his custom at the close of the first class he quoted a brief passage from the "Apology" in which Socrates asked his persecutors to rebuke his children should they grow up caring for riches, rather than virtue. Because the class had interacted so well it did not end early as planned; yet he could with few exceptions still see the familiar subcultural glances of puzzlement and contorted expressions communicating among them a painful expectation of a long grueling year. Despite his minor success, he was skeptical that this year would be any different with perhaps the exception of the freshman girl who would soon be muffled by short-lived curiosity of others who would not tolerate a legitimate love of wisdom in its undying pursuit of truths. Besides, he was aware that the English department was unabashed in its contempt for his small department and inevitably rubbed off on the undergraduate majors. Nevertheless, he was gratified to have this untainted child in his class for the year; he hoped that perhaps his legacy would be that she would convert her major.

He loitered awhile at the desk, absently flipping the worn, curled up corners of his old "Dialogue" text as he glanced down at the class list. He noticed a name; it had a familiarity about it and it had not been checked off for attendance. It was one of many who never showed up. He rustled back to the "Apology"; he was amused by his ancient underlining and marginal notes some of which had been crossed out, others re-vised—watered down. Much of the spirited excerpts over the years of frustration was marginally noted with "forget it" or "skip." He chuckled with self-effacement some of the youthful enthusiasm of his earlier commentary. One in particular yielded strangled hysterics: "Socrates—20th century man." He sighed, and yelped to the dead walls of the room: "O man of Athens—apology indeed!" Flipping several more pages he let his mind slip into Plato's cadence and rode the realm of ideas.

His brain shut down Elgin time. He pushed out from the desk, rocked back the chair and felt the cold slate against the back of his bald pate. He rotated his head to stare out the big fixed window wall. He yearned for the old philosophy building with old double-hung windows that would allow him to poke his head and breathe in the free natural air. Rocking forward gently he eyed the course outline and wondered how far it would take him this year. He rocked the chair further forward and it landed with a thud. He checked his Elgin, extending its chain and pressing its shiny white gold casing to his ear. He grimaced, then shook the watch vigorously; the second hand edged south nervously, then paused. He checked the winding, but it was taut. He shook it again; it started ticking slowly then stopped.

He pulled out the winding stem, but it wouldn't turn the hands; he tried it counter-clockwise; the minute hand moved back and the second hand responded by jittering backwards. He shook it again but the second hand continued its journey back up the northeast slope. He slipped the watch back in its pocket, the old Elgin had finally given in to the relentless track of time. He got up from the desk and went to the big window and pressed his forehead against the pane to look down over the expanse of the campus, cluttered with students aimlessly mobile, wending in out of tall buildings that seemed to be all black glass and no brick framing in mark contrast to the original pre-war buildings two stories high, windows sensibly cased in the security of old brick.

Examining the old watch again, he noticed the minute hand had apparently moved, and the second hand had continued its backward journey to the twelve mark, passed it but stopped at the fifty-nine second mark. He fondled the watch as his tired old eyes burned away the new buildings outside and refocused on the temporary barracks used for classes during the late Forties. The campus magically rolled out its green turf shaded by immense tulip and maple trees. The campus became tranquil but strangely alive with an undercurrent of mature students probing excitedly while gathering round or walking with professors. Other students were stretched out on the grass sunning themselves while reading. Others sat under the trees perhaps reading poetry or engaged in dialogue. Benches along the walks were filled with students reading newspapers, discussing their assignments or the day's politics—perhaps predictions of a Dewey landslide to offset Truman's proposed "socialized medicine." He chuckled to himself wondering if Frisbee had been invented would those students still be wiling away their time in matters of thought. Just as quickly as the scene unfolded it flipped on edge like a giant poster, revealing another face up.

There before his blinking eyes was a huge crowd swarming the Acropolis and to take the rock-cut seats of the Dionysus Theatre. Athenians were everywhere buzzing with anticipation. A small group of youths filed into the first row as though reserved for them. A mobocratic jury with determined expression was seated in the orchestra. The professor's eyes blinked again and popped when he saw himself in his anachronistic garb midst the splendid robes of the times. He moved down the steps of this phenomenon among the masses who were ascending looking for seats. He was drawn to the lower section and found a seat behind the row of youths. They were leaning forward nervously wringing their hands or burying their faces in their hands while others, looking grim, would seem to scan round the massive stadium as if to find a kind expression in the sea of faces. In their midst was a powerfully built youth busily writing on a scroll while another fragile, youngster held the scroll feed frame for him.

The unruly crowd began to chant: "Bring out the prisoner, this vile Corruptor of Athenian youth. Let him appear to face the stern justice of our belovéd Athena." From out of the central stage-building a thin, erect figure appeared between two sentries who halted at parade rest on the edge of the upper stage, and urged the man in tattered robe to descend the steps to the proscenium. The man alone paced the stage as if waiting for the crowd's derision to subside. Each angry invective rode upon its predecessor to the crescendo of mob hatred. Dr. Garret, eyes welling up and hands cupping his ears, squirmed in his seat and wished away this horrid dream that would not, however, dissolve. He stood up, flew from the row and rushed past the jury, which still sat fixed seeming to enjoy the spectacle. Garret ascended the proscenium steps. The crowd hushed in observing wide-eyed this anachronistic interloper. His steady footsteps echoed round the amphitheater as he approached the thin, forlorn bearded man. Garret touched the man's shoulder across the barrier of time. The ugliness permeating was sucked into Zeno's infinitesimal scintilla of time and a strange quiet rushed in. Garret pleaded, "Oh, master and friend to those dedicated to understand this obstinate world, why? With all your bright moments, why must I be witness to this one—the darkest?" Garret looked to the *deus ex machina* and pleaded, "Why not the glorious probes of the *Republic*? Why this damnation of philosophy?"

The deep brown eyes of the sage glistened softly without a hint of surprise. "Why?— ah, the very word I live for! How sweet the word that stimulates the mind and yet despairs the heart. But the merging of the two, so strangely incompatible, forge another for which all who touch the world are truly dedicated."

"Ah, noble sage, you must mean justice."

He nodded and said, "If only my fellow citizens you see here, but for my followers, had learned the lesson as well as you. Truly you must be a friend of the special realm where insight flows without resistance from the sophists."

"You do me great honor, Socrates, but I must confess whence I came the rancor is as great as you face today. Whether out of fear here or indifference there, ideas are kept in the shade."

"Oh, my, and I took you for a man of the future, not the past!"

"I'm afraid I am as you inferred, twenty-four hundred years into the future."

"How sad, I thought surely by then all resistance would have broken down. And yet why should I be surprised in this world of unpredictable action one must face the quaint dumbness of the heart, which I suspect remains, and all generations struggle indefatigably to refine it, to master its wayward bent. Still, there is no rancor here, only confused emotion shorn of understanding and the expansive continuity of time. Look into their faces now shoveled into the abyss of time. They now must wonder what the next stroke of time will bring; for they know not whence they come as afforded you. For we Greeks seemingly out of nowhere brought forth an enlightenment so overwhelming to the nature of the human mind heretofore used as a tool to survive that they feel it is a trick of the gods to inflate our egos as they had poor, proud Prometheus who thought by simply snatching the light of insight mankind, too, would think things divine. Alas, it does not work thus in the field of unrelenting time. Only in the timeless state as we find ourselves within this suspended second—that is, in the realm of ideas—are we free of laborious intellection that in crude time slaves to root out the irrational delusions of Dionysus. Yea, only in this blissful state of timelessness—this wondrous moment of the infinitesimal can the mind truly reflect back onto itself and see glowing Truth." The sage waved his hand across the stadium. "These poor souls you see here having been so swept into the flux that they look into this moment and see nothing but a suspended cloud of darkness."

Garret patted the sage on the shoulder. "Good! Then let us keep them there. Are they not better off in this state of inaction than to experience what they are destined to do next?...Oh, Socrates, come away with me now! Flee from this drop of time and live! Why—as one four hundred years hence will have done—throw away your life?"

"Ah, but is it mine?"

"Oh, I know whence you twist and turn. You have always claimed it belongs to Athens. But in this dark moment Athena does not reside here. It is only through her who looks kindly to your subtle arrogance that flicks light in thinking man. There is no such light here."

Socrates quickly countered, "Oh, but there is! I see it in your eyes." He stroked his beard and chuckled. "You see, Athens is not a place isolated from the linkage of time. You prove that, loyal friend—why, you may be more Athenian than I!— the light in your eye, however, blinds you to the moment—I too once thought that all need only be exposed to philosophy, the divine light that champions virtue and all would become virtuous. I have learned to settle for the chosen few. You need only to look below to the row of youths to carve out more than dark flux in suspension. Lo, the youths before you. See their enlightened expressions, however distraught. There is no confusion, rather a searching look, anticipating a brighter day." He pointed to the youth with the quill in hand. "There is a glow about him—happy impatience poised for the next stroke that will resume the flow of inspiration."

"Ah, yes, I do…he can be only…"

"Precisely, you know your history of ideas. And for him I willingly take the hemlock—even though, I admit, in spite of my ultimate faith in the tranquil calm and coolness of the realm of ideas, I shall miss the sweat of reason."

"Then, for Athena's sake, stay awhile and persuade the mob of your good intent that you labor over youth to advance the promise of the world," the professor pleaded.

The sage shook his head and heavy lips stretched a hesitant smile. "No, my friend, it is ineluctable that history place its marker on the error of man's fear of questioning the ultimate reason for being. The dark side of man, his animal side, still clings instinctively to action of immediate perceptive needs. You are of my profession and apparently as old as I, you then know of what I speak— especially, after centuries, apparently man has not changed."

The professor bowed his head and said with a sigh, "Yes, unfortunately, I suppose I do, but hopefully more have changed."

Socrates touched Garret's shoulder. "Good, then cheer the progress, however little; for, in face of compelling darkness, history always leaves a window of light for those like us. Behold again the youths, already they begin to stir before the others, and young Plato has set his quill upon the scroll…"

Rude time again rushed in: "Throw out the intruder!" bounced the cry off the limestone slope.

"Aye, hoist him back up to the *deus ex machina!*" echoed another, catalyzing all anger to stumble back into time's persecution.

Garret did not cower. He screeched, "Please, furious men of Athens, hear me out! You misconstrue my intent. I am not here in behalf of this vile Corruptor of youth." Socrates' furrowed his forehead for a moment then his eyes lit up and he winked at Garret who continued to address the mob: "Nay, I am here to tell you that this philosopher of philo-sophers—unbeknown to him—needs no kind words, nor public appro-bation. If so, he would be a politician, not a giant of wisdom. I am here to advise the jury not to be led astray by anger which does not agree with the real aim to punish Socrates. Put him to death and you favor him. Exile him and you grant to him the same death sentence because he cannot exist anywhere but in his beloved Athens and will take his own life. But O men of foolish wrath and unproductive hatred, let him live— how he will then suffer! Alive he will never arrive at his darling truth! Oh, the torture of unrequited love! You all have heard this crafty man of sinuous words, yet think that his goal is to corrupt your youths! Again you are deceived: I insist you let him live and youth will corrupt *him* with their flagrant disregard for the good and just. Think not on Socrates as man of integrity whose aim is to reshape the values of this great city. He is a mere boaster. He dreams aloud of Athena and her will to justice as men of hot blood dream of Aphrodite; yet we do not exile, nor surely, sentence to death these men of uncouth fantasy. Why, then, this harmless fool?" Give him more time with hot-blooded youth and soon he will jilt Athena and drivel on, mouth watering, concerning the sensual pleasures of her sister. Then and only then should you contemplate ending his life on the grounds of hopeless senility living pleasure vicariously through those he corrupts.

"Surely, you know how he boasts of placing the values of truth above the value of living. He has often implied that no man living has ever experienced the true worth of life. Not until death he cleverly explains, can one truly know the empty meaning of all the fuss on earth. O citizens of Athens, I alert you to be as cunning as Odysseus himself! Walk not Socrates' path, lest he cast his shadow—that life here shades the window of true life. Give this man the hemlock and you give him want he wants!"

"Let Socrates live!" bounced the cry off the rocky concave.

"Let him suffer as do we in life!" etched another voice into the limestones.

"Death is too good for the likes of him who derides our love of life!' Another rode the crest of the ensuing chant: "Poetic justice to Socrates! Yea, long live the lover of death!"

A juror rose up and beckoned the throng to silence. Unfazed in the bedlam he rotated a determined look to a sea of demanding faces until the busy quill of the youth could be heard scratching the rapidly unrolling scroll. "Do not be taken in by this foreign intrusion—though I must confess this stranger has the sophist's artistry that only Athenians heretofore perfected. Yet I rather think that he does not know Socrates as we do if he really believes our gadfly does not enjoy the sting of living. Oh, how Socrates sucks up the blood of life!

"And why not? Not since his productive contribution in the war has he had to scratch and claw for a living, preferring to sponge off the duped aristocracy which somehow had felt its sons were learning the rich heritage of our noble state. Be not deceived, fellow citizens; Socrates, not unlike this cohort, uses his flapping lips only to smack them later at a festive table to fulfil his true hedonistic character. Wine, food and young boys are all that matter to him—that's his ultimate truth—all else is but a clever subterfuge to that end. You would be fools not to believe that all those yarns he brings to the loom to warp and woof engaging dialogue is anything but subterfuge to shroud his true intent to fill himself with life's pleasures and in the process sting us with words he pretends come from the oracle. The aristocracy itself first hand has come to realize this and thus demands he be exiled, safe from its gullible youth who someday, don't forget, will have their hands on the helm of our ship of state. Allowed to continue and Socrates will have convinced our lads that government as we know it is mobocracy, not democracy, and that if city-state is to endure, the future leaders will reshape our beloved system to the likes this wily, demoniac sage who professes governance to be a mere tool for philosophers to explore their ideas in the realm of practice and a new republic while the so-called mob is relegated to the pens of guinea pigs. If this is what you want, O men of democracy, if this is the destiny you have in mind for your progeny, then by all means let this silly, pesky and pretentious philosopher continue his errant ways." His fellow jurors all nodded approval as the spokesman sat down, crossed his arms and stared defiantly into the crowd.

"Never! To Hades with philosophy! Send him into exile to corrupt our enemies' youth!"

"Death to the wooly sage who dares take away our freedom!"

"End this mockery of the common man!"

"Death to him who will not labor for his supper!"

"Stamp out the fly who infests us with deceitful bites!"

Thus did the throng echo its renewed sentiments throughout the common limestone slope of singularity.

Socrates stepped forward and hailed them to listen to his voice for the last time. "O ye men who once were graced by the owl who no longer nests in her beautiful Parthenon , four flaps of her wings above us." He paused to gesture to the majestic temple. "Does this not tell us that we have offended our belovéd virgin?— that we have violated her pure sense of justice by deriding the just men and rewarding the unjust? Have we not toppled from the statesmanship of Pericles to the piloting of greed destined to wreck our ship of state on the rocks of chaos?" The crowd hooted and jeered. With a wave of a hand, he went on, "Oh, how you do frown on my words, but I beg of you grant me these dying words: I promise not to deceive you as my strange colleague standing beside me has done. He amused me with his satire—I swear he must have gone before the Delphic oracle and pretended he was Socrates; for it appears he knows me more than I know myself! Nevertheless, he has missed the mark: I do not wish to leave this world for my other world of ideas which may be an illusion. If I gamble wrongly, and find myself in Hades that turns deaf ear to dialogue, what else could measure up to the exciting life of an Athenian? But for meditation on the pure idea of an Athenian at his finest, there is no other life worth living. For all the current faults of this city, there is still the vitality that it will again be restored to its original intent, however much we muddle through. And that I shall miss; for I so much wish to a part of its ineluctable renascence.

"It is small comfort to me as Democritus suggests that at my death, I shall return to atoms that might blow across the city and settle on a youth and influence him. O the terrible indifference of such a teaching method! And then there is the terror of accident and chance: what if the youth should sneeze and send my monads wafting north to the barbarians? How more suitable to be nestled safely eternally in the realm of Ideas! I pray to Apollo and Athena it will be so!

"Oh, if I could recapture the belief of my youth! Still,…will come a day—even without your help—when I must give up this tired old body. Why, even now, some days my body aches so I do not wish to rise out of bed despite rosy-fingered dawn caressing my eye-lids with her dewy promises. Only the other day, I crawled out of bed—and despite what you think of my appetite—I couldn't eat a thing, so nauseous was I. I left the house and within twenty feet I had to lie down in the tall grass behind my modest hovel. There I lay contemplating—a term sophists invented as an excuse for doing nothing—on thoughts divine. Suddenly it occurred to me what a pathetically useless thing to do! I asked myself, 'Socrates. what have you done worthwhile lately?' Oh, to be sure, as the eloquent juror has inferred, I am a shiftless oaf! What will be my legacy? I have built no bridges, no roads, no marvelous temples as my productive fellow-citizens have done—why, my last contribution was hanging a shelf for my wife last month and things are still falling from it because I couldn't get it level!

"Is it any wonder than that I idle my time in philosophy? All my life I have urged youth to turn their thoughts inward as I myself have done, thinking the oracle to know thyself was the wherewithal. Yet I confess when I turned to know myself I found nothing there to contemplate! Alas, the fraud I am, for I should have taken my own life then and there in front of the oracle. For living is in the doing and there was nothing for me to do!" Socrates gestured to the youth still busy scratching the scroll, not missing a word.

"As I sat in the grass and had just stopped bemoaning my fraudulent life and ready to stuff a stone down my throat, young Plato here chanced by and saved me from the fate that would have robbed you the joy of execution. He yanked the stone from my lips and rebuked me for being so inconsiderate to take my life as I was already late for my continuing discussion with Zeno and Parmenides. Why this extraordinary young man bothers with me is even beyond our great thinkers to comprehend. Why, he should be home in his splendid courtyard vying with Homer! This bright young man has poetic talent unlimited, yet he wastes it recording my drivel. Though to his credit, he constantly pricks me with his pen and invariably says, 'No offense, venerable master, but would it not be better had you said...?' Of course, I have to agree with him every time because his prose is so penetratingly beautiful.

"Thanks to this young man, I realize that in the event there is not a realm of ideas for me to contemplate when I die, that through the clarity and beauty crafted by the lad's words, ideas, real or not, mine and his, will endure the end of time and render my death irrelevant."

Athens dissolved into the layers of time. Garret looked down at his watch; the hands were whirling at incredible speed. He heard the campus tower clock bong on the hour. The old Elgin slowed and was back to its prosaic path of modern time. He wheeled round from the window when he heard the voice of Yvonne, "Excuse me, Professor Garret."

He peered over his glasses at the little freshman girl and then to a young man in the doorway holding by his side a shabby book, much like his own. He wore a white tourist t-shirt with Athena's helmet blazoned across the breast.

"You must not be harsh on my cousin here, good kind professor for missing class," Yvonne pleaded. "He has a legitimate excuse."

Garret chuckled, "My dear, he needs no excuse if he has truly chosen this class out of *philos*...." He chuckled again. "And to be perfectly honest, young man, beggars can't be choosers, you are welcome in any case."

"Thank you, Doctor,...you see, I was late for your class because I just returned from a summer tour of Athens. I could not wait another day to meet you, though I feel I have known you all my life." He held up the old text. "In my lifetime you have been quoted a thousand times—you see, sir, my grandfather was a student of yours."

"It's true," Yvonne said excitedly, "but not to be outdone my grandmother, my great uncle's sister was one, too!"

The youth added, "Yvonne tells me that you are going to retire at the end of the year. How sad, for as a major in philosophy I shall miss you in the ensuing seven years....Further, I'll not be able to convince my frisky cousin to stay on with me."

Garret's tired eyes shone youthful at the youth, then glanced at Yvonne. "But *together* we shall!...Retire, you say?...Why, what would I do with myself?"

One Very Lucky Day

Thirteen year old shoulder bones highlighted his washed out graying undershirt. Richie tapped the last of the "Breakfast of Champions" into an old Shirley Temple cereal bowl. He took the empty box into the pantry, pulled open the junk drawer and removed a pair of scissors to cut off the top of the box. Reaching up for a rusted canister on the top shelf of a thickly painted cabinet, he dropped in the top with all the others. He figured by the end of the winter or early spring he would have enough box tops to get the mitt being offered but with a pun—the "catch" was that he had to send in fifty-cents along with them.

In touching the checkered flannel shirt hanging over the back of a chair he had put in front of the gas oven he had lit, he was satisfied it was dry enough. He turned off the oven and put on his shirt and tucked it into his dungarees.

There was very little milk in the ice-box. Adding evaporated milk to the bottle, he drew some water from the tap and shook the bottle vigorously. He sprinkled on the flakes—in spite of his mother's rigorous rationing— more sugar than usual to offset the flat taste of the watered-down canned milk. All through breakfast he stared wistfully at the Charley Keller outfielder's glove on the side of the box.

His brother-in-law-to-be had given him an old Babe Ruth glove last summer, but it was several sizes too big for the youngster. He had dropped several easy pop-ups in neighborhood games; his team made fun of him and told him to stop using the glove, but he had no other—besides, he loved the glove. One day during a game, however, as fate would have it, having tossed the glove on the field at the coalyard as he and his team went in for a turn at bat, a crazy Irish-Setter ran onto the field and ran off with the glove. Richie chased the sprightly dog for blocks. The lad never would have caught up with him except that the dog had paused to chew the glove to shreds.

Hurriedly Richie jammed a sandwich into his pea coat and bounded out of the house. He turned up his collar and ran all the way along Hempstead Turnpike till he reached the Belt Parkway. Reaching the ramp, he reluctantly started thumbing a ride. He was hoping that the pretty lady in the blue Chevy convertible would come along again as she usually did every Saturday morning. As a big Buick was slowing down for him, he spotted the little convertible turning onto the ramp. He quickly shook his head and turned down his thumb and shrugged. The Buick blasted its horn and coughed up speed; the angry driver shook his fist. The lad's heart skipped when the blue convertible pulled alongside.

The blonde girl in a light blue car-coat flashed a smile while leaning

over to unlatch the door for him. Her familiar fresh scent tingled his
nostrils as he slid onto the cold leather. "How'd you do last Saturday,
Richard?" she asked with the same true interest of an older sister.

"Gee, it was a good day, ma'am,...got two loops."

"Still, ma'am, is it?...Well, it shows you have respect....Tell me again
what's a loop?"

"A full round of golf,...ma'am."

"Oh, yes, so you did all of thirty-six holes then?...Well, I hope you're
saving all that money."

"Na," he said, watching her slender pearly white hand reach for the
gear knob.

"My, not even enough to see the one at Yankee Stadium you told me
about—your favorite?"

"Oh, I'll manage to scrape up seventy-five cents, including bus and
subway by then. My mother needs the money more than I do."

"Oh, then, that's even better than saving for yourself! Yes, I like that.
Don't ever lose that feeling of wanting to take care of your mother,
Richard."

"Yes, ma'am," he said, lowering his eyes to the floor board in embarrassment.

"It's Carol, Richard; please don't feel you have to be so formal."

"Yes, m'...Carol." Then with a shiver of shame, brushing away his
sandy locks, he glanced over at her beautiful legs rhythmically moving
with her high-heeled feet in control of the clutch and accelerator.

For over two months he had been getting a hitch from this kindly girl.
Only twice had he been disappointed in her failing to show. The first time,
he actually did not thumb a ride for an hour, hoping she would show up.
As a result, he missed the early loops and then it rained the rest of the day.
He decided he would never do that again despite the great but—he knew
she was engaged—tragic crush she had pressed upon his heart. Of course,
like any thirteen year old in love, he would never resent her happiness and
hoped the very best for her. Sitting on the edge of the seat looking out over
the hood, he felt the whole parkway belonged to them this pre-winter
morning. Last summer, even early in the morning as this, the parkway
would be filling up with cars packed with families on the way to the
World's Fair—its final year.

He slumped back to gaze upon the marvelous speedometer. He was
amazed how her little high-heeled shoe could steady the needle exactly
between 30 and 40 throughout the ride. Then he stole a glance or two at
her silk-stockinged legs, and was ashamed. He was never quite sure why
he felt ashamed; nor could he ferret out why he was so drawn to those
shapely legs. All he knew is that they were beautiful and he loved to look

at them.

When she pulled up at the exit near North Hills Country club, she said, "I have to work a full day today, so I'll look for you at the exit across the way about five-thirty. I hope you'll be there." He was speechless in getting out of the car. He could barely choke out a thank you. Arriving at the club, his heart sank in seeing several of the "professional" caddies still in the yard. By the first week in December, all of them were normally in Florida caddying. This meant in this off-season—with fewer members braving the weather as it was —he would have to wait around even longer for a loop, since the old-timers always had first choice and then the older teenagers. Hope looked even dimmer as he gazed up at the graying overcast; still, he sat up on the yard's cold rail fence to look conspicuous whenever a bag dropped out of the clubhouse bag room. He hoped the old timers, rolling dice for dimes and over at an overhang the high school students playing poker for pennies, were not ready to go out this early.

He heard a muffled rattling of clubs behind the Dutch door of the bag room. His heart pounded. He knew from his short experience that a youngster had to be visible and loyal at all times. If one missed a week it would take a month for a young caddy to return to the caddy master's good graces. He stared at the door in expectation. He felt—especially if the caddies stayed involved with their gambling —he had an excellent chance to be chosen since the caddy-master had already left for his winter job in West Palm Beach, and that Gus, the assistant pro in charge of the caddies during the winter, knew Richie better, having chosen him once to carry his bag during a late afternoon nine-hole round.

Suddenly the half door was forced open and two bags were swung out by Gus's powerful arms. He leaned them against the lower door. Richie instantly recognized the bags belonging to the two members who were usually always the first to tee off. They were also the cheapest. Gus looked over at Richie and was about to call him when two old timers in hearing the rattling of the clubs abandoned the game and turned the corner.

"We'll take them, Gus," one who was in his late twenties, said. Richie often wondered how a young man could take to caddying as a career—unless, of course, he followed the professional circuit.

Gus looked surprised. "Fine with me, but this is Two-Tee Kline, you know."

"Oh, sh…, forget it!" The jaded caddy removed his ruddy hand from the strap as if plagued.

The other one called Old Jim—truly old, nearing sixty with the distinction of having caddied for Bobby Jones—looked at the name-tag of the other bag, and swore, "Damn, this one's just as cheap." They both went back to the dice.

Gus beckoned to Richie. "Take Two-Tee, Dick."

Richie jumped from the frigid rail and strutted proudly to the bag. He felt six-feet tall and eighteen when Gus called him that. Gus leaned out and yelled at the card-players, "You fellas, going to run a casino or caddy? One of them so conditioned—the youngest of the group—threw down his cards, picked up his last two pennies and hustled over.

On the first tee the wind was beginning to stir and Richie felt the frozen turf under his sneakers. This meant that these hackers' were going to drive the ball their customary 150-175 yards but the hard surface would bounce at least another fifty yards and quicken the round to give him plenty of time for another loop—provided the weather held up— and still make the exit ramp by five. He was glad his mother made him wear heavy socks, even though it made the sneakers too tight. Richie reached into the bag and handed the golfer, one of the few remaining who still wore knickers, his two beat-up tees tied together by a fish-line. The golfer inspected them and said, "Well, laddie, my tees are still in good shape—should get through the winter." Richie remembered the last time he caddied for him Two-Tee had bragged how he got through the entire summer season with the same two tees.

The youngster's analysis was correct: those two hundred plus drives sped them around the course in less than two hours. Not that it mattered since the weather worsened—bleak, threatening. The youngster was not one to give up easily; besides with his blonde lady he had an added incentive to wait. He folded the dollar bill tightly round the quarter and securely tucked it into the watch pocket of his corduroys and took his place on the cold rail. He withdrew the sandwich from the pea coat and folded down the clumsy Bond bread wrap. Chewing the sandwich—the jelly was iced—he stared at the Dutch-door of the bag room. The card-playing caddy who had been out on the course with him knitted bushy brows, shook a capped head and said, "You're nuts to hang around, Rich, you ain't goin' to get nothin' more this day."

Richie looked up at the dark sky. "Never know....Might lighten up."

"Yeah, sure,...dream on, Pinocchio." Older by a year and therefore wiser, the caddy shrugged and walked out the yard whistling, "When You Wish upon a Star."

It was like the sky opened up! Richie realized that the blonde lady reminded him of the blue fairy he had seen a few months ago in Disney's classic. Freezing from sitting on the rail, Richie started to walk around the caddy yard and tap his feet intermittently. Three old timers moved to the overhang to get out of the cold wind and to lunch on their White Castle burgers. The pro's were the only caddies who had cars—even the older high school kids walked or hitched up to the course. Anyone over fifteen would not be seen dead riding a bike—besides, sure to be stolen while out on a loop. Richie wondered why the old timers were still here and not already out on the course unless they were waiting for some important party still in the clubhouse. Yet who important, he pursued, would be up here on a day like this? Most of the wealthier golfers were already enjoying the courses in Florida or the Bahamas.

Richie heard the Dutch door unlatch and the rattling of clubs. He ran to the fence. Four very impressive, heavy, rich leather bags had been plopped on the cement slab and were leaning against the door. Gus stuck his head out. Looking over at Richie, Gus rocked his slickly combed head and said, "Pope's party, Dick—not for you." Richie lowered his eyes in mild disappointment, but he had learned to accept the bylaws of caddying. Now he knew whom the old-timers were waiting for. Richie had heard of the Pope's party and had seen them once on the course. They played at a snail's pace, but were held in reverence. His young Catholic mind could only think of the papacy in Rome. The truth was that this Pope guy was big on construction and seemed to own all the cement-mix trucks in Queens. Most caddies figured Pope was with the Mafia—easy come, easy go—since he paid an unheard of three dollars and for everyone in his foursome!

Gus did not have to call up the old-timers; they knew the bags were theirs. One older teenager walked up to Gus to inquire about the fourth bag.

"Can't release it yet until they're ready to tee-off. If Old Jim isn't back from his loop by then, it's yours."

The teenager kicked up some of the gravel with a scuffed shoe and yelped, "Cripes, Gus, that ain't fair! I've been waitin' around for three hours! Jim's got his loop."

"Sorry, kid....them's the rules round here," Gus reminded him and closed the door.

The old-timers laughed. "Cheer up, kid," one of them said with a mouth full of White Castle, "you'll get a loop yet." He chuckled and choked on his nickel burger. "Maybe Two-Tee will go a second round today."

"Yeah, sure, I can see myself going out for a lousy two bits in this weather. Maybe not even that for his second time around—more like a dime." the kid growled.

"Well, then, how about six bits?" joined another, whose pale face was a mystery to Richie inasmuch as everyone who caddied never lost their deep tan, which was compounded by winter's constant wind on face and hands. Six bits to Richie was a fortune. Only twice was he fortunate to get a four bit round. Caddies always talked in terms of tips. The flat rate was one dollar and ninety-nine percent of the time a golfer would tip the caddy—even Two-Tee—and very seldom did he give just a dime or fifteen cents. Twenty-five percent of the members were considered cheap because they gave only a quarter. A good loop, which was the majority, paid a half-dollar. On rare occasions a golfer who ordinarily paid fifty cents would give seventy-five cents if he played an exceptionally good round. But even rarer were those who regularly tipped from seventy-five cents to a dollar—the latter referred to as deuce—unless the caddy was terrible and lost a lot of balls or did not "club" correctly.

"Oh, now you're talking?" the kid said. "You know somethin' I don't? Who's left in the clubhouse, aside from these olive eaters."

"Well, I saw the Babe pull up when I went out to the White Castle," the pale faced one said. The other two laughed hysterically. Richie's eyes lit up when he heard the magical name.

"Aw, you're pullin' my leg," the kid moaned, "What would the Babe be doin' here this time of year."

"What else is there for him nowadays? I couldn't mistake his bulk staggering out of the car." The old timers laughed just as Pope's party walked off the practice green and headed for the first tee. With military precision each of the old timers carefully removed the thickly knitted wood sleeve from the driver and slipped the belt over the shoulder and silently marched out to the tee with their respective bags. Richie always admired the career caddies for the way they could wedge their right arm and stretch their hand over the clubs to eliminate the rattle. Gus opened the door and beckoned to the older boy to take the fourth bag.

The yard was empty now but for Richie. There had been another one about sixteen but when he heard that Old Jim was due back, he decided to try the nearby Lakeville club. When caddies started coming back in from their loops, they didn't even bother to inquire what members were still scheduled to come out. They just pocketed the small change of their labor and headed home. A pair passed by Richie; one nudged the other and said tilting his head toward Richie, "Let the kids have the frost-bite...they don't know no better."

A half hour passed before the bag room door opened again. Four bags were dropped out. The lad's heart leaped when he saw the Yankee Logo on the wood socks. But his heart then sank when he saw Old Jim turn the corner along with three other caddies.

The old caddy was pursing his lips. He had seen the Pope party out on the first nine. He didn't even look at the bags; he just continued walking toward his car, mumbling about the injustice of his bad timing. Gus opened the door and called after him, "Don't you want the Babe?"

Jim turned round and frowned, flaring up, "You gotta be kiddin', Gus, why at this late hour he'll be drunker'n a bums' hoosegow! I ain't going to get frostbite fishing balls out of the lake in this weather or traipse through snowy woods for his wild drives....See ya in the spring. I'm headin' for the sunshine state."

The voice of experience scared off the other caddies. They grabbed the other bags, knowing they were good for four bits. The oldest of the group—his woolen cap pulled down over his ears—said to Gus, "Babe's six bits ain't worth the pain."

"Oh, yeah...since when?...another two bits means two packs of butts." Gus said, then turned to Richie. "Well, I guess you're stuck with the Babe, Dick." Gus winked at the others.

Richie jumped over to the heaviest bag. He was smiling ear to ear when he said, "Stuck? — with *Babe Ruth!*"

Out on the first tee, Richie watched the other golfer's taking awkward practice swings because of the bulky sweaters under their wind-breakers. Then he saw the great man coming out of the clubhouse. Old Jim, the great voice of experience, was wrong. The Babe walked straight as an arrow with his customary, snappy short steps. Richie's elation turned to nervous fear when the giant with the broadest, straightest shoulders and biggest head the youngster had ever seen approached and handed him a brown paper bag that was hard as a rock. He said powerfully and coarsely, winking "Zip up my medicine, kid." Richie was so nervous that he forgot to hand him his driver as he put the "medicine" in the golf bag pocket. The Babe slipped off the sock and pulled out the club himself with his massive, hand. The other players were still warming up and the Babe just stood there leaning lightly on his club. The first player struggled to insert the tee into the frozen turf. He blew on his exposed fingers, then looked at the Babe and said, "You'll have to give us a better handicap, Babe,...with this icy weather, you'll be driving the greens today."

"I doubt it; yet you fellas, might be hitting 300 yarders yourself, what with the ice," said the Babe pulling his light sweater down over the bulge to narrow hips. As the first player, several years younger and a bulge that still had some years to go to match the Babe's—hacked the ball off the tee, bouncing some hundred and fifty yards out. The Babe laughed, which to Richie was more like a lion's roar. The Babe said, "So much for theory, old man."

The Babe hit last. He spat into his gloveless palms. Richie then realized this was the first time he ever caddied for a left-hander. Before addressing the ball, Babe wriggled the club in his right hand, but did not take a practice swing. Richie noticed that the tee was unusually high. With a smooth, effortless swing he hit under the ball and it went practically straight up. To Richie it seemed a mile high. His Uncle Johnny told him once: "The Babe's pop-ups were even a sight to behold."

"Too damn lazy to push the tee in!" the Babe growled as he watched the ball take an enormous bounce half as high and land two hundred yards out. Richie had no idea how to club this man, but fortunately the Babe always chose for himself. Besides on a par four it was usually the niblick or sandblaster anyway. Because of the hard turf, the Babe would probably half swing his nine iron. On the first hole, however, because seventy-five to a hundred yards short of his usual drives on regular turf, he chose a mashie. It landed short of the green as planned and bounced nicely hole high. The greens were so fast he three-putted.

On the second hole—an uphill par five about 540 yards—the Babe thrust his tee so that the ball was barely above the grass. He drove a hissing, incredibly low liner that kept rising with the elevating contour of the fairway. Richie held his breath trying to follow it. Its flight seemed like it was never going to come to an end. Then it disappeared beyond a rolling mound. Everybody, including the caddies, except Richie, whistled. The lad was preoccupied keeping his eye on the point of disappearance. There is nothing more embarrassing to a caddy than to have to founder for a ball. Richie was well ahead of the party and reached the mound. His heart stopped; he couldn't see the ball, but he kept walking, though stealing glances here and there, hoping to pick it out. Finally, because he was so far ahead, he had to move to the fairway fringe for the other golfers' second shots. He watched the flight of the golfer's wood shot from a hundred yards back and some two hundred and twenty-five yards out from the tee. It was a powerful fairway shot going just past Richie and rolling down the mound and abruptly back up the inclining fairway about fifty yards in front of Richie. After the rest hit and clustered in the trough behind the first golfer's second shot, Richie still couldn't pick up the Babe's drive. Then he began to think the worst that could happen to a caddy—that he had walked right past it! He turned round to see the Babe following him nonchalantly. The Babe then turned his head to the first golfer asking him what club he used. The golfer yelled over that he had used the brassie.

The Babe yelled back, "Nice shot…good you had the guts to use the two wood."

The proud golfer said, "Yeah, but you'll never get to use one today except off the tee!" They both laughed.

Richie's heart was pounding; he had to move to the side again for the other two golfers' third shots—they still used woods! The other followed up his fine brassie shot with a three iron. All the while, paying no attention to where they landed, Richie kept scanning the fairway for Babe's ball. He continued walking but very slowly, lest he trip over it. He had to stop for one of the golfer's fourth play. "Oh, God, this can't be right!" he muttered to himself. "Please, God, help me find it!" While waiting out the shot, he began looking in the rough. Fear welled-up and he mumbled, "Oh, my God, what if it kicked off into the rough!" Hesitantly he started forward again, mumbling, "Oh, this is impossible!" He was only a hundred yards from the green! Then he saw three balls clustered about fifty yards away. He had not paid any attention to where the other golfers' shots had gone. He glanced over at the party and he sighed in relief as one of the golfers was addressing his ball twenty-five yards back.

His pride regained he snappily forged ahead; he was sure the Babe's was the one in the middle and on the fringe of the green.

"Jesus, Babe! you out-drove our third strokes!" cried out one of the golfers. "You hit that damn ball almost five hundred yards!"

"Yeah, but no right field pavilion to stop it in flight," he said calmly.

As the Babe yanked out his chipper, Richie suddenly got the nerve to say something to him. "Gee, Mr. Ruth, that was a real King Kong Keller shot!"

The Babe stared down in disbelief at the boy for a moment, then his pot belly shook from laughter. Finally he chuckled out, "That's a real doozie, kid—you're as good as Eddie Cantor!...Don't tell me a good-looking little feller like you actually likes that gorilla Keller."

Richie smiled sheepishly. "Sure do,...saw him almost hit the flag pole once."

The Babe grinned. "That gorilla's got to learn to pull the ball. Centerfield at my house is no place to hit the ball."

"I know,...it was caught."

He roared again and then gingerly swept his second stroke near the pin. But he had to settle for a birdie—the elusive eagle putt rimmed round and out.

It got a little brighter out and the party decided to do the back nine. When Richie put the pin back into the twelfth hole. The oldest caddy walked over and said, "You'd better give him his medicine now. He always has it on the short holes. He's overdue."

"Well, he didn't ask for it on the seventh or ninth," Richie said perplexedly. "Gee, do you think I should? He might get mad."

"He's going to get meaner if he doesn't have his Jack Daniels soon!" the wiser voice warned.

The young caddy caught up to his big man. Richie stuttered momentarily, then asked, "Mr. Ruth, do you want your medicine now?"

Babe put a huge hand on the boy's head and tapped it gently. With a soft gaze and light, but raspy voice said, "No, sonny, you're too young to see this old fool take up his worst habit. My swearing and stogies are enough for a little kid like you. Besides, you're my medicine today."

"Gee, Mr. Ruth, no fool could drive three par four greens in one day and the day's not over yet!"

He grinned. "Only a fool would play on a day like this, sonny," he said wistfully. "In my prime, I'd be in St. Petersburg.... Tell you what, boy, the next time I see that Keller feller, I'll show him how to pull better so that the next time you go to see him, he'll put it in the stands for you."

"Gee, Mr. Ruth,..."

"Call me Babe."

"Uh, Babe,... I wish you were still playing baseball."

"So do I, son."

"Yeah, I kinda feel cheated,..." Richie said through misty eyes.

"Yeah, so do I, son,...so do I."

Until he reached the parkway, Richie had forgotten about the blonde girl. He was anxious to get home and tell his family about this incredible encounter with the Babe. He would have been happy to caddy for the Babe for nothing; but he was absolutely flabbergasted when the great athlete handed him a deuce! Actually the Babe did not play as well despite the mammoth drives; still, he played close to his usual game—76.

When Richie saw the blue convertible slow down for him the Babe momentarily faded. But once inside the car he talked to her all the way to the Hempstead Turnpike exit about the great man. As she slowed down for the exit, she finally was able to say to him, "Richard, this is the last time we'll ever see each other. Don't look for me next Saturday. It's my wedding day; and after the honeymoon we'll be moving to Hawaii where my husband will be stationed." She pulled the car onto the shoulder and stopped.

Richie's heart sank and he looked up at her with sad eyes. But when she smiled softly, he did too: he felt so very happy for her. She reached back into the top-well and drew out a package, handing it to him. This would have been for my little brother had he not taken so sick. Of course, to make it especially for you I had to exchange it. I want you to have it to remember me by. I shall not forget you, Richard. You were very nice company for me and helped me get through the loss of my dear brother."

He started to well-up and then broke down and cried. He was ashamed for all the times he had peeked at her legs.

She tenderly brought up his chin. "This is no time for tears, Richard,...after all, you caddied for the greatest today!...And don't you want to wish me well in my new life?"

"Oh, yes, ma'am,...uh, Carol, I really do! I want you to be happy...yes, as happy as I am! You're right, I am so lucky! Two beautiful people—and all in one day!…I-I…"

"What is it, Richard?"

"I just wish, your little brother could have been so lucky."

She hugged him and he felt her tears on his cheek, then she kissed his wet cheek. She leaned over and unlatched the door. "Go, now, Richard, before I steal you. Go have a most happy life—and I know God will keep you healthy."

In his attic bedroom that night he oiled his new Charley Keller mitt Carol gave him. His tears formed little rainbows on the oil. He would treasure this glove for the rest of his life, but only partly because of its signature, and much more so because she had given it from a broken but healing heart. He wished he had asked her to sign it. Were it not for the likelihood of its being stolen from him, he would have chanced taking it up to North Hills the next week to ask the Babe to sign it. Besides, Babe Ruth was not a member and probably would not be a guest again till next spring. His eyes dazzled on the image of Keller pulling one into the rightfield bleachers next season near the bullpen where Richie always sat hoping to catch one. If it happened he hoped he could get the Babe to sign the ball.

He fell back on the bed and kicked off his tight sneakers. He stared at the glove once more before putting it down. It had felt good. He wouldn't be dropping anymore pop-flies. He rubbed his palms together to get rid of the oily feeling. The Irish-setter came to mind. He loved Irish-setters, but that one he hated.

One year later almost to the day, when caddying on the fateful Sunday, he looked back on his most lucky day and was even more gratified that it had occurred when it did and not the day before Pearl Harbor—Carol at least got a year of happy marriage and he a year free of dashed memories—even though on reflection his blonde lady would have been better off had it happened a year ago, thereby remaining safe at home. He prayed for her that night and every night.

Baseball seldom entered Richie's mind for the duration; except for the memories of the '41 season climaxed with Keller slamming thirty-three homers and his dramatic two-out game-winning double off the Ebbet's Field scoreboard in the Mickey Owens classic—and, of course, the lad's memorable outing with the Greatest.

Blind Well

The overhead doors rolled up on command from the flick of his remote. Paul pulled his Cadillac into a neatly arrayed three car garage. In spite of his present abasement, he felt rather good being able to open his car door without banging into a bicycle, or a forgotten doll carriage or the like—the "like" being both his wife's car and daughter's jackknifed in, barely allowing his car any room—of course, it helps when neither was home yet. Still he was proud of his extraordinary gesture last weekend in restoring order and sanity to his sector of home life and tandem was the trip to the fire department which accepted toys in reasonably good condition for their annual fix-up and eventual distribution. How the wealth of one could affect the happiness of so many was a temptation so irresistible that he wondered absently why it was not prevalent—while he estimated he could claim a couple of hundred from his tax return.

The kitchen as usual looked like something out of a magazine ad. "I guess that means we'll be eating out again." He thought back to the days when people actually lived in kitchens. He recalled getting dressed on cold mornings by the stove; his mother would light all four gas burners and the oven so there would be at least one warm room in the house until—with the furnace banked all night—the steam boiler got going again. Once every five years it was a ritual in his mother's house years ago. All the dishes, utensils, pots and pans were carted off to the dining table, along with the canned goods and junk from the pantry so his dad could give the old apple green cabinets a fresh look. "Today, it's an exotic color every year and another try at the latest wood stain or antique craze every other year." He tried the refrigerator: "No beer again—very low status, you know." He grabbed a handful of ice-cubes, got down a glass and headed for the living room where he opened the liquor cabinet retrieved the scotch and poured himself a drink. He plopped into his downy armchair, pried off his shoes and put his feet up on the equally soft ottoman. He gazed at the spacious room, furnished plushly, the mantelpiece crowded with his, his wife's country club trophies, together with his girls'. Only when alone did he really appreciate his home and the success it represented; yet at other times he believed he could be content in any dwelling as long as it fulfilled basic creature comfort and relaxation. He could never shake the haunting irony that in the pursuit of success, one had little time to relax really and to dwell simply in his being. Sustained, however, he assumed it would be boring. "Perhaps, though, it's just as well, Sloan canned me," he reconciled to himself the finality of only three hours ago, although he had known it was coming for several months. "Get out of this rat race...Jesus, though, a lousy half year severance....What the hell, he did kick in fifty thou toward retirement,...conscience got to him...after embezzling the company shares from the fund...son-of-bitch...hmm, my own contribution reinvested...about a hundred thou...practically gone, too!...Better put what's left of it in trust for the kids....Realty says the house is worth three-fifty...hell, more than enough to live on down there...stay up here and we're broke...we'll never change our life-style....Away from it all there's a chance....Kills me... 'under no obligation,' he says,...goddamned Indian giver...I wish I hadn't signed the agreement...still, take it up front, I always say....Be a while before the funds fiscal report comes...Ann's always checking on it...be in Texas by then....Damn! how I wanted to reach the million mark...work forever, not touch it and leave it all to the kids, just like the true blood rich. Aw, start with nothing, end with nothing." He laid his head back and let the turmoil escape.

His eyes resumed their lazy sweep from object to object. There in the quiet his mind drifted to a skinny boy walking along the highway, hoping a golfer would come along and give him a lift to the course. He saw his mother come into his room on a Sunday morning when all the continent slept to shake him again so he could make a dollar that day at the golf links. "Pauly, your HO's and milk are on the table. You forgot to empty the garbage and you never did bring up the ashes. Your apple-butter sandwiches are next to the cereal; don't forget them—you have a long day, poor darling. Be sure not to skip out of mass too early again. I always hear about it from Father Brown."

"Paul,...are you asleep?" his smartly dressed wife wanted to know as soon as she put some packages down on the foyer bench.

"Huh?...No. I'm getting up, Ma." He stirred to sit up, forgetting he had a drink in his hand.

"Paul! Be careful with that drink—we just had it re-upholstered because you wouldn't let me throw out the overstuffed relic." She dashed over and took the tilting glass from his numb hand! "What are you doing home so early?" she asked, obviously annoyed as is wont when men dare transgress the time of women's independent domain. "Why, it's not even six!"

"Gosh, I guess I dozed." He held back a yawn, staring dumbly. "Where were you?— as though I had to ask."

"Oh, just out for a few things," she said with insouciance as she put his drink on the liquor cabinet bar.

"Say, I'm not finished with that drink." He gaped at her dumbly.

She put her nose to it. "Whew! Rather strong." She added some club soda.

"Damn, that's the way I wanted it," he grated, shaking his head and clicking his tongue as she handed it back to him, then he asked out of habit, "Did you pick up my shirts from the chink?— not that I'll be needing them."

"Oh, my, I can't believe I forgot them again! I took so much time deciding on a pair of shoes...then, of course, there were those darling shorts and designer jeans for Tammy, who's slimming down so, isn't she?" She glanced away and smirked. "Oh, you wouldn't know." She strutted over to the foyer to retrieve the packages.

His eyes followed her; he observed the perfectly conditioned shoes she had bought only last month. "You have a closet full of shoes. Those you have on now seem new."

Heading back, she dropped the packages on the long luxurious sectional and replied with a slight scowl, "You too have a closet full....Oh, these....Well, yes, they're nice, but these have a subtle heel." She toed out one of her still shapely legs and looked down; "However, I have so very few flats that flatter the legs."

He nodded, looking down at them. "Your legs always look great."

"I agree—surely, my best highlight; but at my age, alas, who's going to look at them?"

Arching a brow he asked, "Oh?...not enough that I still admire them, eh?"

"You're a dear," she said as she raised her skirt teasingly. "Of course, I know I take it for granted that you do...and I love you for it. Still, a woman must at least take comfort in the pretense that to others she's still desirable —even at my gross old age. Why, even when you had your sundry flings with those girls at the office, you never turned away from me in bed—well, almost never— knowing that I'd be justified in rejecting you, though you were reasonably sure I wouldn't."

"Oh, the snakes of Ireland are wriggling again!...And I never turned away until after you did!" He rose from his chair awkwardly and as if to change the subject reached for a large package on the sofa. With raised eyebrow he questioned, "Shorts and jeans in this monstrous box?" His jaw dropped.

She laughed. "No, heavens, I just mentioned how thin she's getting....No, silly, Marguerite ordered a special party dress from Prim's and asked that I pick it up for her—she needs it desperately for tonight."

"Oh, by all means, an emergency," he said sarcastically. "Funny, how a simple word like need can be misused—or is it abused?" He put the package back down to leave; she followed him to the kitchen, taking his glass and placing it in the sink. "I really wanted a beer, you know," he complained as he sat down at the breakfast nook, and took from the bowl an apple which he stroked on his shirt sleeve.

"Those apples are already washed and polished," she said.

"Just habit everybody adheres to." Then he announced, "I also feel like sinking my partial into a hamburger."

She decided that the lone glass in the sink should be put in the dishwasher; she leaned down to open the door, revealing full racks of gleaming ware. She yelped at herself, "Oh, no!…how many times have I told that dreadful Mabel to empty this before leaving!"

"I'm sure she would have, had the cycle ended before her taxi arrived," he said with his customary cavalier understanding of domestic help—so seldom he thought of them. His mind flashed to the early Thirties: his mother, working as a part-time domestic, on special occasions used to sneak him into the kitchen while the people she served were in high style fulfilling themselves in their grand dining room. Though she had always brought something home to him, it was not the same when it had to be warmed over. For a time in the beginning of his rise to riches, he would boast to the help about his mother having worked during the Depression for a successful lawyer, but now, owing to the aphorism *nouveau* long sent to oblivion, it was a dead recall that he could no longer equate in sentiment for the domestics of the past twenty-five years. "What's it this time?" he asked her, watching her glide from one cabinet to the next putting away dishes and glasses.

"What's what?" she asked reaching down for the utensil tray and shaking her head in confusion.

"Marguerite….You mentioned her special outing—seems every night is special." He bit into the apple. "Ooh, that damn partial." He reached into his mouth to reseat his denture.

"You'd better see Dr. Morris about that partial of yours…cost enough."

"Not a fraction of the orthodontia bills." he said with subdued indignation. "You of all people should not bring up costs."

"I didn't mean in it in that way: I simply meant that you tend to overlook these things, even though you pay good money for the services," she explained as she put his glass in the empty rack. "There that's done." she said proudly as she closed the dishwasher door. She rested momentarily against the counter. "Anyway, a Harvard friend is taking her to dinner." Her tone had become subdued. This was the first year she resented her daughter's popularity. The previous years—down to Marguerite's latter teens—her daughter's episodic life was a source of rejuvenation for Ann: thrilled to observe that one of her offspring was charming to the degree that she could date very wealthy boys. The debut, for which they had redeemed most of their bonds, seemed to be paying off handsomely each time another Ivy-leaguer came to the door. Recently, however, she had begun to weary of her daughter's party pace; what was more, her daughter seemed a stranger to her, bereft of the intimate mother-daughter relationship they had once enjoyed. She feared an alienation between one who always had and one who had and had not.

"Why the face?" He noted the familiar expression of hers. "Your debutante is going places—that's what you wanted, isn't it?" He bit cautiously into the apple and commented in between chomps. "After all,...can't go any higher than Harvard...surely, you wouldn't want someone from Oswego or Dowling," he added with mild sarcasm.

"Must you always rub my nose in it?" She looked up at the clock ornamented by a tea pot. "I admit to my snobbish ways, but I'm also a mother—a concerned one," she said with a tenebrous tone.

"I wasn't trying to be callous," he said with constrained disgust. He got up and flipped the core into the disposal unit and ran the water.

"Lately, it seems you don't have to try—what's come over you, lately?" She searched his dark eyes fleetingly.

"Oh, right," ignoring her question, "I'm the typical unconcerned father who senses that his children are no longer his; the rightful ownership goes to the mother—different blood count, I guess." He took down a fresh glass from the cabinet, leaving it on the counter by the door—she took exception by shaking her head in annoyance—he slammed the door and headed for the door leading to the basement. "I believe I hid some beer in the bar-refrigerator. Things'll be different in Texas...." He made his footsteps be heard as he went down the stairs.

"Texas?" she repeated, but he was halfway down the stairs; she shrugged. She put the glass back in the cabinet. Ann never could understand why his interest in the children did not equal hers. She was tired of excusing him for not having the luxury of time to relate to them. A good share of her busy schedule, however, was self-serving, which she would not have admitted to, for she truly believed that her time was always in behalf of her family. Thus, if Tammy or Marguerite wanted to spend sometime with her, which was seldom, or discuss something with her, when concurrent, for instance, with an appointment with the hairdresser, she would brush them off with: "I'm doing this for you....Surely you don't wish me to pick up your friends at the theater, or meet them at the spa looking like the gardener's wife." Moreover, she detested his obvious show of *nouveau riche*—a term that she resented enormously—his perpetual execution of it was a constant reminder even though she would never acknowledge her own display, which was more subtle. She looked up at the clock again, then went over to the window and stretched her neck to see out. She picked up a towel left on the counter-top and was about to fold it, when she noticed some dust on the Venetian blinds, vexed, she snapped the towel; the blinds rattled. She sat down at the table and wiped the table absently. "That girl never mentions what kind of boy she really wants…nor does she ever mention the qualities of those she has liked. How, then, am I ever to understand her?" She looked at her handsome jeweled watch. "Oh, where is Tammy?"

Her thoughts went back to Marguerite, who possessed not a thread of home-spun qualities: no interest in cooking since her home economics course in seventh grade—a course incidentally Ann thought a waste of good money and surely had no place in a Catholic school. Shopping, which her mother loved, Marguerite, except for herself in conjunction with special occasions, seemed indifferent and would just as soon throw on her mother's blouse and skirt or wear a pair of her shoes before embarking on such trivial matters. Always it was "Mom, pick up my dry-cleaning, stop at the drug store for monthly pons; deodorant is running low; I haven't a pair of panty-hose to my name.…" The day she had received her driver's license she begged to go to the supermarket for her mother. That was the last time she went; her active schedule obviated such errands—tennis date, spa, lunch and swimming at the club—once, though, she dropped Tammy off at the club for her golf lessons—she thought the pro was cute. She possessed a masked coldness in the presence of her aunt's children when they came over to visit their generous Auntie Ann, who always detected the difference between her daughter's natural smile and the one learned from modeling. Ann, though, had to admit the last time her family visited, Marguerite was charming and seemed to take a deep interest in the children. The day Paul and Ann installed their daughter at Manhattanville, they were beaming parents who had never been on a college campus: the first generation from both sides of the family to have reached this high mark. Since, however, Ann had been disappointed: eager to engage in dialogue with her daughter concerning books assigned—Ann was an avid reader—she sadly discovered from prodding her for comments that Marguerite had lost her original love for reading and barely extended beyond: "all right,…boring,…didn't get to it yet…Mother, really, no one reads the *Magic Mountain* anymore—that's what campus bookstores are for; they sell more critical studies than real books." Ann ironically feared her daughter was more a product of environment than of flesh and blood.

Paul's footsteps were lighter coming up the steps; he entered the kitchen with a beer in his hand. It escaped him to look for his glass. "Where is Peggy? Did she get that TV ad?"

"Yes,…she should be home soon," she said indifferently. Ann had been the catalyst, notwithstanding Paul's objection, in launching Marguerite's modeling career. Ann had been quite successful at it herself until she had her first child, a son that died at childbirth. Because she had been so against having the child so early in their marriage and just when her career was flourishing, she blamed herself for losing the child. She never returned to modeling; instead she resigned to housewifery and gave birth to Marguerite three years later. By the time the child was three, Ann had taken her to a professional photographer. She then personally delivered the album and Marguerite to her old agency. "Tammy, too, should be back from day camp—thought she'd be here by now." She consciously ignored launching Tammy, who had not given the slightest inkling, anyway, since the child abhorred the idea of perhaps having to compete with her sister whom she would prefer to continue to admire at a distance.

"You know how Blakely drives—a twenty minute drive is forty for her," he said as he went to the refrigerator and peeled the wrapper off a slice of cheese. "I'm hungry."

"Where would you like to eat?" she asked.

"I'd prefer *what* to where—you sloughed off my cry for a hamburger."

Ignoring the comment, she went on, "I suppose the 'Angus' would be a delightful change."

He held up his beer. "Eat heartily, my dear, for it may well be your last." He shoved down the cheese and sat back down in the nook.

"Oh, lovely talk—sounds like something out of the twilight zone."

"I mean we won't be going out to eat anymore—not as often anyway—your hardworking, smart oil broker husband is broke."

She looked up at him skeptically, "I prefer the twilight zone to this. The heat of city traffic must have gotten to you."

"The car is air-conditioned....No, my love, I'm afraid I'm serious."

She shook her plastered permanant to no avail and laughed. "Now I know the air-conditioning isn't working in your car."

"That's why I'm thinking about our living in Texas." He said solemnly.

"Because of a defect in the Caddie!" She laughed again.

"Don't be a Lucy. I'm *very* serious." A tone she seldom heard anymore since he had more or less resigned himself to their glutted lifestyle and its high cost. He waited for her reaction to his second drop of Texas. She looked puzzled, but not curious to pursue it. He continued, "My dearest benefactor has requested euphemistically that I retire to make room for his dynamic, more educated son, who has all the right connections in the business now."

"Why that's ridiculous! You're the one who built up the brokerage contacts and credibility," she said half disbelieving, squinting at him and slumping in the chair.

"True, and Sloan doesn't deny that; in fact, he's awarding me handsomely by another hundred thousand kick into the pension plan and two year severance," he lied. "Nevertheless, the executives whom I deal with are being forced into early retirement, too, or routed to something less enterprising and being replaced by the younger set with MBA credentials. Not much room for us high school grads anymore—the weeds are being crowded out by a relentless corporate network of ivy."

She screwed her face into skeptic. "My God! How can these upstarts equal experience?" she moaned, leaning forward to rest her cheeks in her palms.

"They can't; but it doesn't matter because this business rests mainly on personal relations and if you no longer have anything in common, there's no way you can close a deal." He nervously spun the can of beer, then looked up at her with a quasi-jovial look. "Can you picture me surfing or skydiving with these guys? Why, just the other day one of them wanted me to meet him at his weight-lifting club—can you believe it? Entertaining these guys is one thing—a show, a ball game, dinner, golf occasionally—but now it's a different world." He took a gulp, then held up the can to her. "*Heineken*—and I used to love *Schaeffer!*"

"And you've been sent out to pasture at fifty-eight! Why, that's positively indecent! I told you not to trust that conniving Sloan; and that you should've started your own brokerage years ago," she said bitterly.

"At the time, it seemed unethical," he reminded her.

"Well, now you know," she whined, "there is no ethics in business. To think that after all the business you brought in and the countless contracts still generating fees—why, it's positively Judaean!"

"Somewhat overstated, my pet...in a way I'm the Judas. After all, I took his money and ran."

"Yes, you gave up too easily...almost as though..."

He interjected, "I knew you'd breach that sooner or later."

"Well, it's true. You never really accepted. Oh, there's no question about your being good, very good at what you do; but somehow you were never proud of your success as I have been. I never understood why. It isn't that you had some secret aim to pursue some other field. Why, if you had another dream, say, to paint seascapes, I'd comb the beaches with you. The simple truth is that you have no talent but to sell."

"I know," he submitted, "there's no denying it. I loved my job; it's the junk that tailed along I despised."

"Would you have preferred working without ample reward?" she intoned sharply. "I suppose this house, the fine clothes on our children's backs, the private schools, the tennis and golf lessons are part of the junk. God, how I resented you for resenting our material comfort as though Saint Francis Assisi were your alter ego; yet at the same time contradictorily reveling in it."

He stared at her blankly for a moment. "I'm not sure resentment is the word—loud, harmless wailing, perhaps." Absently he looked at the label on the can of beer in his hand. "Oh, you know I enjoy affluence as much as anyone;...it's the price you pay...the hyped schedule of fanfare...the relentless growth of the social circle...ours, the kids'...the bullshit.... Most of all, kissing ass...I guess it's not resentment as much as knowing you can't have it all."

Slumping back in the chair, she browbeat him with the drum of her upbringing when he swore. She was never able to ride with the glibness of profanity as simply another empty symbol of a vacuous society. She saw herself in her childhood, cupping her ears while walking by the naughty boys of her neighborhood, closing her eyes to the messages on the sidewalks and school desks, or her mother's flinching before warning Ann's brothers that they would have soap for dinner. "Yes, I suppose you were proud and enthusiastic in the beginning. You loved surprising me with lovely, touching gifts. You approved of my elaborate but necessary purchases in furnishing the house. You inundated the girls with gifts—though mostly boy toys—in their early years." She looked at her watch again; then rose from the table. "I suppose we could have hamburger." She opened the freezer door and searched for the chopped steak. "Oh, Paul, why couldn't you be like the rest of them?"

"Who knows what people are like inside their walls. I can't believe the callouses are that thick that there isn't an occasional blister on one's conscience; still, I know if I were born into it, or passed the brink of just having a taste of true wealth, I'd be the same way," he said as he took the hamburger meat from her and placed it in the micro-wave to defrost. "I hope you have those deli rolls to go with this."

"Sorry, can't afford them," she quipped, "...thanks to your crudeness brought on by your distaste—perhaps some jealousy, as well?— for Marguerite's friends. It was bound to reflect your working relationship."

"What in blazes are you talking about? Marguerite has nothing to with it. The decision of my boss is simply a symbol of our times—the upward mobility of today's generation is papered over with the credentials of the MBA—corporate gain by computer projections, graphics, and inside connections that no Jamaica High School graduate is privy to."

"Well, you did all right without credentials, for that greedy old man all these years," she countered as she unwrapped the chopped sirloin while looking at him over her shoulder. "Don't instinct and wit stand for anything anymore?"

"No, but when they did, I was justly rewarded, don't forget. Too bad we went crazy and spent practically everything I earned."

"You had a lot to with the spending too," she dug.

"I'm guilty, I admit." He finished off his beer and stepped on the garbage pail pedal, squeezed the aluminum can and dumped it.

She turned and said, "Can't do that anymore—cycling remember?"

"Throw-away society—all the junk in the world, including humans, but not bottles and cans!" He reached down, retrieved it, rinsed it off under the tap and left it on the counter.

She took it and placed it under the counter cabinet. "Look at it this way: you're penny-wise. Each bottle and can returned means you're five cents richer."

He chuckled. "But it's our own money."

"Well, at least it's not lost. You still stoop to retrieve pennies."

"Ah, yes, I shall be doing more of that now." He let out a sigh, "Oh, well, you're right;...let's look at it positively—maybe I'm being recycled—the oil business is not the staff of life."

"Yes, you can always bake bread; or eat cake," she joked. Patting on the burgers, she went on, "Seems to me he could have at least made you vice president that he had been promising you for the last ten years, and phase you out with dignity."

"He knew me too well for that, knowing I'd still have my fingers in the pie, leaving the crust for his son. No, he made the right move from the standpoint of his son."

Plugging in the griddle, she offered, " I still feel that if you hadn't popped off so much about today's young people—after all, his son is one of them—he would have been more understanding. Why—when was it a year ago or so?— at a club dinner you had to dredge a family affair—one too many martinis, I suspect—and pontificate on the bratty manner in which your own daughter was relieved when hearing that her aunt could not make the Cardinal's Ball because of the expense of the plate dinner,...and how Peggy went into a tantrum when you offered to pay for her aunt's plate."

"So?...The old man agreed with me that she was ungracious—he still has some of the old school left in him, too."

"But the wife didn't. You heard her comment that the essence of the coming-out is exclusiveness, practically aristocracy" Ann noted surlily.

"What do you expect from someone who actually believes that because she's a Bostonian, she smells of mayflower." He watched her flatten the burger on the griddle. "She's just a bitchy snob," he added bitterly.

"Though I agree, please use some other aphorism," she pleaded.

"So what else is new with you?" He had heard this plea a thousand times before. "I'm going to take a quick shower." He headed for the bedroom suite.

"Better be quick; the burgers will be done soon," she called out after him. A shiver went through her thinking of that time; she herself was every bit as snobbish as her daughter in wanting the ball to retain its homogeneity.

He could hear her heels clicking on the inlaid. It brought back the old days when she was in command of her own kitchen before the long line of domestics over the years. He swept through the sumptuous bedroom suite, much too feminine for his consumption, peeling his clothes on the way to the bathroom. The thought, subconsciously put aside till now, occurred to him as his razor scraped under his chin. "What about the girls?…How will they take this mad exodus? Tammy, of course, shouldn't be a problem at her age, although she probably has her heart set on graduating from that Swellsley Finishing Trap…aw, she'll adjust…she's a young twelve…hasn't been exposed long enough to the trappings.…Then again, they say if you're born into it, it's even tougher;…still, she loves horses and the ranch.…Must stop worrying about fulfilling everybody's wants or I'll wind up reading contracts in the Exxon building for fifteen thousand, instead of nailing them down for a hundred thou. Peggy,… hmm, I don't know…twenty-two, beautiful, thrives on the fast crowd, modeling, out of Manhattanville now…can't see her singing at a roundup fire.…Hell, she's old enough to do what she wants…who cares?…will miss her though." He stepped into the stall and sang "The Yellow Rose of Texas" over the roar of the shower at full pressure. He stepped out in a cocky mood, hopeful that Peggy might go for the adventure of a new lifestyle. "Why, she might even try out for the Dallas Cowboy cheerleaders.…Football gets in your blood down there." Wrapped in a towel he walked into the bedroom.

Ann stood there, looking thoroughly the housewife with an apron over her delicate dress and a spatula dominating the extension of her left hand in lieu of her huge diamond ring. "With or without?" she asked. "It's been so long I don't remember if you take onions." She looked down and screamed, "Oh, Paul, won't you ever learn to dry your feet! Look at my beautiful carpet!"

He said, "We can't take it with us; besides you make it sound like I tracked in mud—I do wash my feet, you know.…And what do you mean?…Of course, I take onions."

"And what do you mean, we can't take it with us?"

"Surely, you don't expect us to keep both houses."

"My God," she cried, "you really are thinking of the ranch!…I thought perhaps to get away for a bit while you feel downcast …but this!…Permanently? …Absurd!"

"Why?…it's not like it's a foreign country.…"

"Some think so."

"Well, even you like it down there."

"Yes, but as a retreat—to get away from the bustle of Long Island."

"Exactly, to get away," he agreed.

"But not to stay in the sticks!"

"Just a nice place to visit, eh?"

She nodded, sighed and sat down on the bed. "It appears you've been thinking of this for some time. I guess I've seen it coming."

He looked at her quizzically, then reminisced, "I can't remember the last time I've seen you in an apron. What's it been…since our first year married?…when you were proud to cook for me."

She shook her head, slightly annoyed. "How would you know…when was the last time you were home for dinner? Besides, you know very well that Mabel goes home early, well before supper." She turned on her heels and said, "Onions it is. You never order them at a restaurant," she reminded him.

"That's because I never order hamburger, lest it embarrass you."

She swung back, annoyed, poised to throw the spatula at him. She softened, lowered her eyes. "I am that way at times, I know." She sat back down on the bed, looked down at the damp stains on the carpet, wishing she had a sponge. "I don't mean to be." Looking up at him, she walled her eyes. "I just want things to be nice. After all, you don't buy your suits in J.C. Penny's. That doesn't excuse it, though, does it?"

"Don't get all uptight over it—Jesus, I was just teasing," he cried. She nodded her head on hearing the Lord's name. He went through the underwear drawer of his dresser. "Blame the damnable Depression."

"Oh, wait!" She jumped up from the bed and put her hand on the drawer. "I have just the thing!" she added excitedly, handing him the spatula. She rolled open one of the closets, then pondered belatedly, "What's the Depression got to do with it?"

"Oh, I read somewhere that our generation is paranoid over poverty. Hell, my family was lucky; they both had jobs and kept them. You, though, with your father dying, you had it rough."

"That's dumb; I'm certainly not a mental case because of it. I might appreciate money for the security…that's about it. Besides that has nothing to do with your calling me a snob."

"I apologize…*both* of us, then?" He shrugged. " But this I do know: if we were so damned scared we sure would have done a better job squirreling it away instead of spending everything we make."

"We did our share—there's Texas and …" She let it escape. "As long as we're roughing it now," she said, though not seriously coming to terms. She opened the closet doors in the dressing area and disappeared momentarily; she re-emerged dragging a large cardboard box. She dug into it and came up with a salty pair of green shorts and fatigues. "Here put these on and relax," she commanded; "might as well do the slumming act right." She reached in again and threw down an old pair of moccasins. "This should add to the evening."

"Well, I'll be damned." He looked at her with a twinkle—he wasn't sure why. "You've kept all that junk!" He rummaged through it. "Even the old green 't' shirt with the 2nd Marines stamped on it," he marveled, handing her back the spatula.

"The pants you can always half zip up under your pot," she estimated, "but the shirt would take a miracle."

"The shorts, too," he clucked, chucked them and put on boxers.

She giggled as he struggled with the remnants of the past. She was surprised that he could get the zipper all the way up, though the navel looked as though it were poised to spew out. She snorted when he struggled with the 't' shirt which stopped under the arms unable to go up or down. They both laughed as she struggled, spatula in hand, to pull the shirt back up over his head. "Perhaps I should leave you like this—in a straight jacket—until you regain your senses." They burst with laughter affected by the bitterly beautiful war years, laughing as they had never laughed before in some thirty years.

Marguerite entered; her white tennis outfit was a stark contrast to her long dark hair, brown eyes and deep tan. "Good heavens!" She looked at her father. "Dad! Are you going to a masquerade or a reunion?" She swiftly dismissed the frolic and turned to her mother. "Did you pick up my dry-cleaning, Mother?"

Ann still laughing, nodded; handed her daughter the spatula and finally yanked the shirt back over Paul's head. She looked at her daughter's get-up. "Good grief, you didn't change at the club!" Marguerite started to shake her head to say she had no time. Raising her hand to suspend her daughter's answer which she anticipated, Ann ordered, "Before you go into one of your tirades on how little time you have to get ready for your date, hop back in the Mustang and pick up some cold beer for your father."

"Beer!" she echoed with disbelief. "You want me to pick up beer!"

"You heard correctly—go! Ask for *Coors*." Turning to her husband, she asked with bland and playful sarcasm, "That's what they drink down there, right, Tex?" Marguerite looked at her mother resentfully, then turned to go, took a step then returned and held out her palm. Ann frowned, responding, "You have your own money—the treat's on you."

Taken aback, Marguerite smiled with some embarrassment and said softly to her father, "Would you like anything else, Dad?— chips, dip?"

"No, Peg, beer will do just fine.…Your mother likes sarsaparilla…maybe,…"

"What is that?"

He turned to the dresser and picked up his wallet. "No, that's okay, Dad; I have money."

"Don't trouble yourself over sarsaparilla, Marguerite; your father thinks it's still the rage."

"Oh, you're on a nostalgia trip, eh?" she said as she left the room. She felt good now instead of resentful as she had normally felt when her mother, however seldom, exercised authority. This errand, she thought, made her a part of her parent's present playfulness. She was certain that they were involved in some prankish orgy of no consequence and since she at times was aware of her wilful alienation, presumably natural in youth's relationship to parents, nevertheless felt petty that she was unable to give to them—she wished she could have had that moment back when she instinctively held out her palm, she would have cut off her arm—just as she had wanted to cut out her tongue after her argument with her father over the Ball.

At the kitchen table Paul and Ann sat having their hamburgers and French fries, which Paul had deep-fried—something he had not done in years. He was back in civilian garb—golf clothes, tried and true moccasins—as his flab could not take the excruciating pinching of his old marine pants. The image of his wife standing before the griddle loitered. She had seemed much more alive and attractive and less statuesque and distant, which he had become accustomed to these fast stepping years. She had made a quick change into an old jumper and shorts. He was amazed how she had retained her slim figure. In his moments of sentiment, he had thought of wanting her always in the kitchen, not chained and enslaved, but as a source of gratification and comfort for him. During their early years of marriage, he used to sit at the kitchen table and watch her lithe body move from item to item and her curved calves from place to place in their harmonious co-efficiency to serve him. But the world did not pause for sentiment or tranquil communication: inner reality always trailed off somewhere in the thicket of interpersonal relations governed by outer realities. To stay on the super highway of success, one had no time for sight-seeing. Because of this inexorable order of things—now disorder, having tasted sour grapes—Paul had to settle for a dozen or more domestics each occupying the kitchen over the ensuing years, expelling him from the intimate beauties of home life, on which he would not have capitalized anyway because his work kept him out to all hours, entertaining clients, and on weekends playing twenty-seven, sometimes thirty-six holes.

However, Ann, too, had been driven from her home—her domain as mother and housewife—because of relentless obligations to the outside world. She had known as a pre-teenager the inversion of fortune when a policeman knocked meekly on their door to inform her mother of the death of her husband. For twelve years Ann had worked assiduously to provide for her younger siblings. Though very much in love with Paul at twenty-five, she had delayed marriage three years until her brother and sister were able to take charge of providing for their ailing mother and young brother. Marriage was thus a painful letdown from the freedom she had expected. Marriage was not only just another job—she could have resigned herself to that when out of love, affection and the caring of a home appreciated—it was more a position that required managerial and labor skills, and an adversary role that effected a deadly distance of swirling objects, rather than close up subjects in her relations with her family, the domestic help, the gardener, the repairmen and the countless frustrations encountered in maintaining image within the circle. Marriage had been reduced to a surrealistic collage of chauffeuring, endless errands, school functions, hostessing, hauling groceries, emergency laundering, dental appointments, boring foursomes, appliance failures, college visits, and a tired bed companion. She did not really know what, but she had hoped for more—or perhaps less. There may now be that hope, she thought, although remote. She knew too—she thought she knew—this was no financial crisis. Ann kept a close eye on the investments the company retirement fund accrued—Paul seldom paid any attention to it because he assumed he would just go on working till he dropped dead—so she was aware that the value of shares in the fund would very nearly reach, if not pass, the half million mark by the next fiscal report.

Sitting across from her husband in a rarefied moment, unhindered by the crisscross bombardment of daily living, she, nevertheless, could not communicate. Thirty years ago when chance teased them with strands from the network of high style, she felt the art of communicating simplistic sentiment waning; only her mother was able to elicit the lost art when Ann would visit her, which was often and probably for that reason: to sustain some semblance of the simple life. When her mother died three years ago, she lost a close friend and her private need to unclutter, however volatile, a life that seemed always under assault. At this moment of silence, she too was thinking of the past in which a carefree, lollipop romance—not without expectations of ice cream in the end—with a man filled with a driving ambition to obtain success bereft of obsession, solely for the purpose of the good life for his wife and progeny—the end to which Jefferson had promised the pursuit. What went wrong?

Jefferson would have told them: in a materialistic society, all things noble, all great expectations are lost in the great pursuit. Had they been able to take a reading of their course to discover that forward is not always the better course, that a walk to the other side of the station to take the returning local is perhaps, after all, the better route, it would not have mattered; for the escape route is ironically for the robust only. Ann had perhaps subconsciously experienced a disintegration within the splendor of the *nouveau riches*; yet all her aspirations hinged on this very success within the pernicious rationale of a society gone ajar, repeatedly slamming a once hearty core to pulpy soap, thus allowing access to bubbles of inconsequence. In his shadow of this giant step back, she felt inadequate, wary. Could she recapture her true self? Could she dismiss with one sweeping stroke all the forces that had given her transitory moments of triumph?— Marguerite's debut and subsequent modeling success as an adult, Tammy's enrollment in Swellsley, her spectacular eagle on the last hole to win the club trophy, that great sense of power walking into a shop and the salespeople jumping to her every wish, knowing that any given moment she may buy out the store, and, oh, those cocktail parties that pumped meaning into ego!   Her initiation into this barrage of upper—rather the very top— middle class was thrilling to her. She had ridden the crest skillfully and with understanding. She was the village sweetheart among the merchants who were charmed by her grace, warmth and patience. At the club the caddies scrambled for her bag, not simply because they were proud to carry for such a beautiful woman who tipped so well, but because she had an air of a kindly big sister about her that had been groomed after her father's death and had not yet been shaken from her style. Gradually, however, she became possessed by the divine right of arrogant station in her circle as her humble origin and sense of gratitude evaporated. The countless phone calls—requesting her presence at charity banquets, invitations to cocktail parties or bridge, golf dates with the oil magnates' wives, obsequious pleas for her to arrange a meeting with her modeling agency in behalf of a neighbor's beauty, or to pressure Tammy's academy to accept one of the club member's children—all fed her ego to the point of no return to where human relations had been a medium for her original warmth and charitable understanding; rather, it pointed to the gridiron of rivalry and the theater of glibness. The private realm had gone public without which achievement, no longer sustained by self-fulfillment and integrity, is dissatisfying, an unheralded event, aching to transpire. Nonetheless, Ann had the uncanny acumen, in her rare moments of reflection, to see through it all—more important through herself—as an endless round of role-playing without identity beyond verbal society's proclivity to name drop within an endless spiral of symbiosis. She used to wonder at times if those with little money were more or less true beings. When her brothers and sister visited, she would observe a more down-to-earth happiness, but mingled with enthrallment of her material possessions and traces of envy. It had bothered her when she concluded that perception of character in the main was built on fortune and not the inverse.

She still reserved sufficient integrity, though, to permit her psyche to be vaguely disrupted by guilt in having indoctrinated her children in values she herself would not wish to possess in her own childhood. In her anxiety to protect them from the ugliness and what was her dread, she had dampened her children's enthusiasm whenever they indicated liberalism toward the other side. Once when Marguerite in her teen years had accepted a date from a young A&P clerk, she grounded her for a month. When Tammy had expressed a desire to spend part of a summer with her cousins—the children of Ann's sister—whom Ann had thought the world of, positively refused, lest Tammy lose sight of her ionospheric destiny, because her sister's station was frightfully common. In this instance, however, she rationalized justification inasmuch as her sister, for presumably the very same reason, only in reverse, denied one of her boys to stay with Tammy for a period one summer.

She looked at her husband and said, "I believe Tammy will rather like this move—she's so much like my sister." She still was not convinced that he would go through with this move, even temporarily, let alone permanently; nor for that matter was she convinced that she would accept it at all.

Paul looked up from his elongated reflection in the shiny coffee pot, wishing he had a beer to go with his burger; he hated coffee with his dinner. He rejoined, "I hope you're right....I'd hate to see unhappiness come from this. You're right, though,...she is like Dot. Here we've been in the same house some twenty-five years and how many times has she moved?"

"I lost count. But I didn't mean it in that way. I see much of my mother in Dorothy, especially now that Mom is gone, she mused."

"I suppose it'll be rough on all of us for a while." He stared at himself in the coffee pot again.

"Paul," she said in a soft, serious tone, "you do know what you're doing?...I mean, you really want to do this because you feel a true need, not just an escape."

"I think I'm old enough to discern the difference. Should I get cold feet, we can always come back." He winced at the thought.

"But what if this house is sold in the meantime?" she asked anxiously.

"I hope it is—we need the equity." He scowled.

"Oh, and move back to Levittown, I suppose," she whined.

"Sarcasm will get you nowhere. Surely to a smaller home...perhaps even a condo."

She looked at him sadly. "God, my beautiful home—just when I have it the way I want it."

He laughed. "This house is never the way you want it for very long. Anyway, you'll love redoing the ranch."

"But we designed it as a vacation home. None of our furniture here is congruent. I hate the thought of selling all our lovely things."

"Well, let's just take it one at a time...time enough, the house isn't even on the market. Then we'll put everything in storage till we're sure."

"Will we ever be sure?" she asked.

"Where's the plucky colleen I married?" He reached over and stole her pickle. "To tell you the truth I'm surprised over your reaction—I expected scrappy resistance."

She laughed. "When we're down there and you're practicing your roping— you know the adage—give him enough..."

"I should've known you were up to something," he chuckled and reached across the table and softly tapped his knuckles on her chin. "Look, if it turns out I've made a mistake, I still have some connections—any oil company would hire me. Even at a fourth of the salary, we'll do just fine," he assured her but unable to mask his diffidence. "But don't plan on coming back, I'm fed up with the city and suburban living. You see, I'm more selfish than noble. I suppose, in a way, I want to return to the good old days when we sucked lollipops instead of sipping martinis."

"I think I might like that," she said in a doubting tone. A poem her father used to recite to her and which was eventually included in her evening prayers, resounded in the back of her consciousness, locking in fears:

> It is said that in the beginning there was
> nothing.
> Nonsense! For then on the drawing
> board was everything
> Locked in—perfect and sublime!—
> Heedless to the storm issuing slime
> That Necessity and Chance
> Would dare advance.

He heard the garage door open. "Marguerite is back. I hope the ordeal of asking the clerk for beer wasn't too humiliating for her." I remember sending her into the deli when she was about eleven—I was in the mood for a cheeseburger when we got home from the club...you never have the old-fashioned American-Swiss. I think you were visiting your mother at the time—anyway, I hand her a dollar and told her to get a quarter's worth of cheese. In the Depression I used to have to go down to the deli under our tentative apartment—Pop had to rent out our house for a couple of years or we would've lost it—and get a nickel's worth. When she returned to the car, I asked for the change. She put out her hand and said, 'You owe me money, Dad. You didn't really think I'd ask for twenty-five cents worth of cheese, did you? I got half a pound.'"

"Paul, you didn't! That would embarrass anybody. Beer is another thing,… after all, she's done a beer commercial—imported, though."

"Of course, that makes all the difference in the finer circles. If you believe the ads—why, even the blue collars are getting picky. God, in my day the guys were tickled pink to have 'Knickerbocker.'"

"Why…is beyond me. It still reeks of poverty," she reminisced.

"Not anymore—beer is in now. Your Irish uncles and cousins from Jersey City still linger, eh? No wonder you're always conveniently forgetting to pick up a six pack for me."

She countered, "No, that's not it at all. Don't attribute a childhood obsession to common sense. You know perfectly well that when I do buy beer, you open it up, take a few chugs and then let it stand to smell up the house, while you've turned to your scotch. You know, Paul, you only think you're down-to-earth. How many times have you pestered me for homemade pea soup?…When I relent and make it for you, you let it go sour in the refrigerator.…Oh, and the humiliation I went through searching hardware, houseware, boutiques to find you a tin pail, just so you could impress my brothers with your nostalgic value in serving them 'good old draught' as the old Irish fathers in your neighborhood had done!"

"Humiliation?" he echoed. "I'm the one who went down to the local tavern to have it filled. The bartender looked at me as though I were the town drunk." He laughed.

"The town phony!" she laughed.

"Gotta shower and change." Marguerite dropped the six pack on the counter along with a small brown bag and reeled to exit, then turned, having noticed his civilian clothes, "Changed your mind about the masquerade, eh Dad? Sorry, Mother, no sarsp."

"Say, what's in the bag?" he asked.

She popped back at the threshold. "Oh, just a quarter's worth of American-Swiss." She disappeared. They looked at each other and burst into laughter.

Later, relaxing together in the den, barely attentive to the television, they scattered thoughts and observations concerning their new fate. Ann, anxiety subsiding as the excitement of challenge welled up, was going through magazines for pointers on how she might mix her northern motif to the Texas ranch, for she was loath to selling all her furniture. Paul was actually enjoying the beer. To Ann's surprise, he did not switch to scotch. "You know, red meat is making a come-back,…why not raise cattle?" he offered.

"Yes, I can just see *you* branding cows.…And I suppose I'd be the one to hit them over the head with a baseball bat," she projected. "We're retiring, remember?"

Tammy came in the front door, dropped her duffel bag in the foyer, then went into the den. She kissed her mother. Ann commented, "My, you have beautiful color…beach living agrees with you." She noticed admiringly that her hair was even blonder from the beach exposure. Her eyes seemed bluer— like her Nana's.

"Yeah, how is it we don't have a beach house, Dad?" she asked as she sat on his lap, hugged and kissed him.

"Too risky—can't get insurance out in Westhampton."

"Doesn't bother the Blakelys," she noted as she took the beer glass from his hand and pretended to drink from it.

"Don't get ideas," he said playfully as he took it back from her. "The Blakelys can afford a hurricane loss …with their millions."

"You mean we aren't millionaires?" she asked apparently surprised.

"I'm afraid we never will be now," her mother interpolated, looking at her husband directly. He grimaced. She was right; she thought: he had little idea of his worth.

Ignoring Ann's remark, he lectured, patting his daughter's sunburned thighs, "Your first lesson in sociology, my pet, is that millionaires are never under pressure to stay ahead of people like us; it is our duty to break our necks catching up with them."

"Such a lesson to teach a child," Ann chided.

"I'm not such a child that I can't get involved in some silly adult matters, Mom. I think I know what Dad means. I should have supposed that they really do have more than we do—quite a lot more, now that I think about it. I can see that keeping up with the Blakelys could be a drag. Laura's closet is twice the size of mine and they're always cleaning out half of it each season and replacing it with new up-to-the-minute fashions. Half my closet is filled with Marguerite's hand-me-downs."

"That's your mother for you; she never throws anything out—except for my things, though not the marine junk." He weaved to catch a glimpse of old 44 driving one deep to centerfield.

"You're very lucky to have a sister with such fine things," Ann reminded her. "Oh, Mother, don't get me wrong. I love Marguerite's clothes. I just meant that the Blakelys just go ahead doing their thing coolly and you just never notice—new car every year, their trips to

Europe—Laura, too, has a big sister, but everything is picked up by St. Mary's for the poor."

"Well, now you know the difference between appearance and reality," her father said with professorial finality as he lifted her off his lap and became involved in the game as Rivers stole second.

"Aw, I don't really care, Dad. I'm very happy and will stay happy even if we become as poor as Aunt Dot."

In defense of her side of the family, Ann scolded her, "How dare you suggest Aunt Dot is poor. They do very handsomely for themselves. Perhaps you could stand a lesson on what real poverty is."

"Oh, the good old days, right, Mom?" she intoned without meaning to be sarcastic.

Ann shook her head; ringlets fell forward—after the burgers she had deliberately mussed up her permanent—she said in a soft tone, "I'm not saying they were necessarily good, but as a lesson in appreciation for all we have today."

Tammy embraced her mother. "I'm sorry, Mom, I didn't mean...Gee!...I love Aunt Dot! I only meant I love both you and dad for yourselves, not for what you give me. Nana always used to say that."

"That's my girl!" Paul blurted as the last out was made and he reached for the remote and clicked off the television. "You're going to love Texas!"

Tammy turned to him quizzically. "I already do! But we never go there anymore!...What's that got to do with it?"

"Your father means that we might live there... permanently."

"Great!" she shrilled, twisting with joy.

"Surely, you'll miss all your friends," Ann interjected.

"I'll make new ones; don't worry about that. Have you been transferred, Dad?"

He smiled. "Yes, I suppose you could say that." He winked at his wife.

"Golly!...this means I can ride my pinto everyday...wear jeans, no more of those stuffy academy uniforms, no more keeping up with Laura..."

"Don't get carried away so—I don't want a cowpoke angel with a dirty face on my hands down there!" Ann objected mildly. They all laughed.

In bed, they discussed their future like they were newlyweds. For Ann it was a chance to regain herself; she had felt for some time that, in spite of the luxurious living that she embraced fully, albeit progressively jaded, there was a need for change—not simply another of their endlessly recurring vacation trips—she had no idea what until now. Over the past few hours, she reasoned—particularly after Tammy's reaction—that when an option comes along one should pursue it when it is at least vaguely clear that existing conditions have gone awry. It was not simply that Paul had lost his job—he could have done very well if he really wanted to—the catch was that he did not want to, apparently for some of the same reasons Ann had tentatively accepted his decision. They saw an opportunity to side-step the quasi-obstacles of their lifestyle and perhaps regain simplicity and calm. It differed from some people in their fifties looking forward to the interment of retirement; rather, they were looking to a recapture of their carefree youth with very delimited, obtainable aims.

He reached over and touched her shoulder. "Apparently I was right about Tam; she hasn't been saran-wrapped for this life yet," he said. "Of course, she's been bratty and demanding at times—and we went right along with it, perhaps even feeding it—still, it's nice to know at least one of your offspring still has a naturalness about her."

"Yes, but I hope you're not implying that Marguerite hasn't any naturalness about her," she answered, rolling toward him. "Naturalness is subjective, you know, and within her culture, I think she's very natural—well,…suitable, comfortable. She does have a head on her shoulders.…Her grades at school improved dramatically her final year; yet it was like pulling teeth to get her to show me her transcript. I thought she had failed a subject or two.…So, she does have intelligence, not just beauty."

He rubbed his palm on her forehead. "You're right," he sighed. "It's unfair for me to fault her because I suspect she will not go with us. It follows the image of a brain on pretty shoulders."

"Oh, she'll spend sometime with us; but that's all you can expect. After all, she's old enough to pursue her own life."

"You're pretty sure, then, eh?"

She tickled his ear absently and said, "Yes,…and why shouldn't she? How many girls have her success so early in their years, not to mention ever?"

"But where will she live? I don't want her all alone in this house."

"Oh, I'm sure she'll arrange to stay with her modeling friends who have an apartment in Forest Hills. It'll be good for her to pay her own way."

"I don't like the sound of it—an apartment in the city!"

"Oh, I've been there once with her on our way back from city shopping. It's a very nice neighborhood and the building has excellent security."

"I wasn't even thinking of that."

"Oh, Paul, You're still living in the Forties! she chuckled. "Don't you trust your daughter?" He stared at her dumbly in the dim moon-cast. "Your silence answers my question," she concluded.

"No, it's for the other girls I don't trust."

"They have fathers too," she reminded him. "Besides, they're very nice, sophisticated, nothing cheap about them."

He reached over for his cigarettes on the night table and lit one. "Natural, eh?— within their circle, that is. No, I'm afraid I'll have to insist that she come along."

"Good, spoken like a real father, but it won't do you any good—she'll only defy you—par for the course nowadays." She propped herself up and cautioned, "We'll lose her if you do, and then, knowing you, you'll probably change your plans and wind up working in New York again for pittance. I've seen our lives rotate round her whims for too long. But you can't expect her to rotate round your whim—it doesn't work both ways."

"Oh, it's a whim, now, is it?...And what do you mean, New York?—there's always Huston, Dallas." He raised himself onto his elbow to retrieve the ash tray. "Oh, I get it. Male menopause!"

"I just meant, dear, that she will look at it in that light. Anyway, it could turn out to be just that—you're not that sure, right?" She tried to search his eyes in the dim cast.

He rolled back, looked up at the ceiling, exhaled his smoke. "Oh, maybe you're right. Why draw her into something that could go awry?"

"Now, let's not make the move with that negative attitude," she chided. She was sorry she had brought it up. She stroked his thinning hair; moved closer to him and caressed his chest. He relaxed; the ordeal of his day was conveniently locked in the back storage room of his mind. He put out his cigarette and reciprocated, gently stroking her thighs. She stretched, squirmed, every muscle in her body quivered and she sighed. They made love as they used to—out of need, not nuptial duty.

She was sound asleep in his arms when he awoke and looked at the luminous dial. It was three in the morning. He eased his arm out from under her; she didn't stir. He was astonished at how restful she was. She was always a restless sleeper. He heard a car pull up into the circle drive at the front of the house. The engine idled for a while then stopped. He waited several minutes for the car door to open and close—to no avail. He got out of bed and peered through the blinds. He could barely make out two silhouettes sitting in a Stingray. "Thank God for those consoles in the middle!" he thought. He felt a double-barreled frustration: he had never spied on his daughter before, believing he never had to; perhaps he should not have had such trust. Now that he was spying, he reasoned that it was justifiable concern; yet what else was there to do? He jumped into his bottoms and went downstairs and flicked off the lamp post light, the act of which was of no consequence. He switched it back on. Her escort's head was no longer in view; but a shadowy hump was on the passenger's side. "That son-of-a-bitch jumped the console and reclined her seat!" he screeched. Enraged, he flicked the light on and off rapidly, then left it on. He saw in the car's interior light, Marguerite pushing her Ivy-league quarterback off after having flung open the door.

The interior light went out as her date reached for the car door and slammed it shut. He had been drinking heavily and was determined not to pass up the play signal to reach the goal—this beautiful prize. He smothered her neck, shoulders, face and lips with wet kisses, despite her knee-kicking, punching, pushing, wailing resistance. The light flickered some more. He reached for the car door-lock switch, jumped back in the driver's seat and started up the car. Marguerite tried to reach the ignition key. He pushed her back. Paul ran out of the house and jumped in front of the car just as it started to roll and then rocked from the sudden halt. Paul went around to Marguerite's side and grabbed the door handle; the young man nervously reached for the dash and unlocked it. Paul and Marguerite simultaneously opened it. He pulled her out. "Nice friend you have," he growled.

"He's no friend of mine—not anymore," she replied unable to look at her father or her date while nervously straightening her hair and clothing after slamming the door. The motor began to rev up, but Paul pulled open the door and peered in at the nervous young man who quickly came to his senses.

"Did you hear that, young fellow? Don't come within a mile of this house or I'll have the village police on your tail."

"I'm really sorry, sir,…guess I had too much to drink," he said meekly.

"I suppose that excuses you, eh? Go find some other bitch to jump!" he slammed the door.

"*Other*! Dad!" Marguerite squealed as the car roared off. "How could you!…Oh, the shame!— And in your pajamas, no less!" She ran up the steps bawling.

His nerves kept his pitch high, though conciliatory as he followed her into the house. "I didn't mean it that way—I was just so damned mad—Oh, hell! What am I apologizing for? Goddammit!…you are a…" But he could not get himself to repeat the word. She threw herself on the large sectional and buried her face in a pillow and sobbed. He turned on a lamplight and knelt beside her and awkwardly patted her head, then gently stroked her soft ruffled hair.

Her sobs subsided; she turned her head and sheepishly looked up at her brute-father, then pleaded, "Oh, Daddy, what happened to you? You never lost control before."

"For that, young lady, I'm sorry," tenderly but not to the point of losing the sarcasm. She dropped onto the pillow again, sighing annoyance. He went on, "But the fact is I took control tonight in face of your defiance and contempt for rules."

She jerked her face out of the pillow. "Defiance!" she repeated.

He growled and flicked her knee. "What else to call it?...out to all hours..."

"Dad," she interrupted with widening eyes, "You never specified hours before...well, not since I was a teenager, anyway. My God, I'm out of college!"

Freeing a kink in his knee, he shifted to the other and said with a contorted expression, "And what have you learned?...to be a woman of the world? Tens of thousands of dollars later and all I've got to show for it is a good-time Charlene."

"Is that all you think of me, Dad?" she cried. "I make good money in a dignified profession—despite what outsiders might think. How many of my friends outside of the agency work?...none! Their fathers never stop paying for them—always vacation trips, purposeless graduate 'matrics', spas and fat farms, golf, tennis, skydiving—fulfilling any fancy just to keep them out of their thinning or greying hair. Do you know Ellen?— no, of course not. Well, she's been engaged three times already and her parents have given an extravagant party each time—the last one at the Waldorf, can you imagine such idiocy? Each one outdoing the previous one and as elaborate as a wedding reception!"

He jumped up and paced in front of the coffee table. "So what are you telling me? I'm a lousy provider—you want more fringe benefits?"

"You see?" She shook her head and bit her full lips, smeared from the rough treatment in the car. "You don't even know me! I have grown some, you know. Not all young people today are spoiled brats—though, God forgive me, I've been one for so long it's hard to break the habit. Yet ever since that fall-out we had over the Cardinal's Ball, it's been nagging at my insides. Last year I finally decided to do something about myself. But it's like going on a diet; it takes an awful lot of will power to unravel all the wrongs and then rewind it right."

He stalled in his tracks, surprised but not convinced, then said callously, "So?...where's the big change?"

"At no cost to you I'm going to take graduate courses at Columbia this fall semester."

"Really?...I didn't know....I assumed you had enough of college and really had gone because of your mother and me."

"Mother doesn't know either. I gave it some thought and realized that the glamour of modeling will someday wear off and that I'll be needing new directions—besides there aren't many opportunities in modeling once you pass thirty."

He was surprised by this; he had never thought of his daughter in any light other than a "poor little rich girl" with nothing better to do than model for the sheer ego-image of it. He sat down next to her and touched her hair for a moment. "Gosh, Peg, what makes you think I wouldn't continue to pay for your education?"

She looked up with a faint smile and said softly, "Oh, I know you would, but that's not the point….I really want to do it myself…to prove to myself that I really want to look beyond the tinsel surface."

"Well, I suppose that's noble," he said lukewarmly. He still had this prejudice against college as being a waste of good labor time—even for his own kin. "But on the subject of tonight I feel you failed to look beyond to the consequence," he clumsily lectured. "Did you think the lawn light switched on and off by itself?"

"I certainly did not think that—I was sure it was Mother, warning me to come in soon. She's done that several times," she noted.

"She has? I never knew…"

"I never would have thought it was you because, either you're not home or get home so late yourself and tired that you wouldn't hear our security alarm if it went off. I forget that you were home tonight. You've been a pretty busy person over the years, Dad."

"And no time to be a father,…is that it?" He glanced over with scowl.

She leaned over and hugged him. "No, I would never think that. All the girls I know have 'busy' fathers—that's the code today. The important thing is to know a father is there when you need him. You were always—well, almost, especially tonight even though bizarre….I must admit that boy was beginning to scare me."

"Did it ever occur to you that fooling around—most of all in a car—can lead to 'scary' complications?…and tonight in front of the house, no less."

"But, Dad, that's the safest place! Would you rather it be in…well, never mind … the fact is it has always been just 'fooling around' in front of the house that way it's supposed to never go beyond harmless necking."

He recoiled. "Why does there have to be necking at all?"

"Oh, Dad, be serious. When a guy spends some money on a girl, he expects some reward. Surely, you know that. The world hasn't changed that much."

He scowled, "Look, I haven't been completely cut off from youth's sub-cultures, you know. Everyday I've seen those young things—yeah, both sexes—that call themselves office workers preoccupied with their sex image in lieu of work ethic, so what if he spent more than some…then what?"

She shook her head playfully and responded with a laugh. "Now, you're being silly, Dad. You know it would never go any further," she added seriously, wrinkling her brow.

His observation reminded her: "It didn't appear that *he* knew it, though."

She grimaced and nodded to the coffee table. "I'm sure he didn't. I'll not pretend, Dad—it's tough for a girl today. Sex is wholesale, or at the very most at bargain prices. But I'm hanging to the ideal until Mr. Right comes along. I'll admit sexuality is important to me, especially in modeling, but sex itself isn't."

He was embarrassed and winced on hearing the dreaded word, but he believed her and was very pleased. Nevertheless, he was frightened over his leaving her to the wolves. He slumped back and seemed to ask the immediate space. "What is it with kids today?"

"Dad, I'm not a kid anymore—no longer your little girl and I hope no longer a spoiled brat. Remember how Mother was so upset with me the first year in college when I behaved like some rich girl who felt no need for survival and consequently barely studied? That too made me upset with myself. I spoke to Nana about it—I loved talking to her; she was so beautifully real!— she told me that just before granddad died, Mom was just twelve then, that his dying regret was that he couldn't continue living to provide his kids with a college education. Well, that did it!...Shame welled up in me. I was throwing away my granddad's dying wish, whether it was a generation past or not. To think I had never known him; a man dead for some eighteen years before I was born and he became a part of me, just as he was an enduring, living thing in Nana until she died. I decided then that I was not going to be some jerk, relying on my looks or the benevolence of an agency, so I opened the books to a new world. So I think I understand your question about today's kids. It is a parent's cry of frustration, but, Dad, you didn't make the world and neither did I. Nor did Mother, though she tries to remake it. I know how frightening it is to be poor. Oh, Mother never discussed it with me, but piecemeal I would overhear Nana and Mom talking about those days. Many times Mother would drive me crazy when she seemed so resistant to a display of naturalness, deep affection or simple fun. Mommy never let us do some of the wild things that others our age had done as a matter of everyday life. It always seemed like Tammy and I walked on eggs or had to suspend ourselves above some dread." She put her head on the pillow, blinked her eyes, then looked at him kindly. "Who knows why values change? Some blame the baby-boomers; others blame their parents for being so busy enhancing the standard of living they forgot to do their parenting. I'm tired of the finger of blame flicking everywhere! I don't happen to believe either. The world just changes under our nose and there are so many forces at work we cannot begin to understand. Things just seem to happen and they're cyclic. I suppose just like fashions; but do we really have to wear them?"

He sat up and heaved his chest; he was proud of her, and shame reared up too in that he never really thought of her as having convictions and theories like some elite intellect; ashamed that he, even though she was barely on the fringe of his everyday thoughts, had claimed her as a possession and nothing more. He said, faltering, "I…suppose…in some way…that is, we all must accept responsibility…but parents the major share…and I don't just mean in parenting, perhaps more so in exercising citizenship by monitoring these events that take us to the bazaar." He felt her eyes on him; he glanced over and thought they had a new sparkle. "You know, Peg, every generation has its fling at youth as it should be, but why do perceptions and values have to change?" He sighed. " Perhaps some generation will take the time to show that because we're in a different period of time doesn't necessarily mean change. I hate it when writers and critics continue to alienate one decade from another. That you were born after and your brother, God rest his soul, before the war, shouldn't mean a damned thing."

She was surprised by him too: perhaps her father went beyond a robot of a programmed society by actually thinking outside the matrix. She was sure she could count on her fingers the number of times they ever had a talk, much less a real one. Her montage of her father's character was from overhearing his conversations with members at the club or with business associates that he occasionally entertained at home and what she overheard was simple hogwash concerning the stock market or the oil industry and occasionally some golf tips and scores. With relatives it was sports, which he pretended to know more than he did since he rarely had the time or interest to become a student of it as now is the case in the Yuppy world and in the blue collar realm, in which sports leisure has become an institution. She looked over at him with renewed admiration. "That's noble, sensitive thinking, Dad, but I don't think there's any support for that kind of effort, although I suppose we could be more discriminating as to whom we elect to public office. A case in point is that fellow they just nominated a few weeks ago—grade B fits him, all right."

"I guess I'm really in no position to preach since I'm retiring and abandoning the world." Her jaw dropped as he went on, "I suppose what I mean is that I don't really give a damn, even though I know I shouldn't feel that way. You know, the only politics I ever cared about was the tax rate. Reagan, though, might make a good president—always liked his movies."

She grimaced, "Ugh, an actor for president!"

"Not exactly—he was a governor, don't forget."

She shook her head, her long hair falling over most of her face. " Except that he was a Democrat and changed coats, I don't really care," she resigned herself. "But I do about you." She swept away her hair. "You say you're retiring! Dad, I can't believe it! I thought you'd go on forever! Why that's just great! You and Mom deserve it. I hope you both take a long trip. Don't worry about Tammy; I'll manage somehow to take care of her." She turned the coin of retirement and saw the lines on his face, more pronounced with his denture partial out, and was saddened how time wrenched its toll. She thought of Nana. She tried to imagine the Great Depression.

Her genuine excitement and kindness touched him; he should have expected a different reaction had he not had this talk. Indeed, she was no longer his little girl; she had matured, apparently in spite of and behind the backdrop of an artificial world. He did not bring up the subject of Texas; suddenly it seemed irrelevant with respect to her. He pulled himself up from the sectional and said, "How about raiding the 'fridge'?"

"Good idea!" She jumped up. "That's the third best way to solve the problems of the world," she quipped.

"Oh, what are the others?" he asked as they headed for the kitchen.

"Drugs and alcohol."

"I'm glad sex wasn't one of them." He laughed, tinged with embarrassment that he could mention the word so flippantly in his daughter's presence.

"Oh, that's number four," she snickered. "Then again a nickel's worth of cheese should be first."

Originally bought on speculation and as a tax maneuver some fifteen years ago, the "ranch" was all but totally abandoned until Paul first got the urge to spend a winter vacation there about five years ago. While on a business trip to Houston in the spring of the preceding year, he had stopped off with plans in hand to arrange extensive renovations and landscaping to make the house more suitable for their kind of living with the exception that it would still retain its rugged motif. They enjoyed their stay as a great change and the kids loved it because they reveled in their "alien" status, as the local kids had perceived them, because they rode horseback eastern style. The summer of that year they went down again, but packed up early because of the brutal heat. Before he left he arranged for central air-conditioning to be installed. The ensuing years, however, had caused little heartbreak—the exception being Tammy—when Ann's hectic schedules, the children's ever higher circles of social and cultural activity, and Paul's business commitments precluded their finding a coördinates aperture of substantial size to slip through and thus escape the bulletin board of unending pursuits.

The decision had been made to drive down in the station wagon, packed with odds and ends, and summer clothes. Paul wanted to drive to get the feel of adventure and closeness to the wild southwest. To his delight, Marguerite, albeit disappointed when she heard of their plans, agreed to spend some time with them, but would not waste half of it in a car as she had to make arrangements at Forest Hills, collate her records for Columbia and remain on call at the agency to ease the blow of tuition, which was new to her. She would fly down the day after they arrived. Paul knew he was "home" when he spotted an old windmill that stood on his neighbor's property. It was a peaceful scene as it turned lazily in the open sky, marred only by oil derricks, which went unnoticed, in the distance. Dusk was approaching and the exaggerated sun laid its magic carpet across the vast acreage; the splendor of the wild stretched its violet hue from the faint shadows of distant foothills. "What a welcome!: Paul whistled. "Long Island was never like this!"

"Fortunately," Ann broke in, as a sense of alienation crept up. "No place to hide if one of those tornadoes they're always having down here rudely rolls upon us."

"Now, don't start worrying, Ann. Remember your own words—let's not get negative," he said with a chuckle. "Besides with all the construction and other improvements to the house, there's no need for alarm. Incidentally, Hon, the Indians have long since gone," he added with a smile.

"Where are all the horses, Daddy?" Tammy inquired anxiously as she recognized the Kimble property.

Paul looked into the rear view mirror. Tammy was perched on top of the luggage, looking out the rear window, fascinated, drinking in the vastness. "One thing's for sure, our horses are safe. Mr. Kimble who's been caring for them at his place has returned them to our stable," he assured her.

"I hope he's cared for our house as well as he has the horses," Ann said.

"No fear of that—he's very reliable," he said confidently.

"I'll bet we're the only people in the world who've owned horses for five years and rode them only twice and not for four years. At least, we got pictures Mr. Kimble sent up to us," Tammy commented as they passed Kimble's line onto their own.

"Ah, home!" he romanced, then glanced at Ann, hoping for reciprocal enthusiasm.

"Perhaps," Ann rejoined calmly. In her renewal for the lure of the southwest and a potential for a different kind of life if not better, notwithstanding her ambivalence, she simply did not trouble herself last week to open the quarterly report from the retirement fund. She had stuffed it in the desk drawer as a deliberate act of defiance. Now she was thinking that perhaps she should have shown it to him as an incentive to change his mind, inasmuch as it was clear they had substantial resources whereby there was no need to change their living habits. On reflection, however, she felt that within her there might have been another reason for not apprising him.

He noticed her subdued tone for the last day or two. "What's wrong, Hon?...not getting cold feet, are you?"

She looked out at the vast loneliness. "No, I guess I'm just tired from the long trip. A decent sleep in our own bed will help." There was silence for several minutes as the three of them were ensconced in perceptions of the vaguely familiar land. He turned into the long bluestone driveway and pulled up in front of the huge ranch house. "I had forgotten how beautiful the house really is," Ann observed. "Mr. Kimble certainly had the grounds tended too—everything has grown so nicely."

"Like I said: he's reliable—nice neighbor to have." Paul started to unload the wagon, stacking everything on the porch, while Ann unlocked the entrance door. She switched on the indirect lighting and was pleasantly surprised that everything was in its place as they had left it; she was proud of herself that she still remembered every detail. Their house on Long Island had been robbed three times during their vacations. Here, she was beginning to feel secure.

She was delighted that the air-conditioning was working, though the evening cool did not require it, it kept the house fresh smelling. She returned to the porch to help her husband. Her spirits returned, though she could not be sure whether it was a relaxing vacation-feeling or a feeling of renascence. She looked at the anxiety in his face and felt compelled to say warmly, "It's good to be home, dear," she said. He smiled triumphantly.

Ann and Tammy went into the kitchen to scrub out the effects of four years of disuse; apparently Kimble had that taken care of too; for the spacious, modernized kitchen sparkled. "Well, now, how nice! All we have to do is to prepare dinner," Ann said airily to her daughter. She went through the supermarket bags and began to put away most of the items that they had shopped for in town. "You can wash the lettuce and tomatoes, Tammy, while I broil the steaks."

Tammy went to the sink and turned on the faucet. "No water, Mom...how come?"

"Oh, of course, we have a well! I guess the pump has to be turned on. Get your father."

Tammy went into the living room where her father was setting up his and Ann's golf trophies on the ruggedly hewed mantel to solidify his intention of permanence. Tammy went through a box beside him and dug out her equestrian team award from Swellsley. "Put this up for me, Dad,...not that it'll mean anything down here the way they rough ride."

He placed it in the center. "Oh, you'll master their style in no time," he said with confidence.

"There's no water, Dad; Mom said the pump must not be on."

Looking at her curiously, "That shouldn't be—we have power....Or,... maybe Kimble left the switch off in the basement." He turned into the hall and opened the door to the cellar. He fumbled for the light switch. It was comforting that the light bulb was still good. He sighed in relief when he saw that the pump switch was off. He switched it back on. The pump groaned for an instant, then hummed. He felt good. Then it began to chug for the prime; the pressure gauge needle went berserk then settled on zero. He recalled that the plumber had told him that he would have to refill the pump after periods of disuse. "Yeah, but where the hell do I get the water from?...Of course, the spring out back by the knoll!" He retrieved a watering can from a shelf over an ancient workbench left behind by the previous owner. He turned off the pump. Outside, he headed for the spring, wary that it might not be there. Normally, little inconveniences got on his nerves, but this was different, challenging. Not since his boondocking years in the service had he ever drawn anything from the earth; yet his moderate wealth was due to others doing just that. He let out a sigh when he heard the trickling water and saw it brimming up from the gash at the base of the knoll.

Back down in the cellar, the thought occurred to him that he had no wrench to open the pump plug. He was disappointed in himself for venturing down here with not so much as a screwdriver. Though back home, he had a toolbox, which he had not opened in years, the need had never crossed his mind. "This is a fine kettle of fish," he muttered. He pulled the chain light over the workbench, but the bulb was burnt out. Rather than steal the bulb from the main fixture, he decided to fumble through boxes of junk under the bench. Rummaging through them in the dim light, swearing interminably, he cut and scraped his hand on assorted tools, nails, screws, plumbing valves and pipes. Luckily in the last box he came up with a Stilson wrench. Angling it to the light, he inspected it and then tapped it on the bench to remove the thumb wheel grooves of rust. He applied torque to the plug but it wouldn't budge until he realized his exertion was to the right. He shook his head over his stupidity and exerted torque to the left; the plug squeaked then relented. He poured in the water, tightened the plug and turned on the pump. It gave a great surge and the needle went up to normal pressure. He was proud of himself. Then the pump began chugging again and the needle dropped abruptly to zero. He stood over the pump for several minutes, but the needle never budged. "Damn!" He threw down the wrench, thoroughly disgusted. "Now, why did I just do that?" he queried in shame, "...mustn't let these things bother me...but, oh,...for city water!"

Ann called from the head of the stairs, "Kimble called to see if we got in yet. He said he found out about the pump from the domestics he sent to clean up." He headed up the stairs. She continued, lowering her voice as he drew nearer and she back-pedaled into the hall, "They had to use the spring water in order to clean the house. He said the plumber would be here in the morning. He tried to get him here earlier today...well, we know how plumbers are."

He followed her into the kitchen and out of futility turned on the faucet; it clunked and belched air. "Dammit!"

"Calm down, Paul." She looked at his hands. "Heavens, what did you do in the cellar?"

"Very funny," he growled, "...obviously nothing." Then he remembered that he left the pump on. He went back down and forgot to duck the low overhead as he descended the stairs. "Shit!"

She heard him. Her eyes rolled up. "God, forgive the language of that man. Oh, my, he'll have a stroke if things don't go well down here!"

He went out to the station wagon and retrieved the beer pail that he had wrapped in plastic and stored under the floorboard compartment when Ann had threatened to throw it out. He took it down to the spring, to contain cooking or drinking water, along with the watering can for washing dishes. When he returned to the kitchen, he was about to tilt the watering can over the sink. Ann rushed over and put a pot under the spout. "No, Paul, I'm not going to wash dishes in cold water. I want it heated on the stove."

"Are you sure there's propane in the tank?" he asked sarcastically. "The way things are going..."

"Now, don't start, Paul; it's not a disaster—and the stove is doing just fine," she added consolingly.

"You're right;...you're always right. I can ride out the storm." He poured the water in the pot and placed it on the range.

"What's this for?" Ann asked, pointing to the pail. "And where did you resurrect it from?— I thought it was long gone."

"It's for cooking or drinking."

She leaned over to smell it. "It looks clear enough, but it has a peculiar odor to it. Dump it in the pot or save it to freshen up with."

"What about our coffee?"

"I thought of that," motioning to two big labeled bottles of water, "I picked them up at the town supermarket. I remembered that the water has a lot of sulfur in it—seems salty, too."

"Really?…I didn't know that."

"You seldom drink water."

He scratched his head. "Now that you mentioned it.…I do remember the coffee didn't taste so good the last time."

"Nor did the pasta, if you remember," she said as she opened the oven to check the steak, then closed it again. "Oh, I must remember to call Marguerite; she doesn't have much vacation time left before that TV commercial and will probably want to fly down right away."

That evening, after squaring away odds and ends they had brought with them, Ann relaxed on the porch. Though anxious and restless from the change, Tammy finally succumbed to the fatigue of the trip and had fallen into deep sleep on the rattan chaise. Paul had just put her to bed and took her place on the chaise and kicked off his old moccasins. "I'd be snoozing in a hot tub right now if we had water."

"Even though Mr. Kimble made our return painless, you can't expect to be pampered out here," she said, while looking askance.

"Except for the water," he moaned. And why shouldn't Kimble pamper us—Jesus, I pay him enough…enough to have taken care of the pump or well before now."

She rocked with some impatience in her rattan swivel.

"Will you stop harping on the water—what's done is done."

"What isn't is what bothers me. I sunk almost a hundred grand in this place and yet we don't have the most basic of utilities."

"A hundred thousand is peanuts today; it's worth three times that. Didn't Mr. Kimble call you last year to ask if you wanted to sell it? If you want to back down, you can always sell it—since you still seem to be on the profit motive—and still live handsomely up north." She was testing him.

"Kimble…that's right…wonder if he's still interested? Aw, without water it's not worth a dime."

She walled her eyes to the stars and sighed. "Now, that's silly! For someone who's been in such a competitive field for so long, you sometimes talk as though you know nothing about business. All this land alone is worth tens and tens of thousands."

He looked over, studying her eyes. "I repeat, not without water. Anyhow, who's talking about selling? I don't understand you: one minute you're up and the next down. I think you really don't want this house."

She dismissed him with the wave of a hand. "Me? I'm not the one swearing and wondering whether Mr. Kimble is still interested. It seems

I'm more willing to give it a try than you are...since a little thing like water has you in a dither. It's obvious to me that you've been spoiled by the northeast. How in the world—even by not doing it yourself—do you think you can farm sorghum and pecans, much less raising some cattle if you don't condition yourself to cope with a new existence?"

"If there's no H_2O to drill for an irrigation system,...then, what?" he asked warily.

"Oh, Paul, for heaven's sake!...Look at the Kimbles—they obviously don't have a water problem—their family's been here for over a hundred years. Besides sorghum needs very little water," she said authoritatively.

"What?" She obviously surprised him. "How the devil would you know that?"

"I read," she said smugly.

"Oh, I know you're a reader—but Texas...sorghum?"

"When you first bought the place, I was curious and sent for material from Austin."

"All these years and you never discussed it with me!"

She shrugged her narrow shoulders and offered, "I guess it slipped my mind, though more likely I did mention it, but you forgot or weren't really interested—after all this place was then but a tax shelter."

"Well, whatever that doesn't discount my worry over the expense....God knows how deep they'll have to drill."

"You don't even know if that's the problem," she said trying to comfort him. She looked up at the great starry expanse. "You never worried about expenses before....Oh, Paul, just look at that sky—it's beautiful! I can't remember ever seeing its immensity before, except in our younger days when we with our lollipops would trip out to Jones Beach in the evenings—even then you didn't get the clarity, the depth and the feeling of such openness,...it's so free!"

"Woman, you make it sound like I cooped you up in a ground floor apartment all our married life. What about the sky over the Riviera or Miami, the trip to Hawaii?"

She laughed. "I guess I wasn't paying attention."

"Still, I suppose, it does have a kind of freedom about it down here." He gazed upward. "There sure isn't any lone star up there—God, the stars sure do pop out at you, don't they?"

"They certainly do. So put your eastern ways behind you, breathe in the air and enjoy the sky so alive—even if you should decide it's just temporary."

He grabbed the end curves of the arms of the chair and jolted up straight. "See? There you go again!" He rebuked, "You really do think this is an impulsive whim!"

She rocked on the swivel for a while, then daintily with her toe pushing merrily left and right in measured arcs. She asked soberly, "I wonder how long the drive from the airport is? You've done it more recently. I simply don't remember from the last time, except that it seemed dreadfully tedious."

"Oh, about three hours if she rents a decent car." He sat back again. "She should be here tomorrow by early evening or late afternoon."

"I still think you should pick her up, or let me go for her," she said with some concern.

"Oh, she's perfectly capable. She's made scores of trips on her own before." He looked over at her and laughed. "And you were the one supposedly unwary about her living in the city."

"I wouldn't go that far; it's just that she would feel more secure with her own kind ."

"*Kind!*...What about *kin*?" He pulled himself up and leaned on the porch stone railing and looked up at the sky. The horizon seemed to stretch out forever but for the partial block from the toes of the Rocky foothills. "Sorghum resists drought, eh?...Well, what do you know. With all the livestock in this part of the country, I imagine it could be lucrative—not like cattle or oil, of course."

"No more talk of profits, expenses and business, please," she beseeched. "You're supposed to be retired—*que sera, sera.* If you're thinking of the dollar sign, this is not the place. Do what you do best and go..."

"Touché—no more New York—though I'd sure like to go back someday to the boss and flaunt him with cattle baron demeanor." He sighed. "Oh, well, reality dictates."

She joined him and leaned back on the slate sill. "Good, I'm glad that's settled."

Ann slipped out of bed at dawn. She put on a robe to meet the chill. She flung open the French doors to the veranda. She was greeted by the vast plains to the west, seemingly lush in the reddish hue and mist of the morning. She heaved in gulps of the pristine air and exercised for several minutes never once oblivious to the strange, new sense of environment. She leaned on the top course of the stone wall and again swept her eyes across the rugged, rolling expanse. A solitary tree stood to the northwest. She popped back to when she sighed with relief as the station wagon freed itself of the Holland Tunnel—the reversal of her feeling when she used to visit Jersey as a child—New Jersey somehow looked cleaner, brighter than it did fifty years ago. Her thoughts turned to when she had ridden through the tunnel with her parents to visit her cousins in Jersey City. She had always preferred the ferry because she dreaded the loss of the sky and air. The tunnel to her was not unlike Proserpina's fate: she had left the brighter side to inter herself in the unfriendly environment of chipped oil cloth on a dingy kitchen table, on which sat the greasy bag of day old buns for which her aunt had always sent Ann's cousin so as to treat the "rich" relatives from New York; then there was in the hall the sordid toilet shared by all the cold water flat tenants on that floor. She loved her "shanty" Irish relatives, but she detested—not their ways, which enchanted her—the hideous fate wreaked upon them and the guilt it foisted on her. The ride back to her world of dolls, lace, steam heat, and with an inviting tub in a pearly white and black bathroom—without that horrid pull-chain overhead—her family could claim as their own. She shuddered, thinking how dangerously close her own family had come to the same fate of a horrid railway flat when her father passed away and the stock market crashed, leaving them penniless but for a small insurance policy.

In the kitchen she busied herself preparing breakfast; she heated the grill; switched on the coffee-maker and whipped up buckwheat batter. She went into wake up Tammy, only to find her dressed—cowgirl hat to boots. "I guess you're ready for the roundup, eh? But before you go off, have breakfast first."

"Oh, I intend to, Mom. Hope the chuck wagon's full…could eat a horse."

"That wouldn't sit too well in cow country, dear; horses are necessary for roundup. Better settle for buckwheat pancakes." She went into their bedroom and woke Paul, who was still snoring; the blankets up to his nose. "Rise and shine, ramrod," she ordered, "and head for the spring; it would be nice to have some water to flush away our grime from the trip."

He peered through two slits and grumbled, "What a way to start the day."

"Ah, but it's nature's way!" she transferred with exhilaration.

After breakfast, Paul washed himself as best he could expect under the conditions; he put on fresh, casual wear and decided not to shave as it would be too painful with the cold water and he was not eager to heat the water. "Screw how I look at the bank," he muttered. He was convinced he would never wear another suit until he was laid out. He stepped out on the veranda, hoping to see the plumber. He decided that after he checked with the bank to see that his bank up north wired the money, he might as well stop at the plumber's supply shop to move him along if he were still there. Ann handed him a shopping list as he got in the car. He noticed the first priority was bottled water written boldly.

Ann and Tammy puttered round the stable for a while, which obviously had not been omitted from Kimble's custodial routine, along with the horses already in the stalls. Ann went into the kitchen to so some cleaning. She cleared away the breakfast dishes, poured the pot of water in the sink and let them soak. She had thought of storing them in the rack of the dishwasher, till she had water again, but then chastised herself for such a petty pre-programmed interaction. She called up the days of the family ritual after supper when her brother washed, she dried, her sister put the dishes and utensils away, and her little brother wiped the oil cloth and swept the floppy linoleum, while her mother worked evenings at Woolworth's. She then decided to wash them right away. There was a knock on the rear door; she dried off her hands and answered the door. A strapping man in his sixties came to the door and handed her a business card as he introduced himself as the plumber.

"Ma'am, I'll have to check out the pump to see that it's okay before I check the line and well outside." He stepped inside and she showed him the way to the basement. She returned to the dishes. She started to towel the dishes when he came back up. "Nothing simple in plumbing, Ma'am—the pump's okay. I'll have to trace the line to the well for air leaks."

While folding in the last hospital corner on her bed, she heard an engine sputter then roar. She looked out from the veranda windows and saw the plumber behind a machine that started to churn up the earth. About some hundred paces from the house, he carefully started to guide the churning trencher. She shook her head from subdued disappointment, then sighed. She threw the spread on the bed and smoothed out the rich velvet. "I really should have one of those rustic patch quilts," she thought.

She went out back to see how Tammy was doing with the grooming. Tammy had already saddled the pinto. The mare in the next stall was excited, kicking snorting, shaking her head, forelock bouncing—apparently eager to be outside. "She must remember you, Mom; she wants you to ride her."

"Oh, not today. We'll take her out to the corral and groom her; she'll like the sun on her back." She went over and steadied her, speaking soft endearments. She edged her out of the stall and led her out of the stable and into the sunshine. Tammy mounted the pinto and followed. Ann opened the gate, released the rein, tapped her neck and the chestnut mare danced gingerly, gleaming beautifully in the bright light. Tammy and her Pinto entered the corral, too.

Ann looked up at her daughter and said, "Prance him about in the corral for a while to get acquainted again before you take him out,…and when you do, stay close to the house and no racing."

"Oh, Mom, for Pete's sake, we're buddies already," she playfully complained as she gently slapped him with the reins to trot. She gracefully managed him about the corral as though there had not been a four year lapse. Confident, she heeled him into a canter. Ann waved to her when she reached the outer circle and then smiled as she passed her by, just as Ann's father used to do when watching her on the boardwalk merry-go-round at Coney Island. She turned to check the progress of the plumber. The trencher had already reached the house. The plumber with a shovel was scraping away the loose earth as he traced the piping back up to the well. He then retraced his steps on his knees as he carefully examined the piping and its couplings. When he reached the house, she could see him shake his head. "Oh, no!" she vented a sigh. He headed for the back door. She called and waved him over as she walked to meet him.

He took off his sweaty cap and wiped the sweat from his eyebrow with the fold of his arm. "I'm afraid it's not a leak or broken pipe, ma'am. I was pretty sure that was the answer because twenty years ago when my father and me put in this well for the old owner, I remembered that he decided against laying a new line to the house. I guess, he thought right—doggone—it's still good, considerin'; but I still advise you put in a new line, while it's trenched out—can't be many years left—I'll only charge ya for the material, since it's already dug. Is your husband around?"

She said, perplexed, "Why are we talking about a new line if that isn't the problem?"

"Oh, right, ma'am, sometimes I don't explain too good. You see, I'm afraid it means the well is dry and I hafta go deeper."

"Oh, my, that's serious, isn't it?" she said, feeling stupid and helpless.

"Oh, no, ma'am, just expensive," he said, grinning.

She did not bat an eye. "Oh, then, do what you have to do; we would like water today."

You don't have to decide on the line into the house yet. I've got some hammering to do." He put his cap back on, then tipped it toward her. "Don't worry, Ma'am, no problem there, reckon you'll be showerin' or bubble bathin' tonight." He headed toward his truck.

"I do hope so," she said inaudibly, but felt mildly offended that he would bring up something as personal as bathing. She thought, "Why not simply doing laundry or cooking—or at least leave it at showering? These service and repair men think they're knights in shining armor without the chivalry as they hold out their hands for their outrageous fees." She watched him back up the truck to the starting point of the trench meeting the well. He got out and jumped on the bed of the truck and started up the huge engine and it rough idled for a while as he rigged a pipe to the hydraulic driver, then coupled it to the well pipe. She walked down to the trench by the side of the house and peered into the trough. She could see that the pipe was scaly from rust. She would not hesitate to tell him to replace the pipes if Paul did not get home in time. She thought better of the plumber and retracted her earlier perception. She walked back to the corral where Tammy was proudly exercising her show-riding skills. Ann thought how beautiful and graceful she looked in her western attire. Her gold hair glistened in the sunlight and her cowgirl hat strung to the back, bounced to the cadence. Ann concluded that she preferred this private demonstration to the stilted equestrian shows and the stuffy riding wear required. She turned when she heard a car approaching on the bluestone that angled around the house to the stables. Marguerite waved to her through the dusty windshield when she braked.

"Oh, what a grand surprise! I never expected you'd be here this early!" Ann exclaimed, genuinely thrilled. Her daughter stepped toward her—graceful and glamorous as always—smiling like only a model can smile; dressed fit for a job interview. Ann felt a volatile quiver of self-consciousness in her floppy housecoat. She embraced her lightly, lest she violate her daughter's crush-proof appearance. It was a wonder to her—after all that traveling. Marguerite, however, pulled her closer and hugged her tightly.

"I took an early A.M. flight out of La Guardia," she said thrilled with herself that she managed so well.

"You must be dreadfully tired."

"No, not at all. I took a long nap on the plane."

"Did you rent a dressing room?— you seem so fresh."

"Oh, Mother, why would I do that? The car was ready and I just bee-lined here. Surprisingly, I enjoyed the ride—the change, I suppose—Texas is not all that bad, after all—more than desert and tumbleweed. When you rent a car in Miami or LA you never really get to see the land. I was impressed." With her pre-occupation with water, Ann wondered if there had been something in the Long Island water supply that made her family so erratic, seemingly a change for the better. She had spoiled her children so over the years she feared they would be alien to natural values. Apparently she had less influence on them than she thought; she was glad that character, after all, was not so susceptible to environment's dictum as presumed. "But I am ready for a bath, Mother, to remove the traveler's stickiness."

"Then you'll have to sit in a smelly old spring," Tammy offered as she pulled up to the gate and dismounted. She opened the gate.

"I'm afraid we have no water," Ann said, shrugging. Tammy clung to her sister. Marguerite pressed her cheek to her sister's hair, warm from the sun.

"My, Tammy, you look like a Texan already!" Marguerite turned to her mother. "So that's what's going on down there, eh?— the well's dry?" she said, motioning toward the truck. Ann again was surprised. She presumed that her daughter took for granted all homes were supplied by the county water authority. In stride, Marguerite said, "Well, Tammy, you and I will just have to ride over to that stream on the north property line."

"Stream? I don't remember any stream," Tammy said skeptically and feeling disappointed that if indeed there was a stream she was not the catalyst of discovery.

"Well, I guess you were too young then; but we did go up there a couple of times. It was crystal clear—then. Oh, Tammy, you must remember. You wanted to play with the cows that watered there."

Tammy smacked her forehead, and screeched with delight, "Of course, Mr. Kimble's cattle drank water there—I remember now!"

"Why was I never told of this?" Ann queried.

"Probably because we skinny-dipped the first time we discovered it," Marguerite chuckled. "Tammy, saddle up the mare for me, while I get into my jeans and, Mom, I'm starving." The two of the them went into the house arm in arm as Tammy retrieved the mare.

Ann relaxed on the porch chaise, watching her girls ride the plains to the north. She traced them, squinting as far as she could see until the bright towels rolled behind their saddles faded away. She started to doze off with the droning of the engine and thumping of the hammer. She opened her eyes when the engine and pounding stopped. Hissing nudged the silence, then a billowy swoosh, a faint smell of gas wafted to the porch—memories of Fourth of July in the old days when her father would send up rockets for his children—then a strong smell, which quickly dissipated in the open breeze. She relaxed again, thrilled that her daughters were actually venturing together, perhaps never again to be truly together. She thought of how she and her own sister had drifted apart, each enthralled by her respective offspring and the pity of it. She wondered how one's child always comes first over one's mother's child: "why should it not be as strong?...coming from the same womb, for heaven's sake, should make Dot and I inseparable!...Peg and Tam at one in spite of eventual marriage and children." In the fading consciousness, she heard the clanging of tools and pipes, "...guess he found water....that will calm Paul." Images fluttered on the edge: the great colorful merry-go-round on the boardwalk, Tammy and Peggy going round and round, waving, smiling, laughing; her husband at the sink masterfully drawing crystal water from a hand pump; her baby brother emerging from a picturesque well sitting in a wooden bucket, his hands outstretched toward his father pulling on the hoist, his mother drew him to her breasts as his father gasped for breath, dying; her own blue brittle baby in the bucket—tossed out. She opened her eyes. The plumber stood over her. He looked as though he had fallen into a grease pit. He was wiping hands with an oily rag.

"I'm sorry to disturb you, Ma'am. I went around back, but you didn't answer. We got problems and have to use your phone—there's no time to lose."

She jumped up. "Of course, you may use the phone. Why are you so full of grease? Go around back again and use the phone in the kitchen—can't have you tracking that goo in my house. What seems to be the problem,…still no water?"

He went down the steps, turned around to her. "Right, Ma'am, still don't have water." He turned round again and stepped quickly, saying, "I must make that call to the riggers. This is out of my league." He shook his head. "Don't know how long it'll hold," he added, muttering as he turned the building.

She went through the house to the back to meet him and to show him the phone and to clarify the problem. While he dialed, she asked, "Will you kindly tell me what's going on? Are you saying we need a new well? I thought all you had to do was to go deeper?"

"That's right, Ma'am," he said nonchalantly, grinning. "but only if there's water there."

"Then it is totally dry?"

"Well, yes,…and no…." He spoke into the phone, "Hello, Mary? Listen, get me Mad Cap on the double. I got an emergency on my hands." He cupped his hand on the phone and said to Ann. "I think you'd better check to make sure all your windows and skylights are shut tight, if it blows you'll have some mess."

"I've had enough of this! Stop with the cryptics! For the last time what is the problem?" she screeched.

"Oh, I'd love to have this problem, Ma'am." He spoke into the phone again. "Yeah, bring a whole team and its rigging. I could feel growing pressure… could be a big one…and those pipes will never hold for very long…you gotta get out here fast and reroute it.…Yeah, I think it's another one like the Kimbles. What?…what d'ya mean I'm like an ole washer woman?…Reckon I know a big one when I see it.…You're just gonna send a geologist?…Cap!…you serious? I don't wanna go near that thing!…You sure it's okay to remove the cap and put on a valve? Yeah?…Crack it, eh?…Yeah, well, okay, I reckon. Get somebody out here quick…don't leave me alone out here with this damn thing."

Ann was so furious with him that she had stormed out of the kitchen, rather than to stand there like an idiot listening to his gibberish. She went out the front door and headed in the direction of the girls, hoping to see them return. Though she had no idea how far they had gone, she was not going to stay around the house alone with that man, who, she was convinced, was loco. As she traversed the rolling plain she also kept her eye on the road looking for Paul to arrive. She guarded her eyes from the bright sun and looked for the girls. The view was distorted from the heat dancing off the earth. She turned her head again to the road, but no car in sight. She looked toward the house; the plumber tilted back the trencher, guiding it to the back of the house. She looked to the north again and thought she saw dust in the distance. She squinted, hoping it meant the girls' returning. She continued walking until the heat started to make her uncomfortable; she paused and looked for a soft patch of grass to sit down on, then thought better of it when the celluloid image of snakes crossed her mind. She decided to head for the shade and companionship of the lonely tree to the west some two hundred yards and wait there. She felt her feet dragging the last few steps; she wanted to just plop, but she looked up to see that no creatures lurked overhead in the branches and circled it, examining the terrain. Satisfied, she sat down and rested against the trunk and breathed heavily for a moment. The dust was still there. The celluloid frame of a stampede fed her anxiety, knowing there would be no John Wayne to rescue her. She got hold of herself and was confident in a crisis that she could reach the branch and swing herself up. "Brave lonely tree," she murmured. She could barely make out the truck but saw that it was moving down her driveway and then parked on the side of the road. "Now, I know that man is crazy!...Where is he going to dig a well—in the road?" A small pickup truck was coming up the road; it pulled up next to the plumber. Then both trucks turned into the driveway and circled the house, as Marguerite had done earlier with her rental, and continued to the back of the house and disappeared. "God, the man can't make up his mind!" With someone else there she decided to return and find out what he was doing now. She pulled herself up, touched the bark tenderly, and headed back. Hooves rumbled out of the dust. She was annoyed that they were galloping but relieved that they were returning. She looked to the road and could see a van speeding in the distance. It pulled into their driveway. The plumber hopped from back of the house and directed the van to the well. The girls spotted their mother and turned toward her, slowing down to a trot.

"Mother, what are you doing out here...getting the feel of the land?" Marguerite asked.

"Mom, do we have water now?— the stream was yucky." Tammy blurted anxiously.

"I'm afraid not," Ann said. "Help me up, Tammy." Tammy slipped her foot out of the stirrup as Ann stepped into it; Tammy steadied her mother's arm as Ann raised herself up and straddled the pinto and wrapped her arms around Tammy's waist. The two horses were spurred off.

"Maybe we should get a swimming pool, Mom—it gets awfully hot down here." Tammy said seriously.

"That's one way to get water." Marguerite quipped.

"I guess you didn't bathe in the stream, then, eh?" Ann said turning around to glance at Marguerite.

She maneuvered the mare abreast of them. "No way,…like Tammy said…it was uninviting, dark and salty, oily. Too bad, it used to be so pretty now there are oil rigs all over the place,…did you know that, Mother?…that Kimble is in oil now?"

"You're kidding! In this beautiful grazing country? Oh, no,…is that what he was rattling on about?"

"No, Mom, really," Tammy affirmed, "he must have a dozen derricks near the stream—they're so ugly. I feel sorry for the cows."

"Who was rattling on, Mother?" Marguerite asked.

"Oh, it's nothing…I guess…strange plumber…something about the well."

"Oh, Lord! Tammy, I bet we too have struck oil! Mother! We're millionaires!" Marguerite ejaculated

"Yippee!" Tammy squealed and tossed her hat into the air. "Hold on, Mom!" she spurred the pinto.

Ann warned, "Tammy, not so fast!"

"Gee, Mother, such kismet!" Marguerite serenaded as she caught up with them. "Some people are just destined to be rich and powerful,…above all,… secure." She leaned forward and twirled the mane. "Kind of a shame, though," she added soberly.

"I'd rather have water," Ann remarked with some sadness.

"Sweet Aunt Dot—why can't she have this kind of luck? God! How could I have been such a brat! I must spend some time with her when I get back.…must make it up to her somehow," Marguerite pined.

"There is one way. Be more like your aunt. If it is oil down there, promise me—both of you—that in spite of the material change, the material that makes character doesn't. I rather like the way you are—that will be riches enough for me and your aunt who's already fortunate to be content with her life."

"You needn't worry, Mother," Marguerite rejoined seriously. "We're kin— daughters of Nana's child. See you at the house, Mom." She galloped off.

Paul had been fretting and muttering, since he drove out of town. "When the hell am I ever going to learn?...Not even sure about staying here...yet I do this dumb thing! Where the hell's the money coming from? Goddamit!...I've got to change...can't keep spending....Shit! Why couldn't that woman save more?...A lousy CD a couple of thou in the money market and checking.... Jesus, I'm glad I was forced to put something away for retirement....Oh, that chiseler Sloan!... Gotta sell the house up there now. Damn, where do I come off ordering a swimming pool?...What a crazy bastard I am."

He turned into his driveway and pulled up behind the van. "Good, the plumber got here," he presumed until he got out of his car and walked to the side of the van and read the decal: *Western Seismographics, Inc.* "What the hell is this?...just my luck the well is dry...Jesus, how deep is the water in Texas that they have to resort to oil exploration techniques?...Ridiculous!...it'll cost me a fortune!—rip off a city-slicker, will they?" There were two men by the well; one younger was pulling up a cable that resembled a small tool cable that he had seen at some old rigs the few times he accompanied his clients. The other older man was studying some samples in his palm and then he dropped the soil into a container, put on a lid, and wrote on its label. He walked up to them. "What is going on here?" he asked not waiting for an answer. "What's wrong with the well...and where in Sam Houston is the plumber?...You certainly don't look like one," he said, staring at the older man, dressed in a light summer suit, though his tie was loosened.

"No, I'm not a plumber—a geologist. You're the land owner of this field?"

That this man of science would use oil jargon annoyed him. He glared at him. "A very disappointed home owner, since it's obvious I have no water yet," he said.

"Oh, Old Pipes is out back driving a new one for you now." Then he laughed and winked at his helper. But I wouldn't be disappointed, sir. It's a little early, of course, but I'll wager you're sitting on an anticline with a good deal of oil and gas. When your plumber started driving deeper, he apparently disturbed a half billion year old formation and some gas found its way through."

"Why that's preposterous in this day and age!...Forty years I've been in the oil business; this is west Texas, sir, there hasn't been an oil discovery in twenty-five years that hasn't exceeded ten thousand feet."

"That's partly true; but the fact remains this field was overlooked years ago. You just lucked out like Drake."

"This isn't Pennsylvania," he said, not to be outdone.

"Granted, it's much deeper than the water well, but from what I've logged briefly, and what my Brunton tells me, it's similar to Kimble's place. Naturally, nothing is conclusive until you lease the field and we drill for truer logging and exploration." His young assistant pulled up the last of the cable revealing a mini fishtail bit caked with a sample of sludge and shale. The geologist carefully scraped the bit, spooning the sample into another container. He bent down and smelled the fishtail. "Hm, hydrocarbon," he murmured with an air of professionalism. He ran his finger lightly across the bit; he tasted it, "Salty, too." He whistled as he stood up to face Paul. "I'd say you had a winner." The younger one closed the valve on the well, then turned it back one revolution to allow the gas vapors to escape.

"You really think so?" Paul asked, trying to hide his growing excitement; he felt his heart pounding. He couldn't control his smile. "Well, I'll be damned. You mentioned Kimble, a neighbor of mine. I haven't been down here in quite a while."

"Oh, yeah…you know his family made millions on cattle; but it took them a hundred years. Thanks to the strange geological happenings around here— most of the experts chalked it up as a unique stroke of luck—he's made more millions in six months."

"Gosh, I wonder why I never heard about it? I get all the journals."

"The company kept it quiet—as well as they could—you know how that can cause a glut."

"Well, I'll be damned—send the company lawyers to me. Lucky I had no water, eh?"

"Yes, and even luckier that no one tried to get you to sell this place. Water well, notwithstanding, someone eventually would've been scratching your land."

"Slick bastard…that Kimble,…another Sloan…Jesus, no escaping the pricks," he thought, looking down at the well; a faint odor of gas lingered. "I'd better see what the plumber is up to. Right now damn the oil, water is of the essence." He motioned to the well. "Is that thing safe? I mean I won't be bathing in a gusher or anything?"

He laughed. "You're as bad as Old Pipes. He was really panicky when he phoned. All he had to do was get a whiff of that gas and he didn't want any part of it. He thought it was going to blow like in the movies."

Paul started to look for the plumber when he jerked around and said, "Oh, I'm blocking your van."

"Oh, we'll be around for a good while yet—we still have a good deal of work with the aldidade for mapping."

Paul hopped over the old trench and grumbled. When he turned the corner he fell into another trench that led to the new well. The plumber's son, who had arrived in the pickup, was already hand pumping the first water. The plumber held his hands under the spout and sipped some of the water, then spat it out. "Another two or three lengths should do it." His son twisted off the pump, while his father started up the hydraulic driver.

"I'm relieved you found water...this time...though I don't think I'd object to a gusher," Paul said in the best of spirits as he greeted them. The plumber laughed politely. "But why are you so far from the house?"

He rigged up another length and jumped from the truck as his son coupled the pipe. "Regulations....Can't be near the septic tank, you know. Anyway, it's no further than it was," he reminded him. "And I wasn't about to dig near the old one. Gas scares the hell out of me, not to mention oil seeping into the new water. Fear, sounds funny coming from a plumber, I know. I was on a job once under a crawl space as tight as a starched shirt at a wake, soldering a coupling; I put my torch down to inspect the joint and grabbed hold of another pipe to swing under and check the other side when the pipe folded under in my hand—it was so damn corroded gas started leaking. I always leave the torch on till I finish checking my work. That day God was with me; it had tilted over and shut down."

"Yeah, He sure was with *me* today," Paul exhilarated the surrounding air with soaring arms as though worshiping the invisible gas.

"Huh,...what happened to you?" the plumber asked vacantly curiously as he increased the power of the engine.

Under the roar of the engine, Paul chuckled and walked away. Noticing him, when she and Marguerite emerged from the stable, Tammy ran toward him. Marguerite waved vigorously and paced behind. She eyed askance the plumber's son. Tammy leaped into his arms, almost knocking him off his feet. "Like winning the lottery, Daddy! First thing is a swimming pool! Gotta have one down here the clubs are too far away!" She rambled.

"Hold on, Tammy, we haven't won anything yet. And we'll get one regardless, believe me." He let her down. "Down here the air boils."

Tammy quipped, "Wow, pools rush in!" She bent down and patted the ground.

"Hi, Dad,...eventful day, eh?" Marguerite kissed him.

"Because you're here so early," he understated, happy to see her.

They headed for the house. He stopped and redirected them toward the front yard. In the excitement Paul had left the groceries and other shopping items in the station wagon. "You girls can take the packages into the house while I put the car away," he said as he continued ahead while they followed and squabbled:

"Gee! We're practically millionaires and still have to carry in packages," Tammy complained in jest.

"When did you ever do it?" Marguerite asked sarcastically.

"All the time for Mommy when I went shopping with her."

"Which wasn't very often."

"More than you ever did." Tammy said as she hopped the trench.

"Yes, regrettably," Marguerite conceded. She thought of her mother's solemn entreaty. She turned her head for another look at the plumber's son and stumbled and fell headlong into the trench. Stunned by the suddenness she lay there limply, one leg over the pipe and her torso pressing the loose earth. She scrambled to get up when a strong bronze hand grabbed her grimy little hand and yanked her out.

"I'm sorry, Miss; it's my fault this happened…shoulda filled it in right away," the tall handsome son of a plumber said. "Are you okay?"

Embarrassed, she looked away from him and clumsily tried to whisk away the damp dirt from her hands, rubbing them on her jeans. "Yes, I'm fine." Her lids forced her eyes up at him and said, "Oh, don't feel that way;…it was dumb. I should have looked where I was going—I knew it was there."

"Sorta forgot, eh?…Reckon ya lookin' somewhere else?" He said, smiling down at her.

She flushed. "Yeah, reckon." She chuckled.

He carried the packages into the kitchen for her and put them down on the counter. "Reckon I'll see you again before you head back to the Apple, eh?"

She smiled up at him; her eyes flashed; embarrassment waned. She said, "Reckon…but not till you get that water hooked up. I'm a mess." She turned and left him standing there, his heart pounding. Ann emerged from the breakfast nook and stared at him coldly.

"There will be water soon, young man, correct?"

"Oh, yes, Ma'am—within a half hour." He looked to the doorway whence Marguerite had left.

"Well, it won't be if you don't get a move on and stand here all day," she said abrasively.

"Uh, yes, Ma'am, sorry Ma'am,…it's just that,…now, I mean no disrespect, Ma'am,…well, you sure have a beautiful filly,…uh, daughter, Ma'am."

"That's not exactly an original observation, young man—but for the gross reference, that is—but thank you just the same," she said sharply. "Now, water, if you don't mind." She pointed to the door.

He smiled disarmingly, and turned on his heels. She flinched and drew up her softer side. "Uh, one moment, young man, please. You and your father have been working so hard out in that hot sun." She went to the refrigerator and retrieved two cans of beer. "Here, both of you take a rest. I'll prepare some sandwiches for you and have Peggy take them out to you." She dazzled him with a smile.

"Oh, yes, Ma'am!" he said airily. "Thank you kindly!" He pressed the cold beer to his forehead and beamed. He swung round on his boots, heading for the door and flung open the screen door, envisioning the advent.

Later, well after dinner, Marguerite and Tammy, having just returned from caring for the horses, were sitting at the dining table poring over swimming pool brochures—Marguerite together with splashes of him. Paul and Ann were out on the porch. "Wonderful feeling to have water again," Ann said. "The bath seemed like a long overdue luxury. She invoked her childhood of her Jersey relatives, eager for the comfort of a bathtub, virtually lined up to take baths whenever they came to visit. Her father used to tease her mother that that was the only reason they visited. After they left her mother would spend half a day scouring the bathroom and scrubbing all the bath towels.

"Even better having oil," Paul extrapolated, as he kicked off his expensive loafers and reached for his scotch. He had decided to throw out his old moccasins. "All these years…wheeling and dealing in oil for the great barons and now I might wind up being one myself—well, partially, depending on the royalties. I'm going to be a tough negotiator, that's for sure—no more Mr. Nice Guy."

She looked over. "There's plenty of beer, you know." The freshness of last night's air was replaced by the loitering odor. "God, they'll destroy the place—I detest those ugly rigs," she moaned; then her eyes lightened. "But maybe there is no oil."

"Not a chance. The geologist's survey practically confirmed it."

Her eyes fell to her hands twisting something in her lap. "I'll miss the natural beauty. And if that's not enough you go out and order a swimming pool.…How in the world did you think you were going to pay for it? Then she looked over at him; a twinkle was in his eyes. "Why, you old fox, you knew…" she hesitated, tasting for the last time what she foolishly thought could have been her subterfuge, "we have close to half a million in the retirement fund."

"You're kidding!" he exclaimed with arched brows. "I was sure we didn't."

"Yet, you bought the pool anyway! You'll never change."

He wet his thumb and whisked it over his shirt. "Well, I knew my tanker would come in." Pointing in the vicinity of the well.

"But the fact is, my dear husband," she said with slight smugness; "from the last statement we do have more than half a million in the account and with the equity....So, you see, all this fuss over oil is pointless."

"Try putting up a stop sign after one has made his first million! I could just see myself having Getty out for lunch at the 21 Club in the Fifties. 'Hey, John Paul, you've made a few million already why don't you retire?' That'd go over real big."

"I'm just afraid this whole thing is going to overwhelm us as it did when…only worse," she said sadly.

"I hate to break it to you, Hon: it'd be worse if we were left with just our retirement—Sloan ran off with most of it. Seems he had an escape clause to recapture his principal and the right to reinvest the gains in anything he damned well pleased and he lost his shirt and mine."

"What!" she jerked her torso up from the chair. "Why, that just can't be!"

"No, I'm afraid it's true—he put it to us — the latest quarter is zero."

"My God! You must contest it! That's your hard earned money! Why didn't the account manager apprise you?" she raved angrily. She hedged her thoughts on whether she would have been so willing, almost cavalier in coming down here on a permanent basis without her little escape clause—the security of the fund had it not worked out here. Yet it occurred to her that it was fortunate she had not opened the quarterly report.

"Sloan had power of attorney and pulled it out. I can't contest; long ago I signed an agreement—that's why he kicked in the fifty thousand as consolation."

"Fifty? You told me a hundred!" She checked herself, realizing that she was getting herself worked up, enmeshed in the same prevailing ways of society. She pined for her mother. She shook her head violently, leaned back hard against the swivel chair, dropped what was in her hands, gripped its arms, toed the terrazzo forcefully and swung herself round and round. "So, this is how the merry-go-round looks from the center," she murmured. "I want to go back to Levittown," she pouted facing him as she planted her feet and the swivel came to a halt. She stared out into the darkness, straining to see the lonely tree.

He laughed. "Warped time frame, my love? No, there's no way we can go back to Great Neck now. "We're going to stay right here and oversee operations or they'll go hogwild. I'm going to keep an eye on the books.   Of course, I'm definitely going back to New York and shove...well, drop on Sloan's desk a vial from the first barrel and thumb my nose at him!...And don't worry with all this land and money we could have the house moved...nestle it behind the knoll or lease it out to the company for their headquarters and build a new one...more to your liking...and maybe an oceanfront condo in Florida...Tammy would love that...and Peg?...why, we could buy an agency in Dallas and..."

Under his drone, her rattling confusion slipped back into the folds of her brain. She saw her first owned home: a Levittown cape cod. Their '41 Plymouth pulled up in front. Paul carried her over the threshold...the bedroom of tender passion....Later,...a baby's room she prayed would come to be.

She looked over at his dream-filled face. "Oh, Paul, it's just not the same thing!...the intent...gone forever," she cried, turning into herself, murmuring, "...more of the same...oh, no...much more...slick...oily...." She gazed up at the starry sky; it was not the same. She thought of her father's recital. She whispered into her heart, "...more...nothing ...not even sorghum....Shhhii...." She looked down through filled up eyes at two lollipops in her lap.

Different Hands

The engine rocked with every stroke. A lanky teenager made one last instinctively calibrated turn of the needle-valve but could not catch it in time and the engine stalled. He braced the lawnmower with his foot and yanked the starter cord. The small engine roared out as though relieved after years of neglect. The industrial arts teacher stepped out the back door to the yard fenced in where the students worked on their cars, boat and small engines.

The teacher patted Ronnie on the back and yelled over the engine roar, "Sounds like new again, Ronnie...." Ronnie cut the engine and removed his earplugs. "Mr. Federico will be pleased —probably won't wait for the spring; he'll probably start right in and mulch his lawn today. You did a fine job."

"All it took was to rip off the head to rid the piston of carbon, Mr.

Walker," Ronnie said modestly.

"All?...Not many know that or what to do about it. Looks like you more than earned your 'A.'"

"That's cool, Mr. Walker, thanks."

"Like I said, Ronnie, you earned it; I didn't give it to you."

Ronnie rolled the mower under the overhang; then put the tools back in the tool room. The bell rang and he dashed out to meet his girl at the commons area. Although both had study hall the same period, they were seldom together; but on occasion his girl would join him in the student lounge when her homework was not piling up on her. Ronnie never had homework—that is, he never did it—since he left private school. Debbie had not arrived yet. "Probably at the locker again deciding on what books to take home," he thought. Ronnie never took books home. He went over to the soda machine and dropped in seventy cents for two cans, then laid claim to their table in a corner of the huge lounge.

"I'm sorry, Ronnie," Debbie greeted him with sad brown orbs, dumping a pile of books on the table; "I know I promised I'd stay here today but I have a social studies test today and really have to study. Can you imagine the first week into the new quarter and he's giving us a test already? Did you get your grades yet?"

"I guess not; my mother hasn't yelled at me yet."

"Oh, I wish they hadn't started that new system...mailing them home like that. The suspense is psyching me out." Her dark silky hair shimmered in the light when she shook her head.

"No way you have anything to worry about," he said confidently, then added, "It'll be my mother who gets psyched out." He ripped open a soda can for her and slid it over to her. "Anyway, what's another test to you—no, big deal, you can study here."

"Oh, it's so noisy;...especially when that crazy Alvin starts...spinning those hard metal records of his," she said between sips of soda.

"Here, use these," he offered taking his plugs out of his pocket.

"You can read in peace while I hold your hand."

She laughed. "Yeah, I know you—that's not all you'll do. No, I'm just going to relax awhile, have my soda and then get a pass to the library. Why don't you come with me? It wouldn't hurt to take out a book, you know—or at least browse."

"Yeah, right, I can just see myself taking out *War and Peace*—did you ever finish it, by the way?"

"Yes, but I must confess, it was an ordeal and I skipped his boring essaying. Anyway, I'm not suggesting that kind of reading, as long as you would just read something else once in a while besides those mechanics books of yours," she pleaded, then took a few hurried gulps.

"No way, Debbie,…just doesn't turn me on."

"Oh, Ronnie, I'll be in college next year and here you'll probably be pumping gas for minimum," she said with dejection, looking over with her customary sad brown eyes while absently fondling her long hair whenever they broached this subject.

"On that again, eh? Bracing me for when you meet some smart nerd on campus and then dump me, eh?"

"You know that's not it; but it does happen. Kids change when they go on to college—and it frightens me. Besides, I always hoped that in the end we'd be up at college together."

"Don't let it worry you—if we split, well, that's life," he announced glibly as his hand nervously brought the can to his mouth. "Come on, I'll go to the library with you and flip through some old issues of *Popular Mechanics.*"

When Debbie was free after school, which was not very often, he would drive her home or they would do a little hand holding and necking as they strolled along the beach. Today he had been looking forward to driving around with her, knowing there was no game and she would not be cheerleading, until the last period announcements blared over "Student Council Meeting Today, Room220 at 3:10"—he knew Debbie would attend. As he climbed into his van parked behind the faculty lane, a short man waving an attaché case and pushing the lawnmower came rolling toward him. Ronnie looked down as the teacher reached for his wallet and pulled out a ten dollar bill. "Here, Ronnie, I want you have this for fixing the mower—Mr. Walker told me what a fine job you did," Mr. Federico said gratefully. "You have no idea the frustration this old machine put me through last summer."

"Oh, believe me, Mr. Federico, I can imagine….It's nice of you to offer, but really I couldn't accept—it's all in the learning and I'm just happy you had the confidence in me to have me look it over."

"Well, you did more than look it over, so I must insist you take it." He stuffed it in his windbreaker pocket and wheeled the mower to his car.

Ronnie climbed out and followed. "Shoot, Mr. Federico, this is embarrassing. I don't need the money," Ronnie pleaded as Federico opened his trunk lid. Ronnie stopped him from lifting the mower and he put it into the trunk for him, deftly removing the handle and laying it flat before closing the lid.

"Thank you, Ronnie; consider the ten as token for courteous delivery service, then." he smiled and patted Ronnie's shoulder.

"I tell you what—how about a 'C' instead?" Ronnie bargained playfully.

"Now you're embarrassing *me*, Ronnie, you know I gave you a 'D' in

English. At least permit me to make amends. I hate giving a nice kid like you such a low grade—why can't you at least try to write some of the assigned compositions." He got in his car and started it up.

Ronnie instinctively tuned in to the engine. and tapped on his window. Federico rolled it down partially.

"Your car needs a tune up. Leave it in the yard Monday and I'll check it out for you—and no charge, please."

"I know you're right; I treat my car like I do my lawnmower," Federico quipped.

"Ugh!" Ronnie laughed.

"Listen, Ronnie, since you want to make a deal,...instead of the assigned compositions this quarter, how about turning in 'how-to-do' pieces? You know, as if you were writing a manual for the layman. You can start with the lawnmower."

"Say, that's cool, Mr. Federico,...thanks!" Federico waved and the car sputtered away.

Ronnie turned a street lined with huge budding maples and opulent homes. He pulled his van into a cobblestone driveway and circled behind the sprawling, rambling Tudor home to the four-car garage. Ronnie was always grateful for the old high style garage that could accommodate his van. Not many of his friend with vans could garage theirs—especially the way they jacked them up. He clicked the remote and nudged his van into the spacious garage between his mother's Cadillac and an original corvette from the early fifties—his dad's nostalgic toy. He headed for the refrigerator and grabbed an apple from the roll-out bin. He hoisted himself up on a counter top and stared out the window thinking of what Debbie had said earlier. If even if he had wanted to he was certain he could not cut it at college. Oh, he knew he could fake it the way most of his friends from last year's graduating class were doing just so they would not, as Debbie had observed concerning him, saddle themselves with barely above minimum wage throughout their lives. Then he felt guilty that perhaps the only reason he asserted a kind of independence was that his parents were wealthy and he did not have to worry about making a living. Still, he reasoned, did he not have enough skill in his hands to carve out a good living wage even when he took on the responsibility of raising a family someday? It was not his fault that he was born rich. He shuddered when he thought of his days in Stratton Academy when he felt like a displaced person in the midst of all those brainy kids—that is, because of their background they had to perceive themselves as smart. If Debbie was going to wind up feeling ashamed of him, then it would have to be. Though he admired her and definitely felt that he was in love with her, he concluded she was not for him if he had to lose his integrity.

Mrs. Terry, Ronnie's mother entered the kitchen, looking like something out of a slick ad from Alderman's or one of those TV mothers from earlier days of television. She was clutching a short piece of computer print-out. "I thought I heard your truck roaring in."

"Jeez, Mom, it's not a truck and it doesn't make a lot of noise," he enlightened her as he jumped down from the counter.

"Well, you could've fooled me—how is it I can't hear your father's Mercedes when he is in and out of the driveway?"

"That's hardly fair, Mom—but I can hear your Caddie. Would you like me to tune it up for you?"

"Don't start with me—I've told you I don't want you working on cars."

He shook his head resentfully and whined, "Aw, Mom, why are you always putting me down?...and mechanics are important people; everybody has to rely on a car."

"This is why," she snapped, holding up the piece of paper. "Three 'Ds', one 'C' and an 'F'—would you like to count them yourself?— and how could you possibly manage an 'F' in social studies and get a 'C' in such a difficult subject as physics?"

"That's easy, Mom—the world's chemistry results in mechanical force."

"Oh, you and your mechanics—you're obsessed."

He looked embarrassed and then asked, "Where's my 'A'? I take six subjects, you know—and what about Phys ed.?"

"I'm not concerned about your ability to toss basketballs and climb ropes. And as far as the other thing goes—small motors or whatever— I strictly forbade your taking that dirty course."

He shook his head again. "It's my best, Mom; it gives me a good feeling. Why, I know I could open up a small engines shop right now and make a good living on it, except I'd prefer auto mechanics."

"Oh, Ronnie, when are you ever going to mature! How could you do this to your father, a surgeon, who had such high hopes for you!"

"Is it really dad or you, Mom?"

"Yes, of course, it's both of us. How do you think I feel when I go to the club or entertain and all my friends are bragging about their children's careers or when they toss around the Ivy League as though there were no other universities in the nation. Now, you listen to me, young man, tomorrow is Saturday and I absolutely forbid you to fiddle around with the cars. Stay in your room and study. O, God, why did I ever let you talk me into allowing you to attend a public school!"

"If I remember right, it was dad who convinced you after I had convinced him. Besides, I hope you're not blaming the school for my poor grades."

"Of course, I am! Why, they don't even have sufficient soap for you to clean your hands properly after that disgusting class you have. I've told you not to come home with dirt under your fingernails and just look at them." She took his hands to inspect and shook her head over them. "My God, Ronald, the grease is imbedded in your pores. Go to the basement and scrub them."

"Hands aren't made just for surgery, Mom."

Ronnie did not technically disobey his mother this Saturday—he simply did not have any books to study with. However, he did write a piece on the maintenance of a mower for Mr. Federico. Since Debbie took the day off owed to her, he finished the report and headed for Debbie's.

Ronnie and Debbie jumped out of the van in front of a used car lot. Ronnie, though having little confidence in used cars unless bought cheaply with the premise that more money was to be put into them, agreed to look at some cars with Debbie to give her an option list for her father who wanted to give her an early graduation gift. Actually her dad was tired of picking her up—most of the time Ronnie did—at her part-time job in the evenings and getting up early Saturday mornings to cart her to work.

Debbie immediately started looking at shiny late model cars while Ronnie fumbled for the hood latch of older cars to look under the hoods. Debbie sighed each time she looked at the prices smeared on the windshields and knew her father would not be willing to go that high. When she observed what Ronnie was doing she came down to earth and decided to join him when she spotted a Firebird at the other end of the lot.

"Oh, Ronnie," she cried out, "come look at this one."

Ronnie followed after her. She was circling the Firebird, admiring its sleek lines and then noticed "Special" scrawled across the windshield. "Ronnie, isn't it beautiful?— and it's on sale!"

"I wouldn't count on it," he said skeptically. "There's no price on it. How much is your father willing to pay?"

"He said about a thousand," she said proudly as though that were a good deal of money, not knowing anything about the current market. But she did know that most of his savings would go toward her college costs.

"Then this isn't for you; they usually want more than that for this kind of car. Kids go crazy for them—especially with the 350 engine," he said in an authoritative tone. "Provided, of course, it's as good mechanically as it looks—even though it's a '77."

She grimaced with disappointment. "Oh, are you sure?" She ran her hand over the long front fender. "Let's ask the salesman, Ronnie, to see what 'Special' means."

"Okay, but you're only going to be shaken up."

They headed toward the mobile office and she said, "Ronnie, you're such a pessimist—but I'm glad you're with me."

A paunchy middle-aged man stepped out of the mobile office and greeted them with a smile and said, "I noticed you're interested in our great weekend special, eh? No finer bargain on the lot than that classic bird."

The three of them walked back to the car, and the salesman unlocked it. "This is in such beautiful condition that we lock it even during the day...real leather and a five hundred dollar stereo system in it!" he declared while unlocking the car door. "Yes, dearie, this is a once-in-a-lifetime chance to sport around town without costing you a fortune. Do you realize what Japanese sports cars are going for today? But this is the Yankee that showed them the way—yes, young lady, this is the granddaddy of all sporty cars. Why, the ones five years old are still commanding five-seven thousand dollar price tags!"

"How old is this one?" Debbie asked, then looking over at Ronnie.

"Oh, about eight or seven," he said coolly, "but the important thing is how well it's been kept and the low mileage."

He held the door open and gestured that she sit in it. "And just look at that gorgeous interior."

Ronnie said, "It's considerably older than that by my calculation—it happens to be eleven years old—it's a '77," he pointed out to the salesman.

"You don't say?" The salesman looked at him dumbly. "Well, it's hard to tell with these cars. Still it's the history of its maintenance that counts and I can tell you this is a one-owner beauty."

He bent in and put the key in the ignition and said to her, "Now watch this magic; look around, no antenna, right?" He switched it to the accessory and the radio blared out Tommy Dorsey's "Song of India"; he quickly pushed the tuner selectors. "That's my boss; he's got every car on the lot tuned to that old band channel."

Debbie coveted the leather wrapping round the steering wheel and admired the cushy, tufted, aerated leather upholstery as she listened to Springsteen resonate out of four speakers. Ronnie shook his head and bent under to check the exhaust system which was badly scraped and rusting out, and there was no future for the muffler either.

The salesman lowered the radio and said to her smiling face, "If you think that's a great sound, wait till you try your cassettes out on this player built into the console with its separate amp. And just look at that stick shift—impressive—yet I know you ladies don't like clutching so it's an automatic just for you."

"Oh, I don't mind shifting—in fact, I rather like it," she said with a trace of resentment.

"Well, then, you're in for a great new dimension—there's nothing like the convenience and smoothness of an automatic transmission, especially GM's—they're the best,...should be, after all, they pioneered it...And what did you think of the radio, wasn't that something?...and without an aerial."

"Oh," she smiled politely, "I know that it's built into the windshield."

"Ah, brilliant girl—yes, you'll go along way in this great car!"

"Perhaps,...what's the price?" she said wincing.

"Do you know the story of the guy who went into the Cadillac showroom?— probably not, you're much too young. Anyway, he asked the dealer what the price was for the model on display. The dealer told him that if he had to ask, then he was not Cadillac ownership quality."

Then he guffawed and said, "But for you, dearie, I'm going to quote you an unbelievable price, if you're really interested—I'm obligated to warn you that this is not going to be on the lot very long. Why, I'll wager as soon as our ad reaches the newsstand this afternoon it'll be gone in an hour."

"Oh, really you've advertised it?" she asked warily.

"Oh, yes, you see, as you must've gathered from the radio, my boss has this nostalgic disease and he used to own a Firebird when they first came out and has regretted ever selling it and he told me if I didn't sell it by tomorrow, he was going to keep it for himself."

"Oh, my really?...It must be a good buy, then."

Ronnie in the meantime had circled the auto looking for body rot which he knew these cars were notorious for, especially, oddly enough, round the cowl and rear window; he was impressed that there was very little. He had gone round to the driver's side and asked Debbie, "Did he say what the price is?"

The salesman looked at him resentfully but did not hesitate. "I was just coming to that, my boy; I was just telling the little girl here, that it's an advertised special....It'll go fast."

Then he faced Debbie and announced enthusiastically, "Yep, this classic has been marked down all the way from twenty-five hundred!"

Debbie sank in the seat "Oh, my!...."

"Ah, my girl, don't look disappointed; you can have it for the fantastic price—mind you, now, from twenty-five hundred all the way down to sixteen-fifty!" He grinned and touched her shoulder, "Can you believe it, dearie? That's eight hundred and fifty off the regular price!"

Debbie looked up and beamed over to Ronnie. "Oh, Ronnie, isn't that wonderful? Maybe dad would go for it and I could pay him the rest with my summer pay!" Then she felt guilty, knowing her parents were counting on her own savings for her extra expenses at college.

Ronnie nudged the salesman aside and reached in and turned the key to the ignition and cranked it momentarily—the battery was low. "Switch the radio off, Debbie, and pump the accelerator a few times—not too much now."

He switched to start again and it cranked and the engine almost caught. Debbie looked over his back at the salesman sheepishly. Ronnie pulled the hood latch and went to the front of the car. Releasing the safety latch under the sprung hood, he raised up the hood. The battery side terminals were frothing with corrosion. He picked up a twig by his feet and scraped some of it off and twisted the terminals to check that they weren't loose. He poked his head around and yelled to Debbie, "I don't think it'll start but try it once more before the battery is killed altogether."

She cranked it; it caught; the carburetor coughed and it died.

"Dearie, don't be discouraged when you come back with your father we'll have it purring for you," he assured her, then he looked over at Ronnie indignantly.

Debbie was euphoric. "Oh, you will? That's just great!"

"Hold on, mister, we're not through looking at others, nor this one, you know," Ronnie reminded the fast talker.

He ducked under the hood again and pulled a thinly insulated wire from a spark-plug and noticed the rust at the base and the grease round the insulator. He checked the engine dipstick; it was low and black. Even the power steering dipstick was low, along with the hydraulic brake fluid. He noted there was no anti-freeze in the overflow chamber so he twisted off the pressure cap and the water level was not visible. He removed the air-cleaner cover and the air and pc valve filters were filthy. His misperception was that the car owner was one of those who polish every week but neglect the service end—until he later discovered the car had been repainted.

He was about to remove the distributor cap to check the points and rotor when the little man came round and cautioned, "Don't do that, young feller!" He tugged on Ronnie's windbreaker and urged him out from under, then he slammed down the hood, muttering, "Who's buying this car?— butt out!"

"Hey, mister, that's my girl and she asked me. If you think you're going to fleece her you're high on something."

He went up to Debbie who had turned the radio back on and had her knees in the seat looking over at the big speakers in the back window deck. He peered in and checked the odometer; it read 07899. He clicked off the radio. She sat back down. He pointed to the odometer.

"How can that be Ronnie?" she said looking up at him with a perplexed expression.

The salesman jumped in, "Oh, yes, that's right; the previous owner told me that the speedometer hadn't been working for quite a while. But he told me the approximate mileage is 48,000."

"How in blazes did it pass state inspection all that time? Is it working now?" Ronnie probed.

"Why, of course, it is—we couldn't sell it otherwise."

Ronnie looked at Debbie who was fondling the leather covered steering wheel again and he said skeptically, "Debbie, don't be taken in by this—obviously, it's the second time around."

"My God, you mean it has over a hundred thousand miles on it!"

"Now, see here, young feller, I've told you what the true mileage is!" he grated. "Don't be putting ideas in the little girl's head that shouldn't be there....We have on file a sworn statement from the previous owner."

"Yeah, right, and I suppose you're willing to sign the affidavit on the title certificate to that effect."

"Well, of course not, we cannot testify to that; the previous owner has already done so."

"And you expect us to believe it?...And what happened to the original owner? Now you keep saying 'previous.' It's a violation of state law to permit the previous owner to write down an estimated mileage that doesn't jell with the reading. It's as clear as day that the reading of over a hundred thousand is consistent with the age and condition of the car," Ronnie said confidently, then bent over and showed him the brake pedal.

"Look, it's practically new! No one replaces a brake pedal unless it's over a hundred thousand."

"Aw, that's hogwash—maybe he was a brake-rider, proves nothing! You've been reading 'Consumers.' We get you smart alecks in here all the time."

"Say, mister, I'm just trying to be realistic about this—I'm not a wise guy. Facts are facts and I'm not saying this car is hopeless. After all, it's proven itself over and over again with that sort of mileage, but it's not worth more than six hundred. Let me jump it and I'll prove it."

"You're ridiculous! And I thought the little girl was serious about buying a car."

"Oh, but I am!" Debbie said in a mild panic.

He reached in for the key and nudged her out of the car as she sighed. "I'm sorry, dearie, but as I said they'll be here in droves soon, I can wait."

He walked back to the office.

She looked at the car again, "Oh, Ronnie look at that paint job—the way the metallic glows! It had to be taken care of."

"It's not the original paint; it doesn't match the original of the trunk interior. Be sensible, Debbie, it's a clunker. Sure, it'll look beautiful in the junkyard two months from now, but that won't be much consolation to you, now, will it?"

"Ronnie, how can you be so sure?"

"I can't really until we've taken a spin in it; but he's not going to allow it. But I do know that it'll take a lot of money to fix it right. Why, just the dual exhaust system alone, if I don't do it for you it will cost a couple of hundred. And I suspect the engine will have to be torn down, not to mention brakes and stuff. Why, doing the work myself it'll still cost over a thousand, I'll bet."

"It's that bad, huh?" she whined.

"Cheer up. There's a nice little Bobcat over there with a five hundred sticker on it. I know they're not glamorous, but it'll get you to school and work. Of course, you'll have to try it out. I suspect it'll need work—used cars always do—and it has 80,000 some odd on the odometer and I know those two liter cube four cylinders aren't the best but if kept tuned it'll get you where you want to go for a year or two....Though, I'm sure, it will need a timing belt, too."

"Ronnie, you make me feel that a car is a bad idea."

"No, Deb, it's just that all used cars are a gamble and I don't want to see you miserable. But if your father is willing to go as high as a thousand, I'd rather see you get something for less and let me put the rest into getting it right, rather than to pick up something for a thousand and then finding out you need brakes and any number of things."

"But I can't expect you to spend all your time fixing my car—and you know how your mother is."

"I can handle that."

"Gee, Ronnie, I don't think I want a car now—or what about the classified? Don't you usually get a better deal through a private party?"

"Yeah, if you really want to scour several towns; but keep in mind: seldom does anybody give a good car away. And once you plunk down the money—and most won't take a check—and the car falls apart a house away, that's it. Of course, these dealers are hardly any better—what with the lousy thirty days they allow you and then when something goes wrong they'll tell you that it was your fault. Still, there's some recourse."

She looked in on the plain cloth interior of the Bobcat. She circled round it and commented, "It's no Firebird—but it is kind of cute."

"Yeah, they're not bad little cars—lousy on gas though. With a light foot you can get almost as much mileage on that Firebird tanker if finely tuned and the engine is decent."

"Ronnie, you're confusing me!" She whined looking longingly over at the bird.

The salesman emerged from the office and headed toward them loitering round the Bobcat. He came up to them and had a big grin on his face.

"You're in luck, dearie; I just spoke to the sales manager and he said you can have the F-Bird for an even thousand. How does that fit your budget?"

Debbie's face lit up, but Ronnie said, "Wouldn't give you a hundred for it without taking it for a spin."

"Hey, boy, you stay out of this! I'm talking to the little girl."

Debbie faced Ronnie, appealing, "Oh, Ronnie, it sounds like such a wonderful deal!"

"Well, the salesman's right, in a way—you're buying it. So come back with your father, if you really want it. But make darn sure your father checks it out thoroughly. And check into the Bobcat, too."

"Now that's more like it, my boy," the salesman interpolated with a twinkle in his eyes, then added, "And, young lady, we'll have it purring for your father. But be sure to hurry back before the afternoon papers are out."

She looked at Ronnie. "How's that sound, Ronnie?…And you will come back with us? Dad doesn't know anything about cars."

"Well,…okay, but you heard my price," Ronnie said to her, looking straight at the salesman.

The salesman frowned. "Now hold on this is a firm rock-bottom offer and there can't be any further bargaining. Your father has to either take it or leave it. The price stands."

Ronnie steamed."That's rubbish! You mean to say if the transmission is slipping, the exhaust system is shot—you know how low slung these cars are—it needs brakes, especially rotors—and you say that's it?"

"Hey, shop for a new car then. All we guarantee for that price is that it runs. Good lord, boy, this is six hundred dollar discount we're talking about…actually $1500 off the original offering."

"Well, you could save us a lot of time if you let me jump it now and we take it for a spin."

He touched Debbie's arm and nudged her to leave.

"Thank you for your time, sir; I'm sure I'll be back with my father," she said wistfully.

"Fine, dearie, but make sure you get back today—it won't last an hour at that unbelievable price."

He headed back to the office as they ambled to the van.

"An hour?…Ronnie, my father isn't even home! He's doing some work over at Nana's."

"Don't worry about it, Deb. That guy is just sucking you in anyway.

With his attitude and desperate pitch the car's gotta be a clunker—just as well."

Since Debbie's father had not gotten home yet and Debbie had already taken the morning off at the dress shop where she worked, she decided to go to work and reluctantly take Ronnie's advice and forget the car of her dream—at least for the moment.

Ronnie dropped her off and cruised around town for a while to see if he could find any of his friends around. Since all of them worked to feed their cars and meet the gruesome car insurance payments there was no one around. He grew envious of his friends having to work for their spend-money and car costs. For some time he had been thinking of taking on a job. He even had talked his mother into giving up the gardener who came every week. But she hired him back because Ronnie had let the leaves get out of hand this fall while he was helping a friend install a rebuilt transmission and engine in a Falcon. He drove out to the junk yards on the outskirts and left Debbie's phone number with each yard in the event they could use a hand after school or on weekends. Had he given them his number, and his mother had gotten any of the calls she would have hung up on them. He pulled into Stanowski's garage for gas. Though it wasn't a self-serve, Ronnie always jumped out and helped himself because he felt sorry for old man Stanowski who had a bad heart. He could never understand why people were so hung up on an education that they felt they were failures if their kids did not go to college. Here Mr. Stanowski had a strapping son who knew automobiles and could make life easy for his father and yet the old man sends him off to learn engineering. Ronnie thought that was crazy.

Mr. Stanowski came out heaving heavily from the garage after Ronnie had already hung the nozzle back up and ready to hand him a twenty. "You didn't have to come out, Mr. Stanowski, I would've come into the garage to pay you. You look like you have your hands full." He gestured to the bays.

"You're a good boy, Ronnie, but why don't you save some money and go to the self-serve station down away. Why pay me two pennies more?"

"Aw, Mr. Stanowski, you're a good one too—don't worry about it. How's George doin' at college?"

"Very good,...smart like you."

"I hope he's better than me! I don't plan on goin'."

He laughed as he gave him back his change. "You fellers...always with the jokes. And you, a doctor's son!"

"Yeah, that's all I ever hear. But everybody's got to live his own life." Ronnie looked over at the garage. I see you got both bays goin', eh?"

"Yeah, customers are draggin', me round today—like that every

Saturday. Just finishin' up a tune up. But that other one's a big job and he wants it tonight. Big date, I guess."

He chuckled. Then he gasped for breath and held his chest.

"Are you okay, Mr. Stanowski?"

"Oh, yeah, I'll just sit a minute in the office…be okay."

Another car pulled up to the pump. "Oh, not right now, I gotta get this one." He headed for the pump. Ronnie intercepted him.

"No, Mr. Stanowski, you go rest, I'll get this for you."

"You will?…Like I say…you a good boy."

He handed him some singles. "Here you might need this for change."

Bent over he headed for the office while Ronnie took care of the customer. After he pulled his van up to the bay. He jumped out and went over to the car the old man had been tuning up. He checked the gap of the remaining spark-plugs and wrenched them in. He removed the distributor cap and could see the old man had installed the points already. He turned the crankshaft to the high point and checked the gap. A box of wires were out so he replaced the old ones as he removed each of them. He cranked it up and checked the timing and it was right on the money. He poked his head in the window of the door and he could see that the old man had dozed off. The bell rang as another car pulled up for gas. He looked in the window but Stanowski did not stir. He pumped in ten bucks worth of gas. He went over to the LTD. The customer had left a note that it died out intermittently and several mechanics had diagnosed it as carburetor trouble and should be replaced. Ronnie shook his head, "These mechanics today—unbelievable."

He started it up and it coughed, spit, sputtered. He shut if off and removed the air cleaner and started it up again. It held freer, then started to flutter. He rocked the butterfly and it raced free again. He was already sure what the trouble was but he checked the timing anyway. Then he ripped off the choke mechanism. And steadied the accelerator it worked fine. He shut it off. The air bell rang again. This time Stanowski emerged from the office. "I'll get it, Mr. Stanowski. He pumped in five bucks. A young woman strolled up and asked if her car was ready. "Is that the tune up job in the bay…the blue Chevy?" She nodded. "Yes, Ma'am, all done."

Mr. Stanowski saw her and stepped as briskly as he could toward her car. He tipped his cap and scratched his head when he saw the hood down and quickly unlatched it, while eyeing the empty wire box on the work bench. When he raised the hood his eyes popped, then looked at the new wires already installed. He looked for the timing gun. Then saw it over by the LTD. The young woman came up to him and asked what she owed him. He scratched his head again.

"Uh, just let me start it up to double-check it, young lady."

He cranked it up and it purred beautifully. "Ya, ya, it's already to go."

The young lady was delighted. They went into the office to settle up.

Ronnie pumped another three bucks worth and came into the office. The blue Chevy lady, with a grateful smile was just leaving. He handed the equally ingratiated owner the singles. They watched her pull out and she waved, coupled with a gleaming smile.

Ronnie handed him the proceeds from pumping. "Mr. Stanowski, I want your permission to go down to the auto parts and charge a choke-kit for that LTD."

"My boy, whatchya been up to?...How long did I doze off? I know you tinker with cars but I didn't know you was this good."

"You looked beat, Mr. Stanowski, so I didn't want to disturb you. My father always says that rest is the best medicine for mild chest pains—that's what you were having again, right? You had better have my father look at you. It's something you can't ignore. It's as bad as forgetting to replace the spark-plugs and to change the oil every two thousand miles." They both laughed.

Then Stanowski said stubbornly, "No, no time for that. Now, what's this about a choke kit?"

"Well the customer has an intermittent problem, so the way I figure it the choke is weak and especially when the car is cold it chokes out and when it's warm I imagine once in a while the butterfly flips causing it to die out for a time. If it were something internal in the venturi it would do it all the time. Besides the carburetor is clean and I checked the fuel line and it flows fine. So I'd like to take the LTD to the parts place with the choke spring removed to see if we get any of the symptoms the customer is talking about. I know with it removed it'll work fine. On that note he claims that other mechanics diagnosed it as needing a new carburetor—gees, they want five-six hundred bucks for these four barrels!— and worse they don't include the choke kit! So he'd have the same problem anyway." I tell you, the carburetor on it is good."

"That's real good thinkin', Ronnie. I told you, you was smart. Yeah, it didn't make no sense to me neither, but I darn near almost called up for a carburetor—good thing I didn't, eh?"

"Right, because I know you care about your customers."

"And you too; so what are you waiting for? Go!" he handed him his wholesale charge card.

Mrs. Terry had planned on eating out Saturday night as was their custom, but since Ronnie had defied her she wanted to confront him when he got home. Because her husband was famished she could not delay dinner any longer. Ronnie's father had returned from an emergency call to the hospital and had not eaten since breakfast. The maid had just finished serving them, and said she would keep Ronnie's dinner warm in the oven.

"The steak is delicious, my dear. We should eat home more often," Dr. Terry said seriously.

"Yes, so you can be near the phone, I imagine," she said.

"No, I didn't mean that; they have no trouble locating me no matter where I am—you know that."

"Only because you're so utterly conscientious by always having that annoying beeper with you."

"I should think all doctors are."

"Humph."

The father asked, "What's our son up to today? I was surprised not to see him out back when I pulled in—he's usually doing something with his van or one of the cars."

She sighed. "I specifically told him not to, but that he should study all day." "And still he took off on me this morning," she said exasperatingly. "I really think we should reinstate him at the academy."

"Good grief, Heather, you're not serious! I mean,…with his grades?"

"That's precisely why. Perhaps they could somehow salvage this graduating year. I'm not sure he is going to make it."

"Oh, heavens, it's still early in the year. He'll shape up," he assured her. "He's simply not qualified for Stratton; besides, what good would it do him—a fish out of water. Though admittedly his grades are nothing for you to brag about up at the club, but they're considerably better than when he was at Stratton."

"Oh, Robert, you've never been supportive. Perhaps if you had he might have developed differently."

"I resent that. True, I've been busier than most fathers, but I've always managed a pretty good relationship with him. Maybe I could have spent more time with him on his studies, but after all, we spent enough dough on tutors and private schools to see to his development. Look, he's a good kid. He's never been in trouble, never any trouble to us—we ought to be thankful—look what some parents have to go through today? No, I can't go along with you, my dear. I've accepted him for what he is."

"And just what is that supposed to imply—that he's stupid?" she blared with a peevish expression on her face, adding, "a hopeless retard."

He reacted with a gasp. "What a terrible thing to say about our son! What I mean is that he is not going to follow in my footsteps; and that he obviously is not college material—though I shall do everything possible to persuade him to at least try some college for a year anyway."

She waved her arms and scowled. "See? Exactly what I mean. You don't see the compromising fallacy of your willingness to send him off to just *any* college. I suppose you had the community college in mind."

"Yes, if need be," he said coolly. "Surely, there is no way he can get into the colleges you would like him to—like all your Ivy league name-dropping friends."

"That's unkind, but perhaps you're right," she resigned with a sigh. "So at least do this one thing for me and call the dean at Stratton—for heaven's sake he's a patient of yours—I'm sure he'll admit him."

"Yes, I believe he would, but it's presumptuous of me to ask, but more importantly it is not in the best interest of our son." He carved another piece of steak and chewed on for a while as he stared at her searchingly.

"Oh, Bob, I know I sound frightfully pompous in wanting the best for our child as only I perceive it. But at least give me this one indulgence. I just have to know if with some proper, stricter, supervision he might just turn around," she said with emotion in her voice as tears welled up. "Goodness, he's our only child!"

"Who's fault is that?"

"Robert, that was cruel." She dried her cheeks with a linen napkin. "My theory went awry, I know, thinking we would be so much better off not dividing our, at least my, efforts. It was foolish of me, selfish, and I suppose,...cruel."

"Yes, all of them. You knew long ago that your dreams weren't going to come true with respect to him and had plenty of time to have more children, yet you clung to this remote hope. And you're still hanging on to it. For God's sake, Heather, you're torturing yourself—and Ronnie along with it. Thank God we have the means to set him up in a thriving business where he will be a respectable member of the community."

"Respectable!...The best grease monkey in town! God, I can't stand the thought."

"You might have to learn to." He chewed another morsel as she held her head in her hands. "I promise to call, but only after I've spoken to Ronnie and he agrees."

"Oh, Bob, he'll never agree to it!"

"Then we will just have to respect his judgment."

"Oh, why must he always have his way?"

"Not always, but as I said before, he's a good kid and deserves our respect. I certainly don't want to destroy his good-nature. Yanking him out in his senior year is rather cruel. You know, I was never much for school either; but I always had this dream to become a doctor and that's what drove me to the books."

"See?...Why, couldn't the same..."

"Because his dreams are in another direction….Oh, perhaps later, he may decide on engineering if the current challenges surfeit. You see, his dream is now—cars are everywhere. And society is crying out for intelligent mechanics."

"Robert, it's so indecent—raising a child to be a handyman to society."

"All of us are in one form or another if we're productive."

Ronnie had closed up Stanowski's. He had been so busy he was unable to go with Debbie about the Firebird; however, he assumed she had not pursued it. The old man hired him part-time even before the customer came for his LTD. When the owner started up the car , he happily discovered the recurrent problem was solved—and for under seventy bills. In the kitchen, having his warmed-over plate, Ronnie was in momentary thought, staring vacantly at his father across from him. "Gee, Dad, even without this new job—and the poor old man really needs me—I just can't see transferring."

"I know, son, it's difficult for me even to ask," the father said apologetically, "but it's so very important to your mother."

Ronnie let out a sigh. "I suppose it is—this job and my friends are important to me too. Still, I could drive home on weekends. Keep the job…see…my friends and Debbie. Yet it seems so pointless. I kinda looked forward to graduating with my friends."

"But are you sure you will graduate? What about those 'Ds' and that 'F'?"

"Oh, you know how I am in the first quarter—slow starting—I'll pick up…always do."

He poured some more milk while his father twisted off the cap to his beer.

"Still a milk baby, eh?…Thought you'd be raiding my beer by now." The father grinned.

"Oh, I do once in a while….Not much of a drinker, Dad—I feel lousy after just two beers—besides, it's illegal."

"How about the other…well, you know."

He laughed, then shook his head. "Of course, I've tried it all—almost have to nowadays. It's not for me. I just don't seem to need a high."

"God, that's great to hear, son," he said, relieved. "What's your secret?"

He held up his glass of milk. "Good parents, I guess; and to each his own, too, I suppose. It probably helps, too, when you have the right girl."

"Yes, Debbie, is very sensible."

"Yeah, she's after me also about college. She's like mom in that way. They're both kidding themselves."

"How can you be so sure?...Ronnie, it's nice to be honest with yourself, but even with that you can't always be sure it is honesty. I mean, have you really given yourself a fair shake?"

"Oh, Dad, believe me, I've tried over the years. Nothing sinks in—not so much that I don't understand the work. It's more that I just don't feel good with it. It kind of strangles me, you know?"

"Yes, I know the feeling—felt that way quite often at medical school—but, of course, I had the dream going for me."

"That's it, I guess—I don't have it....And gosh, Dad, they're so darn tough up there at Stratton. They might not even graduate me."

"I promise to have the dean notify me immediately if he suspects that, and I'll pull you right out, no matter what your mother says."

"Sounds chancy—I could really screw it up."

"We all have to learn to make sacrifices, Ronnie. You'll be doing it for your mother."

"Yeah, but what about me?"

"That's what sacrifice means, son. You have to sit your aspirations in the waiting room. Besides, there's an outside chance your mother might be right and you might just succeed up there. God, Ronnie, you're by no means stupid, and some people don't develop book smartness till late."

"Yeah, too late. And Stratton relies entirely on books—the classics to boot."

"That's where the real values lie, Ron. Look how you're always doting over my '55 Corvette—God, you're worse than I am—there's a magic to old values. It's not that the academy pulls you into the past; it just tries to sustain some old fashioned yet enduring traditions—a proven method of learning. You can understand that."

"Sure I do; but just as some of those kids up on Mt. Olympus wouldn't give you two-cents for your Corvette, preferring the bulky Stingray, I just can't appreciate that learning tradition. Yesterday my English teacher and I struck a bargain. I tell you this morning I couldn't stop writing I was so excited in writing up a manual."

"Well that just proves that you can do anything if you put your mind to it."

"That's just it, my mind isn't there. It's my mother's."

"She's thinking of you—in the long run," the father said. He rose up and dumped half a beer in the sink, then turned back to him and said, "Well, give it some thought tonight and let me know in the morning. Remember, the decision must be yours. I don't know if I ever told you this: I dropped—well, had to drop—out of high school, you know?"

"*You*, Dad?"

"Yes, when your grandfather took ill. I had to run the store for him.

Luckily the school was sympathetic and let me keep up with the assignments in the event I returned in time well before the year was out."

"But you did make it back."

"Oh, yes, but I was prepared not to, in case Pop didn't recover."

"I see."

Yes, Ronnie saw. It was not simply his good nature. There was a maturity about him that germinated within his affinity to the world—the fluid dexterity in which he could labor. He possessed a gift of appreciating, almost philosophically, what the world had to offer in the miracle of its mechanistic structure. Most would despair of this indifference, fear this brute truth; the most they wanted was a spin off they would hope to grab that would yield a cleaner semblance. It is the rare breed who lifts the hood to the world. Ronnie was happy with what was under it. No chance-meeting was necessary, no extraneous fortune. He was merged with its rhythm, like the ancients who went about calmly perfecting the wheel.

"I made brownies for you, Ronnie," his mother said after timidly knocking on his door and entering with a stack of them and a glass of milk.

"You, Mom?" he blurted, turning from his desk where he was working on a finished draft for Mr. Federico.

She chuckled. "Haven't been much of a kitchen mother, have I?"

"Aw, you do okay, Mom—not like some of your friends who play golf five days a week."

She never could stay mad at him for very long. He would always look at her softly with clear but puzzling eyes. "I was furious with you, Ronnie, for defying me this morning."

"Oh, I didn't really, Mom."

He held up his paper for English. "Believe it or not, I did the rough copy of this in the morning before I left to pick up Debbie. I really didn't have anything else to study."

"Oh, Ronnie, we have so many books in the study. Why couldn't you browse through them at least," she pleaded.

He shook his head. "Just not me, Mom."

He munched on a brownie. "Good, Mom."

"Debbie called twice today."

"Yeah, Dad said. I forgot to pick her up at work. She went ahead and bought the car I had doubts about."

"She's a nice girl—and bright." She ran her fingers through his thick hair. She noted for the first time how much it had darkened. "Oh, son, am I so terrible?"

"Don't be silly. I promise to do my best up there—just for you."

"Oh, Ronnie, not for me, for you! And do you mean it? You would do this?..."

"I owe it to you, Mom, to give it a second try. Don't get your hopes up—it's going to be a struggle."

She looked at him admiringly, "Yes, it will be—do your best. I suppose, you'll miss Debbie."

"Got to get used to that anyway—she's going to college next year...been accepted already."

"Oh? Where?"

"At Brown."

"Oh, my."

Ronnie was assigned to Karl's room at the dorm. The dean hoped he would be a help to Ronnie. When Ronnie entered, there were two other boys in the room. Karl with a book in his lap looked up and smiled. The other two looked at him strangely. Karl rose up from his chair and put Ronnie's luggage on a bed.

"This is your coffin....So you're the new replacement. I've been kind of happy alone since my old roommate dropped out. But I must confess that it gets kind of lonely after a while. So welcome to our cozy horror chamber."

He introduced the other fellows, who greeted him indifferently. He edged them toward the door.

"All right, guys, let Ronnie get settled."

They stopped at the door, and Tommy, a short redheaded boy, who seemed no more than fourteen, said, "Now one moment, Karl, maybe Ronnie can help us out on this point."

He looked over at Ronnie.

"Jesus, do you have to bombard him with your trivia now?— give him a break."

Undeterred, Tommy asked, "Ronnie, Jack here," motioning to the much taller boy, "claims that Marlowe was Shakespeare."

"I didn't say that!" Jack noted. "I said that Shakespeare was Marlowe."

"Hmm, a weak point."

"No it isn't. Everyone assumes that Shakespeare had a separate identity and that Marlowe might have fed him his works, thinking Shakespeare was some kind of super Spielberg. I'm saying that Marlowe in fact existed as Shakespeare incognito."

"Well, either way it can't be proven. But at least there is evidence of Shakespeare existing. And no proof of Marlowe living to a ripe old age."

"That's because Marlowe assumed a whole new being and being the greatest literary man on earth, surely had no difficulty creating a character for himself. God, man, common criminals do that all the time. And since he killed someone at a pub, why wouldn't he, rather than like some pedestrian fugitive going into seclusion, burst forth as a renewed creative giant?"

"You should be writing science fiction, Jack," Karl quipped and looked over at Ronnie's bewildered face. "Besides, the fact is both Shakespeare and Marlowe were really Queen Elizabeth."

"*I* should be writing science fiction?" Jack grinned as his long thin arms reached for the door knob.

"Don't distract me," Tom injected. "I want to hear from Ronnie; he at least seems to have some common sense. Ronnie, wouldn't you be prone to think that Shakespeare was simply Shakespeare?"

"Yes," he cleared his throat, "I would take it on faith that he was—it's a part of history, isn't it?— can't think of history as fantasy."

"See?" Tom grinned, reeling round to Jack. "My instincts were right—why, Ronnie here is a chap of common sense."

Ronnie wrinkled his forehead and added, "As for Marlowe, I never heard of him."

The three of them burst into laughter. Jack and Tommy could be heard guffawing down the corridor after Karl had pushed them out.

"That was capital, Ronnie; I love your humor," Karl said as he helped him put away his things.

"I hate to disappoint you, Karl, but I was serious."

Karl broke into laughter again. "Jesus, you're putting me on again!"

"I'm afraid not." Ronnie looked at Karl with an expression that seemed contrite. "I'm sure there are many things you haven't heard of yet. It's just that I've heard a lot less."

"Well, I'll be…Ronnie, you *are* serious! I'm sorry, guy. Really I am."

Karl and Ronnie entered their history class. To Ronnie it was eerily quiet, the members in their school blazers politely waiting for the instructor to finish up at the blackboard. Karl took his assigned seat and Ronnie isolated himself toward the back of the room. He opened his new text and thumbed through it for a while then reached under to retrieve his copy of *Motor Trend* and started looking through as the instructor began.

He became engrossed in an article on classic kits, which got him to thinking about a business where he could reproduce almost any life-size model ever made. The teacher's voice droned. Then he remembered his vow to his mom, and put the magazine away.

"…Empires are forged by cunning men who first appear as champions of the populace. Such was

Caesar's method. True, civilization swiftly advances under the thrust of powerful men, but unfortunately it is at the expense of the private individual who cares only that his will survives to do as he sees fit....Although kinder, a democracy too can impede this will as well as nurture it. The individual must wisely contribute to society as he struggles to retain his identity. Some ironically obtain individuality and greater self-identity by contributing to society; others must struggle to safeguard against society overwhelming him."

Karl was making notes while poring over a heavy book. Ronnie was lying in his bed, palms under his head, staring blankly up at the ceiling. He rolled his head to the side and asked, "What do you find so interesting, Karl?"

Karl looked up for a moment without turning around. "Huh?...Oh, you wouldn't understand, Ronnie; it's Plato."

"Guess you find it dull having me for a roommate, eh?"

Karl dropped his ballpoint and turned to face him. "Hey, I've put up with you these weeks, right? On the contrary, I find you refreshing. One can easily get tired of the same pseudo-intellectual crap around here. You're honest; I like that. Oh, I know I get engrossed in my studies and seem to forget you're here but that's part of the game, and I apologize for that."

"Don't. I should be hitting the books too—God, they're complicated! I wish I had a mind for it—just the sight of a book leaves me cold."

"Hang onto yourself: don't force yourself to be somebody you aren't, Ronnie. Plato calls that meddling with oneself. 'Know thyself is the ultimate in wisdom—let the cobbler make shoes,' he said, 'the just man justice.'"

"Makes sense—though I hope it doesn't mean I can't have a sense of the just too."

"No, but he is saying there are those better qualified to administer justice."

"You mean...like a lawyer?"

Karl laughed. "In a sense, yes, but Plato didn't have in mind the kind we have today. Look, you're good with your hands and would make a crack mechanic or a hell of an engineer. Yet how many are mechanics and engineers today who can't even fit a cog to a wheel?"

Ronnie propped himself up on his elbows, listening intently as he admired Karl's insights.

Karl put down the book. "The world is full of meddlers who are unqualified to labor skillfully or give advice, yet we are at their mercy—especially where it really hurts—in politics, medicine, education, law. I suppose most of us just go along with the power structure because it has a way about it to make us feel inadequate. But it is dangerous, for it is the germ of authoritarianism."

"Sheep, I guess, huh, Karl?"

"Right on, and the worst culprits are in our own teenage circle, which now means anyone under forty—everybody hops on the band wagon. For every freak that goes ape over Michael Jackson there are a million others who beat their chests to the rhythmic chants and steps of the witch doctor; for every sniffer there are a thousand others who will each press his finger to his hungry nostril.... Remember when Travolta was popular?— Jesus, everybody had Saturday night fever!— hopping around like John—a Jerry Louis pathetically serious in his unsuccessful efforts to be like Fred Astaire." Karl made a few more notes, then pushed out from his desk, stood up and stretched. "I think I'll sack-in awhile before I turn to the next dialogue."

Ronnie settled back and gazed at the ceiling again, thinking of his peers here and at home, his mother at the club, Debbie and the used car salesman....He looked over at his roommate, who was also stretched out. "I guess, we're all sheep, huh, Karl?"

"Not exactly, Ronnie, there are the wolves, don't forget."

Later, Karl stirred, opened his eyes and Ronnie was gone. He got out of bed to do some more reading. He went to the closet to get a sweater.

Ronnie's stuff was gone. Karl let out a sigh, "Well, now,...seems the cobbler took off."

Dr. Terry was standing over the hospital bed reading the patient's chart. "You're recovering rapidly, Mr. Stanowski. It was just a scare—no surgery—but you must take the prescription faithfully. I'll release you in a few days."

"Ya? Wonderful! Got to get home to my work. My son got to go back to college. Too smart to do my work."

Terry stared coldly at him. "Oh, I don't mean your son's not smart too. He's a big help to me on weekends...."

"What's this?...My son?...Weekends, even now? Why, where does he stay?"

"Oh, at the shop. He said you folks were away and closed down the house. I'm sure glad you came back when you did."

Terry just shook his head and decided not to pursue it.

Stanowski weakly nodded into the pillow. "No fear he go to college too. My son says it's just as hard to read mechanic manuals as it is the college books."

"Well, don't send your son back too soon; you have to take it easy. You can't be expected to run that service station yet," Terry cautioned.

"I can't afford reliable help full time. Too much college expense."

"Then your son will just have to lose a semester till you recover and think about selling the place. It's too much work for you in your condition."

"Never! All my life I work to send my son to college. I wouldn't get enough for the place to keep us going.... Me no ruin that now. I manage," he said adamantly.

"I can't order you. But I'm warning you: you'll bring on a serious seizure if you persist. Your son is young, he'll find a way to finish college."

Terry left the hospital resenting the old man's good fortune in having a son of college material; yet he admired him for his dedication to that end, even though it would probably kill the old man. He was only mildly surprised to see the van as he turned into the driveway.

His wife was crying in the living room as Ronnie stood over her. She looked up at her husband.

"Oh, Robert, he's back already—couldn't even stay a month."

"I explained that already, mother. I can't afford to miss any more time at the high school. I'm determined to graduate, which I couldn't do there. And who knows maybe I will give the community college a try or take some evening courses next year. Cheer up....It's not the end of the world. I promise to crack some of the books in the study hall too. Maybe there is a world out there that I might be interested in. I'm not going to stop trying."

"But you've promised before—and here you are."

"Now, Heather, what the boy says makes sense; chase the dream away and face the reality of the way our son is doing," her husband advised.

"I'll try, dear, but it won't be easy." she looked up at her son. "You better get resettled, Ronnie; put your things away neatly."

He went to the foot of the staircase and grabbed his luggage and leaped up the stairs.

She raised herself out of the chair and started pacing from one chair to another as if she were trying to make up her mind which one to sit in. "I should've realized that he was incapable of thinking this through. I never should have listened to you when he wanted to come home the first time."

"What more do you want? He's home, isn't he? Do you think if you ordered him to stay at Stratton, the result would be any different. Well, it would be to the extent that he would not have come back here."

"Why, what do you mean?"

"I mean if we had taken a hard line, he'd be out of town by now trying to make it on his own....Even high school would go by the wayside."

"That's ridiculous! He's still a child!"

"In your eyes. and you certainly substantiated that with your comment before—that he was incapable of thinking this through. I think he was magnificent."

His eyes walled about the room. "Heather!...for my sake, would you sit somewhere?...He had made the move for us, then instead of deluding us, he returned with some good positive alternatives. I would call that mature thinking. And you ought to be proud of him, in lieu of thinking of him as someone retarded."

"Must you be so blunt!"

He raised a brow. "Then you don't deny it. You really do think there's something wrong with him. As a matter of fact you always did!"

"Robert, that's unkind! Why, I never thought of him in that dark light. Oh, yes, I've taken him to psychiatrists when he was a boy. And yes, I knew he had a learning disability. But any mother would do the same."

"Yes, that's true but a good mother would accept it and not go on badgering the child. It was Ronnie's strong character that got him through this far, any lesser boy would have folded under your pressure. Now, I'm telling you for the very last time, Heather, put this to rest, and let the boy grow as he perceives himself."

She sat back down on the edge of the chair, wringing her hands. Then she looked up at him with a woefully defeated look. "Oh, Robert, you must think me dreadful. Oh, I want so much to be proud of him!"

The front doorbell rang and Terry went to answer it. It was Debbie and her father, who had a worried look. Debbie with a pained expression on her face and holding her arm looked up at him with helplessness as her father held an ice-pack to her forehead.

"I was unable to get hold of the family doctor, Dr. Terry," he said worrisomely.

"I was hoping you could look at her arm—she's had a car accident. I thought it would be quicker than taking her to the hospital."

"Oh, my God, step right in. Of course, we might have to take her to the hospital anyway....I've been out of general practice for over a decade now but I'll certainly do what I can. You can wait in the living room, Mr. Gilbert, while I examine her in the study. Mrs. Terry is home, perhaps you'll want something to drink to calm your nerves."

He led Debbie to the study. "Oh, Dr. Terry, I should've listened to Ronnie," she cried. They went inside.

Mrs. Terry opened the liquor cabinet. "What may I fix for you, Mr.

Gilbert? You must be a nervous wreck. Oh, why must we have automobiles!"

"Any shot will be fine. Yes, I was scared out of my wits when she came barreling in. Yes, I should've listened as well," Mr. Gilbert said, pacing nervously."

"Good heavens that dear child. What happened?...Oh, do sit down and relax."

"Thank God it happened right in the front yard. She turned to pull in the driveway and wound up on the front-steps. She was so frozen to the wheel that the impact injured her arm. And she bumped her head."

Heather drew in a hefty breath. "Oh, the poor dear."

"The car lost a tie-rod, which Ronnie had warned about."

"Yes, I heard—so that's what she meant?" She handed him the drink. "Oh, please, Mr. Gilbert, you should sit down,...try to relax."

He sat on the edge for a moment, then got up again. "That and the fact that she ignored Ronnie's advice about the car in the first place. We went out and bought a used car that she had her heart set on. Ronnie had said it would need a lot of work. He even put it on the lift for her last week at Stanowski's. And called me and told me not to let her drive it until he could get a chance to reline the brakes and replace the tie-rod—damn I should've listened!"

"At Stanowski's?"

"Why, yes, where he works on weekends."

"Works?"

"Yes, that son of yours is one smart feller! A smart pair of hands!"

Heather fussed. "Will you have another drink? I think I'll have one myself."

A straight drink to her was grotesque, thoroughly unsophisticated. She poured two drinks and handed him his. She held up her glass of straight vodka to him.

Mr. Gilbert held up his glass of scotch to her. "You must be very proud of Ronnie."

In abandonment, she clinked his glass and tossed down her drink. "Why, yes, I am."

The Hollywood Director

One day in the late seventies, a pudgy, completely bald, little man stormed unannounced into the outer office of a Hollywood director-producer. The secretary was too late getting from behind her desk to catch him before he barged into the private office. The director, one of those boy-geniuses who were already making virtual reality in their childhood, jolted up from his desk and demanded an explanation.

"I have a hot film here," the little man said, holding up a video cassette.

"So, you rented a video—now go home and watch it. You're certainly not going to pull up a chair in here and use my VCR." He went to the phone. "Either you go now or I call security."

The little man laughed. "No, no, you don't understand. I'm a film-maker, too; I need you to back it."

"Seems to me, you don't need me if it's already in the video stores." The young director started to dial the phone.

"Please, give me a moment, young man," the pudgy little man pleaded. "This is the only copy I made. To be honest, I am not really a film-maker, but an actor. You see, I've been in four hundred and eighty-two pictures—a lifetime—so I decided to make film highlighting my nameless career, but I've run out of money and especially precious time. I need your marketing and distribution expertise."

"Four hundred and eighty-two films! How is it I don't know you?" with wrinkled brow the young director asked.

"Oh, that was well before your time, sonny," he said with a chuckle.

"Maybe, but I'm familiar with many old flicks and I don't…"

"Of course, you never heard of me…never once got billing." The little man quickly ran to the VCR and inserted the cassette.

"Now, just a minute here, my good man, I was brought up to respect my elders—especially old actors but there's a limit—and you admitted you are not known. So why should I waste my time?"

The old man opened up a stained brown bag he was carrying, and handed the director a sandwich. "This is the best New York Deli corn'beef outside of the Big Apple. Here, sit down; enjoy your sandwich, and take a peek at my movie—I guarantee you'll love it, the sandwich too."

The little man plopped the young director down in the chair before the TV. The young man shook his head in defeat and said, "Oh, well, I am hungry and I do love corned-beef."

"There, you see?…nothing to lose except the film of the decade," the intruder said.

"And my diet!…but what decade?" He didn't have to ask as the screen opened up to a New York City scene of Broadway spangled with moving cars from the twenties. Yet he looked with interest because he was an old film buff. He laughed uproariously when in the middle of the street a short cop, attired in the traditional NYPD buttoned up uniform three times too big, stopped traffic four ways in order to let a little boy, cranking a siren in a toy ambulance, pedal diagonally across the street. Then the camera zoomed up a skyscraper and down again to the revolving doors of an impressive entrance. The camera dollied into the building's lobby where men in derbies or wide brim fedoras and women in floral hats dropped two feet into an elevator that was still bobbing for level ground. They all stared contemptuously at the little curly haired elevator operator who had just been the cop seemed unaware of their presence as he continued pulling on the control stick. The next frames showed the same people climbing out of a three-foot drop to reach the floor while the elevator again nervously bobbed up and down from the operator's continuous efforts to adjust the floor level.

For the duration of the corned-beef sandwich, the video kept spinning out scenes of this same little curly headed actor, whom the director recognized to be the intruder as a young man. The director choked on the sandwich when the little actor was riding shotgun on a stagecoach with an arrow through his ten-gallon hat; then as an endearing little railroad conductor smiling on a romantic scene of a WWI soldier reaching out the window for his sweetheart trailing after him till she ran into a black porter at the station pushing a baggage cart of wooden crates labeled "Explosives To German Sympathizers."

The little actor retrieved a glass of water for the director whose side now hurt from the uproarious cameos. He choked again when the actor metamorphosed into a grubby drunk staggering with a wine bottle through Central Park while two lovers kissed on a bench, at which he sat down, worming between the two and getting kissed on both cheeks. Suddenly the actor was on the second story fire escape of a tenement building mimicking King Kong as early talkies children below with mischievous sound effects tossed up model airplanes at him. Midst the madness of the video tape there was a kind of dramatic relief in which three times he married off well-known stars, once as a minister, a justice of the peace wakened in the middle of the night, and as a captain of a ship at stormy sea; four times he was someone's long-lost uncle; once as a tattered, long-lost father who showed up at his daughter's wedding; twice he was shot down as a World War I fighter pilot; twice he died with a smile and once with a scowl.

Comedy again rushed in as he as a cocky youth fainted upon getting a shot on a medical examination line in WWI; twice he slid down a fireman's pole, and fell off a hook and ladder truck six times. Over a dozen episodes showed him narrowly missing being run over as a pedestrian in the midst of crazy car chases and getting bit by mad dogs. Often he was the brunt of silent and talk comedian's slapstick—dangling from a scaffold atop the Woolworth Building, drenchings from fire and garden hoses, sailing into hallways from gas stove explosions; his nose tweaked, his hair yanked, his ears twisted, his shins kicked, his eyes blackened, his body muddied after being shoved into a ditch, his clothes torn or on fire. In the talkies—over two hundred of them through the mid-thirties—but for one he never had a single line beyond groans, moans, yelps, nopes and yeps.

Excitedly the little old man poked the young director. "Here comes my crowning achievement—the only talkie I was ever in that called for more than one line." A tear rolled down his cheek as he gazed at the petite blonde starlet on the tube. He said, looking over at the director who was deeply engrossed. "The poor darling committed suicide just as she was destined for fame."

"Oh, yes, I recall," said the young man, never moving his eyes from the screen. "Would've been another Harlow—except she met the same fate—indeed tragic."

In this scene, after he saved her from drowning, he lifted her onto a capsized canoe. The up and coming starlet out of gratitude kissed him on the forehead while he raised himself up onto the belly of the canoe. The curly haired actor rolled up his eyes as though he could see the red lip imprint. The role granted him his one and only scratchy, melodramatic utterance: "Oh, my dear, dearest Sondra, at the first sign of a gray cloud my umbrella will be alerted, never will this sacred spot sense the abrasion of a wash cloth or the suds of Ivory!...Forever I shall wear your red badge of love." Then he swooned and slipped off the slippery surface and submerged, only to reemerge with her imprint running down his drenched face.

The corned beef sandwich consumed, the young director belched, laughed heartily, then got up and shut off the VCR, ejected it and looked at the label. Scribbled on it was *My Life*. He looked down at the little man who was beaming with pride as his hairless brow line rose. "It appears you did get caught in the rain without your umbrella," the young man quipped.

The little actor chuckled. "Would you believe, I really did go around the studio lot for several days with the outrageously smeared lipstick on until my next job, and the Make-up department greased away the sentiment."

The director laughed, then asked, "How in the world did you ever compile all this? How long does this tape go on?"

"Oh, I have copies of clips of every movie I ever appeared in—and the miraculous camcorder trained in on the old clips made this tape possible." He grinned with pride. "There's close to two hours."

The director looked at him with sadness in his eyes. "A lifetime in two hours, eh?...How many movies did you say?"

"Four hundred and eighty-two." He grinned from ear to ear.

"Four hundred and eighty-two...my, my,...boiled down to 120 minutes, eh?"

"One hundred and nineteen, actually...perfect for the VHS."

"My, my," he repeated, looking with tenderness at the proud little man. "You know, my good man, this has possibilities—not as a theatre movie, you understand. But it might just go over as a classic video and rental....Yes, it is an important film. Unquestionably film fans should see this. But it will need a preface and technical enhancement from the clips—with your permission I would like to do it."

"Oh, that's very kind of you, young man. But why the preface?"

"It needs someone to inform the viewers on just how important actors like you were and are to the film industry."

"Oh, my!" the little man said tearfully, "Why, you really do think that!"

"You can bet your next corned-beef sandwich on it. By the way, what did you have put in that sandwich?—I can't believe you've affected me this way."

"Oh, it wasn't the sandwich, young man; it was you—I believe that more than ever now—and your love of film—that's why I chose you," the little man said with emotion. "I entrust this cassette to you; I must leave now for my chemotherapy. I hope you like the rest of the video—it's my life, you know—and please do hurry—there's not much time, you know."

After the little man left; the young man canceled all his appointments and spent the afternoon running the tape, searching forward and backward over and over. His side ached from laughter and convulsive sobs for the mixed emoting tour de force. Finally he ejected it, looked at the label again, crossed out the scribble and wrote:

Black Hole Revisited: Rebirth of a Star

Minor Incident

Inside a real estate office off main street suburbium, a married couple in their mid thirties were in the normal state of indecision before signing an agreement. A corpulent, confident agent, slouched behind an unimpressively cluttered desk, contemplated them through rings of smoke from an overworked cigar. He had sized it up as just a matter of custom, a matter of time; he didn't mind earning his commission.

"Believe me, Mr. and Mrs. Dolan, nothing is too good for our children," he   exhaled. "Granted taxes are high, but no higher than any other respectable community. The good people here faced up to their responsibility in providing excellence in education for the most cherished possession—their children....What's a few hundred dollars when it's for a good cause?...Cause! did I say?...Why education isn't charity... it's an investment that pays off in human dividends...more than pride in local colors...it's an expression of   red, white and blue waving in the sky saying nothing is too good for America!" He had wished to raise himself from the chair and to pound his fist on the desk with the elegance of Edward Arnold but knew his great size would not permit it and besides— proud of his record of closings— realized this act would be but superfluous, dead weight to his glib tongue.

"Don't get me wrong," the husband, twirling his cap nervously, divulged apologetically; "I'm not implying that school taxes aren't necessary;...it's just that,...well, when you drove us around town and I saw all those one-storied school buildings scattered about,...well, it just seemed too damn extravagant. In the city, I went to a school that had five stories...and..."

"This isn't the city, Mr. Dolan," the great agent interjected. "Out here we do things differently...better. There are ordinances to protect us from that sort of thing." He rocked back heavily on his chair and swiveled slowly in the direction of a map on the wall. "This is a brave new world a few of us old-timers are working on, Mr. Dolan. Each project-deve- lopment represented by those colorful pinheads is our contribution to modernization."   Drawing on his cigar, then exhaling indolently, he finally rifled, "Isn't that why you're here, Mr. Dolan,— to get away from five story buildings?"

"Apartment buildings, yes!" Mr. Dolan parried hotly, twisting his cap in his hands. "But I still question the trend to put costly maintained school buildings all over the community."

"You're forgetting the savings of having to transport children safely and only a short distance from home. No doubt as a lad you looked out the classroom window and saw the roofs and smokestacks jutting the city sky. Here your children will see grass and other children playing in vast open fields during their recess—isn't that worth the small down payment and the seventy and change a month?" He gazed kindly at Dolan's demure, young wife who was listening while occasionally glancing through a brochure on the house she hoped would be theirs.

She placed a light hand on her husband's shoulder and said softly, "Pat, it's the house we're buying and its lovely setting; we shouldn't look back at the city. I want to get out of it; to be free—that's all I know—and for the money, we won't find a nicer place for the children than here—taxes are everywhere."

"Exactly, Mrs. Dolan!" the agent interpolated. "The days of the minutemen are over—pay we must." She felt offended that he had broken in—after all, she was speaking to her husband. Nevertheless, she ignored the intrusion and after several moments of her searching, pleading eyes, penetrating his, Dolan relinquished and they signed the binder on their future.

They left the office and headed toward a '48 Dodge pickup in the small parking lot. Rubbing his knuckles, Dolan said huskily, "Instead of signing I should've punched him in his fat paunch. God! how I hate those talkers. They make you feel like nothing,...like you have no mind of your own." Smashing his fist into his palm, he announced, "Jesus, Mary and Joseph—one of these days, honey, I'm going to talk up to these guys."

She opened his hand and squeezed it. "We did the right thing, dear, don't you think? I mean you really want to live out here on Long Island—you're not just doing it for us?" She looked pleadingly into his eyes that were turning to their emerald warmth.

"I can't think of a better reason," he said, smiling, "but there's a lot of Irish left in me yet—there's no way I would do it, if I really didn't want to—you know that."

"Tell me, then, Patrick Dolan, do you have a mind to buying a car, too—can't be borrowing my father's anymore."

"Well, now,...I don't know,...starting already, is it?...Could always teach you to handle the truck."

"And how could I get to Mass each day? You heard the agent—the church is more than ten minutes away—by car. You can't very well keep this truck home for me."

"Heck, that's right—sure and I can't have my wife going northern on me by missing Mass. Tell you what: would you settle for one of those wee Henry J's?— we should be able to pick one up cheap, since no one seems to want the little burgers, anymore. Strange, they're great little cars, but most used car hunters think because they were manufactured by the Kaiser Company that they aren't buying American, but German!"

"I thought so, too." She squeezed his hand till her nails dug slightly into his callous palm and sighed, "Pat, I feel like a kid again, walking under the EL with you—hand in hand—and yet, here we are in the open spaces."

"I wouldn't carry it that far, Agnes, after all, Long Island is growing fast—not many potato farms left," he reminded her as he pulled her closer. "Yes,...those were the days....Concrete and steel were all we knew and didn't care. Remember when I used to recite all that romantic stuff when a train passed overhead so you could barely hear me because I felt good but silly saying them?" They reached the Dodge.

Their daughter was sitting on the running board and quickly rose up to open the door for her mother, saying, "Enter the future, Mom." She turned to her father as she went to the driver's side. "Oh, Daddy, I can tell by Mom's beaming face that you bought it!" Their thirteen year old daughter shrilled. as she slid under the steering wheel to the middle of the benchseat next to her mother. Her younger brother, who had been curled up sleeping in the rear of the cabin, stirred from his sister's noisy enthusiasm.

As the mother settled in she turned to her child, brushed back the girl's auburn curls, saying, "Not quite, Patricia, those things take time, but it's as good as ours."

Turning and shaking her little brother, the girl pattered, "Gary! Wake up! Did you hear? Isn't it marvelous? We're going to be country folk! I bet you can raise chicks and rabbits—and most of all have a dog! Just think, you'll be in one of those pretty schools the agent showed us!…Wonder what mine'll be like?"

"Whoa, my pet," her father intercepted as he got in behind the wheel, "we haven't exactly bought a farm, you know."

The boy winced. "Patty, it's still a crummy school—even without nuns!"

His father looked around menacingly and gestured he would give the back of the hand if he did not change his tune in a hurry. "Watch your blasphemy, Gary," his mother broke in quickly, lest her husband lose his temper altogether as he was wont to do.

"The nuns!" Patty echoed as she flung herself back against the seat. "Mother, what am I going to do?…A public school!… I can't believe it…I'll be sentenced to Purgatory!…How am I going to learn anything without the blessed nuns? Public school teachers don't care if you learn—even if they do they don't have the same dedication!"

"What makes you such an authority on public education?… You've never been to a public school." Her father said with a mixture of pride and annoyance. Though he hated his own days in Catholic school—especially in having a taste of public school his first three years because his mother could not even afford the dime a week for text books—and envied his friends who went through the public system, he would not have it any other way. He hated the Marine Corps too, yet never wished he had chosen another branch. He was at first convinced it was a simple matter of pride, then later he attributed it to: "some guys just like doing things the hard way." That is, until he learned the word "masochism." But he was unable to translate the word into 'sadism' when applied to his own children learning the "hard way" because they were, especially the girl, thrilled with Catholic school. Ten years ago he was ambivalent about moving to Levittown when that seemed to be the topic of the day among his fellow-workers in the Bronx. On the one hand, it seemed the easy way out; on the other, he did not want to disrupt hard conditioning of city life. Now he regretted his backing off then: "all this current crap would be behind me."

Patty added, "Mildred goes to public and she says it makes her sick every morning to drag herself there."

"You and your friends." Pat merged onto the road. "Wisdom rests with authority."

Agnes, agreed with the stipulation, "If that authority is the Pope." She glanced at her daughter and observed . "Besides, Mildred was never happy with any school she went to. Even when she went to St.Benedict's she couldn't stand the nuns."

"Oh, how she misses them now! She really appreciates their under-standing, Mother."

"I'm sure the poor soul does." Her mother said, looking out the window. "Going home, perhaps we'll catch a glimpse of your school."

"Oh, I hope it's beautiful!"

"What's beauty got to do with it?...School is school!" Her brother offered, rubbing the kinks in his knees from cramped quarters. "Nothing beautiful about being penned up all day."

"At ten years old you're not expected to appreciate the splendor of am-bience." She said haughtily.

"What?...in heaven's name is am...ambience?" her mother asked.

"Oh, just a word I picked up in reading: it means surroundings, atmos-phere and stuff. It's a kind of setting that can contribute to one's growth and well-being, I guess."

"What do we have here, Agnes,...a philosopher in the family?" Pat joked. "Bad enough she was a welfare worker—now she's way over my head."

"Oh, Daddy, you always try to upset me with your role of ignorance. You don't kid me. You know there's more to life than just sports. And Sisters of Charity don't work for the government. They work for the soul."

"Pat, you never win with your daughter," Mary said, smiling.

"You're so right. She's too much." He thought, "Maybe...na." He thought about relinquishing and letting her stay in Catholic school but thought better of it as the dollar signs from all the needs in buying a home flashed in his mind.

Agnes turned to her daughter and said consolingly, "Patty, it's not that you'll be without the good sisters entirely; the agent informed us that there was religious instruction given by the sisters in the next parish. And the school gives you time off and actually supplies them with a bus to take them there. So you can't complain."

"Oh, he just said that to sell the house—I don't trust the man," Patricia repined.

"Since when? You thought he was wonderful when he showed us the model," the mother rejoined. A jet roared overhead. "I hope that's not often," moaned Agnes, pressing her head against the window, trying to look up.

Gary pressed his face to the rear window and strained for a look. "Wow, an Air Force fighter! Flying low, too!"

"Well, I can't imagine another parish accepting me, a new girl from the Bronx, for RI— can you?" Patricia went on, impervious to the intruding "ambience."

"When the blessed Monsignor Flanagan calls them, you can be as certain as *ex voto* that they will extend to you religious instruction," her mother assured her.

As his father slowed down to read a street sign, the boy, looking at a spacious lot, said, "Say, Dad,...I bet they have Little League here, huh?"

"Oh, I suppose so. That should be a big thing out here."

"Do you think you'll manage my team?" knowing his father, he snickered.

"Hold on there, Scooter,...we haven't even really bought the house, much less moved in."

"Mother!" Patty broke in. "What does Daddy mean? You said it too...that it takes time...how long?"

"It all depends on the V.A.'s approval," her father said.

"I don't understand, Mother." She always turned to her mother for clarification.

"Under the G.I. Bill veterans are granted a government guaranteed mortgage loan to offset the cash needed to sign for a home. Most people need several thousand down to buy a home, veterans don't."

"Are you saying we can't afford it?"

"Patty, that's not your concern. Money matters are for adults. Besides, of course, we can or we wouldn't be here."

"Then why did Daddy say..."

"Hush, child,...just a business technicality."

The father turned down a street with a school crossing sign. "You know, Scooter,..."

"I wish you'd stop calling him that." Agnes objected. "He's entitled to his own generation, you know."

"Pee Wee,..." Dolan taunted.

"Will you stop!" She punched him lightly.

"Gary, you know, I might just be interested in coaching, but I'm not making any promises....Maybe when and if I get work out here, I'll have the time."

"Wow!" Gary fell back in the compartment.

"Maybe next year," Pat quickly added.

Gary followed the jet trail above, then asked, "Dad, when are you going to give up that Tommy Henrich mitt of yours?"

"Ah, 'Old Reliable'! In time, son, that's my youth's treasure, you know? You'll have to earn the privilege."

"Like how?"

"Well, for one thing...making the Little League and proving yourself, or making the school team when you reach the junior high."

"I like the Little League idea better—junior high is two years away!"

"We'll see...but you can't just ride the bench...and you'll have to make the All-Stars."

"Ugh!...I don't like that idea."

"Being a little tough on him,...that's a tall order for a ten year old," Agnes demurred, furrowing her forehead.

"No, he'll make it." Pat's anxiety waned and began to take on a sense of new adventure, of challenge as 'Gentleman Jim' —Errol Flynn, actually— stepping into the ring with John L. His new pride was still mixed with the shame that he had even hesitated to close the deal. "What the heck," he ruminated, "you only live once, so live daring...why not take on a team...why not learn about caring for lawns and fixing things instead of relying on a janitor?...Why, I'll be my own lord!...isn't that what Irish history is all about?...to own their own land...instead of leprechaun turf which might have filled their spirits but not their stomachs...trouble is this might be fantasy land and...empty our stom... Jesus, I don't even own a rake, much less a lawnmower!"

"Pat! That must be the school!" his wife blurted, jolting him from his thoughts.

"Oh, Mother, It's beautiful!" Patty pushed aside her brooding over the good sisters. The aluminum sash and polished brick gleamed in the sunlight as the tall maples lay dormant in the foreground, casting their skeletal shape on the barely greening lawn.

Pat slowed down then eased to a halt. "Just as the agent said—the very latest design. Well, what do you know, Agnes, two stories," he added cynically. "They're getting up in the world. Still, look how long it is—they could've saved thousands just by adding another flight—foundations and roofs cost money."

"Pat, don't be that way—be thankful there are people who still want to preserve the beauty of the sky and countryside. Hard working people deserve a little extravagance." She proudly demonstrated her argument by pointing her finger at him, flashing her light blue eyes.

They continued down the long block and turned at the corner to the side of the building and saw that the sprawling structure ended abruptly. An ancient red brick, three story building, some seventy five feet away claimed territorial right to the rest of the school site. "Ah, now that's architecture!" Pat said.

"Dad, it's ugly—I suppose that's where they'll put me. The senior high school no doubt is the new one."

"I'm afraid you're right, Patty," her mother added, "that's probably why the agent didn't show it to us—he assumed you were of junior high school age. Still, I've seen worse and have attended worse. You'll survive."

"Mother, why can't I stay in the Catholic school system?" she cried.

"We've been through this all before we began our Sunday searches and you agreed to forgo Catholic school to help us with the extra expense of owning a new home." Agnes reminded her.

"I know, Mother, of course,...I'm sorry...like you always say, I'll survive."

"That's my Precious Patricia!" The father rejoined. "Why, you might even like it. It's a solid-looking building, Patty,...see, the keystone reads, 1902...the days when they really knew how to build, and I bet it was even updated by the old WPA in the thirties. I heard they did a lot of work on schools then."

"Twenty year-old update!— sounds wonderful," Patty interpolated, sarcastically.

Her father raved on, "Sure and I'll wager it's good for another forty years. Very sensible of them not to tear it down. The school officials are not completely mad, after all,...though there should be fire escapes."

"Listen to your father, Patty," Agnes maintained; "you can't destroy things just because they're old....Remember when we visited Monticello, how enchanting it was?"

"Oh, yes, Mother, it was beautiful...as a museum and national shrine," she added sarcastically.

Her mother countered, "That's enough! As a symbol of a great man and a great country, just as a school is as good as the people in it."

"That applies to Catholic schools as well, Patty." Her father bantered.

"Yes, perhaps even more so, Mr. Dolan," Agnes agreed. "I'm ashamed of ourselves for ever getting into this unchristian subject of appearances and vanity. And you're right; there should be ugly fire-escapes." She made the sign of the cross; the discussion terminated and Pat headed back to the city.

The Dolans moved into their new home on Holy Thursday. To the chagrin of Pat, before the moving men arrived at the apartment, Agnes had taken the kids to Mass at St. Benedict's—for perhaps the last time there. She and the kids got back in time before Pat could blow off steam. All four Dolans worked together splendidly, busy unpacking at the new home.

Pat could not take Good Friday off; Agnes and the kids finished up the unpacking, sorting things and rearranging light furniture through the day except for Patricia's reading of the Passion to her mother and brother. Agnes, over Pat's objection at Friday's meatless supper, had invited her parents out for Easter dinner. "Jesus, aren't you rushing things a bit?" he had asked her. Having quickly bowed her head from his blaspheme— on this solemn day in particular — she replied that she had never missed a holiday dinner with them and now that she was a Long Islander she was not going to let him use that as an excuse not to visit nor to have them over. He had been upset over that remark as he felt it was entirely unjustified. After all, he got along fine with his in-laws—better than she did as a matter of fact—though the heavens would fall if he dared criticize them in any shape or form that did not fit clearly within the category of humor. Though tolerant of his cynicism, which she attributed to "Irish wit," she was wary when applied to her folks. Margaret and Peter O'Brien were full of the devil themselves, however, and often enjoyed bantering with him. Still, their daughter was in anxiety whenever they got together, fearing the worst that they should become argumentative in sports, politics, and religion—"there isn't an Irishman alive who doesn't relish mixing them," she always said.

"Mother, where do you want the Blessed Mother?" Patty asked earlier in the day, holding a statuette of the beautiful Lady painted in fine blue and white robes with gold tresses peeping from her habit. "Shouldn't we put her in a more conspicuous place, instead of in the hall like we did at the apartment?"

"Yes, I suppose you're right, but you know what your father thinks of those blue eyes and blonde hair."

"Oh, yes: 'Only a heinie could think up a blonde blue-eyed Madonna!'" she said, mimicking her father, "but I also know he doesn't really mean it. Goodness, both of us have blue eyes!" Patricia surveyed what to her was a spacious room. "Perhaps on the mantelpiece?"

"Seems fitting....Yes, I agree,...except...yes, put it there." Agnes sat down in one of the fireside chairs still wrapped in plastic. The chairs were delivered yesterday afternoon with a note from her mother attached, congratulating them on their new home. Pat had observed that they were pretty, but too delicate for him and had counted on placing his armchair by the fireplace until she reminded him that the television could not be put near the fireplace. She reflected a moment on the Lady, "How nice to be able to grow roses, to go to the garden during blossoming and snip one to lay at her feet," she mused. She asked the Lady to help her husband adjust to the long drive into the city.

When he had taken off yesterday to oversee the moving men, who wished he had not bothered, he had insisted that they follow him from the apartment, even though they knew the island infinitely better than he. Knowing him, Agnes had slipped them the extra key. At the first caution light Pat made a complete stop; the moving truck sped by and that was the last of them until the Dolans arrived at the house. The van was already half empty, and they were sprawled on the steps drinking coffee.

"Look at that, would you?— already goofin'off!" Pat growled as he pulled into the fresh, new black driveway.

"They saved us money by not following us; and saved me having to pull out the coffee pot for them. It's tradition, you know, to make coffee for moving men."

"Oh, is it now?…and whose tradition is that?…the O' Briens?"

"Everybody's but yours." She countered. "Fourteen years ago when we moved into the apartment, I served the moving men coffee and buns."

"You did what? A young bride of nineteen prancing about with strangers in our apartment unattended! Jesus, Agnes, what did they think!"

She bowed her head. "No! What would you think is more cor- rect!…And precisely why I never told you!" She steamed.

 Her musing was interrupted by her daughter. "Mother I'm going upstairs to arrange my room now, ok?"

She jumped up from the chair guiltily, as though not entitled to a pause with all the work at hand. "Yes, yes, of course, but first take some towels out of the linen carton and hang them in the bathroom." She took out her egg-white drapes stuffed in a box and stretch them out on the beige carpet, which she had chosen as part of the builder's package before she discovered that all the rooms had to be white unless they opted to pay an extra five hundred dollars for color and another three hundred for trim work. Pat objected to this "Limey demand." He had also protested Agnes' decision to take the carpeting. She had tried to console him by admitting that perhaps when the carpeting got old she would go back to throw rugs or when they generated more income, purchase a nice oriental on sale. He reminded her that there would be no hardwood floors once the carpeting was installed. Nevertheless, she would not waver inasmuch as it had been her dream since childhood to have wall-to-wall like her wealthy friend Dorothy O'Malley had. On her knees she tried to smooth out the drapes to no avail, then tossed them on the back of the sofa. She decided that when Pat installed a washline a fresh breeze and some sunshine would freshen them—she dreaded having to iron them in face of all the work to be done. In the summer, however, she knew she would have to dye them for some contrast. She went out to the garage and went through some of Pat's junk to remove the Japanese rifle and samurai saber hung over from her husband's war days. She put them in the basement behind the boiler. "Out of sight out of mind," she thought, "this will give Our Lady a chance to establish herself and claim her right to suitable prominence in the household."

Easter Sunday came and the house was fairly organized and actually had a "lived-in" look, thanks to the family's concerted effort, particularly Pat's. On Saturday he had risen before dawn and started in immediately on installing the draw-drape hardware, curtain rods and a clothes line for the drapes to air. Agnes was thrilled at the outcome since the wrinkles disappeared. He was so preoccupied throughout the day putting up shelving for the kids' rooms, rearranging the dining room furniture, sliding furniture here and there at his wife's bidding, condensing cartons and papers for garbage pick-up, helping her place endless ware in this drawer and on that shelf—the shelf where Our Lady presided over the industry went unnoticed.

After communion breakfast, Pat was still on the roof installing the television antenna, when the O'Briens arrived earlier than expected, though their usual custom was to arrive an hour or two earlier. The Dolans, however, assumed they would have some difficulty finding the place, which they did, but Pete O'Brien had compensated by leaving the city three hours before the normal hour's drive. Actually, Pete was helpful on the ground by guiding Pat on the roof in orienting the antenna.

While the usual activity of three generations of females in the kitchen went on, Pete queried his grandson on the early baseball season, while Pat went to the nearest deli for a couple of six-packs, swearing under his breath on the way because Agnes forgot his Tudor Ale from the A&P. "Now I've got to pay some Jew a buck more,...and Pete drinks like an elephant."

"Yeah, Gramps, I hope to get into the Little League. With all the stickball I played in the city park I oughta be pretty good."

Pete hesitated a moment to phrase it right lest he dampen his grandson's spirit. "Yes, many good ballplayers are products of city stickball and softball, but until they got into organized ball in high school they didn't really develop into anything much. Today you kids have the advantage of playing organized ball early. But to stay good and develop your natural talent, you still have to keep up with pick-up games almost everyday. City boys like Hank Greenberg and Sid Gordon lived baseball and stickball in their growing up days, of course, you don't remember them."

"No, a little before my time, Gramps, but I feel I know them—I have their cards. Most of the oldies are my dad's."

"Bless you!" Do you have Gehrig, Keller, Reiser...?"

"Maybe,...definitely Gehrig....I'll get'em from my room." Gary ran off.

Pete got up from the fireside, blessed himself before the Lady and moved her more on center. He noted the discomfort of the new chair and decided to settle in the easy chair. Gary returned with the cards and sat on the arm of the chair.

"Well, I'll be...you *do* have Charley Keller! You know, I saw him hit a line drive 460 feet!...would've been a homer anywhere else, except the Polos Grounds."

Wide-eyed,Gary yelped. "Wow! Centerfield at Yankee Stadium, I bet!...was it caught?"

"No, lad, but Dimag's brother Dom held it to a double....Had many an argument with Red Sox fans as to which brother was the better fielder." He shuffled through some more. "Musial, eh?...he's some hitter and still as consistent as ever."

"Yeah, he's my favorite." The boy beamed.

"What?...You're not kidding an old man now, are you? After all, there are all these great younger players—Aaron, Mays, Mantle, Snider."

"Musial is a true lefty, so am I; besides, those guys, though they aren't huge, they're muscular, but Musial is lanky, almost scrawny in comparison and I figure that's about how I'll turn out."

"Well, in my day I cut quite a muscular figure;...still do in fact." He put up his biceps for his grandson to feel."

"Oh, Gramps, I know that. You're still a big powerful man. But what about my father?...He's built like Henry Fonda."

"What's your father got to do with it!"

"A little, I think." Pat said as he walked in with two glasses with creamy heads. He winked at his son. "Got the old cards out, son, eh?" He handed a glass of ale to his father-in-law, put his down by the end-table next to the sofa, retrieved some cards from his son and sat down on the sofa to browse through some of them. "Takes you back, doesn't it, Pop?"

"Not far enough for me; but I still look back at the thirties and forties with fond baseball memories." Pete said wistfully. He chugged down half the glass of ale. "This ale isn't bad, beats what you usually have; the suburbs must agree with you."

"Yeah, I just got it in the village deli—can you believe it the owner is Christian? He robbed me more than the ki…well, than those in the city."

"Well, you guys out here are supposed to be filthy rich, you know."

"Next I suppose you'll be telling me I'll have to vote Republican." He smiled and resumed thumbing through the cards.

Pete laughed. "No, that's as bad as becoming Episcopalian." Then he mused, "I was telling Gary about Charley Keller."

"Oh, yeah…quite a home run hitter. He was one powerful guy…two bats in the batter's circle weren't enough for him. He'd pick up and swirl three or four like they were toothpicks. It was a sad day for me when the Yanks traded him to Detroit—poor guy, was never the same after his slipped disk."

Pete nodded forelornly. "Yeah,…that's one thing we have in common; we both tend to look back on the supporting players that'll never make the Hall of Fame—like George Selkirk."

"Yeah, heck of a player…how about Johnny Rucker?" Pat asked.

Pete's eyes lit up and agreed, "Graceful center fielder with the speed of an antelope. Then there was 'Fireman' Murphy…the guys at the station house loved that name." The nostalgic spell was broken when Agnes called them to the dinner table.

Margaret reminded her grandson to say grace as he reached for his glass of milk. "Nana, Patty always says it," he protested.

"Yes, Patricia does; that's why I'm asking you. The youngest in the family has to start taking some responsibility. You know it, of course?"

"I sure heard it enough times to know it." He bowed his head.

Pat put the carving knife down and thought,…"Christ, she doesn't even give me a chance to carve the meat."

Gary thought for a second, then recited in record time.

"Well, you certainly do know it, young man, but next time slow down a bit and think of the words," Margaret advised; nevertheless, she was proud of him.

"You see, Gary,…" the grandfather joined in. "Saying Grace is like baseball…"

"You and your baseball!" his wife said with a smirk.

"Now, let me finish, Mother," he said mildly vexed. "I'm talking to the boy." He returned to Gary. "In baseball you've got to be thinking all the time. Even the greats like Musial, even though they seem to be doing everything by natural instinct, they're really analyzing every pitch, every play, whether on the field or in the dugout."

"You mean just like a manager?"

"Exactly, good ballplayers manage themselves."

Pat Joined in, "That reminds me of the first time Casey joined the

Yanks and he was watching Dimag in the field and he thought, 'Now what in the world could I say to this guy that he doesn't already know?'"

"'Nothing' would be his answer because great managers manage teams, not great players." Pete added authoritatively. To keep the peace Pat usually yielded. The grandfather added, "So, Gary, you have to think along with the words if they're to have any meaning."

"Well said, Dad, too much rote as it is," Agnes said, thinking of her own upbringing and wondering why they had not given her that advice—with age comes wisdom, she thought. She leapt from the table. "Oh, Dad, I forgot your Guinness!" She went into the kitchen to retrieve one of the bottles she had bought for him the day before. Pat went back to his carving, thinking: "she could remember his damned stout, but not my ale...bless her disloyal soul!"

"Do you know what 'bounty' means, dear brother?" Patty asked with a slight detection of facetiousness.

Gary turned to his mother. "Mom, why does she always try to show me up?"

"She's just trying to be helpful." Agnes looked askance, cautioning Patty, then returned to her son. "Besides, I would like to know on this day of days."

"Well, I know it doesn't mean like in the 'Bounty Hunter'—probably means a sort of kindness. Like I am with you, Patty, when you want to borrow my baseball glove or 't'shirt."

"Excellent, little brother," Patty patronized pompously, "just excellent,...yes, a vast resource of generosity as imparted through Jesus Christ....like our new home, which by the way you failed to mention."

"That's enough, Patricia," her mother warned.

"See what I mean, Mom? She takes a good thing and ruins it!"

"She can't help herself, son;" the father quipped. "That's the philosopher in her...always complicating simplicity."

"Still, she's a brilliant girl, Pat, and you should be very proud of her," his mother-in-law added.

"Oh, I agree...and proud I am. Still, she's often a pain in..."

"Finish carving the ham, Pat." Agnes injected.

"I hope you're not suggesting my granddaughter is a smart-aleck!"

"No, Mom, but Patricia can be overbearing at times," Agnes qualified in Pat's behalf.

Margaret's face drooped. "But Pat too can be overbearing." She turned to her son-in-law. "And what do you mean: complicating simplicity? Bishop Sheen—I never miss a program—certainly is not guilty of that. Why, that brilliant saint makes everything seem so clear!"

"You're right, Bridge—can't argue there — Jesuit trained.... Pass your plates." Pat ordered, doling out thick slices.

When Patty's plate was returned, she said, "Bless us, Our Lord, for Thy gift of family love and our beautiful new residence....And forgive me my trespass in entering public school."

"Last-word-Annie," said Pat.

"Never mind, her sentiments are always in the right place," Agnes rejoined.

"Oh, it's not the place I question...it's the timing." Pat looked over at his daughter.

"Now who's being overbearing, Daddy?" Patty injected.

He laughed. "Like I said, last-word..."

Margaret pleaded, "Really, Agnes, you must try to get her into Catholic school. Father Flanagan said he could arrange it."

"Mother we've been through all this before. There's no school in the district, and I don't want her being transported all over creation,...not at her age. When she's of high school age it'll be time enough — that is, if we can afford it. Besides, Mom, enrolling in public school is not a mortal sin."

"Then it should be! — and surely we can help with the the cost," her mother countered. "Why, they can't even say prayer there."

"Just as well..." Pete said, "What do they know about such things? They're all Protestant Republicans out here."

Through a mouthful of food, Gary wanted to know: "What's so awful about public schools? I'm looking forward to tomorrow...even though I lost a week of vacation."

"That's another thing....They can't even get their holidays right out here." Pete rejoined. "They resent Holy Thursday and Good Friday so they close the schools the week before Easter. Those Republicans are slick devils—and I'm sure the city Jews who've landed out here had a hand in it, too, in order to salvage their Passover."

"Dad, please, not on Easter!" Agnes pleaded.

"Which is it, Pop,...Republicans, Protestants, or Jews?" Pat asked jokingly.

"All three!...and you can bet your St. Christopher's medal that there are some Limey Anglicans on the board of education too," Pete grunted, raising his stout with a massive hand.

Pat chuckled. "Just the same Gary is right! It's no big deal. I went to P.S's till the third grade!...Oops, forced to agree with my in-laws!—I haven't done so hot." They all laughed. Agnes was relieved. Patricia seemed annoyed.

"Daddy, you're the smartest man I know!" Patricia cried earnestly. "After all, you're my father. You did fine with your education."

"Meaning you have no choice?"

"Oh, Dad, you're a last word...Andy." The daughter shook her red curls.

"No, in this case, *I* am!" Pete said half indignantly. "The smartest man is your father?...And what am I a head of cabbage?"

"Oh, Gramps," she said with a trace of embarrassment, "Of course, I meant both of you."

"Don't let your grandfather intimidate you, Patricia," Margaret advised. "Your first loyalty is always to your father."

Pete looked at his own daughter and quipped with a twinkle in his eye, "You heard your mother, Aggie!" They both laughed.

After dinner they gathered in the living room. Patty asked to be excused to do some reading and to prepare for her strange new day tomorrow. Gary sneaked out to the kitchen to catch the Dodger game on radio. Pete could hear subsonics of Vince Scully and could not understand why his grandson could still be faithful to those turncoats. Gesturing toward the kitchen, he said to Pat, "Brooklyn will never be the same."

"Nor will New York, for that matter. No more arguments over the likes of Mantle, Mays, Snider."

"Ah, yes, but the most tragic—nothing to do with the move, then again, maybe it did—is Campy's accident and no more Campy-Yogi comparisons," Pete added sadly.

"Sad, indeed, but the comparison will go on forever," Pat consoled him.

"Baseball on Easter Sunday is sacrilege!" Margaret injected.

"At least we're not watching it!" Pete reminded her.

She stretched the corner of her lips to him. "Humph." She felt the material of the fireside chair. "Do you like them, Agnes? They were on sale at Michaels. They have very good buys, if you're careful. When they heard they were to be delivered to the island they were going to charge me five dollars, until I started to walk out. The salesman had to call the manager when I told them I was not going to pay the city tax either for something that was going to be used on Long Island. So the manager had to okay the credit plan in my name and your address."

"You're a survivor, Mom....Yes, I think they're beautiful!"

Margaret said pensively, "Yes, this modern world...too bad...easy come, easy go...still, it's beyond me why this generation doesn't watch their money."

Pat looked uncomfortable on the sofa. He never sat in it, except when his father-in-law visited. "And your daughter's one of them," Pat rejoined; "she never remembers my cheap A&P beer."

"Agnes is trying to tell you to drink more tea," she said laughingly, then turned to her husband and added, "You should too, Pete; you're too heavy from all the stout you consume."

The two men looked at each other, grinned and shrugged their shoulders in unison as Pat said, "Don't get stout with stout, Pop."

Agnes, ignoring the interlude, drifted back to the chairs. "I saved the plastic covering....They're going back on tomorrow until we're more settled."

"Very wise." Margaret agreed as she admired her own taste again, then winked up at the statuette and said, "Pete took the wrong exit coming out...."

"That's because you gave me the wrong exit," he emphasized.

"Anyway, we got detoured and saw Patricia's school. It's really quite nice, in spite of..."

"Did it have an off-white brick?"

"Yes, sort of tile-ish."

"Well, that's not the school. The one she's going to is the old annex behind that new one."

"Oh, my, what a shame!...That's one more reason why..."

"Mother! Please!"

Pete asked Pat, "How old is this building?"

"Keystone says 1902."

"Oh, boy, that's not good....We were kept busy in the city by those old crackling beauties."

"Really? I thought in those days they were solid," Pat said with some surprise.

"No, facing means nothing...too much dried-out timber in those oldies."

"Now, Pete don't go getting Agnes upset. You were never called to a disastrous school fire. Stop being a Calamity Jane," Margaret warned.

"No, Peg, but many could've been." Then he returned to his son-in-law. "Do they have fire-escapes, Pat?"

"It's only a three story."

"Only? They should have them on two-story. That was always a sore point with us firemen....Because they conducted rigid, orderly fire-drills was no reason to expect order in time of crisis with anybody, much less kids."

"Dad, do you really think Patricia's in danger?" Agnes pleaded with sudden concern.

"No, of course not, darlin'—just an old retiree mouthing off."

"Remember, you said that, I didn't," his wife noted.

"I thought I'd save my darling wife the trouble," he said winking at his daughter.

"Then you should have thought of that before you started—you firemen are like old washwoman." She turned to her daughter. "Now, don't go worrying your fool head off....God will watch over Patricia—no fear of that."

"Yes, Aggie, pay your old dad no mind," Pete said self-deprecatingly. "Those old buildings are like the old ballplayers, they bow out with dignity."

The Dolans were adjusting to their new environment splendidly. Now in mid May, Pat was joining the ranks of the green thumbs by working weekends on his new lawn, watering it faithfully. He added more foundation planting, cursing the stingy builder. Agnes, too, joined in planting annuals and perennials along the walk and driveway. She got Pat to turnover a patch in the backyard for vegetables, since the builder only sowed lawn seed twenty feet behind the house anyway. The kids and she found it total adventure planting vegetable seed and watching the shoots spring up in a week—neither had ever experienced this miracle before. "Just think, Mom, by June we'll be eating our own home grown peas," Gary had said to her one day when they were weeding together. She didn't have the heart to tell them they planted them too late for that. "Boy, I can't wait till that corn is ready! Almost as exciting as the first crack of the bat in spring."

Pat got Gary into the Little League even though team rosters had been chosen and practice well under way. Gary was happy just to be a member of the "Tigers," regardless that the manager was reluctant to accept him so late: "Another 'licorice stick' I don't need." was his comment. Though Pat had little time for his son, he—remembering his reading a tip from Mantle—hung an old truck tire from the garage rafter for his son to swing at to make the manager eat his "licorice."

Patty too was acclimated and had overcome her anxiety concerning school, owing to the early recognition she received for excellent achievement. Because she—like her mother—was good with the pen, one of her compositions was forwarded by her English teacher to the central office for publication in its newsletter, which was mailed to all three thousand residents in the district. On the day of issuance, Patty's picture inset was on the front page under the heading:

City-bred Child Embraces Suburbs

In reading it on the day of issue, Agnes noted a particular—but typically honest Patricia Dolan—observation:

> ....Though I still distress over the loss of Catholic school,
> I find comfort in many new friends and very helpful
> teachers. Time may very well mend this loss completely by

my total adjustment to classes consisting of 15-25 in a class as opposed to 40-50 in Catholic school! Then I may have to resign to the conclusion that it never was a loss that I pined over and that I should have recognized it as an immediate gain....

"O Sweet Virgin, forgive my child!" she moaned, looking up at the Lady. She put the newsletter down on the table next to the fireside chair, which, its mate as well, was still plastic-wrapped. All her school days she had been taught by the "blessed sisters" and here in the Fifties life was changing so rapidly that she feared her daughter would be swept up by the Levittown era. "Was Pat right in resisting it? We could've had a lovely little home in Levittown ten years ago with no money down; yet he feared the change. What was it he said?...Something like...'Give up the advantages of city life—the best schools in the world already built and established, low rent, no headaches, the best sports, transportation—for the boondocks?' Except for the Catholic schools hasn't that all changed, too?...And hasn't he? But isn't she the same Patricia?...Of course, I'm over-reacting....Didn't she admit her'loss'?... and publicly, no less. Mother could be right, though,...perhaps I should get in touch with Father Flanagan...." She picked up the paper and reread it. "Forty in a class...she's right; I never thought of it that way. I was always comfortable with those large numbers...true, I didn't realize it, except that I tended to lose myself in the numbers. Patty is different... more like Dorothy...though not a showboat....Should I call Dotty O'Malley?...Oh, my God,...it's Bernstein now!...Maybe I'd better call the Father!"

Just then Patty walked in. "Hi, Mom!" She put her satchel of books by the stairs and went over to kiss her mother. "Gosh, it's a wonderful feeling coming home to a house like this," she sighed as she turned to head for her room, which was a custom of hers to recopy her class notes immediately after school in order to re-digest the day.

"Patricia, I'd like to discuss this article," she said, waving the newsletter. "It's not everyday that I can speak to a famous author."

"Huh?...Oh, that...didn't know it was out....It's just a composition I wrote for English, Mother,...nothing much."

"If it were they wouldn't have published it."

"Oh, Mother, it's just public relations....Nothing to do with merit."

"Mr. Novak obviously thought it had merit."

"Yes, but he's embarrassing—he's always raving about my writing to the class—I think he just likes my penmanship."

"It seems..." holding up the newsletter again, "that you enjoy the school."

"You know me, Mother,...I just love school...period. Isn't that as it should be? Surely, you don't want me *not* to like it."

"Of course not, I just meant that…well, you seem not to miss your old school."

"Mother!…How could you think that! Of course, I miss it.…It's just that I realize now that teachers are teachers, students are students, no matter what, no matter where.…It's learning that counts. And I've gotten a good deal of it here in less than five weeks. Mildred Lynch was simply wrong about public school."

Her mother concurred, "That much I agree with—I as much as told you that myself."

"So then?…Why the inquisition?" Patty beseeched.

"Now, that's uncalled for. I simply want to know that your head is on right. It just seems inconceivable to me that you can change so quickly by being disloyal to St. Benedict's. What if Sister Justina got hold of a copy of this newsletter,…how do you think she'd feel?"

Oh, Mother you wouldn't!"

"No, but normally, I'd be so proud that I would send it off to her."

"Oh, Mother, you *are* ashamed! Do you think I was that mean?… I…I guess I wasn't thinking…that is,…I wouldn't hurt them for the world!…Gosh, I still miss St. Benedict's terribly!…They were all so good to me there," she sobbed.

"I know that, honey,…if only you hadn't mentioned the overcrowded conditions.…You know how difficult it is for the Church financially to compete with a tax supported system."

"Mother, I'm really sorry,…forgive me?…Still, I felt I had to be honest with myself.…You know how seriously I take my compositions.…And so often at St. Benedict's I'd be burning up with questions during a class discussion or lesson…and quite frankly, Mother, the sisters, trying to handle forty students, simply didn't have the time for the individual."

"Oh?…And here they do?"

"Yes, Mother, they really do." Patty answered in a subdued tone. "Are you disappointed?"

"Yes and no…well, of course not,…I'm glad for you.…I want you to have the best.…It's just…I don't know…I suppose…"

"Please, Mother,…don't fret over this," she said, sobbing. "Oh, gee, how I still miss it—Sister Justina, my friends, the uniform, even the nylons, the Monsignor's class visits and corny, lovable jokes, the Mass in the mornings."

Agnes' spirits rose. "Do you want me to call Monsignor?"

"Oh, no Mother, I don't mean.…Really, Mother, I feel I'm learning more somehow,…something better suited…for me."

Agnes hugged her, then turned to the statuette. "O Holy

Mother!…What have we done?"

Patty recoiled from her.   "Mother! Please!…Don't think I've compromised my beliefs….Please, don't say I've let you down!…I'll be ill if I thought for one moment you…why,…Mother, I'll take the bus for Catholic school in the morning, however late in the term…"

"Now, now,…that would be foolish." She responded with some guilt, drawing Patty to her again.

"Next year, then;…I promise."

"No, dear, that won't be necessary….It was foolish of me to react this way. High school will be time enough to make the change."

"Really, Mother?…do you really?…"

"Look over at the Holy Mother: even though she knew deep within, Her Son was here for a Divine Purpose,…she must have felt anxiety over his decision to change the practices of the day by fulfilling the original intent of His Holy Father.   Mothers are just that way…silly, I suppose,…wary, protective."

"And beautiful!…Loving!" Patty added with a squeeze.

"Life is change….I know that; but that's why I'm so very proud of my faith. It resists change…perhaps there are times when it shouldn't, but I thank God it takes a stand like the rock it is in the shifts of time."

"I love it too, Mother,…and I'm very happy with religious instruction at the convent in Blue Bay. I would never abandon it;…I love it so much….I look forward to it every week." Patty hugged her mother tighter and vowed, "I'll never change, Mother."

"Oh, we all do, Patricia,…but I know yours will always be for the better. Forgive me for upsetting you. It was stupid of me. Here I am blessed with a bright, beautiful daughter who will not always do the right thing in my eyes, but I know inside they will be right for her," she said wistfully, recalling how her own parents had objected to her early marriage after they had built up cash value so tediously in the policy they had taken out on her weeks after she was born with high hopes of her going to college someday. That Margaret had been unable to have more children accentuated their objection. Agnes caressed her daughter's curly auburn hair then gently released her. "Now off you go to your notes. I'll make a sandwich for you and take it up to you."

Patty kissed her again and said, "I love you, Mom….And the Church too." She picked up her bag of books and jumped up the stairs. She turned at the landing and looked down again at her mother and smiled.

"I love you, too," her mother said. "I'm really very proud of you, Patty, …and your article." She thought how much prouder, if she could have sent a copy off to Patty's old school.

At the supper table that evening, Pat, somewhat irritable from fighting the traffic home, finally mustered up some interest by asking Gary how Little League practice was progressing.

"Not bad…the manager tried me out at second base today. Maybe I'll get to play tomorrow night, if Jonathan's late again for the game. He has trumpet lessons that his mother won't let anything get in the way of—even a game."

"Well, good for her. Maybe she's doing you a favor. So you're a regular Joe Gordon, are you?"

Who?…Oh, primitive   history again….Nope, I'm a Bobby Richardson."

"Well, I hope you hit better than he does."

"Got some pretty good licks in."

"Does the coach still think you're a…what did he call you?"

" 'Licorice Stick.' Na, there are plenty of others who do worse than me. He's gotta be desperate to put a lefty in at second base."

"Cheez, that's right…had forgotten about that." His father was forced to admit with embarrassment.

"I hit one almost to the fence!"

"Great! I guess the tire is working, eh?" his father infused some pride, then added, "I hope it wasn't one of those Pee Wee specials that go through the shortstops legs."

"Funny man, my Dad….No, I'm lefty, remember?…it went through the first baseman's glove….No, I swear, Dad, I belted it over the right fielder and he really back-pedaled to get at it, too!…Yep, the name Dolan's going to mean something round the league!"

"Ah, that's my boy!"

Gary turned to his bored sister and said searchingly, "My teacher wanted to know if you were my sister… wonder why?…The name is already known, eh?"

"Oh, are you becoming a celebrity at school already, Precious?" The father asked.

"Why, no, Daddy,…I have no idea why the teacher would inquire about me." She looked at her mother, hoping she would forgive her for her deception.

Gary included, "Well, he said you were an awfully good writer and hoped that some of it would rub off on me,…how about that?"

"I don't know…he probably knows one of my teachers at the junior high." She hoped it was not a lie.

"Disaster! It means I'll have to work twice as hard on my assignments."

"That still wouldn't be enough." Patty bit her lip, wishing she could take back the unkind remark.

"Strange...you must've done something. Did your class visit Gary's school, or somethin'?" the father asked.

Agnes sensed Patricia's anxiety and interpolated, "They published a composition of Patty's in the district newsletter; I suppose that's why Gary's teacher commented."

"She did! When were you going to tell me...either of you?" He searched their eyes.

"Oh, it was nothing, Dad—really." Patty felt betrayed; yet somehow she knew her mother was in command of the situation.

"I'll be the judge of that, young lady. I'd like to see it...this instant."

Patricia pushed back her chair and jumped from the table; looked at her mother with anxious eyes. Agnes nodded reassuringly and told her to retrieve it from the living room table. "Your father is always interested in your school work, though he might not show it often." she added sarcastically.

"Now, pray, what do you mean by that?" he fired back. "Of course, I'm interested in her—in everything she does. Just because I don't understand her half the time..."

She looked over at him with contrition. "You're right, Pat; it was an unkind remark—what with all the traveling back and forth to work and all the work here..."

"Here's nothing, Dad," Patty said self-effacingly upon reentering the room and nervously handing him the paper.

"Cheez!...That's an awful picture of you."

"Pat! How can you say that! It's a fine picture as far as that kind goes....You're awful to say that to her." Agnes said in defense.

"That's okay, Mother; I agree with Dad—it's dreadful. My English teacher took it with the office Land camera."

"I apologize, Precious,...it's not half bad....Wow!...quite a headline there...hmm...let's see...you say: 'Life in the city is very different from day to day activities here in the suburbs...' That's for sure;...can't even get the pink edition of the *Daily News* out here at night...How I miss that, especially baseball time."

"No big deal, Dad, with all the night games they play now."

"Very good, son,...you know, you're right; the night edition hasn't been as much fun anymore as when I was a youngster. Did the Yanks play a day game today?"

"Yep,...they lost. Mantle struck out in the eighth with the bases loaded."

"Man! When is he gonna grow up and learn some bat-control. If Dimag struck out twenty times in a season, he'd consider it a bad year.

This kid—well, he's no kid anymore—does that in a week!" Pat read on: "'Admittedly, we go to school everyday as we do here. But after school there is much to be done in the city....' Oh, and I suppose you mean the fast times of city life?" he quipped.

"You know she's referring to the task force organized by the Sisters of Charity to assist the needy." Agnes offered.

"Oh, that...never could understand why...with all the welfare programs....Well, daughter, I guess you showed them you're no slouch." He put the paper down, leaving unread the "incriminating evidence."

Relieved, Patty sighed. "That wasn't my intent, Daddy." Moments later Agnes slipped the newsletter under a plate which she picked up in clearing the table.

Agnes left the dishes to Patty and Gary to finish up and went into the living room where Pat was going through the mail.

"Can you believe it? The bank wants another three hundred in escrow: the school tax has jumped unexpectedly due to inclining enrollment and that damn new building," he piped.

"Things cost, honey; look at the price of bread compared to five years ago."

"Five years ago?...I'm talking about two months ago. The agreement was seventy-five a month would take care of principal, interest and taxes and then it turned out to be eighty-three and now they want this by next month."

"Well, I have to get ready for a PTA meeting. I guess this isn't the time to ask you if you'd like to come, huh?"

"You're kidding me....When did you join that sewing circle?"

"I didn't. They sent out a flyer urging people to attend an important meeting they're having tonight....They do important work, you know?"

"Yeah, like baking cakes." he uttered unkindly.

Agnes stepped up into a side entrance to a corridor dimly lighted by a row of global fixtures hanging from a yellowing plaster ceiling. She walked along the creaking floor into a sparsely attended auditorium that also served as a gymnasium and cafeteria. Choosing the last row of folding chairs, she sat down several seats in. To her chagrin she overheard one of the few men there say that there wasn't a steel door or girder in the place. A woman next to him mentioned that her plumber had told her that the fire-sprinklers didn't work. Some women on the stage, apparently officers of the organization, were setting up. An expensively dressed woman in her forties, already tanned—either from early boating or vacationing, Agnes surmised—sat down next to her, who was immediately drawn to her elaborate jewelry. "The diamond on her left hand has to be at least a carat," Agnes thought. She looked down at her own hand and fingered Pat's loosely fitted graduation ring, even though he had specifically ordered a pinky ring, knowing she would be the one to wear it.

"We were certainly fortunate last week, weren't we?" the woman next to her declared.

"I beg your pardon? I don't understand." Agnes broke from her thoughts.

"Why, the fire, of course." The woman said perplexed.

"Fire?...What fire?" Agnes asked, dumfounded and somewhat embarrassed.

"Why, my dear,...the fire at the school...here. I thought everyone knew of it, but then, it was kept hush-hush....I suppose you're new here; otherwise, word by the vine would have gotten to you."

"Yes, I am. But, why in the world would my daughter who attends here not tell me?"

"Oh, the school officials are marvelous actors. They let the children think it was simply another drill."

"But didn't they see the fire trucks?...And just how bad was it, anyway."

"Forgive me, dear, I've alarmed you. It was minuscule.... Actually a trash fire in the basement is all it was...and because of all the twist and turns of this old building—one addition after the other—it was well out of sight. And the children are often exposed to fire drills directed by the fire volunteers."

"Wasn't there smoke...smell?"

"Our volunteers are very realistic. They often bring their little toys with them...like smoke bombs."

"My, God!...Look at this place....Can you imagine if it started in here?"

"Yes,...catastrophe. That's why I'm here tonight. Something has to be done," she asserted. Drawing Agnes' attention to a beam overhead, the spiffy woman noted the old wiring running along it and into a large hole in the plaster high up on the wall revealing cracked lath and exposed cable. Then she pointed to the drapes on the stage and said that they were fire-proofed because the PTA had raised money two years ago to replace the old ones. "But if you could see the junk they keep backstage—anywhere from props, paint and gym equipment, you would wonder why we even bothered."

"And to think I almost didn't come tonight. I hadn't planned on joining till September." Agnes bemoaned.

"Well, the mimeo couldn't mention the fire, if it got into the wrong hands the children might panic."

"Oh, by all means…I agree." Agnes had not expected her inauguration into community affairs to be so intriguing: she had anticipated volunteering to accompany a class on an educational trip, or yes, even bake a cake. Her evenings had become progressively boring as she had less to do in setting up house. Pat and she had very little in common on a social level anymore. They seldom could agree on television viewing. She looked forward to "Peyton Place" each week, and he would either sit there with her and criticize every scene or read the paper, turn the pages noisily, throw it down on the hassock when finished, get up to search through his *Sporting News*, which he had read a dozen times before, and start turning pages again. Whenever they engaged in a rare dialogue on events and politics, it was always within his frame of reference and views or the dialogue would come to a close. Usually, however, out of desperation for conversation, she would partake in listening to his views on sports and offer tid-bits here and there just for the pretense of being alive. She even embarked on a study program of Gary's baseball cards, especially the older ones her husband had given him, just so she would be able to interact in the "conversations" that usually devolved into monologue when he would rant endlessly on "yesterday's" ball players.

Following the recording secretary's rapid fire delivery of insignificant notes, the president, a slender fashionable young lady in her late thirties but looking ten years younger, rose to speak. Agnes wondered how she could possibly have any children of junior high age. "When was the last time—if ever—I looked like that!" she thought.

The president, Laura Talmadge, announced with a soft but authoritative voice: "We called this emergency meeting for precisely that reason, if you will pardon the tautology—an emergency *is* upon us. It came to our attention by a concerned citizen, the wife of the school custodian in this building—this alone should tell us something of our school officials—that a small fire had broken out in the this building's basement." No one in the audience seemed at all surprised—apparently the "vine" was efficient.

"Confronted with this, Mr. Tinslow, our dear principal, at first denied it; when we summoned the custodian, Mr. Tatesko, he too denied it occurred until we threatened to call his wife for him to tell her over the phone that she was—as he had put it—a 'hysterical, cackling old hen.'" Then Mr. Tinslow retrenched and said that because it was such a "minor incident" he did not wish to alarm the children, nor the community. She looked up at the high ceiling for a moment and then walled her eyes back to the audience and her tone took on an urgency, "Ladies and Gentlemen, when it applies to the school and therefore our…your…children, no fire is too minor not to demand our immediate attention and concern. The

PTA feels that it must take action against the board in urging them to demolish the building when school is out in June and to make provisions for double sessions next year at the senior high while construction of a safe facility is underway."

"Why not demolish it now—why wait?— I have two children in this building!" one shrilled from the audience. There was some applause.

"I'd put an axe to it this minute, but I'm afraid that's impossible at this time," the president argued sympathetically. "It's much too late in the year and would be disruptive to final exams. Initially, the executive council felt as you did but on reflection modified its position with the decision to insist that extreme precaution be taken till the end of the year by hiring provisional fire inspectors, along with some part time vigilance on the part of the volunteer fire department, to monitor the building during the school day."

A man in his sixties stood up and asked skeptically, "How much is all this going to cost us in taxes—they're already too high and I'm on a fixed pension." There were some groans; only his wife next to him nodded in agreement.

A gentleman in pinstripes and, despite the late hour, still choked to the top button with a garish tie, said indignantly, "The safety of our children is at stake here and priceless; if we have to pay, so be it."

"Yeah, that's easy for you to say; but this old building was good enough for my children; no one gave any thought then. The fact is buildings burn—old and new." The old man countered.

"True, but I'll take my kids' chances in a building of mortar and steel any day," the pinstriper implored, waving his hand. "Besides, look around you: the wiring, not to mention the dried out timber, is ancient and dangerous. Have you no heart, man?—don't you have grandchildren?"

"That's beside the point; I don't want to be forced out of my home."

The president said consolingly, trying to regain control. "All right now, please, gentlemen,...the taxes will not be prohibitive...I assure you, sir." She went on to inform them: "The state pays for over ninety percent of the construction costs, we will hardly notice the increase.... And I'm sure you agree that is a small price to pay for the well-being of our children." She smiled, looking softly into the elder's eyes, and added, "You will not lose your home, my good man....we would not permit it."

Disarmed the senior citizen said, "Well,...I...don't want you to think I don't care about the children....It's just...you know, how taxes keep going up? I'm just concerned...perhaps I'm being selfish, but it's rough at our age."

Deeply respectful, she inquired, "Oh, gracious, don't think that, my…oh, excuse me…what is your name, sir?"

"Parisi, ma'am."

Continuing her gentle, consoling voice, she went on, "Mr. Parisi, we understand the plight of the senior citizen in a growing community such as ours. But you have my word, we do not intend to allow the community to lose our elders, who have done so much to prepare the way for us to enjoy decent living. Our organization, together with the teachers association, is lobbying at the county seat to reduce taxes for our elders on social security and pensions. Please feel free to join us in our endeavors, Mr. Parisi, on both issues."

The man sat down and reached for his wife's hand; she smiled; he squeezed her hand and said, "Seems like an honest lady."

"Oh, yes," the wife replied, "and charming."

"Except the county doesn't control school taxes," he explained to his wife.

"It doesn't? Oh, my that's by far the biggest share of our tax bill."

"You bet—seventy-five percent."

"Of course, Mr. Parisi, lest I deceive you, this current lobbying effort does not affect your school tax. Still, it is a beginning. As God is my witness, I announce here and forever, that we will not end our efforts to assuage the elderly's tax burden. You are too important to us to abandon you."

"Well, now, she certainly didn't have to tell us that," the wife said. "I trust her completely."

The president went on to inform the audience of the board meeting in two weeks and that it was very important that they turn out in large numbers because the board would try to foil their proposal as an "over-reaction to a minor incident." She filled them on the time and place, and the strategy once there: to remain calm but persistent. Lest they not be totally committed, she continued with a strong emotional tone, "The truth is this: the 'minor incident' without the good lord's grace could've led to a great tragedy, a *major* accident. Because this building is so vulnerable, as the good gentleman pointed out earlier, it is simply stupid and immoral to gamble with our children's lives. Now, I know some of you have children in the high school and will not like experiencing double sessions and will feel as though the high school is being shortchanged—but what alternative do we have? Surely, we do not want the Parisis' tax and those of similar plight to rise unnecessarily, so why the added expense of having pre-fabs transported on site for the duration of construction when we have ample quarters in a beautiful new building next door. Moreover, why should the junior high children be subject to the indignity of those horrible boxes? Also double sessions actually reduce taxes, thus, at far less cost we have better facilities for all.

"I cannot stress enough," the president pleaded, " how important it is that you attend the board meeting. Turn off the television that night and drag your husband along. We must impress the board members—overwhelm them if need be—that we mean business and are ready to force a referendum if they do not cooperate. To accomplish this massive presence we need more than you who are present tonight. The entire community has to be behind this to convince the board that we are most fearful of a *major* incident. We'll need volunteers to organize a telephone chain. Others are asked to write letters to the board and administration, to the faculty association, to *Newsday*, and our local *Herald*. Speaking of the *Herald*, I see Mrs. Tiffany, the publisher, is present, ready to assist us in news coverage."

The woman next to Agnes rose and announced that the story of the fire would be on the stands tomorrow now that it was decided to be made an issue. "I also pressured our fire-chief, who as you know is my husband and editor, to condemn the building in next week's editorial." There was enthusiastic applause—an outlet of relief for the faint-hearted who felt out on a limb.

"How in heaven's name did you arrange that, Jessica?" The president asked happily. "After three years of conservative views!— why, he was even against the senior high construction!"

"What he editorializes on is seldom my concern—I must admit rarely worthy of my time—as long as he doesn't make a damn fool of himself." Agnes winced and tugged on her ring midst the laughter. "After all, it is my family's paper. When he goes against common decency and fair play, then I put my foot on him and threaten to fire him. In this case, however, I simply refused to sleep with him."

The overhead beams seemed to shake from the roar of the laughter. Agnes looked up at her with open-mouthed bewilderment. Jessica sat down; her smile dissipated when she noticed Agnes' stunned look. "Oh, my dear, did I offend you with my crude language? You mustn't mind. I'm always at the top of my head...I dwell there comfortably....You should try it;...you seem too tense, too thoughtful. I am very uncomfortable in rare moments when I go deep....It isn't worth the agony. That's why when I go boating I stay in the bay."

"No, really I'm not offended,...taken aback perhaps. I'll get over it. I suppose, in a way, it was funny." She managed a subdued smile.

"I understand;...not your way. I respect that,...well, I don't really," she laughed. "But you're entitled...by the way I'm Jessica Langley."

"Agnes Dolan....Moved in from the Bronx a month or so ago."

"Dolan?...Dolan...why you must be the mother of that beautiful child that was in the newsletter today?...Oh, isn't that awful of me?...like saying, Harry Truman, the father of Margaret." She chuckled.

"That's me...portends my future, I suppose."

"She must be a brilliant child...she certainly can write. Perhaps I could use her on the paper this summer. She can probably proof better than I. My husband's not that good at it either, he's always letting mistakes slip by. But I've really been wanting to get some junior high level interests going. Readers get tired of the same hackneyed high school level stuff. They're so beautifully innocent at the junior high age."

"Oh, what a marvelous thought. Patricia would love it!"

"So that explains it;...your manner, I mean,...so very Catholic. That's just wonderful, my dear;...well, that is, as long as you remain a comfortable minority,...we need you....the world is being overrun with the likes of me, you know, all too secular."

"I hope you're not calling me a narrow-minded prude," she said in subdued resentment coupled to a vague smile.

"No, surely not!...Well, then again maybe I am, Agnes, but in a nice sort of way. I suspect you're happily married."

"Oh, yes." She did not hesitate.

"There!...You see?...total, natural, equilibrium. That husband I spoke of is my fifth...just another sex partner and an editor as a bonus."

"My, you are frank...or is it, honest?" Agnes said with a mixture of revulsion and admiration.

"Actually, I prefer the former;...honesty is perhaps reserved for you."

Pat was already in bed and snoring when she slipped into the room; she was relieved. She quietly undressed and slipped into her robe and went down into the kitchen to see that the kids had done their chores. She put the finishing touches to their work. She put a kettle on for tea, took a pad out of a cabinet drawer, turned the radio on low and sat down at the table. She doodled for a moment; half listening to Frank Sinatra's "Stranger in the Night." She reflected, "I never liked him when we were kids and he was the rage...but, then Pat hated him...still, his voice wasn't really that good during the war...he was just about the only one around....Oh, well, who cares, really...much better now, though;...well, I should hope we all get better as we get older." Her digression faded, then wrote "Dear Editor." She got down a cup, started humming to the song, dropped a tea bag in and poured the boiling water, dousing the tea bag gently, humming absently while thinking of her opening sentence.

A half hour later, she eased into bed. She lay there somewhat restive, thinking of the letter, the meeting—Jessica and the gentle, but commanding president. She finally dosed, only to be waked by Pat, who took sex; she got nothing. It had not always been that way. To Agnes sex was a communion through which a part of themselves could transubstantiate. When Pat announced there would be no more children and he began to wear protections, its spiritual beauty turned to physical vulgarity and arrant sin. She became but a cold backdrop to his passion. Afterwards she would lie in the dark whimpering over her sin as he flushed down the toilet what could have been life. She likened herself to a common whore and when she would reject his advances she hoped that he would become frustrated and seek his pleasure elsewhere. He never did; instead he would cruelly persist until out of fear and fatigue she submitted as a matter of course. Tonight she rolled over and instead of tears and penance, she envied Jessica.

Agnes was glad Pat balked at attending the board meeting. "He'd only embarrass me. He'd get up there and rant and rave about how high taxes were already that he would be just the defense the board would need. I'd never live it down," she thought as the Rambler—Pat never did locate a Henry J—choked and backfired toward the high school. The telephone chain and letters must have worked because the parking lot and the curbs embracing the school were jammed. Agnes had to turn down a side street, which was also crowded with parked cars. She found a spot; careful not to block the driveway, she edged close to a Cadillac. She bumped it slightly. To her embarrassment someone got out of it. It was Jessica.

"Don't fret over it, Agnes;...what's a scratch on a bumper," she said as they walked together to the school. "I've bumped it plenty myself."

"I feel awful....It's such a beautiful car," Agnes agonized.

"That's why I trade them in every two years, so I don't get attached to them. Some people carry on with their cars like they were pets or spouses."

Agnes held her hands as in prayer. "Still,..."

Jessica dismissed her, "Oh, hush,..." and changed the subject, "that was a fine satiric letter you wrote....I was very proud of it....I guess you aren't just the mother of a famous daughter, after all." She laughed.

"What?...Oh, yes, I see....That's funny. Did you really like it?"

"Very incisive. I liked the line about the real estate agent, especially....It fits old Tom ...that grasping son of a..."

Jumping in quickly, Agnes said, "You know him, I gather."

"You can bet on that. ... He and all his cronies that bought up half the undeveloped land around here." Inside the large board room at the new school, they sat up front next to Laura Talmadge who greeted them warmly.

"Oh, it's gratifying to see supporters. From the looks of this crowd,

I fear the opposition outnumbers us," Laura said warily.

"Yes, it seems Tom got all his cronies together, but that was predictable," Jessica said calmly. "Nevertheless, it seems we have a good many concerned parents as opposed to the so-called concerned taxpayers."

Laura glanced at the opposition and said, "They have my sympathy on that score, but gracious, times are changing and needs are growing....And what greater need than the education of the young?"

Agnes thought of what her husband's reaction would be to that. "I'm afraid," she offered, "that most see education through the eyes of the past as a hard-earned privilege, rather than as an inherent right. They resent paying for those who abuse education; they know education costs more because there is so much resistance to learning. Nor do they perceive the process as an elaborate building with exotic facilities. Why, just the sight of a yellow bus makes my husband see red. 'What's wrong with these kids out here?' he would say, 'If they want an education they should be willing to walk to school. In our generation we walked, you know.'"

"In the city you could, and if not, there was cheap public transportation," Jessica pointed out. "But it's true, even out here there was never transportation and some had to walk as far as three miles. But again as Laura said, times have changed."

"Oh, how well I know that!—dramatically in the almost two months since moving out here. And I certainly wouldn't want my children wasting half the day walking to school. Still, I do know how some people feel about so-called frills; I felt the same way when I sent my children to Catholic school that always seemed to get by on minimal essentials."

"Oh, my, don't bring that up, Agnes! You sound like you're in the wrong camp," Jessica revealed.

Agnes laughed. "No, I'm just being the devil's advocate. As a mother I want what's best for my children and see nothing wrong with improving conditions. After all, it was kind of drab when we were in school." Nevertheless, she thought otherwise, when it came to Patty and hoped that when she finished with the junior high she would still want to go to a Catholic high school. "You know, I lived in the city all my life and because we always rented—my parents too—school taxes, taxes of any kind, for that matter, were never brought up—except city sales tax, that is. The city-dwellers always thought of school as free, never thinking that built into the rent was their share of the taxes—kind of like now when the tax is built into the mortgage payment one isn't as conscious of it."

"Ah, there's the rub," Jessica chirped; "most of the old guard have paid off their mortgages and therefore must pay the tax bill directly. Yes, it's a matter of perception—especially when they no longer have children to send."

Laura in reaction qualified, "That perception won't be reserved for the elders; for when the young begin to see their mortgage payments increase each year, owing to school costs, they'll join the old guard. That's why it is imperative that we get the junior high built now—or it will be never."

Pat rose from his armchair during a commercial and went to the refrigerator for an ale. "Dammit...she's done it to me again!" He slammed the door. He went to the back entrance for his jacket. Went back into the living room to shut off the TV and headed out the door. At the deli he took a cold six-pack from the display case and walked over to the counter. The owner said, "Getting to be a habit, Dolan,...wife forget again?" Pat begrudgingly handed him two dollars. Then he caught pink in the corner of his eye. He looked over by the stacks of papers—there was a lonely pink edition of the *Daily News*.

"I don't believe it!" A pink edition!..."

"Yeah, but it's from last night," the owner said. "I was in the city last night—I go in once a week for kosher items in behalf of some of my customers—and thought I'd buy a half dozen to see how it would go. Well, I tell you I got back at eleven o'clock and by the time I closed at twelve, that was the only one left. A lot of city folks around here. I could've palmed it off with the morning edition today, but I kind of like having it around." He handed him his change.

"I'll take it ...didn't get a chance to buy a News today." He opened his palm fingered a nickel.

"Na, forget it. Take it....Say, do you ever read the *Herald*?"

"No way, the *Tribune* is for Republicans like you."

"No, alien, I don't mean the city paper....Our own local paper....it's been hot the last two weeks....All about the fire at school."

"Oh, that...that's all I've been hearing about at home."

"Yeah, well, now you can read from the horse's mouth. Your wife's letter's in it...but I suppose you read it already."

"My wife!...No, I haven't read it....She never mentioned it. What the hell is going on here?...first my daughter, now this." He reached for the *Herald*, handed him a dime. "I hope you realize it's killing me to pay a dime for this rag."

"Yep, I know, just like the ale...but we all have to make a living. I pay a hell of a lot more school tax than you do to keep up this store. And I'm not about to agree with your wife and pay anymore."

"I'm with you on that." As soon as he got home, he lit the lamp and sat down on his hassock, pried the cap off his ale, chugged on and searched for the letter.

Having heard his father come in, Gary, grinning ear to ear, came down the stairs. "Where were you, Dad? Guess what?"

"Gary, can't you see I'm busy? No time for guessing games," the father bellowed.

"You're always busy. How many times have you promised to show for a game?" He turned and jumped back up the stairs, yelling, "You were supposed to guess that I hit a home run." He slammed shut the door to his room.

Pat, unfazed, began reading the letter:

> In the smoke screen of the fire, a recent inspection of the Junior High School by the PTA Committee on Safety has inconsiderately produced a rash on the thick skins of the Old Guard in town. It seems the Old Guard does not agree with the committee's findings that the dinosaur-building is a hazard. In spite of the Eternal Guard's wail for baby-powder to soothe this rash, our hard-boiled committee closes its ears by maintaining its right to justice and reason and by refusing to relinquish to emotional nonsense. Nor will the committee mollify the overgrown darlings with their favorite lullaby: "O days of yore, O sweetened lore, let ye endure forever more, despite those who yell for more."
>
> The committee concedes that what was good enough fifty years ago was indeed very good, but the committee argues that the physical thing of that which is good cannot remain so forever in a world of decay, which thankfully can be remedied by reasonable progress and the spirit of the state willing to defray most of the cost. The fact is, the school, though sufficiently sturdy to withstand winds short of summer's breeze, is no match for a match. The charming brick is merely veneer; basically it is an overgrown wooden shed, housing three times as many children than its original design at the turn of the century. Granted extensions have been added but additional staircases were not, posing extremely dangerous possibilities. In face of this, the village's influential sphere led by the Bay Realty, which incidentally sold this writer a home, and at the time boasted that nothing was too good for our children—and then strangely rephrased it as "nothing is too good for America!"—has fought the PTA tooth and nail to the lethal point of organizing a committee of its own under the guise of "Citizens for Tradition's Beauty." More appropriately, it should be entitled Citizens for Unlimited Greed, preserving the portrait of George Washington in the mildew of their palms—no helping hand here for our children's

well-being. That's why the PTA is looking for helping
hands among those concerned for their children.

Dolan threw down the paper in disgust. "What in hell am I raising in
this goddamn town?...A houseful of Judases... Joyces!" He opened
another bottle and stormed out of the house and jumped in his truck to
head for the senior high school.

Foundering through the many corridors he came upon the board room,
outside of which were several smoking with ears straining to hear what
transpired inside. Pat merged into a noisy, grumbling, argumentative
crowd. He looked for Agnes. Then took a seat near the back, amid shouts
of "Sit down!" which he thought were addressed to him, but actually
meant for a speaker in the crowd, who responded, "I'll sit when I've had
my say."

Pat felt out of his league, "Christ, how I hate this!...people have
nothing better to do than play-act democracy," he thought. "That's the
beauty of the city—no one gives a shi...." He strained his neck, looking
for Agnes. "Why does she have to be a part of this...she's no match for
a crowd...but because now she's a big shot, ...published writer!...thinks
she towers over others...it's just not like her." He took in some of the
Founding Fathers on the wall. He was able to read the inscription under
Franklin: *Think not to elevation, and if you need speak, imitate Jesus and
Socrates.* Each of the faces within his view, expressed its own claim on
discontent. Each pair of eyes flashed its own level of motivation—that of
principle, sacrifice, self interest, economics, duty, anger, liberalism,
conservatism, showmanship.

The president of the board finally gaveled them to order. "Please, let
us behave ourselves. Now, let the good man speak." He nodded to the big
man who was being heckled to continue. Just then a short, slim woman
with long brown hair, highlighted by auburn streaks, rose slowly from one
of the rows up front.

"Forgive me, Mr. Chairman, but may I request that you exercise the
same democratic consideration for all of us; inasmuch as you did not
resort to your privilege of power when Mrs. Langley had the floor before
but never had a chance to be heard." Agnes sat down again as
inconspicuously as she had risen.

Jessica sitting next to her shook her hand. "Good girl!...You sure have
become a suburbanite in a hurry."

Pat was stunned. "Sure and that couldn't have been my sweet, quiet
wife! The leprechauns are playing tricks!" he moaned to his third ear.

The president assured her, "You are right, young lady, of course. If I
left the impression of unfairness, I shall rectify it by giving Mrs. Langley
the floor immediately after this gentleman." He gestured to a big man in

work clothes.

"As I was saying, I'm an electrician and have done several rewiring jobs on the old building and I can assure you it is as safe as this new building, and because I worked with contractors I can say that beyond any doubt that old gal is a sound, sturdy building that will out-live this sickly new one here."

Jessica blurted out, "Oh, you're a doctor, too? Does this new building have high blood pressure...the foundation developing varicose veins? Will it suffer from a heart attack in the near future? Or was it pieced together by Tom Wilson's sleazy subcontractor-friends? Fortunately, the truth is he had nothing to do with this new building."

"Mrs. Langley! Control yourself or I'll have to ask you to leave. Now I assured the young lady you would be heard, but not in this manner you have just portrayed. There will be no insults tossed across the room." The chairman's eyes drifted from Jessica to caution others round the room.

Pat noticed the real estate agent several rows in front of him rise to ask rhetorically, "Mr. Chairman, I know this is needless to say, but, of course the scathing comment directed toward my associates and me will be stricken from the records?"

The chairman concurred, "No fear of that, Mr. Wilson, and I apologize that it was said at my meeting."

Agnes popped up again; Pat buried his face. "I, too, apologize, Mr. Chairman, for my friend's runaway enthusiasm, however well-intentioned." Agnes said in atonement. She sat down and said to Jessica, "I'm sorry, Jessica, but we have to remain cool and collected. Remember what Laurie said."

"Oh, damn!... they're railroading us," Jessica said, then turned to Talmadge sitting next to her. "Jesus, Laura, get the floor and speak our case before they overrun us. Don't be so damned patiently rational."

Laura looked over calmly with barely perceptible smile on her face and said, "Heed Aggie's words and stay calm. We must leave it to rational persuasion."

Jessica waved her off. "Humph, there's no reason to — economics! that's all it is, you know."

"Is that what you think of Laurie—too rational? Why, you think the world of her," Agnes said in a harsh whisper.

"I know, I know, but there are still too many wolves around, like Wilson, for instance, and up on the dais was that Petrie fellow who conned you so eloquently."

"Oh, Jessie, what else is there to do? I don't want any part of this if we have to be mean and transgress dignity. I've been sick over the aspersions I expressed in my letter. ...And my sanctimonious plea to the board, apologizing for you, as though you were a naughty little girl."

"Good grief, girl! Don't come to pieces now. You're dealing with small-time politicians; they wear people down by wasting time and feeding on their own morsels of pettiness while others starve on their ideals. And you're right I was being naughty, ok? Now hang in here—I will too and leave it to Laura."

Wilson with a good deal of effort had pulled his great hulk from the chair, and with caution sat down again. So that when he had heard Agnes' remark he thought to let it go. When, however, he settled in, he reflected that he could not let a good thing go by. He leaned forward against the back of the chair in front of him and said with great glee. "Mr. Chairman, that sweet Mrs. Dolan who so nobly apologized for Jessica, throws darts with equal venom as her letter in Jessica's scandal sheet proves."

"All right, Mr. Wilson, You've thrown your dart," Petrie observed.

Pat boiled in his own blood. "I'll throw... it won't be a dart...something like bare knuckles or cat o'nine tails at the miserable bastard!" he muttered under his breath.

The chairman turned to the women. "Now, Jessie, you have the floor.... Please be careful."

"You never wanted me to be careful when we were high school sweethearts, Phil." She said before rising to address the board. The tense atmosphere threw off a coil or two from her remark. "Now that I mentioned the good old days....I'd like to remind you natives of this hamlet that we no longer boast as the pride of the indigenous. We have invited our new residents to live here with us for our mutual benefit. It is true that we find the requisites of a dynamic community stressful at times; and feel that the new generations are a bit demanding and should be content with what we had all our lives. True, most of us so-called natives started kindergarten in that old building and stayed there for twelve more years and graduated. Times have changed; we cannot expect realistically to turn the clock back. We have a commitment to the newcomers, and with their support, we can make this village a thriving, happy community—and we better live up to that or suffer the consequence of eternal conflict like so many other villages go through that are divided by so-called natives and city people.

"Let's face it: the building is too damned old and we should've taken that into account when we put up this building by designing it to accommodate the junior high children as well. Well, we didn't; and though must of us learn to live with our mistakes, I prefer to learn by them—so let's demolish the old dinosaur next month and end this nonsense. I just want to say one other thing—and to my husband's chagrin, I don't care how many advertising accounts I lose—I'm tired of the special interest groups that have gotten rich patching up that old building all these years—the electricians, the plumbers, the painters, the plasterers, the bricklayers, the floor-layers, the carpenters, the glazers—and for what? It is still a dying building and we ought to put it out of its misery and ours." There was a round of applause as she sat down.

Agnes reached out for Jessie's hand and commented, "I wouldn't call that irrational!"

Wilson shouted. "Now who's playing doctor, Jessie?"

"Doggonit, Tom, I warned you. Now they'll be no more of these outbursts." Chairman Petrie scolded. "Now if there are no more comments from the floor we will hear a presentation from the president of the PTA, Laura Talmadge. Pat was on the edge of the seat, then eyed the Franklin inscription again.

Poised and impeccably arranged as usual, she approached the podium. "Chairman Petrie, members of the Board, Superintendent Lane, and members of the community." Though she had index cards in her hand, she seldom referred to them during her delivery. Instead her warm but determined eyes were everywhere, lighting on the audience: each person present feeling self-consciously certain he or she was being directly spoken to. "Judging from the large turnout it is clear that a crisis is upon us. A crisis so urgent that it is unprecedented in affairs of this school board. For we are not—as important as they are—here to discuss matters of class-size, lunch programs, updating textbooks, more gymnastic equipment, busing—none of these, but rather, to discuss the ultimate truth of life and death." Her voice trailed off, almost brokenly. Her eyes seemed to emit a pleading, hurting soul; she cleared her voice and continued in increments of alarm, "In your hands, ladies and gentlemen, is the fate of three hundred and fifty children. There is no cause to debate having guards at cross roads, safe drivers busing our children, competent dieticians in charge of our children's lunch menus, or teachers of competence and high moral standards. But when it comes down to the very basics of our children's housing wherein they spend five to six hours and longer, we become obscenely cavalier. How can you expect parents and citizens of conscience to be cavalier over a near tragedy?

"Many have said that the PTA is being melodramatic about an insignificant event that was never out of control. I thank God for the wisdom and coolness of those who were involved in protecting our children from potential danger. Nevertheless, the fact is, the PTA has rationally viewed this event as portentous to the extent that we are driven to act in averting something of cataclysmic proportions. Ladies and gentlemen, it is simply realistic concern and nothing more. By the grace of God we have been flashed a sign—a message from the sky—that compels us to act now, for there may not be another chance. True, it was as Mr. Tinslow stated but a minor incident; but are we to infer that we are to wait for a *major* incident? Assuredly I for one will not.

"Now, the board has stated that the budget is finalized, the voting next week; and a referendum is out of the question for this year. Give them another year to study the proposal and its implications, then perhaps next year there will be action. I submit to them this: had the fire not been a 'minor incident', had the building been gutted, what then would they do? Study the proposal for a year? Of course not, emergency situations generate immediate action. I appeal to you, gentlemen of the board to act under urgent contingencies; for this is surely a matter of extraordinary implications. You see Thomas Paine's portrait there on the wall; but do you see, I mean really see with the mind, his inscription? 'What we obtain too cheap we esteem too lightly.' Who is here so rude that he could withstand the death of a child for a ten cent saving per hundred dollars of assessment and spit in the eyes of that portrait? Who is here so callous that the specter of a child's painful death could be purged from his mind and the resounding words of the venerable Thomas Paine be herewith erased from the conscience? I take great comfort in answering no to these questions: surely, there is no one here who would answer with a yes. The wheel of fortune has renewed its spin, God help us all when it stops again."

"Good heavens!" Jessica leaned over and whispered, since there was dead silence, "Forgive me, Aggie,...she's a trouper, all right."

"Oh, yes, splendid statement—not too rational, I trust?" she quipped. Every member of the board and all eyes in the audience watched her return to her seat. The superintendent leaned over to the president, "We'd better get our tails into executive session. Anymore like her and we're duck soup." Just as the board prepared to adjourn by gathering up their folders and the president raised his gavel, he heard:

"Hold on there, I'd like to get a word in," Pat boomed in a nervous voice.

"I'm afraid that's impossible, sir; the meeting is adjourned." Petrie commanded.

"Over my dead body!...As a taxpayer, I'm telling you it isn't. Now, hear me out."

"Then, it will have to be...your...well, I'm not going to get grisly. We have much work in executive session, including the PTA proposal."...He rapped the gavel. "Meeting is..."

"The hell it is!" Pat pushed aside several pairs of knees while scrambling out of his row and moved down the aisle menacingly toward

Petrie.

Petrie dropped his gavel, nervously tugged on his tight collar, then wiped his brow. "All right, stay where you are and say what you wish but be quick about it, but it's off the record."

"Off or on doesn't matter; what counts is that you and the members listen and listen good." He pointed to Talmadge. "This one is a charmer; I have to admit I was under her spell for a moment…"

"Uh, oh,…who's this jerk?" Jessica bounced off Agnes.

"I'm not sure you're ready—I know I'm not—that's my husband."

"You poor thing!…The masterful type, I see…cute, though."

Pat looked at the PTA spokesperson kindly for a moment. "Don't get me wrong, Mrs. Talmadge, I suspect your heart is in the right place and I admire your concern for the children. But you haven't been honest with us. You and that lady over there sitting next to my misguided wife…" (Agnes looked askance then turned away and bowed her head.) "are trying to convince us that the building is too old and dilapidated to last as much as another year. Didn't you listen before to the man who's worked on this building many times? Oh, true, he doesn't have your eloquence—and you can wager your last shamrock he doesn't have your looks." (Most in the audience laughed, which broke the tension brought on by this intruder.) "He assures us the building is soundly built. I agree with him; workers from that era really were craftsmen who took pride in their skills and labor, building things to last and last." He looked up at the ceiling, pointed to the walls, waved his hand to the windows behind the board. "Not like today,…here, put together with asbestos, aluminum and glass…"

"Patrick Judas Dolan!" Agnes shrilled as she leapt from her chair and unleashed a decade of pent-up emotion. "You dare reveal yourself before the public and pass among them your two cents as though they were a fortune, rather than from your fanciful mint? Pray tell, when was it the Holy Ghost came upon you with this extensive wisdom of the junior high school, since you have never seen it from less than a thousand paces? Or could it be that the leprechauns had carried it to your doorstep and you toured it during a commercial break between innings?" Her heart pumped furiously from the moment at hand, but her brain ricocheted with the consequence thereof. Petrie appeared cataleptic, his gavel frozen in his hand. Superintendent Lane tried to get his attention, but Petrie, motionless, nevertheless, was transported by the cadence of her voice. "Tell these fine, but under-privileged people, the magnificence they've been without by not being privy to the glorious architecture of city schools that all were so finely crafted by immigrants of European guilds, and though making but ten cents an hour somehow they remained true to their craft even though brutally exploited!...And tell these good people, too, the blessed Talmadge colleen, that how dare she presume to answer her own question when here stands a man, my husband—the public confession I needs suffer for my honesty—who indeed would dare spit in the eyes of the venerable Thomas Paine!"

Mr. Lane ripped the gavel from Petrie's clenched hand and rapped the table but wishing he could rap it on her head. "Enough of this family squabbling! This isn't a divorce court. The adjournment stands."

Pat looked at the superintendent indignantly. "Family squabbling, you say? Where may I ask do you see a family? Divorce you say? And where, then, be the spouse? For surely there is none here! Now, I have come to speak my mind, as that gentleman there, who at the moment seems indisposed, has agreed; thus, speak I will, 'tis that simple." Lane turned to Petrie, who was absently bobbing on the surface of family tension, he shook him and demanded that the meeting be adjourned.

"Uh, uh...." Petrie turned his eyes to the small woman who now was seated, her head bowed, revealing only the glow of her hair shining chestnut in his eyes. He said softly, looking concerned, "Madame,...uh, Mrs. Dolan,..." he raised his voice, "Mrs. Dolan, I believe, should..."

She raised her face barely but her eyes fully, "There is no one here by that name."

He threw up his arms, and turned to Pat. "Mr. Dolan, under the circumstance, I do not feel that you should continue."

"The circumstance is simply that I finish my say, nothing unusual about that, sir," said Pat simply but sternly.

"Well, I thought, having upset your wife as you did that maybe you should take her home."

"You seem like a very noble man, Mr. Petrie, and I 'm not suggesting that you may be hallucinating but I have no wife as you just heard. I am going to finish." Dolan nodded to himself, turned round and the audience joined in with scattered nods.

Petrie was going to appeal to the audience, but there was obviously no assistance comming; for everyone seemed screwed to their chairs. He shrugged; then turned to Jessica and was satisfied that she seemed to be comforting the distraught woman and held his hands as if in prayer. "Continue, Mr. Dolan,...and may there be mercy." He said, despite Lane's protest.

Pat returned to Laura. "Take heart, then, good lady, that the building in question is safe." At first, though not visibly shaken, his voice was measured and subdued, but then, ever conscious of the alien spouse across the room, he developed anger in tone and pitch. "The incident you referred to hypnotically as some kind of message from Providence occurred, I assume you know, from the meanest of sources—garbage and the stupidity of its handling. There was nothing providential about it at all: no crosses burned on the lawn, no dramatic boiler explosions, no great flash fire in the gym, while children thankfully were outside on the sports fields, not even children inconvenienced in the showers by poor plumbing, there were no seventh graders buried in rubble of beams and plaster, no shocks were suffered by an eager student plugging in a movie projector for a teacher, no loose bricks falling on anyone's head, no one fell through the floor to the coal bin beneath. The only thing your committee and those big blue eyes of yours could uncover was garbage. The truth, my dear lady, is that the incident was due to negligence that could happen anywhere, when trash is stored in a basement." He turned away from her and spoke directly to Petrie, who by now was elated. "I leave this with you and your members, sir: that you order your custodians to put the damned garbage outside the building where it belongs." Most of the men and elderly women applauded.

Petrie said with great enthusiasm, "You have my word on it, good man.... The trash will be outside in the morning and thereafter." He turned to Lane. "That's an order effective immediately." Lane nodded in compliance. Petrie returned to Pat. "Excuse me, sir, for resisting you before. You have contributed immensely to your community toward resolving our problem. I just wish that..." looking over at Jessie and Agnes, who seemed rather composed, "you had specific support from other quarters. I hate to see something like this happen, after all, it's just a game of politics."

Pat could not resist salt in the wound. "Oh, I beg to differ, Mr. Petrie; It's more than a game from those quarters of bored housewives turned serious." Hooting burst out.

Lest Dolan's support be doomed, Petrie raised the gavel and rapped it with resounding finality. "The meeting is adjourned." Lane sighed with relief, and gathered up his folder.

Pat swung on his heels to make a rapid exit. Laura stood before him with a cryptic smile. He felt his reflexive being collapse momentarily as he was drawn to those eyes, though not busily sparkling with purposeful quest as before, luminous from the well of despair. He gently waved her aside and left.

"Masterful, indeed he is...and rotten, too," Jessica announced as they began to file out, " but most of all a smart son of a..."

"That he is—not the rotten part or the other reference, though." Agnes added. "You have to know him...and accept his Irish temper."

"*His* Irish temper, did you say? My, God, *you* were the one who scared the wits out of me!"

"We Irish do it to scare the devils out of us."

"Well, he seems to me to be still full of the devil."

"Yes it appears that way; but it works both ways. At least I got the devil out of me."

"If you ask me the way to handle him is to starve him sexually....It'll serve him right."

Agnes mustered an embarrassed laugh. "Oh, I'm a different breed from you, Jessica, I take my marriage vows seriously—not always honestly, though."

"Sure, the old 'obedience' clause, inserted by men!...Oh, Agnes, I had high hopes for you. Especially when you went at him the way you did. Now you'll go home and be his rag doll."

Talmadge, her eyes had lost their lustre, weaved her way to them. She said without a trace of resentment, "Telling speaker, your husband. I guess we lost that one."

"No guessing about the outcome of the executive session...it was just what they needed to thumb us down." Jessie said.

Agnes said compassionately, "Oh, Laurie, I'm truly sorry; I know how hard you worked on this...and as for my husband...heavens!...Why was he here to begin with?...I left him with the TV."

"Wilson's telephone-chain...it was more effective than ours....I felt out-numbered. Don't worry about it, Agnes;...you're not responsible for your husband's actions." Laura consoled her.

"I'm not so sure about that. ...Something triggered him to come here...but he hates Wilson. ...and he would never—no offense, Jessie—read the *Herald*."

"That's two things I have in common with him already," Jessica quipped. "Well, then, perhaps he's a typical male, checking on his wife to make sure she's not having an affair."

Agnes blushed. "Oh, Jessie, you're dreadful!"

"Well, Jessie surely does know men," Laurie added.

"I'm not sure anyone really knows Pat," Agnes added despondently

"Does anyone...really know the other or himself for that matter?" Laurie said vacantly, looking at the crowd in front exiting the building, though in her perceptive reality it was an invisible force of betrayal.

When Agnes returned home, Pat was in his armchair reading the sports section of his pink edition, as though everything were normal. She hung up her coat in the closet and walked across the room to the Lady, paused before her then sat down on the edge of the chair, twisting his ring. He looked up from the paper and stared cruelly. She lowered her eyes and twisted the ring furiously. He returned to the paper. She sat nervously in the dead silence, but for his turning of the pages. She pushed her rump back into the chair and crossed her legs and started absently to kick out her calf back and forth. She noticed a run in her stocking, uncrossed her legs and touched the run above her ankle, and murmured, "Darn!" She rose to head for the bedroom.

He looked up. "Where do you think you're going? Sit down," he ordered. She sat back down on the edge, and began fingering the ring again. He returned to the paper.

She mustered the courage between sighs, to say, "Am I to sit here like a little girl while you read your paper?"

"Yes,…and because you are a little girl, I'm going to read to you." He put the News down and picked up the *Herald* folded back to the opp. ed. page. She yanked and twisted the ring on her finger. He searched the page for a moment and then read: "'…the school, although sufficiently sturdy to withstand…summer's breeze, is no match for a match.' Now, what kind of hysterical rot is this?…Are you bewitched by that Sheba or that Doomsayer?"

"Certainly not I have my own mind, you know?…And please don't refer to Jessica and Laurie that way—they're fine women." She answered phlegmatically as she lowered her eyes and pulled on her ring. "They as I are simply concerned for the children's safety."

"Bullshit fiction!"

"Pat!" My Lord!…Why, you've never been this crudely profane in my presence!"

"Well, you've never made a fool of me before!" Surely, there are more ways than that to show profanity as you so proved in your language tonight."

"I?…what of you?" She sensed her blood warming. "Profanity, do you call it?…when I try to defend you from the devil himself!…And pray, what do you call that Benedict Arnold speech of yours?"

He smirked. "I had no intention of saying anything, till that blonde hussy…all I wanted to do was pull you bodily out of that d…arn place."

"You would've gone that far?…and disgraced me in front…"

"You're darn right I would have!— just as you surely had no reservations about insulting me before all those people. You have no business there…it is not our world."

"True, true, our world…where there is no Pat O'Brien, only Knute Rockne; no Gary Cooper, only Lou Gehrig; no Errol Flynn, only Gentleman Jim Corbett. …Arthur Godfrey, you say? Oh, no, Bill Stern, you say…Walter Cronkite, you say? Oh, no, Mel Allen, you say…. And what say to an evening out with Audrey Hepburn? No, my dear, Red Barber tonight."

He protested with a grin, "Oh, now, Audrey Hepburn—that's a different story—and I suppose your world is now that of Brenda Starr?"

"This is horrid truth, not fiction! You haven't been in that building....I have—it's a disaster," Agnes hotly observed.

"I never hear Patty complain," he contested.

"What do children know? They are without fear."

"Hysteria, you mean. We haven't been here two months and already you're carrying on like a crazed celebrity or somethin'...like you own the town." In disgust he threw down the paper.

"We both own a piece of it, Mr. Dolan. That is why it is our duty and right to protect it against the unscrupulous."

"Oh, and I suppose I am on the side of the unscrupulous," Dolan grunted.

"You said it. I didn't. But you certainly fell into their hands."

"What do you mean?"

"By attacking that...hussy, as you put it...that dear, angelic woman, whose only concern is the well-being of our children. ...Totally, unselfishly committed, as she has none of her own."

"Then, by Jesus," he went on, in face of her bowing her head instinctively, "she should have! Probably belongs to one of those Planned Parenthood pips. If she knew the costs of raising a family she'd soon hose-down her mighty ideals and feel the pressure of taxation."

"Pat!" She targeted her eyes to the ceiling and quietly beseeched, "Oh, dear Lord, control my husband's flying tongue."

"Oh, for sure you'd like that so you can defy me and fill yourself with blarney about your new-found friends."

Her tiny jaw dropped. "Darn you! The poor woman lost her only child in an auto accident; the child was burned to death."

"Gosh, that's awful!" he said as the fire within waned.

"Yes,...awful things happen," she reflected. "That is why we should do everything possible to prevent them."

"But wait a minute. ...Don't you see?...Unselfish, you say?...why she's more motivated than you are!...She's paranoid."

"Patrick Nicholas Dolan....for shame! May I convince the Holy Rosary Society to pray for you! Were I not Catholic, slandering a saintly woman like that...would be unforgivable!"

Laura standing before him rushed to his consciousness, then stored a rattling panic to his conscience. He rose awkwardly and crossed over and kneeled before Agnes to reclaim his partner; he put his hand on her shapely calf and caressed it; rested his cheek on her thighs. "What's done is done....The devil with it all....Let's go to bed and start this night all over." He drew his hand on her calf up under the back of her thighs and slid his other arm under her shoulder blades and began to lift her, when he felt a thrust from her arms that set him back on his haunches and he tumbled to the floor.

"The devil, indeed!…Bewitched am I.…Not on my soul will I permit the stain of Satan's ale, not on my flesh will I permit the lips that spoke in violation of God's Will Be Done." She pressed her foot on his stomach and headed for the stairs.

"This is the thanks I get for my loving Christian forgiveness!" he said in crescendo.

She turned and put her hands on her barely noticeable hips, "Forgiveness now, is it?…And what is there to forgive?…That I made a fool of myself in your myopic, Irish eyes; that I want to protect Patricia and you don't; that I called upon Almighty God to be my own person; to reach into the Constitution for my rights to say what's on my mind?"

"Aw, you're out of your head—all of a sudden you're a politician!" He reached for his ale that he had forgotten to refrigerate when he left the house for the school. He ripped off the cap with his opener and guzzled it, half of it came back up. "Ich, it's warm as birdbath on a summer's day!" When he had returned from the school and guzzled down the two of the three left he had not noticed their being warm.

"Oh, Mary, my beautiful carpet! So help me I'll not forgive you for this Patrick Dolan!" She ran into the kitchen for a sponge and towel. She heard the front door slam, a moment later the truck starting up. "Good!… could be that's what's ailing him; he hasn't tied one on since we came out here."

Later Patty softly knocked on the door ajar to her parents' room. "Are you awake,… Mother? May I come in?"

"Yes, dear, come in…just lying here awake." Agnes reached for the lamp on the night table and flicked it on. She propped up her pillow and sat up. "What's on your mind?"

She sat down on the bed. "I heard you and Daddy arguing…and then he left the house."

"Yes, those things happen when two people are in love. …They always wind up hurting each other. No one has ever found a way out of it."

"I just finished reading the *Song of Bernadette*…it seems so unlikely that people could have hated such a beautiful soul."

"Envy does that. It's usually the root, too, of people in love. They marry because their souls are one, but they're always fighting to retain that separate identity." Agnes said wistfully.

"It's really a contradiction, isn't it, Mother?"

"Oh, now, that's for sure. We know that we are individuals and should act accordingly; yet when we do without consultation or what isn't clearly for the benefit of the other, resentment and distrust comes on the scene."

"That's why you reacted to the newsletter the way you did?"

"Why, yes, I suppose, I did. Foolishly I felt betrayed by a loving daughter."

"That's how it was with one of the nuns in the book, she felt as though God had passed her by in favor of Bernadette; and the resentment and envy built up to such an extent that she literally hated this loving saint....I don't think I like the idea of falling in love, Mother....It sounds so frustrating, at times so ugly."

"And beautiful and meaningful, don't ever forget that. ...You'll see," Agnes counseled in a soft motherly but authoritative voice.

"But to see you and Daddy like this...frightens me. Two beautiful people, who are all my life, the mirror of my being, fighting over a stupid school. If I had stayed in Catholic school all this would have passed you by, I'll bet."

She swept back her daughter's hair and touched her young blossoming cheeks. "Perhaps, perhaps not...and there's still Gary, who'll be in that firetrap soon. Goodness, child, don't start blaming yourself. We'll get over it, we always do. The mirror isn't shattered...cracked a little maybe."

"Still, it's so much more terrifying to see two people in love have a falling out than the violence of people who hate each other. I mean, that oneness you spoke of is usually how I see and think of both of you....Like Our Lord on the Cross...so pathetically torn asunder by Himself....I just cannot get myself to believe that such an event had to be."

She patted her daughter on the head and again brushed back the ringlets on her cheek, noting her auburn under the soft lamplight resembled her own dark chestnut. "Your father is right, Patricia; you are a philosopher. But remember this, whether Our Lord had the power or not, it was not in the order of His purpose to save Himself—after all, He was here to save us....Don't think so much, Patricia. Now go to bed and dream little girl dreams—leave the mirror whole."

Meanwhile, careful not to wake him, Laura Talmadge gently lifted her husband's arm tossed over her, and she crept to the edge of the bed, reaching for her robe. She went into the den and switched on a light. She crouched before a built-in cabinet and retrieved a photo-album. She rocked back and sat on the carpet and thumbed through the pages. Tears welled up as she wistfully gazed at the pictures of her beautiful child. When she came to a picture of her husband holding the child and standing next to their old car, she clawed at the picture, ripped it out and crumpled it. The album slid off her lap and she cried profusely.

Right elbow on the bar, his head cocked and his cheek contorted by his fist pushed up against it, his left hand fiddling with a half empty mug, Pat drifted from the 12½ inch TV eye and was plunged into a vortex of his wife sloshing in his consciousness on whose outer rim was the bartender perched on the rung of a stool and rapping the *Admiral* box, hoping for the sound to return and the snow across the screen of a boxing match that was on. Pat's mind bobbed the tide of their life together and waded toward the beach of their innocence—those high school years of courtship that were so gleefully painful to him, her resistance invincible, and the early months of marriage when both of them were still excruciatingly virginal.

As his mind edged toward the beautiful inevitability, Pat barely felt the heavy slap on his back that the fat hand of Wilson had delivered when he entered with his electrician friend. Nor did he budge when he heard "Good work, lad, you really did a number on that bitch Talmadge."

So immersed was he now in the great advent when at long last she had said in the most sultry terms he had ever experienced: "Oh, yes, my love, oh, yes,…now!…" The boxing announcer squawked momentarily from the bartender's jolt, then silence reigned until the bartender grumbled. He rapped it one last time and shut off the set. Pat's elbow slipped from under his jaw; he blinked his eyes and guzzled down his ale. He grunted and asked for another draft of *Ballantine* as he refocused physical space and got up, staggering momentarily, more from the deep stupor of his thoughts than from the ale, and headed toward the jukebox. He slid in a quarter and pushed repeatedly key 98 from the "Oldie" selections. He resumed the same position at the bar and started humming along with Frankie Laine's "Jezebel." He caught a glimpse of the blimp floating toward the men's room; this aroused his curiosity and waited to see if it would return from dockage. Wilson did return to his table. "No, Frankie," Pat muttered to the strident singer while wriggling a finger unnoticed at Wilson, "that's the SOB that caused all this.…You're all wrong…it's not Jezebel who's to blame." Dolan smelled the noisome cigar, reminding him of the real estate office, and observed the cloud of smoke surrounding the two men seated. He recognized the other as the electrician who was speaking when he had walked into the board room.

The bartender instinctively made two drinks and took them over to them. While straining to listen in on them, Pat was still getting echos of the song, together with the TV which the compromising bartender had turned back on again after serving the new arrivals while muttering, "Maybe this time the old TV wreck will last or pray for a quick knock out."

"Joe, it was a good thing for us that the Board wouldn't go along with that proposal to have a special vote. Of course, I knew it never had a chance—just the same, I'm glad it's over." Wilson vented and puffed smoke across the table triumphantly and half emptied his drink.

The electrician rubbed his eyes and quelled a cough with a hefty drink, then said, leaning over, "Yeah, when I got back from the john that dumb bastard over there was moving in with the clincher....I was worried when that spiffy dame started talking....Christ, that gal has everything— she could charm a monkey to give up a banana," his cohort jabbered.

"Yeah, but she had no luck," gesturing to the bar, "with Dolan over there—he's a tough one." Wilson was certain.

Pat nodded agreement to Frankie Laine and toasted the Talmadge dame to the pugilists on the snowy screen. Then he bent his ear again to the pompous agent's voice: "True,...you never can be too sure with board members, Joe. ...They're a spineless breed. Do you know another new building would make it impossible to sell another house? I have a tough enough time as it is to convince people that our taxes are reasonable and stable inasmuch as all the construction for schools was over. Of course, I'm exaggerating about never selling another house...damn good at the trade. I work by Barnum's code. When I'm ready, the town'll have a school."

"Well, so am I—good at my trade—but if they ever tore down that building half my income would be lost. There's no way I could underbid those big contractors from the city. Even if I could the electrician's union would be down on me so fast to hire union help...and there go the profits. I tell, you Tom, I got a job at that dying school Saturday that'll cost, em plenty. You wouldn't believe...the insulation on the wiring in the boiler room;...it's so..."

"Christ, Joe, keep your voice down!" Wilson warned, gesturing toward Dolan. "In fact, idiot, let's drop the subject. Order another round."

Joe jumped up to the bar and ordered the same double-scotches. "Business must be good out here, eh?" Dolan asked in a carefree manner.

"Oh, yeah, always a living."

Dolan added, "Yeah, If it's anything like the city—I've seen many an electrician pull up to a job-site in a Cadillac or Lincoln."

"Oh, sure those city-union guys make a pile of dough, but when you're in it for yourself...even with expenses, though tough, you can do as well on some jobs."

"Such as the old junior high, I suspect." Pat went on, "You know, I know one electrician who bought an old Packard Clipper and had it restored—it cost him a small fortune—of course, he can afford it being an electrician—but it's really beautiful. In fact, I worked for him for a while, but I didn't like it; have to crawl into too many tight spots."

"Oh, yeah, part of the trade," Joe agreed, then extended his hand. "I'm Joe Johnson."

"Pat Dolan here. I saw you at the meeting tonight."

"Oh, yeah, gee, I almost missed your act—too many damp places raised hell with my kidneys. When I got back there seemed an awful lot of confusion. I didn't know half of what was going on."

Dolan chuckled. "You didn't miss much....Say, I guess, you've found yourself in many a tight crawl space, huh?"

"You betcha life. I got a beaut Saturday where I've gotta squeeze in behind a boiler—even though it's shut down for the weekend, it holds its heat."

"Good for the kidneys, Joe, eh?"

"I guess you got me there. But then I've gotta climb onto a beam and snake the wiring through a dozen or so joists," Johnson added.

"Sounds like a big building," Dolan said with a snickering echo.

"Oh, that's for sure, Pat." He picked up his refills and said, "Say, I wanna thank you for that little talk. Wilson says it was a great help. You really kicked those sweet little asses." Joe winked at him.

Pat raised a brow. "Those?...I thought she had one ass; besides that's not my style to kick asses. She seemed like a very nice woman."

"Yeah, I'd sure go to bed with her!—anyone of them, in fact. Talmadge, though, seems a little too perfect for me. You know that peanut butter blonde, the hefty one who spoke after me?...Now that would be a big treat!...But I tell you I've always wanted a small one like the other—my woman is almost as big as me—it must be somethin' to play with a little kitten like that purring in your ear." He pointed to a news cut with a poison label above it, posted on the bulletin board behind the bar that contained nothing else but an index card advertising a Henry J in mint condition. Pat strained his eyes and finally focused in on his wife's letter.

"Yeah, old boy," Joe went on and obscenely panted, "she would be somethin'!"

"Why, you son-of-bitch...you ain't never gonna experience that!" He hurled the ale in Joe's face, hopped off the stool, leaned way back and roundhoused Joe squarely on the jaw. Johnson, as big as he was, grunted shock and crashed to the floor. Pat with a menacing glance turned to the bartender, "Get that goddamned letter down from there, burn it...and hand me that index card." The bartender in shock immediately complied.

Wilson came puffing up to him. Pat was ready to deck him. "Whoa, now, Sugarfoot!...I'm not built for this sort of thing. What the hell happened?"

"Your friend here has a dirty mind." Pat turned on his heels and bolted out, leaving "Jezebel" alone with the bartender and Wilson still gaping from the Irish cyclone. The bartender handed Wilson a pitcher of water. Wilson dumped it on the unconscious body. Joe crackled and wobbled his head.

Wilson frowned at him and asked with annoyance and surprise, "What the hell did you say to him?"

Joe propped up on his elbows, shook his head and rubbed his jaw. "Damned if I know....Jesus, I've never been punched like that before...Goddamned scary!"

"For Christ sake, that Irish bastard was on our side," Wilson reminded his cohort.

Still on the floor nursing the right side of his jaw, he groaned, "Christ, what a left-handed hammer!" He stared at Wilson stupidly. "On our side?...has a weird way of showing it....All I said was I'd like a night with that bitch that wrote the letter in the *Herald*."

"You stupid, bastard, didn't you know they were married?... Goddammit! They were at each other's throat tonight!"

"Guess, that's when I left to take a second piss."

"Shit, you couldn't add 1+1 if you didn't have two apples with you! Piss off and get the hell home. You've had it for the night."

The bartender laughed. "He sure has—more than he bargained for."

Dolan drove up to the old school; his curiosity had been piqued. He searched for its entry, found it down the opposite end of the new school and pulled into a small parking lot and continued round behind the building. There was a small yard. He could detect with the spread of his headlights a railing around what appeared to be concrete steps leading down to a basement door, the top of which was barely ground level. There was a late model car parked inconspicuously next to a large Dumpster. "They'll put that to use now, instead of the cellar," he thought. A shadow darted away from the Dumpster to the car as he approached. His headlights illuminated the figure of Laura Talmadge, now frozen in her tracks with her hand on the car door handle.

"Mrs. Talmadge, I can't believe it!...What in the heck are you doing here?"

"Huh?...uh,...I...left...some papers here the other night and thought perhaps I could retrieve them."

"At this hour? And in your bathrobe! For God's sake, Mrs. Talmadge,... it's almost two in the morning!"

"Yes, very silly of me,...I know ...uh, I couldn't sleep, so I thought I could do some work...should really wait till tomorrow, huh?...I must seem weird, eh?" She absently swung a large ring with some twenty-odd keys. Realizing what she was doing she put the keys down and behind her back after the fact.

"They look like school keys, are they?"

"What?...Oh, yes, I...I often need to go in the building, the organization sometimes uses several classrooms for various projects, you know."

"In your bathrobe? Jesus, Mrs. Talmadge, what's ailing you? And if it had to be, then, why didn't you go in since the papers are so important to you?"

"Huh?...Well,...to be honest I was frightened. I mean, the building is so dark and large."

"Your husband should've come with you. God, why would he let you out all alone so late?"

"Don't be harsh on him, Mr. Dolan. He was sleeping....I didn't want to wake him." She rattled the keys and fumbled with a handbag. He pointed the flashlight to assist her; from the glare Pat noticed keys in the ignition. He also picked up a strong smell of gasoline.

"If you're looking for your car keys, they're in the ignition."

"Of course, how stupid of me!"

He wondered what had happened to the magnificently poised woman he had seen earlier in the evening. He sniffed again. "Are you having carburetor trouble, by any chance? I detect a strong smell of gasoline."

"Gee, I really wouldn't know, Mr. Dolan." She opened the car door, and Pat realized that the gas was coming from inside the car. He spotted a gallon can on the floor in the back.

"Mrs. Talmadge, never carry gasoline in the car like that! It's dangerous enough in the trunk."

"Please, Mr. Dolan!" she pleaded in a vanquished, sobbing lament. She let go the handle and pushed closed the door with her hip, tossed the keys and handbag on the roof of the car, and pressed her forehead against the misty window and sobbed. "I know all too dearly what the horrible attributes of gasoline are capable of doing to a...a car, Mr. Dolan." She rolled her forehead against the glass.

"Ah, now, I know something is bothering you, Mrs. ...first name is Laura, isn't it?"

"Yes, Mr. Dolan,...Pat, right? Better to go by first names—in this awkward moment—I'm ashamed," she intoned, then chuckled nervously and pulled her robe closer to her throat.

"Laura, I'm really sorry if I insulted you at the school. That look of yours...God, I felt like a heel,and then when I found out...is that what brought this on? I should've let events take their course. Heck, what's another increase or two in taxes. Everyone's out for your buck—they'll get it all, too, one way or another. So why shouldn't the school get it first?" He put his hand on her shoulder and the ends of her hair tickled his hand. "But it's not just me that's troubling you. This situation here is bizarre—you're up to something."

She sighed from untold depths. Then her sobs became uncontrollable. She swung around and embraced him, startling him momentarily. She clutched at him with a frenzy, then became still, breathless. His arms encircled her. She stirred, scrambled out of his arms. He dropped his arms and stepped back. She looked up at him, again with watery eyes, he could barely detect in the shadows but for a glimmer coming it seemed from a rage within her; she drew his arms round her waist, then rose up on the ball of her feet and threw her arms round his neck. He felt her golden hair caress his stubbly cheek and her hot convulsive sighs on his ear as she whispered, "I'm so ashamed." Her robe loosened and her soft quivering body pressed in to him. "I fear you are right." Her hair moistened, softening his stubble as her tears seeped through the thin golden veil. She clung to him harder and cried, "Oh, Pat, I'm so miserable!...The gasoline,... don't you see?...I...I...O God! I'm going crazy!...Pat! Pat!" She hugged him tighter, clutching fiercely; he thought her delicate frame would shatter from the strain. "Oh, Pat!...Please squeeze me;...protect me...from myself!...my wretched soul! Hold me, please...and forgive me!"

He held her as he had long ago held Agnes to absorb within him the implosions of her moods. "I understand,...Agnes told me about your daughter. I'm so very sorry for you. It seems I got in your way twice tonight. I don't regret this time. God!— You were going to burn the building!"

She withdrew her arms from round his neck and slipped them round his waist and buried her face in his chest. "O God! O Pat!...forgive me...both of you!" They stood there in the mist, and in the great shadows of the dinosaur—she in her innocent search for comfort and security; he in his rarefied charity, which began to succumb to primitive motives and he was ashamed.

"God sent me an angel," she said. He gently released her and drew her arms slowly from round him; he touched her face, caressed away her tears, kissed her hair and forehead and tenderly pulled away from her. He ducked into the car. "Is that the only gas you have?...We've got to get it out of the car. I'll take it with me on the truck."

"Oh, Gosh,...the other can...I panicked when I heard your coming and I dropped it somewhere by the trash."

He stumbled around for it; he didn't want to trust his luck with the flashlight, lest someone detect them; he was beginning to feel vulnerable in more ways than one, and wanted to leave in short order. He found the can; it had spilled over. "It lost about a quart, but don't worry it'll evaporate quickly, not a trace by morning." He retrieved the other from the floor of the car and lifted both onto the pickup.

"Oh, you're so good!...I hate to think what would have happened had you not come along." She stretch up and kissed him on the cheek. "I shall never forget these moments." She promised.

"Oh, but I want you to," he replied. She seemed disappointed. He went on, "Put it completely out of your mind. Call it sleep walking, the dream side that stirs the monstrous thing in us that we all want to stifle. But not this way, Laura; you'll be ruined. Don't you see?— this way you too will be burned, consumed — not free you! I know the feeling from the war. Oh, you feel good at first when you lash out but it comes back to haunt you. Only nature— chance—gets away with it. You have conscience. Shake off this thing, Laura. This old dinosaur will outlive us—learn to accept it."

"Oh, how I've tried! But the awful possibility taunts me....I'm haunted by her cries, her little body in flames....I imagine her cries while they cruelly devour her. Oh, my baby, my poor, beautiful baby!" She threw her body on the hood and cried convulsively with repeated muffled echoes of the headwaters of her sorrow, "My baby!"

He gently drew her into his arms again and held her tightly for but a brief moment; he subdued the primal glands and was again purified by true sympathy. She squirmed to bury her face in his chest and murmured, muffled by her lips pressed into his jacket, "I needed this, you, so very much. By God's good grace—His strange, awesome path—it was destined. My husband ...seems like ages ago...no longer could withstand his own pain and guilt to comfort me. Unfairly, intolerably, I suppose, I expected him to feel with me the vast, horrible abyss."

"Men aren't the same," he said. "I guess we never really see—with the heart—not with real substance, anyway;...probably why we invent our little games, so's not to see." He gently released her clinging, tied the belt round her robe and eased her into the car. He held the door ajar, uncertain she was yet conditioned to leave. He leaned in and stroked her blonde hair glowing softly in the door's light. "I wouldn't be totally honest if I said I know what you must be going through: I know there aren't any words." Still, in the war he had seen the devastation of flame-throwers; he had felt the awful loss. He could not touch what she was feeling now; he knew what could not be bridged; yet from his side of the shore, he felt her pain. He saw her dragging herself from the river's turbulence and falling exhausted on the other side of the shore, heaving heavily, crying out to all the gods in the history of human consciousness, "Why, why, the awful, awful cruelty of life doomed to destroy itself?"

She was leaning back on the seat, breathing heavily, her head on the back edge, listening for the stirrings of tragedy in the shadows of the building. Slowly she rolled her head toward him, her blonde tresses gracing her temple fell to her cheek and he sighed from the recesses of another realm, another time. "Pat, I can't explain it …but at this moment where there seems to be no before, no after, I feel somehow in love with you! Isn't that weird?"

"No, I don't think so. I suppose we all have those moments when we are in someway wrenched from what's real—good or bad. I'm like a teenager madly in love for the first time whenever I see Audrey Hepburn on the screen."

She turned the key in the ignition. "Well, Audrey, notwithstanding, I am at your bidding, Pat. If there is ever anything and I mean, anything, I can ever do for you, I shall, with my entire being."

He reminded her again, "There is something: just promise to forget this night."

"I shall, I promise. Oh, your …our dear Agnes is so fortunate!"

"Another thing, these keys…" He slid them off the roof. "Did you come by them legally?"

"Oh, my, what will I do with them?"

"Leave'm with me I'll get rid of them."

"O Pat, don't go getting yourself in trouble over me!"

"I'm already in trouble over you—with my wife. Why do you think I'm out till this hour?"

"Oh, my goodness, I do breed trouble, don't I?" She started up the car and backed past the pickup. She stuck her head out and said, "Oh, about that promise …I'm afraid I'll have to break one part of it—I shall not forget you."

Pat sighed ambivalently as she finally left. He wouldn't forget either: he would be forever grateful to her, for she had awakened in him a tenderness and a true feeling of warmth for one in need of love and understanding as he had so often shown in behalf of Agnes as she for him—before Time's winds, lashing the check and balance of sensitivity to the other and immersion of the self, tilted the delicate symmetry. Though he wanted to rush home and just admire Agnes in her sleep, he was drawn to the monster, in part by Johnson. He went down the steps and tried a dozen keys before he found the right one. Before entering, he went back up a few steps to survey the area. His truck was nicely tucked into the shadows, not a living thing stirring but for the presence of this monster that threatened his contentment. He was careful not to turn on the flashlight until he closed the door behind him. He bumped into a large thing as he turned from the door; he turned on the flash: it was a large barrel on wheels.

"Now, will you look at this?...filled with paper. These guys are begging for trouble, and blocking the exit, to boot." He edged up the basement stairs and entered a corridor. Old lighting fixtures lined the walls. He observed that one was not secured to the wall and the wiring had snaked out of an aperture framed by chipped plaster and lath. The floors creaked weirdly as he walked. "Hundreds of pounding feet on this old flooring six, seven times a day ...Patty's, too!...To be sure there were but two staircases: A city block apart!"

He peered into one of the classrooms, chancing the flashlight only momentarily. "Oiled wooden floors, of course, what else would they be?" He headed back to the basement. "God help us, if the kids ever got trapped in here. I wonder if those old schools in the city, like Pete said, are just as bad?...Aw, he's probably right...when things get old ...like the clunky Rambler ...it's time. Why not give chance a shove?"

He returned to the basement, searching for the boiler and found the wires overhead. "Jesus, look at that, will you? They really *are* down to the copper! Those bastards...how could they, knowing this?" He foundered back to the door, opened it carefully and went up the steps slowly. "Sweet Jesus, is that a police car going by the other side of the fence? Jesus, Mary and Joseph, what if they spotted the pickup!" He waited to see if they would come round the building. He hopped in the truck and waited. He decided if he heard them coming he would take one of the cans and proceed to put gas in the truck, telling them his wife had borrowed the truck during the day to pick up their daughter, and that he had been working late and his wife left him a note to wake her up and she would drive him in the family car to get gas, but since he had gas in the garage for the lawn mower and being the nobleman he was he would not wake her and hoofed it here with the cans. In trying to get his story straight in his mind five minutes had passed.

"Jesus, they'll be ready for another round if I don't get moving." He rifled through his toolbox under the seat and found a propane torch, scratcher, and insulated pliers. He went back into the cellar, found a step ladder and lit the torch and proceeded to burn away the frayed insulation of the wiring, following it joist after joist. Here and there with his insulated pliers he pinched the wires gently to appear as though they had shorted, causing a fire. Then he clustered as much flammable junk as he could find along the wire's path and was about to put the torch to the paper from the barrel he had strewn under the junk. Suddenly he twisted the valve on the torch. "What the hell am I doing?…I've gotta be off my rocker! Christ! Talmidge bewitched me!"

He ran back to the truck for insulation tape to wrap the wires. "If that son-of-a-bitch, Joe, does his job in the morning, he'll pull those wires anyway." He started back down the steps when he heard a thunderous crash which vibrated overhead. He panicked, and screeched, "Jesus, maybe this damn building is alive! Christ, did she come back…that crazy Laura?" There was another explosion. "I'd better hightail it out of here!" He relocked the basement door and shoved the keys in the Dumpster under the refuse, muttering, "No use for these now." Flames roared above, devouring the tarred roof, forcing jet black billows of smoke into the graying sky. He ran to the truck; the door handle was already warm. "Gotta get this out of here before the gasoline explodes, too!"

He noted that the flames had not reached the narrow drive behind the building leading to the parking lot, so he barreled through, hoping to exit unseen, unless needed in which case it would look better if he were in the parking lot near the exit than behind the building and subject to questions. As Irish luck would have it his window was rolled up as the truck sped along the narrow drive and another great blast came, showering his truck with glass from the windows above. "Laurie sure as hell didn't do this!" He turned the corner into the parking lot. There still wasn't a soul in sight! "Maybe I'm the one having a nightmare!"

He barely got his truck onto the street and backed away from the parking lot ramp and pulled into the curb, when the sirens went off and people, hastily garbed or still in their robes and slippers, were running from the residential area, the next street over from the schools. Pat jumped out of the truck to blend in with the onrushing crowd. He noticed a metallic glimmer on the edge of the school lawn. He walked toward it and could see that it was what once was an airplane wing with the Air Force star. "Well, I'll be damned …how about that?— on its way to the base not far from here, no doubt.…Lucky it missed the new building." He sighed in relief, "Good, girl, Laurie, safe and sound in bed having a restful sleep, I trust, dreaming of her message from the sky come true."

Great throngs from all four corners of the small community joined in the great spectacle. Huge flames lapped at the helpless structure burning out its insides that grated, popped, rumbled, then tumbled. Other hungry flames lapped and blackened the wooden frame windows and the once mighty, stately white doors now red with coals. The great heat from inside propelled brick loosely mortared from their fifty year old berth. They clacked and cracked falling at rapidly progressive intervals. The last remaining roof rafter, some distance from where the jet fighter apparently had plunged, caved in, and a great sector of the wall tumbled out against a once proud maple whose leaves were shrinking from the immense heat.

When the firemen first arrived, hoses hooked, they moved in toward the dying, dinosaur, raised their hoses and the great streams boiled and steamed as the fiery tongues lapped at them playfully. Driven back by the intense heat, all they could do was to stare at the awesome marvel of the spectacle—none but a few from the city had ever seen the likes of its magnitude and intensity before—hardly knowing where to begin it had spread so rapidly, though graciously contained within its own walls. They decided all they could do was to wet down the premises, carefully monitor its breadth; and form a defensive ring round the high school. Anxiously the volunteers waited for the neighboring fire districts with better rigs.

Within thirty minutes from the time of the initial explosion that Pat had felt there was not a roof timber arched to the sky, not an ornate sash to admire, not a welcoming door—nothing left but remnants of brick stepped erratically like an ancient ruin and leaning in or out while jackal-like flames lapped the inner remains. Fifty-six years of bustling, interactions of life's success, failure, young love of some or no consequence, knowledge—its grandeur and its pain—all clinging to the enduring ambience of the structure's spirit turned to cinders and smoke in less than a half hour.

News traveled that the Air Force pilot had bailed out and was safe. Some cheered; others cursed him for shifting his inevitable fate to the fate of a community. Pat wondered, if school were in session would the pilot have chosen the same fateful path.

Saturday at noon Agnes drove up to the Little League parking lot in a Henry J. She stopped and turned off the ignition and with the same excitement when her father had bought her first and only bicycle, exclaimed, "Pat! it handles like a dream! And it truly is in 'mint condition'... why, it's as good as new! I love it!" She leaned over and kissed her husband on the passenger side. "Thank you, dear,...you are full of surprises, aren't you? This one—and by all means, the rose—I like."

"Yes, I'd say it was a great buy ...perhaps even a steal." He said, thrilled that she liked it so much—and the rose. "What the heck," he thought, " someday I'll build a den on the back and hang the sword and rifle—hidden from your lady."

"Not half the room back here as the Rambler," Patricia whined, "still preferred to that smoking, wreck, though."

Pat shook his head, but smiled, turning to Agnes. "Does that mean I've finally done something right in her eyes?" Agnes shrugged.

"Daddy," Patricia said, touching his arm, "a daughter doesn't think in those terms—a father is a father. I guess I am stuck with you. Or is it stuck on you?" They laughed and got out of the car, Pat grabbing a shoebox on the front seat. The three of them strolled to the field where Gary and his team were warming up. Patty ran ahead to catch up with some friends, who were excited over the prospect of moving into the high school. The parents strolled as one—arm in arm.

"You know, we have plenty of room now—what do you say to having a native born Long Islander?" Pat asked.

Agnes beamed in disbelief. "Do you mean it? You're not just saying that to round out a perfect day."

"I suppose in a way I am; but I'll mean it tomorrow and a year from now. Not much beyond that, though," he chuckled, "we're getting on in years."

"I love you, Pat....I really do so very much," she burst with a sigh and squeezed his hand. "Uh,..." She hesitated, squeezed his hand again. "I know I haven't been,...well, you know ...responsive. But I feel free now! So very much in the world. Pray, why not?...The world is mine." Gazing lazily at first at a row of courtly iris, which to her meant heralding the advent of the rose, she gulped in the air and exhaled slowly. "Oh, look how beautiful the iris are! Oh, Pat, we never planted iris!"

"I'm afraid I did...It was to be a surprise....I didn't know they wouldn't come up till the following year."

"O God, who cares ...to think you did it for me! Besides, soon the roses will be in bloom!...Meanwhile, I have your rose at the Lady's feet. Oh, yes, Pat, it is now!"

"You mean it ...really?"

"Yes, Pat, O yes, yes,...now!...Well, when we get home, of course." They laughed, then hastened their pace. Pat saw his son shagging flies in the outfield. He called him over. Agnes continued ahead, knowing this is one of those exclusive father-son moments.

Gary came trotting over. "Son, I'm real sorry about the other night. I went out of my head," the father said with deep regret.

"Aw, Dad, that's okay. I'm just happy you're here to see me play. Guess what?...Oops, there I go again!...I'm playing rightfield today! The coach said the Pirates have two big left-handed batters that can hit'm a mile, and wants me ...ME ...out there to tighten up defense! Not exactly All-Star material yet, but I'm getting there!"

"I'm proud of you, son....You're an All-Star in my book." He reached into the old shoebox he was carrying. "This is a fitting day...what with your playing rightfield...for you to have this." He carefully extracted a glove folded over its pocket. "It's still a little oily; I've been freshening it up. The pocket is as deep as it ever was." He handed it to him.

Gary threw down his other one. "Tommy Henrich! Golly! Tommy Henrich! ...I can't believe it! What a right fielder he was, eh, Dad?"

"One of the very best. It might be a bit big for you, but you'll get used to it."

"You're the best, Dad!" He was about to hug his father when a fly ball was hit his way. He took off after it and on the run speared it with "youth's treasure."

Pat whistled, waved to him, picked up Gary's old glove and put it in the box. "Who knows?...I'll oil it up for my new son....Who's on it? I don't remember." He turned it over and looked for the signature barely visible from scuffs and oiling. "Sandy Koufax...wild arm; still,...lot of promise." He looked for Agnes; she was at the refreshment stand, talking to Jessica and Laurie, both of whom had been faithfully flapping burgers, rolling dogs and popping open soda since the season's beginning. He observed that Laurie was smiling, chattering, laughing in the matrix of body language totally relaxed and free.

"That was quite a jolt you gave me the other night, you Irish bastard." Pat recognized Johnson's voice and when he felt a hand on his shoulder, he reeled to do damage. The electrician jumped back. "Hold on there...gotta regular Billy Conn among us. Just wanted to say that I'm not going to apologize..."

"Nor am I."

"But I did deserve it." He grinned and extended his hand.

Pat's left came down. With his right he grasped the electrician's. "I thought you had a job today?"

Joe's eyes dropped. "Na, turned it down....Thought I'd watch my youngest play."

He snickered privately. "Nice thought," Pat said with little trace of sarcasm. He turned and headed for the refreshment stand. Laurie beamed when she saw him approach. "Have a burger and a coke, Mr. Dolan,...on the house...in celebration of a very successful night."

"That's a cryptic remark!"

"On the contrary, just being honest. Good riddance to the relic," Laurie said calmly.

"It's hardly the means we wanted." Jessica said, puzzled. "I think you're getting giddy over the school fire."

"No, Mrs. Langley,...Mrs. Talmadge is just fine....She's right, you know. I changed my thinking: the building had disaster written all over it....Besides, the Air Force will bear the brunt of much of the cost—our insurance robber barons will see to that." He put the shoebox down on the refreshment counter by Laura, slipped out Koufax, and stole a wink at her. He put his arm around Agnes and drew her close. She responded with a secretive hug, and they headed for the benches.

Laura glanced over at them; she flinched but was convinced he would black out the night. She turned away from Jessica so she would not see the tears rolling down her cheeks. She took the box and was about to throw in the waste container when she removed the lid. A rose peeped up at her.

A half mile away, the board and the administration, galvanized by a major incident, were furiously making contingency plans to finish out the school year with some semblance of order. The business at hand, however, was far from orderly, which, in face of the mammoth task before them, was excusable—not even the most heartless reporter would elevate the intra-organizational disarray to a level beyond a minor incident under the circumstance.

In a special Tuesday edition of the *Herald*, after the long holiday weekend, it was reported that double sessions would be in effect on Thursday and would continue that way until construction on a new junior high school was completed. Lest there were many like Pat who did not read the *Herald* nor bothered to listen to community messages on radio, the board had voted to have on Wednesday its decision written in the sky—penetential compliments of the U.S. Air Force.

Sailors' Voyeurism

T tailored uniform swung his club smartly with one hand while resting the other cowboy-style on his 45 holster; the other MP in fatigues let his stick hang from his garrison belt while pin wheeling his M-1 round nimble fingers. They sauntered down the Yokosuka's thoroughfare, confident no swab-jockeys on shore leave would violate the Occupation's curfew, yet itching to find an offender so they could confiscate some cigarettes.

In the shadows of a kimono and curio storefront, two sailors pressed against the window as though frozen while the marines passed by. "Don't start that damn hill-billy humming again," one sailor whispered huskily to his mate who was breathing into a half empty beer can.

"Aye, mate," he gulped as he rolled one side of his face to the window with Japanese writing all over it and tried scraping off the strange lettering.

"Keep quiet, Tennessee! You can't scrape off what's inside, you idiot....And what the hell is the matter with you? Can't you see they're the same bastard gyrenes that bushwhacked us out of one house already. If they catch us again — it's the brig for sure."

Tennessee rolled his head to his mate. "Oh, yeah, Joe, the ones that aren't really like the navy's shore patrol. I heard from the scuttlebutt that these guys are combat marines and they hate this chicken duty."

Joe, relieved that the marines were out of sight, said, "All the more reason to be careful if we're ever going to get laid tonight."

Tennessee squinted at the window dimly lighted. "Say, what is all that shit over there? — they all look alike."

"Aw, Red, don't they teach you nuthin in Tennessee? Thems Buddhas."

Hey, let's break in and steal a couple for souvenirs and a kimono for my girl back home."

Joe shook his head in exasperation. "Oh, yeah, that makes a lot of sense. Those marines would dash back and club us like cattle...."C'mon, let's get movin while we can and head for the whorehouse our P.O.[1] told us about, you know the fancy one."

Red nodded, took a final draft from the can. He crushed it and raised his arm to throw it. Joe grabbed his arm. "You dumb ass, throw that and I'll kick your teeth in. Marines are ear-trained; they'll jump all over us." He took the can and quietly placed it on the walk.

"Na, they're a good block away," Red in stretching his view from the shadows, speculated.

"That's nuthin to fast movin marines." Joe hugged the storefronts as he edged down the sidewalk beckoning to his mate to follow. "I think that house is the next alley up from here."

Stealing one last look through the window, Red asked, "Hey, Joe, what's Buddha doing here anyway? I thought he was from India."

Joe replied, as he yanked Red's arm, edging him along the building, "Aw, all these Orients think alike.

"Yeah, but the Indians,..." He chuckled. "Indians! — jeez, that sounds weird, Joe."

"What does?"

"You know, when you say Indians, you think of..."

"Johnny Mack Brown and his feathered friends, I know," Joe extrapolated.

"Anyway, India Indians don't have slanted eyes and yellow skin — so what the hell is Buddha doing here?"

"How the hell do I know? I'm from Jersey....Now, forget it and let's find that house and get some — we've had too much sea duty and I'm hurtin."

---

[1]Petty Officer

Red relinquished. "Roger and out, but I still don't get it." They paused at the end of the storefronts.

"Well, if you looked hard enough you's see that they fattened up Buddha and slanted his eyes."

"Oh, yeah, like their fat wrestlers!"

Joe peered into the alley. "Bingo! This it!"

"How can you be sure — it could be any alley."

"No, the P.O. said it's the only one with fancy lanterns." They turned into the dimly lighted corridor flanked by rows of houses whose eaves seemed to overlap onto the next.

Red observed, "Jeez, this place looks like Knoxville's nigger quarters....Can you imagine what an atom bomb would do to these shit houses!"

"Wouldn't need that; just a single napalm would cover it, Joe piped. "Ah, look! — that's no shit house!" He gestured toward one large house clearly separated and set back from the others; it was gayly illuminated. They cautiously looked around before crossing over to the wide wooden steps leading to a porch bedecked with artistic lanterns.

"Boy, this place must be jumpin....It's the only one with lights behind the shit paper windows," Red mused.

"Yeah, busy all right, look at all the shoes lined up by the door," Joe noticed.

Red added, "And they're not all shoes; plenty of clod-hoppers — that means civilians. Say, I don't see any G.I. shoes."

"It's probably for a reason. I doubt that any marine or sailor is stupid enough to leave them out for kids to swipe or for the MPs to spot them."

Red, stroked his chin and said, "Gosh, that's right; we can't kick them off or we'll be sitting ducks."

Joe agreed. He knocked on the door. Suddenly all the lights in the house went out.

"Jesus, they're going to bushwhack us!" Red yelped.

"Na, the damn marines run this town. The P.O. tells me that the whorehouses are warned not to open for sailors," Joe said in sizing up the situation, while shaking the sliding door.

"Maybe we shouldn't chance it, then." Red took off his skewed cap to wipe his forehead. When he turned around to check the narrow street, the same marines were coming toward them on double time. "Joe! We're cooked! They're back."

"I ain't come here to give up now — besides, my balls are hurting. I gotta get some ass." Joe shook the door again. "Christ, open up."

A voice on the other side squealed, "Nyai, we...Geisha...nyai gollies!"

The marines jumped the steps, the one smartly dressed, pointing the club at them; the other inverted his rifle, menacing the hapless sailors with the butt. "Well, swabs, to enter a place like this," the one with the club stated with authority, "you must've gone back to the ship store for more cigarettes."

"No way," Joe said, turning toward them. "When you frisked us earlier and cleaned us out, we was humbled — felt like the Dodgers in the '41 World Series." The other marine slung his rifle on his shoulder and began to frisk them. "You know, the routine, jockeys, up with the bell-bottoms so I can check the socks." The sailors complied; there were no packs stuffed in their socks. The marine looked over at his mate, "Damn, it seems we struck out this time....What'll we do with them?"

The marine in tailored dress, noted, "We ain't pirates;...can't take their money....Besides, they're going to need plenty we're they're going." They both laughed.

Red gulped, "You're takin us to the damn brig, eh?" The marines laughed again and went back down the steps.

"Balls hurtin--that's precious," said the club marine.

"Aye, and they'll be swollen back at the ship, too," remarked the rifleman. They guffawed all the way out of the alley.

"Whew, I can't believe they let us go!" Red vented.

"Aw, all they care about is cigarettes for the black market." Joe stretched a look down the alley to make sure the marines were gone, then turned to the door and resumed shaking it.

The voiced squealed, "Nyai, nyai,...Geisha!"

"Bullshit! Open up!" Tom yelled back, and almost shaking the door off its track. Gradually the lights came on again. The door rolled partially open. A tawny elderly woman peered round, waving a veined hand, while beseeching them, "Nyai gollies...we Geisha,...Nyai."

"What the hell are you talkin about, old lady?" Joe snapped. "We'll see for ourselves, Mama-son." He rolled open the door all the way. He stepped in and motioned for Red to follow.

"Nyai, nyai," the woman screamed, pointing to their shoes digging into the soft straw mats.

"Yeah, mama-son," Red said as though she understood. "Like walking on straw hats."

Joe shook his head. "She wants us to take them off, jerk. Where's your oriental manners?" Joe began to unlace his shoes.

The old woman screeched, "Nyai loom, nyai, no loom!" She motioned to the rice paper doors surrounding the entry.

"Oh, I get it...no room, eh?" He grinned at her and pulled off his shoes, got up and headed for one of the doors.

Red stopped him. Jeez, man, are you nuts? What if there are marines in there? We'll get our asses whipped with their heavy belt buckles."

"I doubt it. I think it's strictly for Nips. The old lady would have called out the marines if they were here," Joe assured himself. "Probably why the MPs let us go."

Well, I guess that makes sense," Red agreed, but then thought, "Wait a minute if it's strictly for Japs maybe these gals have the clap or worse. I sure don't want to chance that — our ship heads for the states in a week."

"What do you use for brains, boy? Japs are very clean and probably more so for their own kind."

Red smiled and sat down to remove his shoes. "I sure need a woman, too."

"Then anchors aweigh, mate!" Joe slid open one of the doors. The sailors stepped in. Two Japanese men with robes over their business suits were on their haunches round a low tea table. Two young girls, beautifully bedecked in colorful kimonos accompanied them. One was coyly feeding one of the men a rice cake. All four spontaneously rose up, bowed their heads toward the intruders. The two men eyed each other as they bowed and simultaneously they discreetly moved toward the door, easing themselves round the much taller sailors. The mama-son was heard pleading to the two men as they hurriedly left the house.

The sailors motioned to the girls to sit down. They knelt closer to the hibachi to oversee the rice cakes. The sailors awkwardly squatted by the table. The mama-son entered and tried again to explain herself but they did not understand. She in an authoritative tone addressed the girls. They both blushed a somber innocence. The woman threw up her hands and left the room.

"This floor is cold on the rump," Red commented as he reached for a pillow once occupied by one of the predecessors.

"That's why they sit on their legs, you dope," Joe reminded him as he himself tried to bend his legs back. The girls laughed. Joe reached for the nearest one; she recoiled, but decided to move closer to him because of the heat of the hibachi. He dropped his hand on her knee just as Mama-son reentered.

She squealed the same tune, "Nyai gollies...Geisha!" She tried to remove his hand from the girl. "What are you worrying about, Mama-son? Her kimono is as thick as a pea jacket!"

The woman shuffled round the table, repeating: Nyai gollie...Geisha...hubba, hubba...nyai!"

Joe laughed and put his arm round the girl whose wary face turned to alarm. She wormed out of his grip, jumped up and briskly went to the corner of the room where a samisen leaned against the wall. She cradled it in her arms and began to pluck. The other girl rose up and began to dance delicately to the twanging rhythm. The old lady chuckled and clapped her hands; her tone changed: "Y'e, y'e...Geisha, Geisha...nyai gollie!"

"What the hell is going on here? Joe yelped and leaped over the table to reach for the dancer. "We're never goin to get laid at this rate!"

Red jumped up and prevented him from interfering with the dance. "What do you think you're doing? The dancer is mine; you made your pitch for the banjo player. You gotta be cool, man, they're classy gals. You gotta give them time, finesse them."

"What gave you culture all of a sudden? Besides you got it wrong; they're finessing *us* right out of our hunger for sex! — they're damn teasers!" Joe sat back down on his haunches in frustration. Mama-son sighed in relief and left the room.

The sailors seemed to succumb to the Geisha charm as the girls elegantly performed with an incredibly demure style. Joe and Red contented themselves by eating rice cakes while observing the performance with growing interest. The door slid open, Mama-son entered with a steaming pot of tea. "No, no!" Tom cried, " Saki, saki...we want saki to loosen up the girls."

Nyai saki,...Geisha...tea." She smiled as she poured the tea.

Red said, "Jeez, this is no whorehouse — it's a damn Japanese convent!"

Joe lowered his head and groaned, "Just our luck to get hooked up with confirmed virgins."

Mama-son laughed. "Oy, Geisha...nyai hubba hubba...nyai,...no gollies!"

Red blurted, "Jeez, I think she means girlies! — like the girly magazines back on board ship."

Joe, staring into his tea, growled, "I'm afraid so — and I bet our P.O. knew it all along — damn joker."

Red added, "And the marines."

Chow Down Easter Morning

Just before Easter of '45 we were on our way to Okinawa—of course, we didn't know it then. We were playing poker over a mountain of ammo and under an LCT chained topside. Though cramped and suffering neck and back pain from being so hunched over for hours at a time in this

Charybdis, we claimed territorial right to this sleeping quarter and poker haven as there was no space below deck. The China Sea was kicking up its usual fuss.

"Now hear this, Gyrenes, Mess call, but don't all line up at once!" the P.A. of LST 772 (I think that was the number) resounded off the flat bottom of the LCT. We continued playing a few more hands before we crawled out of our casino—what's the difference whether you stand in line or idle on deck? There's not much one can do on a ship designed for tank transporting and its skeletal command. An LST is not a troop ship but somehow the command horned in half an infantry battalion! The galley was made to accommodate no more than seventy or so men—and on shifts at that—let alone over four hundred. As a result when we got in line—if lucky enough to find the end of it—they would run out of mess after twenty minutes and we would have to wait another fifteen minutes for them to finish cooking another round before the line started to move again.

Nevertheless, it was well worth it because after island-hopping anything barely resembling appetizing chow was a major event. We marines gave the Coast Guard a lot of credit for knocking themselves out to see to it that we got three mess calls a day. Those cooks from Brooklyn worked round the clock to keep us content. They probably figured we'd eat a hole in the tank-deck if they didn't.

Virtually the whole crew of some thirty men came from the Big Apple, and they never pulled any punches complaining to us how unfair it was for the Coast Guard to be out here some fifteen thousand miles from the Brooklyn Navy Yard. Though we never bent a sympathetic ear, most of us agreed that it was a raw deal—after all, we didn't join the marines to pull duty in the states—each to his own trait, and if they were cowards, then, hell, they ought to be accommodated.

Normally the crew ate first, but being cosmopolitan Brooklynites many would join us in the lines and relate to us hicks their escapades with the hot dames from the big city—even though some of us had spent a weekend in New York after boot camp. Most of all, though, they loved to brag about their beloved "Bums" back home. Soon names like Ducky Medwick, Dixie Walker, Dolph Camilli became shiphold words that we later used as nightly passwords on the foxhole line at Okinawa—that is, the ones with 'r's in them like "Du<l>och<a>, <L>eese and <L>eis<a>." Besides, some of the crew didn't feel as though they were making any sacrifices arriving late for mess; they could still break in the line near the scullery to beat their gums with us on how bad the food was. Hell, when they were stateside most of them ate in the automat or grabbed a bite at Nedick's before heading for Forty-second Street, so they weren't exactly connoisseurs.

In contrast, we marines thought we were being served at the Waldorf. The cooks aboard were gourmets to us and made those powdered assortments taste like fresh, delectable victuals—not like the marine cooks on the islands who half the times didn't even bother to add water to the powdered potatoes and eggs.

When we card jocks approached the steaming serving counter we got high on the aroma alone, so long had it been since we were treated to the likes of synthetic home cooking—in fact, not since Camp Lejeune or Parris Island where what they lacked in quality they made up for in quantity; there they always had "seconds call." Moreover, the ship's freezers—under double guard—were loaded with fresh meat and every other day we were literally overcome with the savory juices of hamburger, lamb, or pork, and chicken on Sundays. Steaks were stowed away for our last meal aboard when they planned a D-day banquet of steaks and fresh eggs for pre-dawn breakfast. We figured for that occasion the ones first in line would be having morning mess at 2200 hours the night before.

A short redheaded coast guardsman gunner in front of us got indignant when a marine on mess duty was about to ladle a bowl of soup for him. "Na," he growled, "tired of the same old dumpling soup!" I looked at the mess-marine pleadingly, and he tipped it into my bowl then ladled a second dip of the delicious soup. The coast guardsman passed up the kidney beans and rice too and I benefited again by getting a double portion. Though entitled to two biscuits, he only opted for one reasoning, "Hey, I'm not from the brig! Waddya think, I'm on five days bread and water! Nothin' lately but doughballs comin' out of me as it is." I edged my tray toward the marine on rice and biscuit detail and he sympathetically threw the blue shirt's on my tray in addition to my two. They were the most delicious biscuits—helped by the fresh butter, can you believe it? Butter!— that had ever collected South Pacific mold. My mouth watered when we approached the fried chicken. The marines on mess duty were not permitted to monitor this choice prize. The scullery "maidens" themselves doled out the golden poultry. I couldn't believe my ears when the blue shirt said, "Just one little wing, mate—sick of this damned chicken every Sunday." I promptly nudged him and pleaded, "Shucks, mate, let him pile it on! I'll relieve you of it as soon as we get to a table....And cut out the bat sh ...droppings, jockey,...don't pass up the apple pie!"

Licking my chops at the table, I scraped off a drumstick and breast from his tray, together with his apple pie—I swear, he didn't even want the apple pie because it was made from dried apples! So satisfied was I that I invited my benefactor to our poker circle. He was heating up with excitement that he could be privy to the likes of us. You'd think we had given him tickets to his temple Ebbets Field.

While one of us flicked out the hand of five card stud, the blue shirt said in a tone like a twelve year old hanging out with teenagers, "I never met anyone suicidal in my life before! Us guys from Brooklyn value our lives, you know. And here we now got a ship-load of yooz maniacs and it grabs me as good as Errol Flynn's Charge of the Light Brigade!"

Well, that little city-slicker won the first pot to our disappointment because of all things he had thrown a Butterfinger into the stakes against our K-ration "dog biscuits." It was my deal next and I was determined to deal from the bottom when I saw that crazy guy throw the Butterfinger back in and keep the K-ration chips! He started eating them! "Cheez, these are delicious!" he cried. We all looked at each other as though we had a doozer of an overseas mental case on our hands—and this New York swab was calling us suicidal!

After the game I tore into my Butterfinger. Smacking my lips over this island happy treat, I was ready to unroll my blanket on top the ammo and sack in till the next mess call, when the blue shirt asked me if I could get hold of anymore of those delicious cookies. "Cheez, jockey, you don't mean those K-ration-chips? I mean, they're not fit for consumption except in an emergency. I mean, you have to be suffering from malaria or battle fatigue to hanker for them—even on the front lines we avoid them till the C-rations run out."

The guarsman dismissed me with: "Well, I tole ya, gyrenes was screwy. They're almost Kosher, I tell ya." Hell, one good deed returns another, so I opened my pack and gave him a box. "Holy Abraham, man, they got cheese in here too!" he yelped as his eyes popped.

"Aye," I said, "that's one thing you can say for them, though it's so chemicalized it doesn't taste like cheese—sort of like eating boot tongue with moss."

I saw him again in the chow line for the evening mess and he and his mates were all chomping on the dog biscuits. Apparently it was a great thing to them—sort of a novelty. I suspected they were bored with the ship's baker.

That night we relieved the midnight watch down in the tank-deck and the Corporal of the Guard warned us to be on the alert—five cases of K-rations had disappeared.

The way I figured it those Brooklyn jockeys earned those cases of K-rations. They fed us a great D-Day meal of steak and eggs! This "breakfast" had to begin at 2300 in order to feed all the troops before they climbed in to the amphibious tractors. Moreover, the "cowards" saved our lives on Easter morning, which was D-Day, when their gun crew shot down a kamikaze aimed at the LCT topside and the plateau of ammunition underneath.

Piltdown

A little man in eastern clothes topped by a derby hesitantly went through swinging doors of the "Western Outpost," a large taproom and dance hall and the only place in this small town of Piltdown to get a bite to eat. So early in the morning the place was empty but for a large gunmen at a table near the window. The little man removed his derby and rubbed his bald head and went up to the closed bar, serving as a breakfast buffet this time of day.

A young lady greeted him. He was taken in by her sweet face but her long cascading red hair was prominently in play. "Can I get you coffee, sir? You have to serve yourself for the eats."

"Yes, thank you,…black."

She came back with a large mug of coffee. "You're a stranger, I gather."

"Yes,…got in on last night's train. I'm a salesman."

She beamed beautifully to soften her words. "Judging from your clothes, I hope you don't sell clothing. Not much use for eastern wear out here."

He laughed. "No, not entirely, occasionally I get an order. I'm in farm equipment mostly."

"Then you got off at the right town. Plenty of homesteaders and ranchers in these parts. The general store doesn't carry much except for shovels and stuff. Most get by on what they brought with them."

"That sounds promising." He picked up a plate and spooned into a warming plate of scrambled eggs. Then he looked around. "This is a strange looking restaurant."

She chuckled. "But the food's good. Actually it's an entertainment post. The girls take turns handling the breakfast bar, and on Sundays we change into respectable dress and serve families after church. The rest of the time we are dance girls for the heavy drinkers."

"My, my, you look…well, I don't mean you aren't beautiful to be one, but …what I mean is that you don't look like a dance girl."

She laughed. "I don't think you'd say that if you saw me in my costume."

He laughed too and stared at her. "Right, I'm sure of that. It's just that …well, gosh, you have such an innocent look about you." She broke into laughter.

The large man overheard. "That's because she is!" he boomed. "In my book, she's the town angel." Then he laughed, adding, "Of course, not many read my book."

The little man overcame a startled look and smiled. "I read it, sir; I'd say you're right."

"There aren't many in town who would," she said. "In fact only one besides the marshal here...." She chuckled. "And he can't read."

"Come on over and join me, stranger," the marshal urged. The stranger complied after he doled out some breakfast on a small plate.

At the table the little salesman watched awhile as the marshal wiped his big plate clean, then wiped the egg from his gray moustache. The marshal held up his empty coffee mug, and said simply, "Cressie."

The salesman said, after he forked some egg, "My, these eggs are good."

"That's because Cressie makes them. She's a great little gal—known her since she was knee-high to a toad."

"Yes, she seems very competent—and beautiful to boot," the stranger said as he looked out the window to the waking town.

"None prettier than Cressie, that's for sure." The marshal patted her slim arm as she put the fresh mug before him and reached to remove the plate and empty mug.

"Oh, you're just prejudice, marshal because you've known me so long," she said with a blushing smile. "Don't forget Jennie."

"Yep, she's a pretty one, for sure." He nodded. "But just the same...."

The salesman let out a cry, "My God, who's that?...Is he an Indian?" He gestured to the window through which he saw a crude dark-complexioned hunched figure loping his horse down the street. "A world of contrasts. Here we're talking of beauty and I swear I've never seen anything as ugly as that."

Cressie said, "Be careful that could be a very good prospective customer. Neither the marshal nor I think of Jeff that way. Besides, how could you judge him from a distance and his hat pulled down?"

"The instant configuration of the...man, I suspect....Oh, but forgive me. It was cruel of me. It's just that it...he startled me," he apologized. "I guess, I startled you. After all, look at me. Especially here in the west, I must look like a clownish little fool out of his element."

She chuckled. "I'm glad you said it and not me....It's good you admit to it...." She stared into his eyes flinching from embarrassment and added in defense, "Jeff is not the elephant man, you know,...and no, he's not an Indian;...some kind of aboriginal blood in him, though. Besides, they don't come any nicer than Jeff."

"Yep, Jeff's a kind young man. Ugly, I grant you, but you pay it no mind; he's a fixture in these parts, though he still scares people." The marshal said good naturedly.

"I think it's the other way around, marshal; they scare *him*," Cressie said with subdued petulance. "And those who still taunt him can't equal the good what's inside him."

"Aw, I know, Cressie. I know he ain't so ugly when you get to know him....Still, I don't see you datin' him any."

"That's because I see him as a brother."

"By God, that's right!—you two have seen a lifetime together." The marshal jolted as she went back behind the bar. He reached across the table and pulled the stranger back from straining his neck to follow the huge roundness of the rider's back equaling the haunches of his draft horse that he often rode yoke-free. "Yep, I've known Jeff since he was eye high to wheat's whiskers when his folks first came to settle in these parts. They were simple, hardworking homesteaders. Decent law-abiding they were, and believe it or not it rubbed off on Jeff natural like. All the town folk round here liked him even though he was homelier than a mule. He was always doing nice things for people—like lending out free his great strength at harvest time after he'd put in more than a day's work at his Pappy's. Why, he helped me track down horse thieves. When he caught up with them single handed, he let one of them go because he said he was only a boy who just needed a horse to pull his plowshare for his poor widow mama's fields." The marshal took another gulp, then chuckled. "By God, he let him keep the horse, too! Then, would you believe, Jeff paid for it!"

The little stranger shook his head. "You sure know how to make a big mouth from the east feel humble."

"Nix, don't feel bad—you're not the first one to rush an opinion. Shucks, folks who know him still look at him as though they were prancin' round a side-show," the marshal comforted. "But I tell you, he's a fine boy—well,...man now. He got that way not only from his folks but a kindness inside I never saw in anyone before. When children would make fun of his looks when he was a mere boy, he never got angry. He'd just quietly go home to his folks who would comfort him—and what's more love him, especially his mama. He worshiped that fine, homely woman....I think she was Eskimo of sorts. The father was a white man, but not much to look at either. Yep, Jeff thought his mama was beautiful. And, you know, in her kind ways, she was....Her Christian name was Mary; she understood him. Yep, a decent man he is. The whole territory likes him, though, as I said, they all look at him as though he's some kind of freak. Real kindly goodness gets under peoples' hides...especially since he was decorated by old Ulysses himself."

The little man's eyes popped. "You mean the president!"

The marshal looked proud, then spread a smile of tobacco stained teeth. "No, the general."

"My, my,..." the salesman murmured, looking out the window again for the strange hero, "decorated, you say?...Must've been something."

"Yep, young Jeff practically licked the rebs all by himself," said the marshal rather proudly. An old man with a badge on his hat poked his head over the doors. "Looks as though my deputy, Gabe, is hankerin' for his grits. I got to go back, so Cressie can fix'm up special for him. She gives old Gabe the royal treatment."

"Deputy? Didn't I see him working baggage at the train station last night?" The stranger scratched his head.

"Oh, yea, for years he's been doing both. Neither the railway nor me has the heart to retire him." He rose up. The stranger gazed in awe at the length of the marshal's body. "Say, you don't deal in guns, do you? I don't cotton to that. Hard enough keepin' the peace without the whipper-snappers comin' in with new fancy guns."

"Me?" The salesman laughed heartily. "Never so much as held one in my hand....No, marshal, almost everything but—from the latest design hoe and plowshare to fine carriages of the seventies line."

Going out the doors, the marshal turned and said, "Not likely you'll sell any plushy carriages to these simple folks."

After the Civil War Jeff returned to his family's homestead to find that both had died. He was devastated: throughout the war his drive to survive was his parents. Though alone, despondent and wondering what the purpose was, he slowly began to work the farm in deference to their memory. Except for the war years, he was never anywhere else anyway. This would always be his home. Only dimly does he remember early childhood when his father owned a store in a Canadian logging camp. His father was forced to sell and cross the border because the customers continually taunted and ridiculed his wife and boy.

Upon his return, Jeff first worked just a small plot and retired early in the afternoon to sit by their graves into dusk in a mournful void. Cressie out of kindness and their childhood familiarity would sometimes ride out to the farm and sit at the grave-site with him. Gradually he took on the tilling of another field and by the second growing season he was working the entire acreage from dawn to dusk. In this second year's harvest he once said to a hired hand who helped pitch the hay and pick the late corn and was complaining about the lack of rest: "Taint no mere farm to me. This here's my Ma and Pa's shrine. I'm goin' to make it as beautiful and busy as I know how."

Then and ensuing years at early harvest time he would go up on the knoll overlooking the cornfield and place on their graves the first two ears of early summer's picking. "They'd be proud of this here corn," he once told the marshal who drove out Cressie to the farm during this annual ceremony.

"Knowing your Ma and Pa," the marshal corrected, "they'd be more proud of their Jeffy."

Jeff vented a heavy snort, but then laughed raucously and said, "Yep, by thunder, you're probably right, marshal, but Pa sure loved Ma's cornbread and Ma loved makin' it for us."

"She sure did make a mighty fine bread." The marshal nodded jerkily. "She damn sure gave me aplenty...kindest woman I ever knowed."

"She certainly couldn't have been kinder to me....She taught me how to cook and bake," Cressie added, showing a smile for the far past.

Now, after five years of incessantly and humbly working the farm, Jeff dimly became aware on the persistence of his hired hand that he should find himself a woman. Added to this was the perception of the hired hand's wife who would cook and take hot lunches and suppers out to the fields to them just as his ma had done for him and his pa. The spiritual pleasure gotten from pleasing the souls of his parents by continuing their work was losing ground to physical gratification lacking in a man of thirty-five. Of course, since childhood he had the occasional companionship of Cressie. But he too looked upon her as a sibling and friend. Yet when subconsciousness reared up in the loneliness of night and he would anguish over her and curse God for making him so ugly he knew he wanted only her—an impossibility, he was certain.

Gradually he took to frequenting the town on Saturday evenings and soon found distant enchantment in the opposite sex—particularly the dance girls at the Western Outpost patronized by cowboys with a month's pay in their pockets and miners who struck just enough to drink and gamble away a weekend. Of course, he knew that he would never find a mate there; but Cressie was his lodestone. He thought considerably about a woman through the catalog as the salesman had suggested. But he decided against that because he was certain that any woman who looked upon him would get on the first train back east. When the salesman said he could easily get him an Oriental bride, he thought about it, then concluded, "Even they are too pretty and delicate for me."

Although he consciously made it a point to cover his eyes when Cressie would perform as a solo in her scanty costume, he could not escape the moth-like attraction he had for her.

One Saturday evening of his awakening and quietly drinking volumes of beer in a corner partially blocked by the bar and between a curtained entrance, he heard   pleading from a familiar voice. When her voice became shrill and seemingly desperate, he got up from the table, hesitated, then with measured steps headed for the curtain which he drew open. He peered down a long dark hallway: a tall gunman—whom he had observed last week as a heckler of the ladies' performance—was mishandling Jeff's lady of song and dance who was struggling to free herself from his grasp. Suddenly they fell to the floor. She started to scream but the tall man muffled her quickly with one hand as he busily began to tear Cressie's flimsy costume of cotton gauze and silk.

Jeff shook off his numb feeling from too much drink and clumsily rushed down the hallway. With his great apish hands, he clutched the gunman's collar and yanked him clear off Cressie and hurled him six feet down the hall along which he slid on the seat of his pants until his head met up with the heavy vanity where the ladies did their last minute primping before entering the floor of emotionally hungry men. Jeff turned back round and dropped to his knees, stared dumbly at her while wrestling off his coat to cover the sobbing Cressie who nevertheless seemed impervious to her torn garment baring her breast to which Jeff had never before been privy. She looked up with grateful eyes that instantly turned to jerking surprise in purveying his countenance; for in all the years of their relationship she had never been this close up. He helped her up and carefully placed his giant coat onto her bare, narrow shoulders. Even through the thick buckskin his calloused hands felt her sensuous fragility; a shiver accentuated a sensation never before experienced.

She bent back an eye to one of his hands still on her shoulder and she quickly moved out from under as she skirted past the unconscious gunman. She paused, let out a mixed sigh that he was out cold but still breathing. Instinctively she tugged on Jeff's arm, then recoiled. "You had better leave here quickly. Ranker has a terrible temper and won't hesitate to retaliate with his gun. You came to the rescue so quickly that I doubt he has any idea who did this. So please, dear Jeff, leave now."

"Well, I sure hate trouble, Cressie, you know that, but are you sure you'll be all right?" His eyes riveted to her gorgeous shiny hair, which he had always admired, but the feeling was different this time. He was sure it was the drink.

She looked up at him—ashamed of her previous reaction—as though she had been studying his crude features for the first time. "I'll be fine; he's leaving town in the morning."

"That's tomorrow but what about now—when he wakes up?" He felt her eyes on him but he could not look directly at them. He had never been but for his mom this close to a woman before—yes, for the first time but for his anguishing nights—he saw her as a woman of his passion. He was ashamed. It was unfair to Cressie—why, even the proprietress of the general store would avoid him and have one of her clerks wait on him for his supply order because he was so repulsive looking. He shook his head as though this phantom would escape him.

"That's true; I'll walk you out to your horse and then I'll go to my room till the next performance. Perhaps by then he will have cooled off," she said nervously.

"And if he don't? And why do I hafta leave, anyways?" he asked.

"Oh, but you must! I told you Ranker has an awful mean streak and deadly with the gun! I'd never forgive myself if you got hurt," she pleaded, looking softly up at him—he was only a few inches taller—as though she saw in his soft, curious eyes a denial of his self-conscious ugliness. She knew at this moment that she now could look upon not just a brother but a man.

"Shucks, Cressie, that don't bother me none, you know that."

"Of course, I know that, you big ox that fought in the war. But you said before you don't want any trouble," she reminded him.

"That's right …"

"Oh, don't you think I know that you hate to hurt people? But this man is a killer."

His dark eyes bulged from surprise as much as they could with his large cheekbones and finally he sputtered, "Huh?…Then why are you with him?…Doggone it, Cressie, how many times do I hafta beg you to get out of this hellish place?"

She snarled at him. "Oh, sure, and come live off you for the rest of my life! Even a real brother wouldn't want that. You're entitled to your own life, Jeffy. Now, stop worrying about me."

He shook his head vigorously. "Not till I know you're safe."

She laughed and then tugged on his arm urging him to the exit; she parted the curtain. "Oh, Jeff, a girl can't ever be completely safe in a place like this—anywhere, for that matter." They crossed the floor weaving in and out of tables. Men, drunk or not, pawed her as they went by and tagged her with flirtatious remarks. She simply ignored them and hustled Jeff out the swinging doors onto the rough planks of the deck-walk.

Jeff felt awkward and embarrassed; he scanned the street thinking all eyes were on them. He felt the stars were echoing laughter under the black vault. He thought of those dreadful times in his boyhood when shopping with his mother the town children would scoff at him with apish antics and shrieks. Cressie was the only one who treated him normally—perhaps because she first laid eyes on him when she was only three and he, though nine at the time was but a few inches taller. In a territory of many tall, lanky cowhands, it bothered him that in his adult life he still felt as though he was a fence-post driven into the earth. By the same token being pile-driven to the earth gave him a sense of security and affinity to the soil.

She looked both ways, then up at him. "Well,…where's your horse?"

"I'm not leaving you!"

"Oh, Jeff,…please! He doesn't fight even by the rules of war." He was ashamed again. He didn't seem to be listening, so glued was his eyes again to the shiny red hair. "Please go home," she pled again.

"If he's that bad," he responded shaking his head, "that's sure all the more spore for me to plant my big feet right here." His boots thumped the planking. "He sure don't treat you by no rules."

She protruded her full lower lip, then said, "Stop worrying. I know he has a temper, but I can handle him once he's cooled down. Besides, he drank too much. He doesn't usually treat me like this. You're a …man, you must know."

"No, I don't know. No man oughta beat up on no one, a defenseless girl 'specially." To Jeff there was only one way to treat people and particularly women and that was with respect—the way his father taught him indirectly; for his father treated his mother as though she were a goddess and even though Cressie as a child sometimes would hit Jeff, he would never retaliate.

She looked up with surprised admiration at now a man whose face and stature belied gentleness. She had always defended him when there were those who ridiculed him. And when he returned a hero; there were rumors hat he had fought like the savage that he was. She would laugh at that but secretly she feared its possibility. She thought there was some truth to the jungle law of war erupting one's ancestry. She could now see in him the gentle being as a man that she had always seen. A gentle corner of her mind had always overridden the revulsive instinct for his appearance, and she touched his shoulder. "Jeff, you are very kind to think of me, but please don't be stubborn …why, I'll never see you again if you stay and get yourself killed." His eyes glittered. For the very first time he touched her hand differently, loiteringly, yes, even lovingly. She went on, "Of course, I can't say the same thing for you. I see the way you won't look at me when I perform."

"Aw, you know why. In this dinky costume. And all those dirty eyes staring at you…and dirty hands touchin' you. I hate it. Why don't you just come home. So I know you're safe. You know, ma would want it."

"I've already told you why I won't."

"Then be my housekeeper. I'll pay you."

"Oh, Jeff, you're so sweet. But we both have to lead our own lives."

"I'll cover my face; you won't ever have to look at me ever again.…If you never want to lay eyes on the awful likes of me, I'd understand."

"Oh, Jeff, you mustn't think that. And it's an insult to me if you think that!"

"But you're so beautiful ...and I'm ..."

"Hush." She surprised herself by putting her finger to his drooping mouth. "Promise me you'll leave now and I shall look for you next Saturday. Come early before I have to work and we can supper together,..." she paused for a moment, looking at him with compassion, "in my boarding room."

He grinned and couldn't resist touching her withdrawing fingertip. "Gosh,...Cressie,...I think you mean it." He wished he could embrace her. He brushed back his hemp-like shock and laughed for lack of a better tact.

"Of course, I do. Now run along,...please."

He acquiesced and headed for his horse calmly, though his heart was pounding in expectations.

The next Saturday was a disappointment. When he went to the boarding house and asked for Cressie, the matron laughed. "Whatever for?...Could it be you are a monkey in her act?"

"We're suppose' ta supper here," he said naively, ignoring her comment.

She broke into hysterical laughter, then recovered to say cruelly, "You mean she was going to feed you bananas out back with the horses, don't you!"

"Please, ma'am, I'm used to these jabs, but I'm a heap serious. Where is...the...lovely Cressie?"

"Lovely, is she?" she repeated with a raised brow. "My, she's stooped this low, has she?" She squinted at him and said, "Don't waste my time, big— whatever you are—I'm sure she's at the Outpost already entertaining the riffraff a little better than you. I grant you, though, they're still raunchy, primitive."

When he arrived there Cressie scarcely acknowledged him. Still, for a fleeting moment when she came within inches of his table with song and dance, she pulled down his hands from his eyes, winked and smiled at him. That gesture carried him through the next week's chores, thinking of her constantly. That Cressie had conveniently forgot her promise to sup with him was erased from his mind.

The following Saturday, he finished work early and made a conscious effort to freshen himself more. An immeasurable moment of thrill went up his spine when this evening she had faintly squeezed his hand. It mattered little to him that she had immediately withdrawn her dainty hand as though repulsed from the feeling of hot granite. It bothered her that she had felt this way. After all, she had held his hand countless times without such a thought—that she thought about it is what bothered her. She left him abruptly in this bliss while she moved sinuously to one drunk to the next, professionally unmindful of the pawing, aggressive embraces, obscenities, and stifling proximity to the general uncouthness. To her surprise, admiration for him swelled because he had never been one of the sleazy pack.

Other Saturdays in Ranker's absence took place indeed. Her tiny hand remained in his rugged hand longer each time as she by degrees visited his table in the corner for longer periods. No longer was it the feel of granite, rather the security and warmth of a hearth. At the last of these precious moments, she reminded him of Ranker's impending return. His hands were sodden from the thought of losing her even though he was realistic enough to know that he could never have her other than in these fleeting moments.

Nevertheless, another weekend, two months since their first encounter involving Ranker, while plowing the thawing fields, he looked up at the sun for a sense of time. Though it was a cool day, he was drenched in sweat. It was still early for him, yet he decided to quit work. He unhitched his horse, leaving the new plowshare sent by the salesman to the elements and jumped on the draft horse and aimed toward the barn. Inside, he hitched the horse to the wagon. He thought he might as well get some supplies this Saturday, since he felt going to the Outpost would be a waste of time. Still, he had to get there early to watch out for her in case Ranker had returned. Owing to the anguish of his nights, out of desperation he had another reason for making this a special night. He lumbered about pulling items from drawers and closet, muttering as he did so… "socks, new hat and boots, brush my suit …ah, my bath …the hot water." He gripped the big pot on the stove, pouring its contents into a large wash tub half filled with cold water. Having dropped his soggy clothes, he doused his sweaty body into the tub. He looked down at his coarse, hairy chest and moaned: "Boarding house woman!…Awful you are, but so right!" He scrubbed himself vigorously as though he could suds away the ugliness. Finally he stepped out with renewed vigor, careful to dry his large feet, lest they again be black from the earthen floor.

An hour later, dressed, his beard combed, he exemplified the bumpkin on his way to church. Humbly treading his parents' still undisturbed room, he took from a small box a bronze ring. He had seen gold bands on other women, but thought bronze a truer metal. His mother had once told him that sun rays were the only gold people were entitled to, and by tilling the land the true nuggets would turn up naturally in the soil just as God's fruits.

When he left the house, he tried desperately to straighten his posture, which seemed to bend forward even more from the tightness of his coat around his shoulders—apparently the salesman didn't measure him too well, he thought. The fact is, the tailor back east did not know how to "fit an ape." The coat looked as though it had been boiled—his long heavy arms extended way beyond the cuffs, accentuating his immense hands. From starched discomfort he hopped onto the wagon and started for the dusty road leading to the town. He stopped the wagon at the end of the cornfield and walked up the trail to the graves. Head bowed in the solemn air hanging on the knoll, Jeff noticed a gallant crocus peeping out from under his mother's stone. Carefully he stepped over the grave and picked the stem of purple bud, placing it gently in his breast pocket. Suddenly and ominously the bright afternoon sky became bleak, and the thunder rolled from a distance. He shrank in awe as the dark snarling sky shed a gloom upon the graves. He turned back down the trail to the wagon. He looked over at the brown, rolling fields—the gleaming plowshare stood alone, nosed into the softened earth.

Fastening the horse in front of the Outpost, he saw her going into the town lawyer's office. He wished he had the courage to stop and talk to her; instead, he turned to the swinging doors instead of heading for the general store. Supplies were the furthest thing from his mind. He was surprised to see the Outpost half crowded this early. He sat down at his lonely table and one of the "dancers" came over with a large mug of ale that he had always drunk. He asked her if she would get him a glass of water for his flower as he drew it from his pocket. She chuckled and said, "Jeff, you are the strangest...yet, there's something close about you."

"What do you mean, Jennie?"

"I'm afraid I don't know myself....I guess, I mean you're so darn gentle in a funny sort of way." She turned toward the bar, and came back shortly, immersing the flower in the glass. "There, but too bad Cressie won't get to see it." She fluttered her lashes. "Ranker's back." She disappeared behind the curtained exit to join the other girls preparing for their performance.

Jeff had noticed the tall man at the bar talking and drinking with another gunman, but it did not alarm him in the least but for the exception he felt was ominous for Cressie. However, Ranker finally caught Jeff in his vision and left his drinking partner to amble over to Jeff's table. He stopped short and widened his stance ominously and moved his hand toward his gun. "I hear you've been seeing Cressie? There must be lemming blood in your ape veins, homesteader. I haven't settled the score for you sneaking up behind me; now, I come back and hear you've been after my property."

Jeff stared up at him vacantly. "Nobody's property to nobody, Ranker. And who I see is not your business." Jeff's hands slid off and under the table.

He snarled and laid his hand on the handle of his gun, "Cressie is my business."

Jeff writhed a wide nose. "If you mean she's your concern, then you have a dumb way of showing it the last time I saw you with her."

Ranker eyes squinted as his hand gripped the handle of the revolver. "Yeah, the last time…is why I'm here."

"Too long ago to worry about it, Ranker. It wouldn't be a good thing for you to draw that gun here. The marshal wouldn't like it. He's strict about that."

Ranker removed his hand and tipped back his hat. "I don't need it for you." He reached over the table and grabbed Jeff's lapels. Jeff felt his jacket rip up the back. Jeff gripped Ranker's hands and squeezed. Ranker let out a yell and released his hold and backed off. "By God, you *are* a gorilla!" he said, rubbing his hands, smarting from the powerful crush. Then quickly he grabbed the ledge of the table to tilt it up and over onto Jeff who quickly caught it and reversed its momentum back to Ranker who had to back away to avoid the table crashing down on his toes. He drew his gun, but Jeff jumped over the table on edge and body-slammed Ranker to the floor. He took Ranker's gun and skimmed it along the floor.

Suddenly the brass band blared and the girls entered on cue while Jeff scrambled to look for the crocus. The girls laughed as they danced by Ranker flat on his back. Then Cressie came through the curtain and gasped momentarily in seeing Ranker laid out, knowing full well what it meant as her eyes tried to scan for Jeff, but she had to fall into the opening dance routine. When the brass subsided and the girls moved in and round the tables to hustle the men to buy them drinks, Cressie saw Jeff emerge from the floor with a flower in his hand and then move to another table a good distance from Ranker. Jeff had put the flower in another glass of water. She vented relief and wanted desperately to go to him, but the pianist banged out her honky-tonk cue and she began to sing. Her delivery was coarse and untrained, but it was suitable for the rugged clientele, and the scanty costume she wore. Jeff was transfixed—he could not get himself to cover his eyes. He thought there was never a sweeter voice, nor a more beautiful vision as she sang and slinked from table to table. Her heavy perfume dispersed the smoke-filled air and defied the thick odor of beer and whisky. She projected a phantasmal beauty as she snaked about and coiled and stretched to every drunken howl and edgy paw, for at this moment she was queen, not just a cheap dance hall girl. To Jeff she was a goddess who was the causality of his sleepless nights and lotus-eating days. He thought, "Such thrills ain't turned up in soil!"

She undulated round but kept her distance from both Jeff and Ranker as she sang:

> Along the vineyard trail
> The bursting grapes enjoy
> While lovers fife and rail,
> To the baton and lyre boy.
> Still, Love is all there is
> Withstanding nature's lechery
> But even this will fizz
> When Bacchus plants his treachery!

But then she soared above this foreboding lyric and looked softly across the spacious hall at Jeff:

> Farewell O darkened nature, death!
> And on the hardened breast from winter's sting
> Sing and dance to the lyre's skip of spring
>
> While sowing in the crust love's regaining
> breath.

Jeff, so arrested, wrapped his big hand round the glass containing the crocus; the glass shattered; his hand bled—an outlet for his pining heart. The brass band blared again and all the girls gathered including Cressie to the opposite end where long tables were left unoccupied for them to jump on and dance freely. Men by droves stumbled up to the tables for a closer view and within arms-reach.

Ranker finally lifted himself from the floor and staggered over to the bar. He uttered to the younger gun-slinger, "That thick bumpkin is one strong son of an ape! It's like he's anchored to the floor." He got the bartender's attention and pointed to a large earthen mug and the a special wine cask behind the bar. The bartender took it down and filled it with the rich red wine.

"Why didn't you gun him down?" his friend asked. "I wouldn't mess around any other way with a powerhouse aborigine like him."

"Oh, that will come; you can bet on it.…But right now I got to get the satisfaction of beating the tar out of him." He slid the mug over to him. "Take this to him. Tell him it's my symbol of truce. This stuff would put a lion to sleep."

"I don't know—what if he starts with me? So help me I won't hesitate to gun down the savage."

"No, chance …sure looks savage, but he's not the kind …too dumb," Ranker assured him. "Besides, the old marshal will be on you like a young cat."

Jeff had reached into his pocket and was staring at the ring when the gunman placed the wine before him. Instinctively he placed the ring on his pinky tip and drank down the wine in one phantom moment. Within an instant another mug was before his drooping eyes and he sucked it dry. He finally looked up but not to see the source of the wine but to look for the source of his new life. He could barely distinguish Cressie from the other dancers on the tables. The wild orchestration rolled over his ears like a crashing wave. He imagined Cressie a mermaid splashing about on the deck of a submerged ship and he with a trident in hand rode a dolphin above her as she looked up with a bubbly smile. Her beautiful hair turned to seaweed and from buoyancy curled upward, tickling his feet. High above loomed a nervous shark.

He looked over at the bar. There Ranker was staring at him with a mocking smile. Jeff dropped his eyes to the ceramic mug: in soft relief a pastoral scene of a vineyard spangled purple against a clear blue sky; swiveling it round to the other side revealed the same scene with winter's gray sky and lying on barren field was a maiden whose breast was being ravaged by a black clawing paw. Seized by the image and strong wine, he dashed the mug to the floor and shrieked over the noisy band with a jungle cry of a distant past. He rushed over, breaking into her dance; the music locked in the heavy air. He grabbed her arm.

She felt the sweat and tackiness of his bloody hand. "Jeff, what are you doing? Go sit down and behave yourself." She struggled to break loose.

"I ain't never..." he slurred; " 'Cause ...the devil's back ...and you ain't doin' no more dancin' for him ...and the rest of them, too!"

"Oh, Jeff, for your sake, please leave—I'm frightened....No telling what he'll do! Please ..."

"No! Me and you both are goin'—pronto." He pulled her along to the swinging doors, midst jeers and cheers. No one, however, dared challenge him; for they had never seen this likable oddity in such a rage.

At the doors she stepped in front of him and held him fast to protest. Looking up at him with apprehension and then glancing quickly over at the bar, she pleaded, "Let me go, Jeff, you poor, darling soul. You're drunk! You never drank too much before! Don't you understand? He'll kill you!"

He squinted through the blur; her endearing concern convinced him all the more that she was not what she seemed to others. Then her face contorted as she looked over his shoulder. The last thing he heard was her cry.

Ranker had come from behind and smashed a jug over Jeff's head. Jeff slumped to the floor as Cressie, shocked but caring, could not break his heavy fall, hurling her out the doors. She screamed and reentered, dropping to the floor to cuddle him in her arms. She looked up at the wild clientele to intercede, but they were held in check by the drawn gun of Ranker's confederate. Ranker pushed her to the floor and grabbed the unconscious Jeff by his lapels and dragged him through the doors and out onto the deck and kicked him into the muddy street.

Cressie noticed a subdued glitter on the boot-scuffed floor. She picked up the bronze ring. For a moment her eyes followed the continuous trail marks of dispersed sawdust from dragging Jeff; under the lower plane of the swinging doors she saw a flash of light in the street. She struggled to her feet and pushed out the doors into lightning, silhouetting Ranker on the steps looking over the squirming body in the mud; she heard thunder rumbling overhead. Another flash and thirty feet away a tree cracked thrice under the bolt before crashing against the lean-to over the walk. She squeezed the ring in her palm and looked up at Ranker, her eyes burning into his. She slashed his face with her long finger-nails, then skirted round him to head for Jeff. She knelt by his side—Ranker's protests and black silk-stockings muddied, notwithstanding—and tore off feathers from her bodice and wiped his grimy face. From behind came an abrupt tug on her long hair now drenched and she fell back on her haunches. A knife's edge was at her throat; she closed her eyes and thought only of Jeff's safety, lying helpless with this madman loose.

"You so much as squirm and I'll cut your head off. You're not worth the trouble—a bitch that has feelings for that animal—why, you probably slept with him! I wouldn't even let you breathe on me now!" He then relentlessly cut off her hair near the scalp. She winced when in spots she could feel the blade scraping her scalp. The last handful he threw onto Jeff's face. Ranker laughed grotesquely. "That and a little flour paste will help hide that ugly mug for you." He turned and went back into the Outpost; he was disappointed in himself that he lost the will for final vengeance. Actually the faster gun of the marshal was in the back of his mind.

Jeff opened his eyes to lightning flashes and could feel the raindrops tickling his flat simian nose. He heard the familiar grinding of his rear wagon wheel. "Won't never get around to fixin' it." he thought absently, and then he groaned from pain in his head. He felt his head; it was bandaged. Struggling to sit up, he turned round painfully and to his surprise saw Cressie up in the driver's seat. "What in blazes happened, Cressie, what am I doin' here…and what's more, what are you doin' ?…" he questioned like a wide-eyed lad as he attempted to climb up on the seat. "I was suppose'ta be doin' the rescue."

"Now you just stay put. I promised the marshal I'd look after you. Now lie back down." She reached back and patted his beard.

"But the last thing I remember is you not wantin' to do nothin' with me." He scratched his wet, muddy beard. "And what's the marshal got to do with it?"

"He ran Ranker out of town and probably saved our lives, that's what." She check-reined the horse onto the trail of the farm.

He rubbed his head. "Oh, yeah, Ranker—I guess I didn't do you no favors. I sure got caught off guard."

"Well, now that it's over and if Ranker does stay away, I'm glad you forced the issue," she said matter of factly.

He felt dizzy and settled back; the moon was breaking with the clearing sky unraveling the trail to home. He took one more look at Cressie to see that he wasn't dreaming. At first he thought the soft reflection round her head was her silken hair but then realized it was a satiny scarf. He had never seen her beautiful hair covered before; then he realized it was obviously because of the rain. He was about to rest his head when he jumped up again and looked up at her. "Why did the marshal ask you to take me home?"

She reached down at him. His headache jumped from his head when he saw the ring on her finger. "Because I wanted to. Besides, you told me my job at the Outpost was over."

Half emerging from his stupor, he queried, "I did?...Why, yeah, that's for darn sure."

"So that's why I'm here and to see that you will be okay....Well, of course, you're okay at least when the swelling goes down and the wound heals. I'm really here because ...well, I like you, Jeff, you're not the like the others."

He said with a slight chuckle, "That's for darn sure."

Ranker's toady, Tex, rode into town at noon. His hat was tipped to cover his face. The street was fairly empty at lunch hour. He tied up his mount under the sign *Sam Hull, attorney at law*. A short, heavy set man opened the door eagerly and waved him inside. The confederate looked over both shoulders before entering. The attorney assured him, "Don't worry about the marshal he takes forever to eat his lunch."

"Just the same, I sure don't want to meet up with his guns," he said taking another look up the street before closing the door behind him.

The attorney laughed. "He's the best man, all right." He then snickered.

"You best have something important on your mind, Sam, for me to chance coming here....I don't want to fight my way out of here. That damn marshal's too quick for me," Tex said with a worried look as he sat down by the desk.

Sam grinned. "Well, now, Tex, that's quite an admission—and with the marshal in his waning years at that!...You shouldn't be carrying a gun then. You know how the old tiger is about sidearms in town....Anyway, it's important, all right—the sum total of which is five thousand dollars."

Tex whistled, leaned back on the chair and agreed, "That's a heap important. Start talking."

Hull paced behind his desk. "There's a weird old miner that comes into town every now and then to get drunk and buy himself some time with one of the girls at the Outpost. He really wants Cressie, but between looking over her shoulder for Ranker and the fact she never liked the old man, she wouldn't sleep with him for any price."

Tex's chair slammed back on all fours. "What this got to do with us? Ranker's through with that redheaded bitch. We're doing fine in the next town with our card games. And no marshal with no peace-keeping ideas."

"Five thousand in gold would take an awful lot of winnings," the lawyer reminded him. "Hear me out: The codger some time ago came in here to have me draw up a new will, since his only kin died, and made Cressie beneficiary of his holdings."

Ranker's man leaned forward with interest. "So now the old man's dead, eh?"

"No, not yet."

"Well, what in tarnation..."

The attorney sat down behind the desk. "That's where you and Ranker come in; but it has to be made to look like an accident."

"What good will that do?"

"Everything. You see, the old man stipulated if she marries, unless it's him, before his death, the will is void."

"Shucks, where's the problem; no one's going to marry that whore. Then all we've got to do is take it from her when the old man kicks off. In fact, how can we track him down?"

"Now you're cooking, but remember, the old coot made sure the will is void if he's a victim of foul play, so it can't look like murder....There's another matter. She's planning to marry that damnable homesteader. Can you imagine?— she doesn't care about the money."

Brash Tex let out a horse laugh. "The gorilla! I don't believe it!"

"It's true; she's gotten some kind of religion in her bones now," Hull conjectured.

He laughed again. "That ain't religion, man! There's a word for that kind of animal worship, ain't there?"

"Regardless, it means the end of a small fortune for all of us, if Ranker doesn't do something."

"Why don't I just rob this old miner?" The rambunctious gunman queried.

"Can't....He's a wise old owl. He's been shipping the gold to a bank in St. Louis where his kin had lived. He wouldn't even trust our bank."

Tex removed his hat and scratched his head. "Why you tellin' this now. Why not sooner when me and Ranker was still here?"

The lawyer flushed and became uneasy. "Well, I thought…that is,…"

The gunman grimaced. "So you wanted it close to your vest but got a nervous heart, eh?"

"Maybe, but I'm not a violent man," he admitted, wringing his hands. Actually Hull had earlier visions of Cressie accepting him after the old miner died. Hoping to be in a position eventually to embezzle her fortune.

"Well, no doubt about us gettin' cold feet," Tex bragged.

The lawyer got up and went to the window. He was astonished by the strange procession outside. "Speaking of violence, you better lay low. There's more than the marshal you have to worry about." Hull directed him to the window.

Curious, Tex bolted from the chair and joined him at the window. The new couple rode by in a fancy new carriage that Jeff had ordered through the little salesman. Cressida in a new, modest dress sat straight, serene and delicately held the reins. Some tresses now were easing out from under her bonnet. Jeff, in spite of his bowed spine, strained his short, thick neck to be on a plane with his source of exultancy. His narrow eyes glanced at her marvelous profile as though in disbelief that after six weeks from her ordeal she was still with him.

The gunman guffawed with bravado and patted his holster. "Yeah, I know he is one strong son of an ape, but no match for this."

"Just the same, Tex, don't get involved, now," Hull warned, "or you'll mess up our plan. Don't underestimate the ape be as cautious with him as with the marshal. You better go and tell Ranker to get a move on."

"Shucks, I can handle a bumpkin.…When is this fantastic event takin' place, anyway? Not that I believe it's really goin' to happen."

"In a month."

"Hell, Cressie'll long be gone before that," the young gunman snorted.

"No, according to the marshal, who's going to be best man, it's serious."

Tex snorted again. "That's a laugh—best man to an ape!" He beat his chest and jumped up and down.

"Cut the antics! I tell you it's happening. We can't chance that Cressie will change her mind."

"Maybe the ape'll will change its mind—if it had one," Tex scoffed.

"Will you be serious, if she marries we lose."

The coming wedding raised brows in town: Some thought it was a hoax and that Cressie was up to something; others out of a cultist whim hoped it were in fact true because they looked upon Jeff as a freak of nature and they would love to see the actual event of Beauty and the Beast materialize. On the other hand, there were a few who perceived in Jeff a harmless, affable man who was the savior of Cressie's soul. Regardless of her adult behavior, most liked Cressie since her childhood until she joined the rowdy and infamous Western Outpost. For the most part, however, she was still the personable little Cressie on Sundays when the Outpost was transformed.

She had been an abandoned guttersnipe and most took her to heart in the early years—particularly Jeff's mother who wanted to adopt her, but the town officials would not allow such a pretty child to become a member of the ugliest family the west had ever seen. To them it was worse than white parents adopting a half breed or Indian child. Nonetheless, the mother often cared for her, seeing to it that she did not go hungry and reserved a corner of the barn for her to sleep. Cressie was appreciative, but because she was left to the tumbleweed by her widowed mother she was determined never to be dependent. When the attorney, Hull, informed her of the old miner's will, she saw this as an opportunity to become truly independent, knowing that the old man's lungs would soon put him in the grave.

Her attitude changed, however, when Ranker dealt her the final blow of humiliation. She realized that her livelihood directly or indirectly was dependent upon the worst kind of men; and when she did come into modest wealth, she would still be their target—even more so. She was now convinced that there was no escaping women's dependence on men in the hard environment.

Jennie one day rode out to the farm and told Cressie she was looking forward to being the "maid" of honor. Jennie, unlike Cressie, had no inner thoughts that the relationship with Jeff was unnatural. She observed how kind and gentle Jeff was and believed it was the best thing for Cressie. In fact, Jennie herself was intrigued by Jeff. She had long ago rid herself of the "sideshow" syndrome of this man whom she could now look upon and readily respond to the good in him. Her experiences with the wolves at the Outpost convinced her that they — even the dashing and handsome — were basically pigs. She said to Cressie that had she not known that Jeff adored her, she herself would want a life with him. "After all," she said, "mothers who have ugly children don't drown them." She reasoned that the natural attraction of their own flesh and blood precludes such action. And why not carry that to another level: "why just kin—and love people for the good in them? And Jeff is certainly good." Belatedly Cressie began to understand.

It was this frame of mind that gradually led to her acceptance of Jeff as a man and lover, rather than simply her lasting friend. The simple but noble perception she had of his exterior since childhood seeped into her psyche which leaned to deducing that if she could love him as a brother because he was always good to her, then why not as a husband? Is it not preferable to love someone who truly loves than to pay the price of appearances? Besides, she reasoned that it was more than gratitude—and certainly not pity—that she retained her relationship with him all these years. She had always sensed that the gentleness about him sprung from a truly loving spirit that contradicted his craggy appearance. And now alone with him these two months, the cragginess dissolved, leading her to believe that in her weak moments her perception of him belonged to the town's perception, not hers.

Cressida's early childhood memory of Jeff's mother awakened. In living with him on the farm, each morning she cut fresh flowers to arrange a lovely bouquet for the mother's grave. She was not as elaborate with the father's grave but she did not forget him. One morning when she was fixing flowers at the grave site, Jeff walked up the hill while admiring her bob glistening in dawn's jealous light. But he could never look upon her new hair without a feeling of rage. The dark image of Ranker loomed and he stopped in his tracks to clench his fists and pound his chest. He continued up the trodden path and in her glorious presence he became tranquil in forgetting, if not forgiving.

"You know, Jeff, I've often wondered if I could fuss over my own mother's grave. I hate her so that I doubt it."

"You mustn't feel that way, Cressie," he said softly kneeling beside her. "She loved you, I'm sure. Things happen we don't understand. I know she had a good reason. She could've been very sick—maybe even contagious and felt it best to free you."

She chuckled. "Oh, Jeff, you're just too darling. Only you would think of that." She hugged him. "Let us pray that our marriage, gesturing to the tombstones, will be as loving as theirs." In silence they prayed. A warm breeze whistled in and out of young applauding foliage in the fields; low in the sky cawed a crow as it darted across the pink sun. They went back down the path hand in hand. It was now so natural to Cressida to hold his massive sweaty hand and to look up at his leathery adoring face.

Inside the house, Cressida—just days before the wedding—was opening gifts from neighboring well-wishers. She was like a child on Christmas morning, which she had never experienced. She held up a flimsy nightgown from Jennie. Jeff smiled sheepishly, then looked the other way. She laughed. "After all this time, you're still shy! I love it!" She thrust her jaw and pecked him on his craggy beard. "Ooh, I must trim that for you." She went back to the packages on the table and stood a long one on edge. "This is just what we need, Jeff. I want you to hang it for me, so you can keep your beard trim all the time."

"What is it?" he asked scratching his beard now that she made him conscious of it.

"Why, it's a mirror, silly."

He lowered his head. "I don't want it for me....I know, you should have one....I'm sorry, I didn't think of one all this time. I was being selfish."

"I've done just fine with my hand mirror....Really, now, you must get over this, Jeff. I just wish there were a mirror that could reflect your heart, then you would see how handsome you are."

"You are the one with the heart, Cressie."

She began to strip the paper from the mirror, then carried it to the wash stand. "There, now you won't leave soap suds in your beard."

"Gosh, Cressie,...I don't know if I'm ready to look at myself every morning —bad enough I have to see my reflection in the basin." He scratched his beard again.

"Oh? But it's all right for me to look at you each morning, eh?"

They both had a hearty laugh, then he went for a hammer and nail.

Their camp on the other side of the ridge, Ranker and his companion from a hillside high above the cornfield, looked down at the farmhouse in Jeff's vale. "What are we waiting for?" Tex aired impatience, "Let's go get her!"

"I can handle it myself, Tex. I want the smelly animal to get his hopes up a while longer. Then I want to see him pant in pain when I take her away before he had a chance to lay a hand on her."

Tex snickered, "Reckon you got new strings in your banjo, Ranker. Before you were sure he was into her....And now, hell, they've been living together alone for two months!"

"Living *off* him, you mean," Ranker corrected him.

"Anyway, keep your head; you've got a train to St. Louis to catch," said Tex. "This is supposed to be business only."

"Who's running this?...I know, and you have an appointment with the miner and see that you do it right and soon. If the old man gets wind of Cressie leaving town, he'll change the will in a hurry. So saddle up while I take care of my end."

While he hung the mirror, Cressie noticed he never once ventured looking at himself. He quickly turned to put the hammer away. She stepped in front of him; grasped his shoulders and turned back around. "Now, look at yourself, Jeff, and see what I see—never mind what others see. It is what I see that counts."

"Aw, Cressie, I know what you see."

"No, you don't....Now look." His eyes slowly turned askant and focused on the reflection of her beautiful smile. "See, it's not so bad now is it?"

"No, your smile is beautiful."

She slapped his shoulder and pouted at the mirror. "I can't be in the reflection all the time. You must learn to see only you in it. You're a big boy now."

"It would be a lot easier for me if you were in it always."

She laughed. "Oh, Jeff, I take it back it. You're still a little boy." She sighed and propositioned, "Okay, I promise for a week I shall always be in the reflection but no longer than that....Now, you stay put while I get the scissors. And I want you to follow what I do in the mirror so that next week you can trim it yourself."

As he indeed watched her every move in the mirror, he couldn't believe how slim and narrow she was compared to the immensity of his torso. He flinched, thinking about what they would do on the wedding night. He was fearful of crushing her. He prayed to his god that he would be gentle.

"There! See how good you look!" she said as she stepped back to admire her work.

"Yes, Cressie, maybe I do look good—all because of you and I just don't mean the beard....It's 'cause you make me feel I'm good." Outside the cows and sheep seemed restive. "I'd better go see what that's about out front," he said. He hesitated for a moment—still unable to rid himself completely of his public figure even with her—but then kissed her on the cheek.

"Hurry back,...my husband soon to-be," she said softly. He closed the door behind him and she added, "Yes, my darling, come back."

Ranker stole into the house from the back. She checked a scream. "How dare you!"

"Speaking of daring, you're putting on some act here," he snarled.

"It's not an act. I demand to know what you are doing here."

"Maybe it's time for the barber again," he snickered.

"You're a comical stampede." She laughed nervously.

"You won't be laughing if you don't pack up now and come with me."

She fell back against a table while gasping. "You can't be serious!"

He grinned diabolically, "More so than you are with that animal you're keeping on leash." He stepped toward her.

"Don't speak of him that way!" she chided. "Take one more step and I'll scream for Jeff."

"He's a dead man if you do." He adjusted the gun in his holster.

She hid her fear. "You're forgetting the marshal. He'll see that you hang."

"We'll be long gone from his territory. A posse can't chase a train."

"Train?" She stroked her cheek. "So that's it. Sam Hull opened his big mouth." Then she chuckled nervously. "But that won't do you any good. When the old man finds out, there's no beneficiary, you buffoon."

"He won't find out. Tex is seeing to that now." He laughed with a vicious twang.

Her face contorted. "Oh, my God, you're worse than I ever dreamed!"

"Then you'd better come now or you'll see worse."

Her eyes filled up; she lowered them to the floor where Jeff spent hours laying it over with polished planks to protect her dainty feet. "I ...I just can't leave him; it would break his heart. Oh, Ranker, just go; you can have the money when the time comes. You just can't kill that poor old mixed up man —murder nullifies the will."

"That wouldn't do any good if he lives and you marry this tailless primate."

"I promise I won't marry Jeff. Just go!" she pleaded.

"Gotten kind of religious in your pasture days, eh?...No, Cressie, I can't, don't and won't trust you, nor the old man. So get packed now or come as you are." He slid a hand inside his coat. "I have the will. Besides, I know you're scheming, too. I know you can't love anybody but me." He reached out and pulled her into his arms. He spit wet kisses on her neck. "Oh, how I miss your hair. I was a damn fool to cut it."

She squirmed and struggled midst sighs of weakness. "Don't do this!...Oh, Rank,...dear,...how could you?" She drew up her hands and urged his lips to hers as she hungrily opened her mouth and he wedged in his tongue. Suddenly deep from her heart a spirit cried and she pulled away her sucking lips while reaching for his gun.

His hand quickly circled her wrist. "Bitch!" He pushed her and she went sprawling over the table. "If you don't want a double killing here right now, you best move pronto! I'd like nothing better than to kill both of you—the hell with the marshal and the money!"

She struggled to her feet and closed her eyes. Momentarily she uttered inaudibly to her inner self, "It's over; I knew it couldn't be true." Her eyelids parted and she stared coldly at him. "We'd better go now before he returns." She removed the ring and gently placed it on the table.

Jeff flung open the front door just as Cressie was putting on her cape. Seeing Ranker struck him dumb even though he saw a horse out back. Then he turned his eyes quizzically to her. Cressie concealed her anxiety with a cold front. "I can't go on deceiving you like this. I'm deeply sorry, Jeff, it was cruel of me. But you know what I am."

"It's not true!" he cried desperately. "I know what you are now—with me. You are no longer the other one."

"No, Jeff, people don't change. I still love him—in spite of what he did." Her eyes dropped to the floor as did his.

"Sure, gorilla, she just needed a place to hide out till her hair grew back," Ranker broke in with a laugh.

Jeff raised his head, clenched his fists and started toward Ranker who quickly drew his gun. Cressie gasped and stepped in Jeff's path, clinging to him. "No, Jeff, you mustn't! It's not worth it. *I* am not worth it....Please, Jeff, again I'm so sorry, but the minute he walked in here I knew I still loved him, strange as it may seem to you. Do you understand, Jeff? All these weeks with you and I missed *him.* Yes, Jeff, I still love Ranker, not you!" She beat her fist into his barrel chest. "Do you understand what I'm saying? I missed *him,*" she became hysterical, "*Ranker* I missed, *Ranker* I love!"

Jeff's rage limped; he bowed his head and turned away from them. "I'm just an old fool. I guess, I always knew....Should'a tried for the mail bride route." He said tremulously, "Go! Go now,...please!"

Through tears Cressie saw his big hands, her fleeting comfort, flexing, then move up trembling to cover his face. She heard like a distant moan from beneath his hands. She held a sheer scarf to her breast, then let it fall at his feet. She turned to Ranker. "Put that gun away." With a scowl, he complied. She took nothing but a pressed iris from a book. They left.

Pounding hooves dissolved as the crushing pounding of his heart increased. Left in the terrifying emptiness, Jeff reached down to pick up the scarf. He sat down at the hearth and peered through the thin material at the faint embers from the fire the night before. Her image garbed in her wedding dress rose from the smoky embers. She was rustling through his cornfield, long beautiful red hair emulating the wind swept veil. Then a whirlwind touched down leaving in its wake bent stalks. Wrapped in wet corn silk was a corpse invaded by flies and its maggots. He pulled himself up and staggered to the table. He fondled the ring for a moment, then flung it at the mirror, cracking it. He went out the door to visit the grave site.

Jeff returned to the hard-working, lonely reality without Cressida. He never gave up hope, however. Every evening after his supper he would drive into town in her carriage to meet the train, unrealistically looking for her to be on it. Although he had to pass by the Western Outpost, he would never stop in. Jennie soon learned of this ritual and would stand outside and wave to him; he would tip his hat but never stop to talk. Weeks flowed into fall. In spite of the long hours of harvest, he nonetheless would continue to meet the train and Jennie would still be there waving to him.

Occasionally, he thought of dropping in on the marshal and have a chat but never did.

Months flowed into early winter. This evening he felt it his duty to stop by and see the marshal who had always been so kind and helpful, and for another reason. After the marshal commiserated for a while, he told Jeff of the old miner's death. "Seems he fell into one of his old mine shafts and cracked his head," the marshal said, echoing the unoffical report. Gabe who's known him a long time discovered him."

"I've seen him at the Outpost; he was always there. It seemed to bother Cressie. Yet all he ever did was ogle her. Harmless though…poor old man."

"I'm not so sure about that. I never liked the old buzzard. There was somethin' strange about him—somethin' in his eyes that could draw a snake out of its nest. You shoulda seen the mean look on his face, though cold dead. And when Gabe lifted his body onto the pack horse, he said he weighed a ton—choice nuggets strapped to his legs. But I don't believe he fell. I think Ranker had something to do with it. Still can't figure how the death certificate got to St. Louis so soon—Hull, too, I reckon was in on it. You know, Ranker left his young gun-slinger behind."

Jeff leaned forward on the chair. "Uh, when did you see *him*?"

"Oh, the deputy located him some time in the fall when he dropped off supplies for him. Gabe and he go way back."

"Uh, no, I meant the gunman."

"Oh,…not for a good while. I lost track of him. But I know he was still in the hills," the marshal said confidently. "But why …did you see him?"

"Uh,…I …but why would Ranker want to do that?" Jeff asked.

"Reason enough …same as why he took off with Cressie."

"Cressie!…I don't understand," Jeff heaved.

"The will …seems the old man had her in her will. That is, if she didn't marry." The marshal had been hesitant about informing him, thinking it would confuse him even more.

Jeff tipped back his hat and rubbed his low forehead. "Then that means she didn't go with him because she loved him; she went because of the money!" His eyes brightened. "Maybe now she'll come back."

"Hold on now, Jeff; even if you're right, it doesn't make a whole lot of difference putting the money before her love for you. Besides, if she did feel that way, she didn't need Ranker."

"Maybe she thought I'd get mad and hurt her," he deduced simply.

"You hurt someone, much less Cressie?" The marshal laughed. "There'd be diamonds in the old man's hill, too, before that ever happened. No, Jeff, you couldn't be violent with anybody—except Ranker."

Jeff slowly nodded, then his eyes distended and he shook his head. "No, marshal,…the kid you mentioned—Ranker's second gun. I caught him in my house, digging under my new floor where I hide my money. I hit him over the head with a poker. When he came to, I asked him how he come to know where my money is. He told me Cressie told him. I went mad, not believin', and shook the devil out of him; then he drew his gun and I had to knock him out again—but not hard enough, I'm afraid. I went to the barn to fetch the load-wagon to take him here for you to lock him up, but he high-tailed it. So you see, marshal, I'm not so peaceable—because I went after him and killed him with my shot-gun. You can put me in jail now. I got his body on the rig."

The marshal almost fell back off his chair behind the desk. "Jeff, he broke into your home! You had every right to take the law in your own hands."

"But I didn't kill him because of that but 'cause of what he said about Cressie!"

"And did Cressie know where you hid the money?"

"She was the only one who knew."

"So?"

"I feel bad because he must a told me the truth; yet I killed him."

"But then again why didn't *she* take it herself when she had plenty of chances to when she was with you? No, Jeff, I don't think she would've told where the money was unless made to."

"Oh, no, you think Ranker is still being cruel to her?"

"Ranker is Ranker."

"Then that's why you think she went with him?…No choice?" His heart pounded. "God, I wish I knew where she was!" he cried, shaking his head and staring at the floor. The marshal looked away. Then Jeff asked, "But how does the old miner fit in?"

"Ranker gets him killed; Cressie gets the money and he gets it from her."

"Takes it, you mean!" Jeff buried his face in his hands and moaned. The marshal went outside, checked the body, then sent a young lad riding by on his pony to fetch the undertaker. He returned to Jeff.

He put his hand on Jeff's back, still hunched over as Jeff absently stared at the floor. "You blew one big hole in him, Jeff."

Jeff jerked his head. "I didn't want to, marshal; but when I caught up with him; he drew his gun again."

"I know. That kind lives by the gun, but think they ain't ever gonna die by it…especially the young ones like Tex," the marshal said, lifting him up by the arm. "Why don't you have a stiff drink at the Outpost while I tend to the body? Forget about all this and then go home."

"Not just yet. Got the train to meet," Jeff said, moving to the door. "I reckon you ain't gonna arrest me, eh?"

The marshal smiled, shaking his head, and sat down and rocked back on the chair. "You know, Jeff, you got to forget Cressie. She ain't ever coming back. She's a rich woman now—that is, if Ranker lets her live."

"Marshal, don't say that, please. He must care somethin' for her. And if she does…love him, he'd just hafta let her live. If I knew where she was, I'd see to it that he respects her."

"If I learn where she is, I ain't tellin' ya.…Look, Jeff, why don't you take up with little Jennie? I tell you, she really likes you. She'd fill your loneliness."

"Yeah? An old ugly ape like me?"

"Now, don't you start believing this mean old taunt'n town. Cressie didn't think so. Why shouldn't Jennie see you for what you really are?"

Jeff pulled on the brim of his hat. "Yep, maybe so. She waves to me every night, you know." The marshal nodded. Jeff added, "Maybe some day I'll give up on hopin' she's a-comin' back." He eased the door open. "I'll just walk over to meet the train and come back for the wagon."

Jeff headed out the door. He glanced briefly at the gunman's boot dangling off the edge. He headed up the covered walk. Jennie was standing there. He tipped his hat.

"You're not in the carriage now, Jeff. You have no excuse not to stop and chat with me," her eye-lashes fluttered while she spoke. But he observed with curiosity that they didn't flutter like they did during her routine at the Outpost—there was a little girl innocence now. He gazed longingly at her silky hair—not unlike Cressie's—though jet black it was tinged a burnt red in the sunset. The rage swelled up within when he thought of Cressie reduced to mutilated tassels. "Why don't you visit us anymore, Jeff?"

"I'm not much for drinkin', you know that, ma'am…uh, Jennie," he uttered, awkwardly, tugging on his belt.

She pouted. "I know that, but still, why can't you come in and see me once in a while. Are you still that crazy about Cressie that you don't know I exist?"

"No, Jennie,…Shucks, you're a …wonderful …a real sweet girl. You was always nice to me—not like most of the others in there. But you're so nice I hate to think ya goin' out with a clumsy ox like me. Gosh, I could break you you're so darn little and soft like."

She laughed. "I don't think so, Jeff. You didn't ever harm Cressie. She always said you were the most gentle of all the men she knew. I can see that because of the way you act. You're so darn nice and polite. Despite your size, you could never be rough. Why, except for that bully Ranker,

I never saw you get mean with anybody—not even those who were mean to you. No, Jeff, I'd feel safe in your hands, just as Cressie did."

"Gosh, Jennie, you're kinda like my ma. I don't mean…well, you know, you're so much prettier …I guess what I mean is that you sound like her—so nice and soft, like a little bird. I mean like ma who showed a nice feeling, you know, she was like, like, you know, real love-like."

"Jeff, maybe you take after her more than I do. She brought out the love in you.…Just as you're doing to me right now."

"Yeah? Really?…Oh, but what about Cressie? She'll be on this train.…I gotta feelin'."

She reached up and touched his face lightly and gazed in to his brightening eyes. "Jeff, you're so darling in your simpleness that it pains me. She's not coming back. And even if she wanted to, she couldn't."

"No, Jennie, she's gonna be on it!"

She lowered her eyes and said grimly, but softly, "Then I'll always be alone."

"No, Jennie, you can come live with us. I don't want you working here anymore, either."

"So I'm like a little sister to you, huh?"

"Yeah! Right, just like a kid sister! And we'll both be good to you, Jennie,…me and Cressie, you know that."

"Yes," she said sadly and turned to the swinging doors.

He called after her, "You get ready. We' re gonna stop by and take you home with us. Don't you forget now." She turned and smiled with a quizzical eye.

He headed for the station—his usual heavy stride became sprightly. The image of Jennie's smile lingered even though Cressie's stepping down from the train was in the forefront of his mind. He was certain now that she left because coerced, and perhaps she still had feelings for him. Turning the corner, he heard the train whistle and could feel the rumble under his feet. His heart skipped as the train thundered in.

Before it came to a halt and exhaled its steam, Ranker standing in the well saw Jeff and quickly, before Jeff saw him, ascended back up the steps and jumped off the other side of the train. Jeff looked into every window. The train of fewer than six cars was virtually empty. The train screeched to a stop; only a young couple got off and went directly to an awaiting carriage. Only one old lady climbed aboard. Jeff moaned disappointment but continued along, staring up at the dusty windows until he reached the caboose. He bowed his head, sighed and turned on his boot heels.

Down the line behind the engine the door to a freight car creaked open and a fresh pine box was slid to the edge. The old deputy rolled a flat cart up to the car. A trainman dropped down from the freight car and helped

Gabe, wearing his other hat, ease the long box onto the cart, then he climbed back up and closed the door.

The train started up again. Jeff trotted along side it, checking the windows again. He bumped into the baggage cart. "Watch out, idiot!" Gabe cried, then looked up. "Oh, it's you, Jeff....Mighty sorry about this."

Jeff looked at him perplexedly. "No, my friend, don't...I walked right into it."

The old deputy-station worker shook his head and smiled a little "At a time like this you apologize?...No, big fella." Gabe pointed to the box. "The body ... I'm really sorry. I know she meant so much to you."

Jeff's square jaw dropped. "What are you talkin' about, Gabe?"

"The body,...what else...and where's your rig?" He handed him the shipping papers. "Look, it's for you....That's why you're here...and been every night for as long as I can remember,...right?"

Jeff glanced at the papers. "Gabe, you know, I can't read. What's this box got to do with me?"

"Jesus, Jeff, you can't be that stupid!...This is Cressie!"

Jeff stepped back in shock. "No! No! It can't be!"

"Gosh, Jeff, I thought you knew."

"It's gotta be a mistake!" Jeff cried out. "Open it!"

"Now, don't go crazy on me. It's against the law—I'm a deputy too, you know."

Jeff felt the edges of the coffin and tried futilely to pry it open with his hands. "Get me a pinch-bar!"

"Jesus, you don't want to that! Get the undertaker," old Gabe pleaded.

"Get it, Gabe!" Jeff said menacingly.

The old man reached under the flat bed and pulled the crow-bar from a rack. "You shouldn't do this, Jeff....You don't know how long it's ..."

"I tell you it can't be, but I gotta know." He quickly pried it open and slid the lid down from the head end. Gabe gagged, covered his nose and swiveled round and bent over. Jeff howled as he stared down at what was once Cressie. His nose sensed no stench. Cressie could only smell like flowers. He touched the cold folded skeletal hands. He put his stubby finger in her open breast wound and sobbed. He withdrew his hand and dropped his head on the lid and cried.

The old man overrode his revulsion and ventured toward him to put a comforting hand on his shoulder. "Gee, Jeff, I'm really sorry that you had to find out this way." He muffled under his hand. Then he braved the decomposition by removing his hand from his nose and added, glancing obliquely into the coffin, "She was a sweet kid—no matter what others thought—that's how I always remembered her. Just a nice kid who had a hard life."

Jeff backed off from the lid; and gently pawed the old man's cap. "It didn't have to be." He reached into his pocket and drew out the ring. Carefully he freed her finger and slipped it on. He touched her hair; he was grateful that the curly ends were at least to her shoulders. He put the lid back on and with the back of the bar drove the nails back in. He put his hand on the old man's shoulder. "I've gotta go back for my wagon at the marshal's. You won't leave her alone?"

"No, Jeff, I'll be right here when you get back." Gabe fondled the coffin. "Many a time she used to hang around here. Many a night as a young'n, the poor thing slept here at the station. Yep, Cressie's like family. I won't leave her for a second."

An hour later Jeff and Jennie were driving out of town with Cressie's coffin. Sam Hull from the shadows beheld the broken driver and heard the coffin vibrating from the wobbly wheel, whirling an eerie cry:

> Bury your love so it'll rise;
> Hurry your love to the awaiting skies.

His face writhing from sweeping inner pain, the lawyer ran back up the street, muttering penitence, "My God, my God, what have I done!" He pushed his way through a group of cowhands coming out of the Outpost. One of them tripped him and Hull fell against one of the studs supporting the overhang. The cowboy laughed, whipping out his gun and firing dangerously close, splintering the stud.

Sam Hull scrambled under the swinging doors, and wormed along the grimy floor, crying: "Judas! Judas!" He picked up a dirty piece of bread and stuffed it in his mouth. He snaked toward the bar, lifted his palsied body, and shrilled to the bartender, "Well? What are you waiting for?" The bartender looked at him curiously. "The wine...the wine, you fool!"

Jeff was leaning on the shovel that tossed the last of the burial. Jennie clung to him. "This is a beautiful setting, Jeff. Cressie never had a home before. She has now,...and is at sweet peace ...as sweet as the corn that will grow down yonder next summer." She looked at the bottom of the trail where the marshal was dismounting and began walking up the path.

The marshal squeezed Jennie's hand, then put his arm round Jeff. "If it's any comfort to you, Jeff, at least you know now that she's not alone. Cressie's with two of the nicest people I ever met."

"Thanks, marshal. I'm sure ma and pa will take care of her."

"No doubt. Your ma finally has her daughter now."

"Gosh, that's right!" Then Jeff looked down at Jennie. "And another." He managed a smile. She clung to him even more. "It was nice of you, marshal, to pay Cressida a visit."

"I have two reasons for being here tonight. Rumors have it that Ranker was seen in town. I wanted to make sure he wasn't lurking here somewhere."

Jeff tossed the shovel and pushed Jennie away. His jaw and fists clenched.

Jennie cried out, "No, Jeff, please let it alone!"

"Jennie's right, Jeff; I'll handle him," the marshal agreed.

"No, marshal, this is my job....I just have to."

"Marshal, no, don't let him!" Jennie beseeched, clawing the marshal's vest.

"I can't, Jennie; I know how Jeff feels. I owe it to him for my dumbness in not killing the bastard before." The marshal glanced over at Jeff. "You be mighty careful; he's quick."

"Oh, marshal, how could you?" Jennie cried and ran down the path. The marshal's eyes followed her.

"Maybe you should leave it to me, Jeff. She's a good girl. I'd hate to see more sadness."

"No fear of that," Jeff assured him. "Yeah, Jennie's sweet, all right. And I sure don't want anything to happen to her. I gotta make sure of it myself."

"Two thousand and a closed mouth—that was the deal," said the tall man dressed in his usual black, head to boots, except for a red vest. He dug into a saddle bag slung over his shoulder and removed a bundle of cash on the lawyer's desk, which shook a small figurine of blind justice.

The bedraggled lawyer reached to steady it. With insomniac stare, Sam said ponderously, "No, Ranker, take it back; I don't want any part of the blood money."

Ranker grinned down at him. "And I thought lawyers were a realistic lot." Ranker without hesitation stuffed the cash back in the bag.

"Not when it comes to murder."

"Hell, Tex killing the old man didn't bother you."

"That was different. He was a worthless piece of trash."

"Oh?...And Cressie wasn't?" Ranker grinned. "What do you call a woman that lies down with animals?"

"Regardless, she was a work of art. Beauty shouldn't be destroyed. You had no right. She would've gladly given you the money if you let her go."

He suddenly thundered. "I did her a favor: she would've returned to him." His face writhed and his body shook.

"So? She meant nothing to you obviously."

"The idea of them together did mean something,...disgusting!" he groaned, still ruffled. Then he snapped out of it: "I thought we were clear about this. Here I am being honest by returning. I could've stayed and kept it all."

"You came back to see about Tex, thinking the old miner had more stashed away—I wasn't born yesterday—otherwise, I'd never see that cash." Then he laughed. "You'll never see Tex again."

"I'll find him."

Sam chuckled, then burrowed his forehead in the heels of his hands and whined compunction, "Why did you have to kill her?— it was totally unnecessary. She would have kept quiet—she never really wanted the old man's money, anyway." The lawyer looked up at Ranker. "She had a conscience, you know."

"Dangerous thing—conscience," Ranker countered curtly, looking down at the nervous hand of the lawyer softly tapping a large book on the desk. Ranker leaned over the desk and grabbed him by the throat. "I have a little conscience myself for your good deed; so you better leave town for good and keep your mouth shut. I don't want the marshal on my trail."

"No!" the lawyer stressed, "this town is my life and here I die." He got up and turned to the filmy window, gray in the dawn.

"Then you have your wish." From his holster he drew out his long-barrel Colt. He flipped it the air and caught it at the barrel end and stepped round behind the desk.

The lawyer winced when he felt Ranker grip the back of his collar. He knew—his lips quivering, then stretching to a smile as his eyes rolled up, "Cressie! Forgive…" He slumped forward from the crushing blow on the head. Ranker held on to him, and another blow splattered blood from out the skull. He let him fall to the floor. Ranker squatted and turned him over. The lawyer's lifeless eye stared up; the other rolled down his cheek.

Ranker left the office and swaggered calmly across the frozen waking, wheel-rutted street. Suddenly his hand moved to the bloody butt of his gun when he noticed in the morning's gray shadows, a wide-shoulder figure slumped in a wagon and cradling a shot-gun. Ranker quickened his pace when he recognized the homesteader who tipped back his rumply hat and stood up in the driver's deck. Ranker gripped the handle of his gun tighter and stopped several steps from the hitching post by his horse and stared suspiciously at the man, who bit off the end of a straw and spat it out of his heavy lips. "That's right, Ape man, spit it out. You got a reason for being here in town this early?" Ranker growled.

Jeff slowly gripped the gun-stock in his large hairy hand. "You know why," he said gruffly. Besides,…been here all night, waiting.

Ranker moved behind his horse and slowly drew out his gun as he focused on the shot-gun drifting in his direction. "Look here, oaf, you got it all wrong. Maybe a little prank, but that's about it—I didn't *have* to send her back to you, you know."

Jeff nodded in grimness. "I know I'm dumb, but not when it comes to you!" Jeff shot back with fire in his eyes. "A cruel joke to you....A broke heart wasn't enough.You had to stab my heart, too; but I'm glad you did."

Ranker smiled and chuckled. "My, my, you actually opened your package, eh?...Well, you see?...You got what you want, and I got what I wanted out of this town." He patted his saddle bag, then flung it over his steed's flanks. "You can breathe easy, ape man; I'm riding out of here." Ranker glanced over at the marshal's office.

With the shot-gun still hanging loose, Jeff responded angrily, "The only thing that counts in this world, you ain't got."

The tall man laughed. "Say, that's right. You got her now—forever." Ranker laughed again. "Dust finer than gold's—yep, human dust and a woman's at that!" He laughed hideously while reaching up for the saddle horn. The shot-gun jerked toward him; Ranker stepped into the stirrup and pulled himself up drawing his gun and firing in fluid motion. From the roar of the gun, the big draft horse jerked its head but Jeff had the rein secured to the brake handle. But Ranker's mount reared up, snaked and, sidled the trough. Ranker's second round went wild. Jeff twisted round momentarily as the first round nicked his arm. Unfazed, he steadied his bulky frame and fired both barrels to Ranker's head. Ranker was literally jolted from the saddle—his hat and gun flying; his right stirrup flew up; his foot slipped out and he soared five feet from the flank of his horse, his back landing up against the trough. His body quivered, his half-torn head rolled along the edge; his glassy eyes drawn to the slimy water glazed over with a sheet of ice. The homesteader calmly wrapped a kerchief round his bleeding arm, then gently wiggled the reins and the wagon headed out of town.

Having heard the shots, several townspeople ran to the scene and gathered round the body sitting in the frozen mud. The marshal with gun in hand, who had been observing from the swinging doors of the pub, started up the street. Nonchalantly he moved through the small gathering and kneeled beside the body. He signaled to old Gabe, now wearing his deputy hat. Gabe emerged from the crowd, hopped onto the walk and stopped a few stores away under the undertaker's sign. The Marshal stood up and watched the wagon edging out of town. He knew Jeff would seldom be seen again. Jeff's work here was finished: the sun shone golden on the homesteader's broad, round shoulders, but soon shadows would be behind him—only the sunny memories of Cressie would lie ahead.

The marshal picked up the saddle bag and whistled to himself when he saw all the cash. He knew Jeff wouldn't want any part of it; he thought to himself, "I'll put it in the bank for Jennie. They deserve it. They got a long life together."

The marshal waved away the gathering and headed back to the Western Outpost, wondering, now that Jennie was gone, too, who would make breakfast.

Prepare Ye The Way of The Lord

Santa seemed on every block. Life, color, light were everywhere belying the evening's dark, heavy sky. Caroling floated on snow flakes. Smiling shoppers were eying decorated windows as children were pressing against panes flaunting busy toys. Last minute shoppers were rushing into stores while others were rushing out on the way to the many things left to do at home. A thin woman, looking worn and clutching the lapels of her flimsy coat emerged from the bustling shoppers in whom she felt no affinity. She sneered at the last Santa tinkling for alms before she turned into a dark side street. She tightened her grip on the collar and seemed to sink into her coat as the snow lighted on her heavy makeup. The street barely acknowledged the approaching holiday but for a few windows from the tenements aglow with lighted wreaths. As she turned the corner an immense Christmas tree in the dooryard of a church illuminated a gold upon the falling snow.

Boys heavily scarfed and coated flung open the church door and immediately dug for frozen missiles and engaged in happy combat in front of the church. A clergyman followed and playfully threw a few snowballs himself, then shouted, "Off with you now and return at midnight with your angel voices."

The boys scampered off. Some brushed past her and beamed broadened cheeks as they wished her good cheers. She sunk deeper into her coat.

From the steps the clergyman waved to her and buoyantly said, "Merry Christmas, my child." She did not turn her head and quickened her pace into the darkened shadows of closed shops and headed for a neon light flickering on the far corner of this church street.

She descended the puffy steps of a café, which on any other night would be alive with beer and wine, song and dance. The door was stuck; with some hesitancy she pushed hard against the door. The gaily decorated wreath fell onto the wet rubber welcome mat in the vestibule. She hung the wreath back up carelessly. She noticed most chairs were stacked on tables. She brushed the snow from her coat and shook the flakes from her bleached hair and descended the two steps.

Crossing the empty dance floor, she sat up on a bar stool and eased out of her coat, revealing a red blotch on her neck and barely perceptible bruises on her shoulders. Mechanically she draped her red coat on the backrest of the stool as she stared into the mirror behind the bar. She snarled. Over the bar mirrors was a painting of silhouettes on a mountain against a backdrop of angry flames. Removing a compact from her handbag, she flipped up its mirror and brushed away the circles under her lifeless eyes with the heavy mix. From a crumpled pack she drew out a bent cigarette and let it hang from chapped lips. It was discomforting. She balanced the cigarette on the bar ledge and traced her mouth with lipstick. Digging deeper into her handbag she came up with a heavy, masculine lighter. Its top tipped back; she thumbed the wheel but it barely sparked. She spun the stool round the desolate, mocking tryst—faced the bar again and tapped the lighter on it. Leaning over a centerpiece of shiny holly to look down behind the bar, she broke the deadening air by blurting, "Bartender!" Tailed to this, wailed the start of Christmas music from a jukebox at the other end of the bar.

A youthful bartender reared up from behind the jukebox and rolled it back in its place. He brushed back his rather long brown hair and scratched his trim beard as he moved back behind the bar. Easing up to her with a warm smile. She flinched and fondled the lighter. "Good evening, Ma'am, and Merry Christmas to you," he said as his smile broadened. She squeezed her lighter.

"Give me a scotch on the rocks," she ordered bluntly. He chuckled and rolled his blue eyes as he turned to take down a tumbler. She tried the lighter again; the flint was gone. She watched the scotch splash over the ice, then looked up at him. His warm blue eyes splashed into her cold ones like soothing eye drops. She dug into her handbag.

"Oh, that's okay it's on the house Christmas, you know."

"No, I didn't know. But I wasn't going to pay for it, anyway," she said, pulling out an empty book of matches.

"My, you're as cold as your drink. You should have some egg-nog I made—might lift your spirit."

"Don't have any except the spirits in this glass." She pulled out of her bag a folded memo, looked at it, put it back and said, "A Ugo called for me." She snickered, "Original, anyway, get tired of John....I trust you're not him."

He laughed to hide his embarrassment. "No, but so-called Ugo mentioned he was expecting a visitor...should be back soon." He flashed a glare but then washed it away and reached in his pocket for a lighter similar to hers. He struck it and edged it toward the bent cigarette still hanging from her lips. She sucked on it as he lit it. "So tell me, little lady,...why?" he asked, looking at her with quizzical eyes that seemed to clear away the puffs of smoke. Her cigarette hand met her cheek and she looked up at him strangely not surprised by the question. "Seems to me you should be home with your family," he said softly but unable to subdue a trace of indignation.

Her eyes dropped to her drink; she tinkled it with the stirrer. The rough edges of the cubes were gone. "Don't have one— not sure I'd be home if I had a family."

"I can't believe that," he said with kindly assurance.

"Oh, I mean, if I were truly what I am."

"Family doesn't see you for what you *think* you are that's the strength of it."

She laughed absently. "You don't know my brother."

"Why don't you call him?"

"That's impossible; besides, I am what I am." She scowled.

"You could try to be what you feel you ought to be," he urged graciously, trying not to sound self-righteous.

"Only the strong can do that," she said with a sigh. "There's no real privacy in my line of work—tough to grapple with the past in starting anew."

"Oh?...Then you *have* tried?"

"No."

"You could try a new town."

"This is a new town. It follows you."

"Sure, you don't take it with you?" He rang with bitterness from a shift in his perception of her.

"I suppose, hard to change, you know," she said coolly, peering over the rim of the glass.

"Granted, but surely tonight makes it easier, doesn't it?"

She crushed out her cigarette and replied, "More profitable during the holidays."

He abruptly turned away and walked to the swing gate and made a few more selections on the jukebox. He returned and said coldly, "What is profit if the soul is bankrupt?"

"Don't preach — you're kind of nice and I don't want to dislike you," she pleaded, curiously searching his blue eyes.

"I'm sorry. I know it's none of my business." He dipped into a bowl of egg-nog and sipped from the dipper. "So you kind of like me, eh? I'm glad....Why not try some of my egg-nog?" He offered the dipper.

She screwed up her face and grunted, "No thanks, not my style."

"You know, you're right about privacy...guess you do forgo it when you engage in...this sort of thing."

"Well, I didn't exactly mean I'm a street-walking exhibitionist!"

He chuckled and took another sip of his proud mix. "Oh, I didn't mean that. It's just that your success depends on word of mouth and performance—men talk, you know. That's how my boss found out about you."

"One as holy as thou shouldn't be listening," she reminded him sharply. "And by the way, you're one to talk why aren't you home decorating the family tree?"

He dropped the dipper back into the bowl and reached for her hand and squeezed it gently. "Sounds hypocritical, I know, but I need the money. I'm sorry, I don't mean to cast stones—there are always contingencies, I suppose. It's just that it saddens me to see you like this so awfully alone. Why can't you treat yourself to the grand feeling of decorating a tree in your own home? Everyone is entitled to that."

She gnarled and snickered, "Haven't had a tree in years." Her face softened. She glanced up at the painting, then her eyes moved to a leopard's head near it; incongruently icicles hung from its mouth and a white sprayed wreath was round its neck.

He touched her chin and urged her eyes back to his and said gently, "It's not the tree in itself. It's the value of breaking out of yourself, a time to feel good, draping a little sparkle over the world."

She laughed with sarcasm. "There's plenty of that in fashion and jewelry."

He shook his head. "Not the same. It's not like looking in the mirror before an important date...more like projecting a feeling, not an image."

"I have no feelings." She vacantly sipped her drink; to her surprise, she had barely touched it.

"Oh, all us have...some have to stir it up once in a while," he said good naturedly.

She asked for another ice cube. Ignoring tongs he picked up a cube and warmed it in his palm, then gently dropped it into the glass. He reached for a towel. She observed how smoothly glazed the cube was. She said, "Well, there's nothing left to stir, just like these ice-cubes will be forever lost."

"Ah, but they're not lost; they transform." He reached over and squeezed her hand again; he searched her eyes.

She let her hand dwell in its warmth; she thought his hand should be cold from the ice. She accepted his searching eyes, thinking of her brother. She extracted her hand, then glanced up at the painting. "Interesting that in those silhouettes you can't tell whether they're facing us or the raging fire. Either way there's no escaping the blisters of life."

"Perhaps,...but with help," he said half quizzically.

"Perhaps, but that's buried now," she looked into his eyes and saw the past.

"Only you can bury it."

"I wonder." Still staring at the picture, she saw Vietnam's tongues of fire.

He turned his thoughts away. "Do you like my music? I fixed the machine to play Christmas music all evening for the people without charge wouldn't be right to put a price on it."

"What people?" she chirped.

He chuckled. "Well, there's you. I guess the wise ones are home."

"True, I never had wisdom," she said solemnly. "For that matter seldom seen as a person."

"Forgive me, I wasn't implying...still, everyone should be home," he added wistfully.

"Well, then. why aren't you home?" she asked.

"Believe me I would but I'm just a part-timer—had no choice —already told you I need the money."

"Oh, I guess I wasn't listening....And ...and I suppose you think I don't need it, eh?"

"I need it for college."

She scowled at him. "I suppose that justifies it, eh?— whereas I'm just a call girl whose needs are the nearest drug dealer."

"Said the wrong thing again," he said apologetically, slapping his forehead in rebuke. "But you could be less crude, you know; why refer to yourself that way?" He held up his hand. "Forget it. I don't want your answer. He deviated and added, "So do you like the Christmas music?"

She drank half a tumbler and put it down hard. "It's all right, I guess." She took a few sips, tinkled the cubes, then toyed with the stirrer. "Got any livelier?"

" 'Rudolph'...'Jingle Bells.'"

"I mean Rock in Christmas."

"Now, why on this night would you want that crass nonsense! Don't you feel the holy spirit underlying you?" He grimaced in disappointment.

"Holiness has passed for me. I don't want to be lulled," she snapped, "like an infant in swaddling clothes." She finished her drink.

"Beautiful sentiment is humbleness. It's affected people for two thousand years."

"I wonder why? Surely people don't want to be humble."

"Oh, but they do!" He reached for her glass. "Are you sure you don't want to try my egg-nog?" She shook her head vigorously. "Too bad," he moaned.

"I told you I don't want to be lulled by anything smacking of the holiday," she rejoined. He refilled her glass. "Take a real, hard look at me," she rasped. "I've been roughing it for years. I've been humbled plenty, but never humble."

In a way contradicting himself: "Still people know it's good to be humble. The trouble is they don't trust the other guy to be that way."

"Yes, nice guys finish last like Dukakis," she said bitterly.

"Still, he lost nobly."

"Oh not humbly? He sure was humbled sitting in that tank."

He had to laugh at that. "I admit," the youth said, "there is much misunderstanding and apprehension about the word. But it doesn't mean you have to be an idiot even though Dostoevsky showed that it is perceived that way because in this material world humility is idiocy. Ah, despite it, to be humble in face of arrogance is to be noble in the end."

"Wow, that's a tall glass full!" She nodded emphatically. "Oh, you're Joe college for sure," she said with a half admiring smile. "But I do know about the arrogance of clients....Yeah, I've been pushed around, betrayed,...defiled by classy Johns." She gulped down half a glass, then hopped off the stool, disturbing her coat. "How old do you think I am?" The youth's face reddened. "No, really, it's okay," she said assuredly as she pirouetted before him. "Go ahead look me over good!"

He sheepishly looked away and stared at her coat slipping off the stool from the spinning. "Your coat will get soiled."

"Never mind the coat it's been through worse. Look at me...how old?"

He looked over and saw what he did not wish to see: "Twenty- five," he lied.

She laughed hysterically and spun back to the bar, picking up her drink. "You're a horrid liar, a jelly fish!" She finished the drink, then added, "But you're a sweet boy who means well."

He dipped into his egg-nog bowl again and sipped the foam. "All right, you're thirty—satisfied?"

She tinkled her glass. He put down the dipper, tonged fresh cubes and poured her drink. She looked at him admiringly and said, "You really mean that, don't you, thirty, I mean?"

"I'm sorry, but I do," he said with genuine contrition.

"You *are* a sweet boy. Most men think I'm forty of course, they say thirty-nine. They suffer the illusion that an older woman is in her prime."

He leaned forward. He asked, "How old do you think I am?"

"Oh, I don't have to think, I know: same age as my brother ...was."

"Was?" he perked.

She reached for a cigarette. He was ready with the lighter. She touched his hand, strong and warm. He lit it. "Your lighter is like mine," she noted.

"Not exactly a lighter for a lady," he said.

"Lady!...My, you are a master mix of off-comments and real flattery!" she ejaculated. "But why do you have a lighter? You don't seem to smoke."

"For my customers like you....Really, it's for my pipe."

"My brother smoked one too." She picked up her own lighter, fondled it, looked at it wistfully. "They sent this back from Nam with his other belongings including his pipe."

He squeezed her hand. "Oh, my God! I'm terribly sorry."

"Forget it; it's history now."

"One can't forget history."

"I suppose. But when I lost him, I lost myself." She tucked her brother's lighter in her bag. "When our parents died in an auto accident, he worked like a saint to keep me out of a foster home. He was only a kid himself. Like my mom he was gentle with me; like my pop he was firm. I was 'May' when he was gentle; 'Mary' when firm which was most of the time, I'm ashamed to admit. Though I loved him deeply I never really appreciated him till he died."

"Ah, yes, the story of life and death, I'm afraid," he commiserated awkwardly. "Didn't you have any relatives to take care of you?"

"Oh, yeah ...apparently *they* felt they didn't have any," she snickered while squinting at the leopard's head. "When I received his insurance money, I spent it madly. I guess I thought I was entitled to squander his money as they squandered his life. But I knew I was wrong. From his grave he taunted me crying out 'Mary, Mary' in a firm, angry voice. Yes, I knew that had he lived, he would have gone to college not just for himself, but to secure comfort and dignity for me." She chugged down her drink and then tinkled the glass. "What a mess I've made—what a betrayal of his memory."

"Then why continue this betrayal?" he asked candidly.

"I'm too deep in the muck."

"You can be pulled out and washed off." He could have bitten his lip for that last thought.

She looked at him indignantly, then rattled her glass. "You can start by washing my insides with another drink."

"You've had enough, Mary."

"Oh, no—unlimited fringe-benefits go with the territory," she reminded him. "It's part of being a well-primed middle aged woman."

"I didn't mean it that way. I just think you should be careful and work on doing your brother proud."

"No use...you said it yourself. I'm a dirty thirty, in need of a wash. Ironically I'm a wash out," she said resignedly: "in high school, I remember, we had to memorize a sonnet by Shakespeare. One line stuck in my mind all these years and it's not difficult to understand why that is....Alas, '...besmeared by sluttish time.'" She laughed from the belly. "Fits me beautifully, horridly!" Then she sobbed into her palms. The youth, distraught, filled her glass. She looked up ingratiatingly. "Thirty-two. Do you hear? Thirty-two! Look at Jane Fonda for Christ's sake! She must be fifty! I'd have to play Katherine Hepburn in 'Golden Pond'!" She licked the empty glass drink and then folded her arms on the bar and demanded another drink. He ignored her. Then she buried her face in the fold of her arms, pushing away her handbag.

He eyed the lighter and took it to a drawer behind the bar to replace the flint. He softly patted her pate in returning and said, "Cheer up, May. It's just as easy to face the world with a new look as it is the other way."

She bolted up. "Oh, you think so, do you? Well, I've tried. Believe me it isn't easy. I suppose like you say, one can't do it alone. My strength died in Nam."

He reached out for her hand. "Oh, Mary, that's bunk, a cop-out! Why, you're still a young woman and very pretty ..."

She withdrew her hand. "Don't make me laugh. It would take a Hollywood makeup man to make me pretty again. And what do you mean—cop-out! My brother was everything to me."

"I'm sure he was; but you don't show it now. What would he think of you now? Why, the poor, brave guy died in vain. He fought for you more than he did his country."

"And to think I called you a sweet guy!"

"To be sure, truth is bitter," he said softly. "But in the end it sweetens life."

She looked up at him tearfully. He noted her eyes could be beautiful. She asserted, "You college boys have all the answers." Her hand crept to his. She speculated, "Tell me, you seem to have understanding. Would you want me, knowing what I am and you were near my age?"

"In time perhaps," he weakly admitted. He was a little ashamed.

"Bitter truth indeed!...In time!" she echoed. "Perhaps!...Time...my worst enemy!" She rolled her forehead on the bar edge.

He stroked her hair and was repelled by the sticky spray. "Correction," he said, "you are your worst enemy. Time can also heal it need not always destruct." He held up her brother's lighter, tipped the cap, struck the wheel and it flared. "Look, your brother's eternal flame, but you have to keep it that way. In the final analysis it is up to you and only you to set things right again. Others can help, but only to help you help yourself. Yes, I can help you to make peace with your brother; yet you must really want to."

She sat up, reached for the lighter and smiled wistfully. "What do you mean make peace with my brother? He's dead what difference does it make?"

"Is he really? Not with you he isn't you admitted that. You know he cannot rest in peace because of what you are now." Mary bowed her head. He slipped his hand under her chin, urging her to look at him squarely. "May, be honest; would your brother want you here tonight…any night?"

The door forced open. A heavy set man stepped in stomping the snow from his galoshes and shaking the snow from his turned up collar. Kicking off the galoshes, he went up to the bar, shrugging his shoulders at the youth. He said in a tone of disappointment, "I suppose, I should've closed down. The office party never showed up, eh?"

The youth shook his head. "No, guess they had too much at work. With the stricter laws, I suppose they decided against two or three for the road." He offered his boss an egg-nog.

"Na, Steve, give me the same as the little lady's." He removed his gloves and placed his hand on her shoulder. She recoiled, though his hand was not cold. "Hi,…been waiting long?…My wife stuck me with decorating the tree while she and the kids spent sometime with my in-laws. Just as well now we have the rest of the night to ourselves. Did Steve take care of you okay?" She looked down; her glass was still empty.

She turned to size him as she was wont to do when meeting clients for the first time. His looks were passable, but his nose was too long and bulbous. She hated to fight a big nose in love- making; her cheeks smarted after a while. His heavy build too would leave her with muscle aches in the morning. At last she said, "He—Steven, you say?—was charming company. His helpful conversation was well worth the wait."

"Oh, he psycho-analyzed you, eh? Yeah, the college boy is notorious for that. He thinks he's everybody's conscience."

Steve heard and laughed. "That's what we bartenders get paid for, right, '*Ugo*'? Still, I like to think of myself more a philosopher than a psychologist."

"And why is that?" asked Mary.

Steve took away her empty glass. "Psychologists are busybodies; philosophers lean to universals."

"That's a mouthful, but I gathered you lean to the former," she said with sarcasm. "You certainly zeroed in on me." Steve chuckled and gave her a thumb up.

"Either way," Ugo interpolated, "it's systematic confusion." He gulped down his drink. He seemed anxious. He turned to her. "They say you're high performance."

"They?" She thought back on what the youth had said about the wagging tongues of men.

He swigged his drink. "Well, you know, Marvin. He's a customer of mine too."

"I never make it a point to remember names; all are John," she said coldly while squinting at the lettering on the stirrer. "Even yours, though inventive."

Ugo squinted skepticism. "Really? Not even the Johns who perform as well as you and turn you on?"

She shook her head. Steve noticed that not a hair stirred. She said, "Nor do I keep score—all the same to me."

"Wow, you're that good, eh?" He grinned lasciviously.

"No, I just do service for those whose wives can't."

"*Won't*, you mean," he growled.

"Whatever." She poked the stirrer at him, then stared at its logo. "Strange name to have on this—'Inferno.'"

"Kind of fitting to me hope *you* live up to it," he said as he pawed her. She didn't bother to recoil as she dwelled on the youth, who kept his distance washing glasses, yet somehow she felt his proximity.

Ugo noticed her preoccupation. He turned to the youth. "Doesn't look as though you're going to earn your pay tonight, Stevie. Head for the kitchen and tell Joe to make some sandwiches just in case someone drops in, then tell him to go home to his old lady. I'll be in my office but I don't want to be disturbed you got me?" The youth nodded, but contorted his mouth. Ugo tugged on her arm. "C'mon, baby, we'll finish our drinks inside."

She shrugged him off. "What's the rush? let's stay awhile and listen to the Christmas music the boy of sentiment is playing for us;…besides, I don't have a drink. The busybody there won't serve me anymore." He gestured to Steve.

The boss stared at both icily. "Well, maybe he's right,…but, see here, girl, you're expensive. You're here to entertain me unless you don't like my money, in which case you can pay for the drinks and get the hell out of here." The youth, drying his hands, grimaced and wrung the towel violently, threw it down and went in the back. This was the first Christmas Eve that ever depressed him. He wished he were home with his family. He no longer heard the music.

She glared at her client and rasped, "Don't be a Scrooge." She grabbed his drink and guzzled it down, hit the glass bottom of the glass hard on the bar and demanded, "I want another drink."

"Plenty in the office, bitch. I'll fix you one there."

"No," she squealed, "I want Steve's gentle hand to mix it."

"Hey, what is it with you? You a cradle-robber?" He wrenched her off the stool.

"Easy, you hood, I'm not your inventory," she screeched while swinging her arm round to smash him.

He laughed, catching her arm in flight. "You are tonight, my pet, though why I pay for a pedigree and wind up with a mutt-bitch is not my idea of Christmas."

"Haven't seen the C-notes yet! I might just pay for my drinks and leave."

"Why, you little phony you wouldn't turn down two bills if I were a gorilla!" He grated as he jerked on her arm.

She laughed hysterically while fighting him off. "You *are* a gorilla!"

Steve emerged from the kitchen and quickened his pace toward them. He pleaded, "Give the girl a break, boss. Jeez, it's Christmas!"

"Well, I'm, not Santa!" the boss stared at him menacingly. "And you watch your tongue, boy; stay out of this!" He grabbed her blouse by the breast line and urged her toward the office door.

She squealed, "Like I said, *gorilla!*" Haplessly she punched him; he felt nothing with his heavy coat on.

Steve interjected, "Aw, boss, can't you see she's had too much to drink? Let me get her black coffee."

She shook her head and waved her arms, squealing, "Oh, no, not on Christmas, Stevie! Let me try some of that warm spirited egg-nog of yours!"

Ugo, John or whoever snarled at him and warned, "You need this job, kid!" He tugged her along and she grabbed the end of the bar. Her blouse tore. He stumbled back with remnants in his hand. She screeched and crossed her arms over her bare, still firm bosoms.

Steve ran to her side with her red coat to throw over her shoulders. She started to sob. He turned to his boss. "You'd better forget your plans for the night, boss. She's apparently not in the mood—must be the season. Why don't you go home to your wife and kids. I'll lock up."

"You'd better not forget you have a job, you college freak," the boss scorched as he pushed him aside and jerked Mary to the office door.

She looked back at the youth who was momentarily taken aback. "Steve, it's all right. Don't lose your job over me. I'm not worth it—too late for me."

Steve clenched his fists and yelled, "No, it's never too late!…Your brother…no, never for him." He stepped resolutely and gripped Ugo's collar and forced him against the office door. His boss had never seen those happy blue eyes turn to ice before. "It's Christmas, boss. Go home to your wife."

"Ugo" cocked an ear: he heard the Christmas music for the first time. He looked over at the leopard but saw only the wreath and the icicles, then rolled his eyes to Mary. His dark brown eyes seemed to brighten. He smiled, reached into his pocket and retrieved a fifty dollar bill. He stuck it in her belt; took one final look at her bosoms, then smiled. "Buy yourself a new blouse, Mutt." He looked back at his employee. "It *is* Christmas, kid. What the hell, you're right. I belong with my wife. With a little holiday tenderness she might perform." He reached up to Stevie's vice grip. Stevie relinquished and stepped back. Both looked on as the boss went to the front door and nonchalantly squeezed back into his galoshes. With a broad smile, he buttoned up his coat and said before departing, "Lock up early kid; it's Christmas for you too. Take tomorrow off we'll keep the place closed for the day." He wheeled round and left whistling "Jingle Bells."

They faced each other and laughed. Steve went to the kitchen to shut down while she struggled to tuck up her blouse then put on her coat. He came back and switched off the outside neon. Going to the jukebox to flick off the service switch, he hesitated when "Drummer Boy" came on. "Oh, this is my favorite....How about that egg-nog now, May?" he added, moving behind the bar.

"Love it, as you implied: much more fitting especially now," she said wistfully. He poured the drink into a mug for her.

He half filled the dipper again and raised it toward her. "Here's to your brother may he now rest in peace." She softly clinked his dipper, then took a sip, looking warmly at him over the rim of the mug. He went on, "Yes, you've done him proud this great night. Let us hope it spills over to many other nights." He raised the dipper again.

"Yes, perhaps it isn't too late, after all," she said half hopefully, again raising her glass mug in acknowledgment.

"If we were to think it so—too late, that is—with every case of human frailty, there would be not much point to this holy night, now would there?" He put the egg-nog in the bar cooler, doused the dipper, her egg-nog mug and turned off the bar lights except for the advertising sign over the cash register. In the dimness, the fire in the picture now seemed under control. At the jukebox he paused for the carol to end. Waiting for him at the door she gazed at his face illuminating from the light. She sighed, smiled.

He switched off the jukebox and put on a mackinaw, reaching in for his pipe and pouch. He pulled open the door. The wreath fell into the snow. He shook off the snow from the holly and handed it to her. "Here, when you get home, hang it on your door to welcome the world that is good." He lit his inverted pipe with the lighter which she had seen her brother do so often.

She pressed the wreath to her breast. "Home?"

He tapped his forehead. "Of course, you don't have one!...Well, you heard your Ugo, I have the day off tomorrow. We can catch a bus and go to my folks for a real Christmas."

"Oh, I'd love it, but are you sure your family would?"

"There's always room at the Inn." He laughed. She glowed.

He saw a radiance in her eyes as though from out of the past. Her cheeks crimsoned youthfully from the contact with the fresh, tingly air. Her sprayed hair seemed to soften as the snow flakes conditioned it. "You *are* beautiful!" he said elatedly as the snow danced prankishly on his lips traced with egg-nog. "Yes, yes, a radiant twenty-five, in fact."

"You're very kind but foaming at the mouth," she said, then chuckled. She pulled out a handkerchief and gently wiped his lips. She beamed up at him as he reached for her hand. He squeezed it several times; he puffed his pipe happily as they headed up the street, which did not as before seem to cast any shadows in the whiteness. The snowball skirmishers were now angels in a choir. Carols pierced the night, melting the flakes gravitating to the leaded stain-glass. For the first time she saw the tree and the gold lights in front of the church. Steve's warm hand in hers reminded her of how her brother always held her hand when they walked together. "Yes, I do have family," she sighed under her breath. She blinked her eyes and tears welled up as she imagined her brother standing by the tree under the golden shimmer, smiling peacefully.

Spring Sale

Burt was always handy with tools—well, most of the time, unless his thumbs got in the way. This Saturday he finally wrapped up the job of painting their bedroom after incessant prodding from his wife, Lanie, who had selected the paint at Sears two years ago, hoping he would get around to covering up the discoloration loitering for thirty years. Lanie had painted the room then— still a youngster of thirty-six. To Burt painting was for women and faggots. A man was designed to do something more utilitarian with his hands than to waste their strength on meeting the cosmetic needs of women. Their bedroom served them well regardless of the original cream color now sick yellow with puffs here and there of nicotine tinge and sharply outlined variations from changing family pictures on the wall and furniture locations over the years. Lanie, however, reminded him that the bedroom had been freshly painted when they moved in forty years ago and was apparently conducive to a more vital life, since they had conceived five children within six years. "Though I surely don't long for anymore children and certainly don't wish to carry on like honeymooners in bed, it would be pleasing to gaze up at soft pastels before drifting off to sleep."

Anyway, he dumped all the rollers, brushes and cans and roller pans in the garbage can out back, muttering good riddance to them. He strolled through his yard and checked the ravages of winter. He raked up some twigs and acorn shells that the squirrels left behind. "Why can't those little buggers shell them in their hideout?" he grated to himself. "If those bushy-tail rats shake the bunches off my grape trellis again this year, I'm putting poison around."

For thirty-five years, he had been threatening to do that, but Lanie would never allow him "to offend God's creatures"— but more importantly, she observed, it was too dangerous with the children, and divers dogs they had had over the years.

When he had reminded her that there was no dog anymore since the kids had grown up and married off, she countered, "Well, we have to think of the grandchildren now and their dogs." Then she added peevishly, "Of course, we never see the children anymore." Burt always shook his head over this comment she habitually made—especially one day last August when she reflected this sentiment, and he had not yet recuperated from having the kids over for a barbecue on the Fourth; the twenty-two grandchildren had run him ragged to the point that during the summer he hoped that the Labor Day sales come-ons, especially school clothes, would be so outrageously and attractively misrepresented that the whole crazy brood would spend their day shopping and stay away—they didn't.

He decided it was still too chilly to be doing outdoor work so he headed for the basement and gathered up his plumbing tools to undo his son-law's botched hook-up in his absence last fall when he was hospitalized for gall-bladder surgery. Lanie had talked her unskillful son-in-law into installing an old faucet that her husband had lying around the garage with the rest of his forty year accumulation of hardware and lumber from the endless projects he saddled himself with after every annual IRS refund check. The first thing Burt did when released from the hospital was to check his son-law's work. "Jesus, Mary and Joseph, Lanie, why did you ask him to this? It leaks more than the other one. Not only that he's got the cold water on the left! Damned teachers what the hell do they know about plumbing—or anything for that matter!"

After bending over the kitchen sink for forty-five minutes installing new washers and then turning the valves under the sink back on, he was satisfied that the washers worked perfectly—except for a drip now and then. He said, he thought, to his wife who earlier had been at the kitchen table browsing through a Sears sales catalogue, "There, Lanie, good as new." He turned around and she was no longer there. He walked through the house and found her in the bedroom. She had been shampooing the blue carpet to remove the pink paint stains and was now busy scraping the globs off the windows. She was pleased that the faucet no longer leaked, but added, "I almost burnt my lips last week drawing a glass of water—can't you do something about switching the cold water where it belongs? The grandchildren could scald themselves. They're all coming over next week for Easter dinner, you know."

"Don't our kids ever spend a holiday in their own homes?— at least you'd think they'd go to the in-laws once in a while; it's always us!" He went back into the kitchen and squeezed himself under the cabinet. Forgetting to turn the valves back off, he applied torque to a compression nut, instead of turning to the left. His powerful hands and arms cracked the slip washer and it started raining down on him. Frustrated and swearing at his daughter for marrying a teacher, he tried tightening it more and he cracked the nut as well. He turned off the valves and stuck his head out of the cabinet looking disgusted just as Lanie returned to resume her thrill-reading of the spring sales. "Well," he growled, "I guess it's time to buy one of those new fangled single-lever faucets you've been pestering me about. Is there one on sale in the catalogue?"

Noise and confusion thundered from the back door and his middle daughter's brood jumped the steps into the kitchen, the mother following. "Oh, what a pleasant surprise!" Lanie rhapsodized as she bounced about the kitchen hugging all five of her daughter's energized children before accepting a kiss from her daughter, Jean. Being the "middle child" Jean always had to make the overture in kissing her mother, who, on the other hand, always gestured melodramatically in greeting her other children—especially the boys. "So what brings you here today?"

Jean said, "Oh, the usual, Mom; I've come for the discount card…have a lot of Easter shopping to do." Lanie, a retired Sears employee, had a lifetime 10% discount card and whenever her children shopped they took advantage of it—charging their purchases in her name and then when the statement came in they would settle up. Lanie was a whiz at keeping records and whenever there was a question like—"Gee, Mom, are you sure that was my purchase and not John's wife?"—they would always yield to her wisdom.

"Ah, yes, never pay full price! As long as my ticker holds up, eh?" She had said that a hundred times to her children the hundred times they came to use the card. Though utterly delighted that they used the card freely, she would always remind them of her heart condition and that someday the card, if not her, would be missed. "Well, since your father needs a new faucet I think I'll go to Sears with you."

Jean seemed disappointed. "Well, I hadn't planned on taking the children. I thought I could leave them here with you; it's so much easier…so much more can get done that way."

"Fine, leave them here. Your father can't do anything until the faucet is here anyway, right Burt?"

Burt looked up with ambivalence as he was greeting his grandchildren who were busily tugging on his work pants and belt or jostling with him. Burt was always elated to see his grandchildren as long as he was not stuck with them and could head for the cellar or garage on the pretense of a "project." He masked his scowl with a nod and a vacant smile. "But don't take forever—I know how you two get lost in the store."

He headed for the TV in the living room to turn on pro-bowling. The kids followed him in after they raided the cookie boxes and the grandmother broke out the soda cans before she and her daughter left for the store. The kids were fascinated with bowling for about two minutes; then each took turns getting up from the floor to change the channel whenever a commercial came on. Each time the grandfather bellowed that they change it back, but after some twenty minutes he yielded, dividing his time watching an old movie with them and staring at the digital clock that incongruously stood along side a thick 78rpm album on a long forgotten console phonograph.

After another hour elapsed the movie ended to his relief—and much to the relief of the middle child who had been pouting through-out because the others would not let her watch old re-runs.

Restless, he ordered them to put their coats on and he paraded them out to the garage, handing a man-size lawn rake to the next eldest and two toy rakes to the tiny tots. He rolled out the light garden cart for his favorite, the middle child. Her broad smile overrode her perennial pout. Pruning shears went to the oldest boy. Not much got done; but at least plenty of play-time and energy were expended outside the house—tossing weathered acorns at each other as they rolled and wrestled on the lawn. Their coats were littered with dry, mulched leaves. After a half hour the kids one by one started disappearing into the house under the pretense of having to go to the bathroom. Of course, Burt knew they were raiding the cookies and watching TV again. Left alone, he put the things away, fiddled with some junk then went back inside. He looked up at the clock on the kitchen wall and moaned. He chanced dismantling the old faucet, hoping they would be home soon. The faucet was so corroded that he stripped the threads on the fitting under the sink where the supply tube connected, but he managed to remove the faucet without chipping the porcelain sink too badly. He was certain the new faucet would cover most of the chipping. Looking up at the clock again and shaking his head and mumbling profanities, he sat down at the table and rustled through the catalogue. He was delighted to see that the ball-action faucet was indeed on sale. After a while and growing impatient, he went into see what the children were doing. In spite of the cookie crumbs, leaves and acorn shells littering the floor, and soda cans making rings on the tables and on top of the TV, he was content—at least they were quiet.

The little ones jumped up when they heard their mother pull into the driveway and ran to the kitchen door. Lanie and Jean returned with half the inventory from Sears. [It is miraculous what a 10% incentive, together with a sale, can do for the shopping spirit of women.] Mountains of bags and boxes were deposited on the dining room table as Jean opened each before her children to check her expertise in estimating sizes. Of course, each pair of shoes, each dress, sweater and jacket jelled with the intuitive, measuring eye of motherhood. Lanie, too had to break open the bags to show her husband the wonderful bargains she had gotten for all their grandchildren.

With each bag he expected a box to emerge so he could get right to work installing the shiny new and modern faucet. His patience at an end he demanded to see his faucet.

"Oh, that,..." she said as though the farthest thing from her mind, "they can't deliver till Monday."

"Deliver?...What the devil are you talking about?...a little faucet you couldn't carry after carting all this home?" he queried in a distressed tone, gesturing to the mountains of sales items on the dining table.

"Oh, yes, that's right the faucet!...Well, they didn't have it in stock. Besides, I couldn't resist the offer—what with the fabulous sale and the 10%, I saved all of thirty dollars!"

"Are you telling me we have to go the weekend without water in the kitchen—why didn't you just forget the sale item and buy whatever they had?"

"Oh I wouldn't pay list price!"

"Sadie, for God's sake, this is an emergency and you still get your 10% off! And how could you save thirty dollars on a fifty-nine dollar item? Furthermore, what's the difference?— just what you bought for the grandchildren could have paid for a crate of faucets!"

"I'll have you know everyone of these was on sale—and I still got my discount," she said as she held up to her breast a toddler's sweater.

He shook his head in disgust and reached out his hand. "Give me the card, I'll go get it myself."

"Oh, no, you can't now! Everything's signed for. I 'm not passing up a thirty dollar saving because you can't wait a few days. Why, do you realize the deal? Heavens, along with the single-lever faucet and a beautiful walnut-stained cabinet with a Formica top, they're throwing in a new kitchen sink!"

Vincent's Moment of Truth

A handsome Irish setter sat squirming in anticipation at the roadside while the school bus approached. When the bus did not stop, passing by the farmhouse, the stately animal ran after it barking at its wheels. After a good run the dog stopped, cocked his head in perplexity, then slowly almost reluctantly turned toward the familiar tractor going up the trail cutting through a variegated vegetable field. The oddity of the tractor's job at the moment forced him to abruptly turn away. Suddenly the setter turned round and ran as though desperate round the vegetable field and beyond in the direction of a huge hill in the distance.

A thin book under his arm, Vincent, a youngster of about twelve had cut through a wooded path on his way home from school. Since the early grades he had often taken this route instead of the school bus. It was not his nature to join the pandemonium on the bus. It was an extension of school, which, when breaking from it, he wanted the calm of his own nature's space. Ordinarily, except for severe inclement weather he would bolt from the school and head for the wooded trail. For weeks, however, he did take the bus; he could not force himself into the woods since the last time. On this Friday afternoon, however, he was drawn to it again.

As he stalked further into the shadows, he examined—with hesitant eyes nonetheless—every foot of underbrush along the twisting path. With every step another thread of his shirt clung to his thin, prickly sweating body. He felt the awful nearness of it now and felt his flesh rise. The brush now took on its own individuality as he sensed the familiarity of the vicinity. Slowly, unnerved, he parted the huckleberry bush—there it was! His blood chilled, distilled, then burst forth like a river overrunning its levee. Letting go of the huckleberry, he scurried to a bend in the path, then pulled up. He looked back, bit a fingernail and retraced his steps. This time he extended his leg and spread the bush apart with his foot. He stared down at the mystery. There was no nest of flies; only a few scattered green ones remained to scavenge, along with busy ants crawling over the skeleton of what was once a cat. He relaxed his foot; the bush snapped back. He stooped over for a closer look. Picked clean was somehow comforting; not like the other time when he stumbled on its carcass being mercilessly marauded—maggots all over, rotting, stinking. Vincent shuddered at the image that would stick with him. He stared down at it with a strange compulsion, a strange empathy. Choking, sobbing, he turned from it and bolted to the near fringe of the woods where the sun dispelled the dark shadows, and the dense, dark green of the interior woods transformed to welcoming pale green of sparser branches interlacing a clear sky.

Croaking crows in a nearby cornfield hovered over a rabbit invading their territorial rights. The rabbit took off disclosing its cotton-tail at swift interludes as it dashed out and through the disturbed verdure of the rolling plain. The lad heaved a sigh, seeming to denude his oppressive wrappings, and freely began to whistle in the open air. A half mile ahead was Gulliver's Hill. The boy's imagination saw it as a huge grave under which the giant held his breath for centuries, never to exhale his finality. From the hilltop appeared the excited Irish setter on the run, descending with flapping ears, stretching its long energized legs and fanning tail. It greeted its master with unwieldy paws upon his shoulders. The boy stumbled backward while the dog's loose, eager wet mouth and tongue showered the lad with happy affection. The boy soothed his companion and then placed the book in its foaming mouth. "Now, don't get it all wet, Rex." The setter pranced ahead with show dog regality while both advanced up the hill.

The lad paused at the top and sat down on the huge jutting outcrop. The boy was sure it was Gulliver's head that stretched up in disbelief to check that he was truly dead and not just tied up by the Lilliputians. The dog already half way down the descent, looked back as though confused. It went back up to return to its master's side. It dropped the book and then barked as though recognizing the horse head on the cover of the book. The lad took its snout in his palm and looked into its sad, almost questioning eyes. "I know, Rex, I know," he said softly. He patted him lightly on the head in empathy, for he understood what lurked in Rex's nervous make-up. The lad often wondered what went on in the unanswered folds of an animal's brain as he himself so often questioned the unanswered.

The lad looked down into the valley of sundry farm homes distant from each other. He focused on his own and the green barn behind it. Tears rolled down his cheeks, which he rubbed into the sleeves of his gray cardigan. The setter gently retrieved the book when his master slid off the rock and resumed his trek into the valley. The usually lithe lad, felt as though something were pulling from behind.

They went round the white house to a rear gate through which the dog and lad entered a gravel path flanked by lilacs. Strangely the aroma of them frightened Vincent. It never used to. He kept his eyes to the unpredictable pattern of gravel, lest he gaze upon the lilacs. He did not know why...until loomed his grandmother's wake. Arriving at the steps of the back porch he took the book from his companion and flipped it on a swing chair. They both proceeded to the green barn, its tall white doors wide open. The boy and dog entered the accustomed darkness and slipped past an ancient, dust laden tractor used for parts. Rex led him to the stalls. His heart was in his mouth when he saw the empty stall and freshly hosed-down floor. He gazed round the cluttered barn. Tears again welled up. Scratches came from below where the setter was clawing a heavy plank. The distraught lad squatted and held his setter which commiserated with the boy's sadness. "I guess, he's gone, Rex—Whitey's really gone!" the boy cried. His companion whimpered and gently pawed the lad's knee, then sadly laid his handsome red head in the crook of the boy's embracing arm. Rex felt the warmth of the boy's cheeks on his collar, then slipping off and burrowing into his proud rustic coat. Rex did not respond to the fingernails digging into his back—he would not whimper, nor stir from the mild pain inflicted by his distraught master. Nor did the boy's sobbing—not totally unlike the annoying buzz of a fly that would flutter its ears—distract from the animal's stoic stance; for the faithful setter instinctively sensed he was needed. His instincts associated the lad's venting of pain with his own whimpering when hurt or frightened and runs to Vincent for comforting sympathy.

Vincent rose up to the drone of a distant tractor. He ran out of the barn. Rex followed him. The increasing roar of the tractor froze Rex in his tracks, dispiriting the animal which cowered, whimpered, squirmed, crouched with chin on its paws, eyes lifeless as he watched Vincent bravely running ahead. Though afraid of the tractor, Rex suddenly flexed upright, his lean body flaming in the sunlight, and the great animal heart beat in unison with the fluttering fright of his master's. Rex would not take refuge under the porch; he raced to catch up to the boy now dashing madly over the fallow field. Some twenty paces behind, the setter abruptly stopped and sniffed chunks of earth that had been agitated by the deep treads of the tractor's tires. His busy nostrils scraped the soil and he crazily zigzagged between the tracks. He sneezed and yapped, trying to shake white hairs from his snout. He cringed and turned round to head back to the house, but then reversed himself, loping back to the scent. He extended his fanned tail and feathered paw at point. His young master had disappeared into a trough of terrain. In spite of the fearful instinct of the missing link of a once happy triad, Rex regained his courage, barked after the boy, then ran toward the tractor.

The lad cried, trying to get the attention of his father who was sitting on the tractor, whose blade nosed into a mound of freshly dug dirt. His father shifted and the huge black Cat moved a great pile back into the excavation whence it was unearthed. The boy waved his arms, trying to get the attention of his father. But the crown of the mound slid off into the excavation. The boy screamed at the sight of the small avalanche and climbed the mound as the tractor backed away in preparation for the second pass. He called at the top of his lungs, "Dad, no, no!" His father so preoccupied to end the grim task shifted the great machine forward again.

The boy jumped up and clung to the massive earth-moving blade. He raised his feet as the hydraulic power lowered it into the mound for another scoop. The lad was immersed in churning earth, and from the immense weight was hurled and deposited into the half-filled pit. Rex scampered up the mound, barking grotesquely, senselessly at the imposing blade. The father, startled, cut the engine and jumped from the seat.

"Trying to kill yourself, Rex? Or is it to pay your respect?" Rex slid down the mound and sniffed the fresh earth. "Get away from there, you mad dog. Let Whitey rest in peace!" Vincent's father ordered. Rex went on sniffing in panic, then scratched the dirt, barked and went into his graceful point. The father gaped at the dark hair uncovered. "Oh, my God, what have I done?" He jumped and slid into the pit. He scooped away the soil and held his dazed son in his arms.

"Please, Dad," the boy groaned, "I've got to see him!"

The father hugged him. "So bad, that you almost got killed! No, son, let him go. Why, you knew it was going to happen—yet you couldn't get yourself to visit old Whitey in the barn, knowing he was half dead. I was hoping I could get this over before you got back from school."

The boy pressed his face covered with grit into his father's chest, muttering, "I know, I know, I was scared, a no good coward."

"No, my boy, it was just that you loved Old Whitey so much. Don't blame yourself."

"But I should've been there to comfort him in his final days. I hate myself for not showing I cared."

"Nonsense, old Whitey knew, believe me." He held his son tighter and lifted the boy's chin. "You proved that you could face up to it. Come now, help me finish the burial—still have the topsoil and sod to do to make it a fitting grave. Whitey would like that. You don't have to see him to show your respect." The father carried the boy from the pit and helped him onto the tractor. Rex stood on the edge of the pit and watched the cat's great paw seal up the last scent of death.

On the ride back the boy turned to look at the grave; he was thankful that it did not rise up like Gulliver's. He noticed that behind the tractor a chain was dragging along. "What's the chain for, Dad?' he dared to ask.

"Huh?" The father turned round briefly. "Oh." He braked the cat and jumped down to roll up the chain.

His son persisted, "What did you use it for?"

Climbing back onto the tractor, he said, "You don't want to know, son."

The boy bowed his head, then turned and looked at his father squarely. "I do, Dad. I'm okay."

"Well, son, you're dealing with more than half a ton. There's no way the pickup hoist could handle that and its bulk. I know it sounds crude, son, but I had to drag him with the tractor."

"The boy grimaced. "Gee, Dad, it must've been awful for you—all alone like that. You should've waited."

He smiled down at his son. "I would've if I knew I was waiting for a man." He reached over and brushed some sand from Vincent's shoulder, then squeezed it gently.

"Well, Whitey's in his final resting place right here on our land." The lad said, as mixed feelings welled up.

"Right, son, most wind up in the glue factory."

They rode the rest of the way in silence and when the tractor reached the green barn, the boy abruptly leaped off and ran to the house, scampering directly up the stairs to his room, Rex right behind him. The lad cried into his pillow while Rex laid his chin on the edge of the mattress until his young master cried himself to sleep.

Down in the kitchen, the boy's mother said, "Go get Vincent for supper, Rex. I've let him alone up there long enough." Her husband nodded in agreement as he went to the sink to scrape his plate into the pail underneath.

"You're right, mother; he's got to get over it."

She prepared a plate for her son. "Yes, but not completely, you know."

The setter jerked himself from his own meal to dash up the stairs. With his damp snout Rex nudged the boy's arm stretched over the bed. Vincent stirred. Rex ran to the corner of the room and picked up the book he had retrieved earlier from the porch and dropped it on the bed. Vincent sat up and stared at the book on the veterinary care of horses. "Don't know if I'm ever going to read it now."

At the kitchen table, idling over his plate, Vincent heard Rex outside scratching on the screen door. "Gee, Mom, I'm not really hungry, may I be excused?" His mother turned from the kitchen sink and nodded. He went to the door and peered through the screening where Rex was sitting upright with a lilac in his mouth. He went out to him, kneeled down and hugged him.

"You're right, Rex; it's time." He went to the gravel path and picked more lilacs glowing a pinkish violet. Vincent and his companion headed for the fresh patch of carefully laid sod rising modestly, fittingly, matter of factly, in the setting sun.

He Will Prevail

Maria Mason, widowed by war, took down a bright color coat she had hardly worn, folding it into a carefully kept department store box; its lid sparkled with Christmas wrapping. She put it under a small Christmas tree, from which she stepped back to review, then rearranged several ornaments. She was about to open a wrapper of icicles when the doorbell of her small apartment rang. A teenage girl, sad brown eyes on the edge of tears, stood in the doorway shaking the light snow flakes off her kerchief and frayed coat, saying, "I'm late, I know, but my mom is very sick."

Maria took the girl's coat and said with genuine concern, "Oh, Denise, my dear, you shouldn't have come." She hung the coat on a hanger in the entry closet.

"No, my brother is home with her now. And I couldn't disappoint you," said the slender girl, virtually the same stature as Maria who was in her late twenties.

"Well, I'm glad of that," with a sigh Maria said, taking the girl's kerchief and draping it over the coat.

"Besides," Denise said, "we both need the money, right?— especially Christmas Eve."

"No question there," Maria said with a smile.

"There is one thing, I have a prescription." Denise took it from her handbag. Would you mind dropping it off? I didn't want to be even later."

"Of course, Denise, but you shouldn't have delayed something so important. Your mother needs it. I'll have them deliver it right away," Maria said with urgency, taking the prescription from her.

"Oh, please don't bother," Denise rejoined warily.

"It's no trouble and too important to delay it. Besides, I'm sure the drugstore will close early tonight on Christmas Eve and I won't be home till late."

"But, Maria, I can't pay for it." She flushed with embarrassment. "I was going to pay for it later from my sitting money."

"Oh, Denise,…no problem…I'll deduct it."

"I have no idea what it's going to cost!"

"Hush, Denise, stop worrying. The important thing is getting your mother well."

"Oh, Maria, you're so kind. I wish I could sit for you free," the girl said, her long brown hair fell forward as he she reached for the icicles on the coffee table. "I'll finish the tree for you."

"How nice—that'll be big help, even though it is small this year," Maria said, then added a sigh.

Denise's eyes lowered to the floor as she moaned barely audibly under her breath. "Yes, I know — compared to last year's."

Maria swallowed hard and went for her coat in the closet. "Jimmy is napping right now, but he's so anxious that he'll soon be up pestering you."

"Oh, never is he a bother. We'll get along fine."

"Yes, of course, as you two always do.…Still, on this day he could get out of hand."

Denise laughed. "Only normal …but I'll warn him of the Brownies lurking and watching."

"Well, I've got to run or I'll get a pink slip instead of a bonus." She chuckled. "Fat chance the latter for a part-timer, eh?"

"Oh, Maria,…with your training and education, it bewilders me," Denise said.

"For the time it meets my needs, Denise. Besides, I really enjoy it." she said as she put on her kerchief and left.

Though her bus was due, she continued down the street to the druggist. Because of the shopping rush, she knew there would be another bus soon after. The store was crowded, that is the toy and decorating aisles where prices had been slashed. She would have been tempted to browse and pick up a toy or two for her son had she the time. She chuckled at the thought that when her husband was alive she used to think shopping was a drudge. More accurately she subconsciously resented it because she had sacrificed her career for her child. Now she would eventually resume her career because of Jimmy.

Peace of Mind—your pharmacist is the proprietor was the sign behind the pharmaceutical counter. Maria said, "I'd like to pay for it now and have it delivered."

The woman behind the counter winced. "On Christmas Eve?" She went round the glass enclosure to her husband working on other prescriptions. "Can you imagine, this customer wants it delivered!…And our delivery boy never showed up."

"That's because I gave him the day off, Lori.…You know I always deliver them myself on Christmas Eve."

She giggled. "Oh, Simon, you will never change!" she said, looking up the price in a fat book.

"If she's going to pay for it now, add a few dollars to it." He winked. "Chances are they'll be no one there to tip me. She'll probably get lost in last minute shopping."

"One of these years, Simon, you're going to find the ghost of Marley at your doorstep!" Lori giggled again, went back to the counter, wrote down the address and rang up $18.75.

Maria gulped and handed the clerk her last twenty. Maria returned the quarter from the change and said, "This is for the boy."

Snow flurries began undulating again as Maria, waiting for the next bus, turned to the large department store window through which she eyed many times before the electric train display. She heard a little boy's voice: "Gee, dad, I hope I can be a train driver someday." She glanced over at a man rubbing a suede glove over the boy's snow topped hood and heard: "That's engineer, son; but better to be a commuter."

She turned her perceptions inward: feeling guilty in leaving behind her husband's train-set when moving off the base after her husband was killed in action. She rationalized that it took a man to understand the intricacies. Actually in her husband's family tradition, it was "Santa" who set up the trains round the tree. There would be no Santa: she had reasoned that it took a man and a boy to set-up and fully appreciate the intricate network of tracks, crossings and villages. The interplay of son and father gave each security and a feeling of power. Snow flakes met tears; she retrieved a handkerchief.

In the Swanson's large gleaming kitchen, she was mixing egg-nog. She said to herself, "How nice of Mrs. Swanson not to notice I was late — Christmas spirit *does* touch even the rich!" While checking the cook-book she slowly sprinkled in nut-meg. She sampled it— perfect! Placing the bowl on a tray with glasses, she carried it into an immense, plush living room, handsomely decorated for the holiday. Carols floated out of the rich mahogany cabinet that had been moved from its customary place to make room for the ceiling high Swedish pine bedecked in luminous splendor. Two young teenagers were hanging the icicles—a crowning achievement for the youngsters since they had been forbidden to touch the tree until decorated by professionals. The lad turned to his sister and cautioned, "Don't put them on too heavily; you won't be able to see the tree."

She looked back indignantly. "Oh, we'll still know it's a tree!"

"But not the same tree to suit our parents. It cost them plenty to have it done right." He relieved her of some icicles and deftly hung a strand at a time.

She yelped, "Oh, you're being ridiculous — positively Sroogean!"

The girl turned from her brother and said buoyantly, "Oh, here's Maria with the egg-nog!" Turning to her mother who was sitting at a desk writing last minute greeting cards, she pleaded, "Mother, may we have a mug?"

The well-dressed woman nodded absently while she said to her husband engrossed in *Fortune* magazine, "Of all the people to send us a card, dear, the Terrys! I crossed them off our list years ago when they stopped sending. I suppose they have a new secretary who found our address in some old file."

The husband continued reading, but said, "Good, maybe we'll get their account again!"

The youngsters skipped to the table on which Maria placed the bowl. Maria poured two delicate glass mugs for them. They tasted it and grimaced.

"Too sweet," the boy said.

"Too bitter," said the girl.

"It's perfect," said Maria, smiling as she poured two more and placed them on a small silver tray to take to the heads of the mansion.

The lady accepted hers and sipped it indifferently. The master of the mansion waved it aside and demanded a scotch and soda.

As Maria was mixing the drink, she heard from across the room "Not too much soda, Maria." Then she heard Mrs. Swansons voice, "Maria it's nearing midnight; you and Herb may start placing the gifts under the tree. You'll find him out in the garage fixing the star for the Nativity scene on the lawn. Then you may wake, the children."

"Oh, no, Mother, those little dearies will pull everything apart!" the girl bemoaned.

"Yeah, Mom," the boy joined in, "can't you wait till we get to open ours first?"

The mother looked up knitting her brows. "You're forgetting family togetherness. Why, on Christmas it would be sacrilege!"

In the garage crowded with four large automobiles, two sports cars, and old toys strewn about neglected, an old stout man was hunched over a work table. He was dressing two tiny dolls in patched clothing. The perfect craftsmanship far outshone the dress, as though it was meant to be. He was humming to himself a distant carol:

> Wrapt in arms,
> Nestled in breast
> Soft as silk
> White as milk
>
> In these charms
> Felt He so blest
> He did wail:
> "I'll prevail."

Maria entered and smiled warmly. "I see you finished them — I'm sure the children will love them."

"Yes, that they will — they're still real children — haven't been too spoiled yet." the old man chuckled

"Did you fix the Nativity star?" she asked

He laughed. "Just had to change the bulb again. The so-called professionals couldn't figure it out, I guess." The old man's eyes sparkled and mumbled, "Poetic justice is sweet!" as he finished the dolls and handed some wrapping paper to Maria. "Would you mind wrapping them I am awfully clumsy with this sort of thing."

She laughed as she took the paper from him, "Nothing could be further from the truth after looking at the delicate work you've done with these dolls."

Having settled the dozens of packages under the tree Herb and Maria left the spacious but cluttered room. They heard the Mistress shout above the Swing band records that replaced the stack of carols that Maria had put on before: "John! Wake up! The children will be down soon."

Herb signaled Maria to follow him to his basement room. "This won't take long." he promised. They walked along the dingy basement hall till he opened a door. He flicked on the wall switch and the tiny room danced with spangled splendor; toys were interspersed on shelves, benches, a large canvas bag in the corner was spilling over with more smiling, colorful toys. The room was enchanted and insulated from the gloom outside. Maria blinked her eyes in disbelief as she scanned the room; a miniature Nativity scene was secured to the wall. Fresh pine aromatically filled the air from many wreaths on a table. Multi-colored lights dashed madly across the ceiling as they blinked on and off. There was a tree top angel strewn on the work table. It reminded her that she forgot to get one for her own tree; but she decided she would not mention it to him. She looked at him in wonderment. He answered her quizzical glance proudly, "Soon I pluck the fruit of my labor the moment the orphanage in the city comes alive with joy on my arrival tomorrow morning."

"Oh, Herb, you're wonderful!" she said honestly. She eyed a handsome clock on the wall; below it was last year's calendar.

"Oh, I don't know about that," he replied; "after all, I merely repair, do-over, or touch-up what's been thrown away. Most of what you see here has come from this very house just like the tree top — and there's still plenty more in the garage I haven't gotten to yet." He was a little annoyed with himself at that last thought; but consoled himself by adding, "I'm not as young as I used to be." He pointed to a large carton on the floor and requested, "I wonder if you would mind wrapping this for me? It's kind of special."

She took some paper from the table and wrapped it dexterously, only asking for his assistance to turn it over since it was rather, heavy. "Do you have any ribbon?" she asked.

He laughed, "No, that won't be necessary. It looks Christmasy enough."

She noticed an unattractive tiny box. "My this is so tiny, but it can't be jewelry because the box is so unattractive — looks more like a Sear's parts box."

He laughed. "Yeah, I sure have plenty of those."

"But if it's to be a gift, you must put it in a better box than that." She eyed the table for another box.

"No, it serves its end. But it *is* a gift and I'd appreciate it if you would wrap it attractively for me. In fact, so attractive that the receiver will not want to unwrap it!"

Maria chuckled. "How very strange you are at times!" She chose a silvery green wrapping paper out of the mountains of boxes and paper on the floor.

His eyes lighted up as a thought came to him, "Oh, I almost forgot to show you something!" he jumped airily to the closet and held up a bright red suit with furry white collar and cuffs. "Complete with boots and a hat with a tassel. My tailor friend made it for me at cost! I was actually getting embarrassed wearing those shop-worn department store discards that never fit right—what a Christmas this is!" he was ecstatic. "Quickly, help me on with this!"

Upstairs, Maria entered the younger children's room first and woke the two gently: "Open your eyes little ones; it's Christmas!" The church bells tolled in the distance. "Listen…the bells are softly tolling the good news of the Christ Child's birth and the rebirth of happiness for all children all over the world." Maria turned on the lamp by the beds.

The gold curls of the little girl of seven danced in the soft light as she stirred in her bed. She looked up at Maria who had been a mother to her for almost a year. "Maria," the seven year old uttered sleepily, "Why do you wake me. I was dreaming of a beautiful Christmas, I had just hung up my stocking over the hearth and was waiting for Santa and wishing for a cuddly little doll to peer over the top of the stocking, and Tommy was roasting chestnuts in the fire — just like the song said — oh, they tasted so good, so warm!"

"Well, I can't promise you chestnuts, but there's someone to see you — an old friend whom you used to know in your earlier years, Maria said seriously.

"Oh, really! Who? — is it Santa Claus? — has he really come back?" She turned to the bed next to her, whispering heavily, "Tommy, wake up!

It's Christmas Eve!"

The little boy, not quite four, rolled over mumbling in the pillow, "So what, Christmas doesn't mean anything around here."

Maria turned to the boy and said, "Now, Tommy that's not true! Your Mother and Father give you everything including their love. It's just difficult for some people to show a childlike interest in Christmas. Your mother and father are older than most mothers and fathers of children your age. Also they are very important people—many things are on their minds, they cannot possibly live only for you. Yet you are what matters most to them—in this way all mothers and fathers think alike. I'm sure when your big brother and sister were your age Christmas was different— it had that young spirit little people like you and me and my Jimmy cherish so much. So try to understand when you go downstairs; show them light in your eyes, joy in your voices — make them feel young again." Tommy cracked a skeptical smile. Maria announced, "And now a little preview of Christmas—look!"

Santa came in; in one hand he had two Christmas stockings filled with candy, cookies and yes, chestnuts and the two wrapped dolls in the other. The children were wide awake now. They were bright from this prankish spirit. They suspected it was Herb; and when the dolls were unwrapped they knew it was he — but it did not matter, That the game was played was all that mattered. They played along with Herb, sitting on his knee, reading: on a long list for him to remember next year; testing his knowledge of the names of his reindeer— he knew them by heart—reminding him not to forget kind old Herb who for some unknown reason needed another paint-set, for it seemed, when they would sneak down to the basement, where Herb was making funny noises, while talking to himself, he would emerge from his room with a tiny artist's paint brush in his hand. Santa laughed jovially; they laughed blithely, and then they leaped out of the room to the head of the stairs.

> Their eyes like stars that peeped on Jesus' night
> Out-twinkled human reason's deadening light.
> Down the stairs the children elfishly danced,
> Arm round arm these two in unison pranced.
> Into the room's dead air hanging heavy
> They stirred swiftly in name of an infant's levy—
> The lasting spirit of smiling youth and hope—
> On brother and sister it did interlope.
> Bravely mid stale sentience they plunged;
> Starchy siblings' frolics soon expunged.
> The children first danced round the tree—
> Their parents amazed by the spree—

Bouncing onto the arms of chairs
Unsettling years of stuffy layers.
Puzzled at first from parental smiles so new,
They rubbed their lids and could see it was true.
Holiday jaded by their resistant sage
Bogged by deceit of the modern age,
Mom and Dad abandoned snobby ways,
By rediscovery of this festive phase,
Thus they fell into the season's routine:
Dad leapt up like he was again eighteen,
To the floor wafted Mom's last minute cards
And all understood this fanciful game of God's:
That all to make merry like in children's yards;
So that this most happy family holiday
Inspires globally staunch felicity everyday.

Herb and Maria then went to the kitchen. It was time for Maria to leave. She went to the closet in the pantry. There on the top shelf next to her purse was an envelope: she was grateful and put it in her purse.

Herb was sitting at the table opening his envelope. "Twenty dollars! That will help pay for the suit," he said thankfully.

She poured him a cup of coffee. She put on her coat and said, "Sorry, can't have coffee with you or I'll miss the last bus. Be careful not to spill any on your beard."

"It's too bad you couldn't have managed to sleep in," he said. "I still can't understand why they object to Jimmy's being here— they have more room than they know what to do with—besides they're never home."

"Oh, most of the time I get home early—I can't complain. My home— though it's only a three room apartment—is much too precious to break up anyway. Well, I must be going to relieve darling Denise. Merry Christmas, Santa."

"Oh. I almost forgot! — your lovely baby-sitter." He went to his work table and retrieved a necklace, dropping it in a tiny felt box. "Mrs. Swanson threw this out, but I fixed the clasp good as new. It would be more fitting for the girl, even though the pearls are really just opal."

"Oh, you are truly Santa Claus!" She kissed him on the cheek and started to leave.

"Uh, Maria,…wait a moment. I'll walk down to the bus stop with you."

Outside the snow was carpeting the land. From the house laughter pierced the cushioned silence. "Maria," Herb hesitantly began, "you won't think me Santa when I tell you this—it's even harder after what you've done for those children."

"You mean the Swansons have released me?" she guessed. "I knew it'd be only temporary. I've faced worse news, Herb—I'll manage; still have most of Ray's insurance;…besides, it's time for me to return to nursing and real money."

"The agency got them a refugee from the Philippines. She'll be here tomorrow." He knocked the ashes from his pipe; marring the pure beauty of the spreading mantle. He frowned, then added, "They didn't have the nerve to tell you face to face. It amazes me how people throw out things—even people. I guess I'm next."

She turned to her friend and said, "If you are, surely, they'll regret it."

In the hall to her apartment Maria fumbled for the keys and the envelope, in which were her wages and a ten dollar Christmas bonus—she had hoped for a severance token. She figured her baby-sitter' s fee for the day. $4.50. She had to laugh — Denise was going to purchase the prescription out of this! She folded the ten dollar bill and turned the key in the lock. Denise was awake listening to midnight service on the radio and gazing at the little tree that she had finished decorating for Maria.

Denise was thrilled on receiving in addition to the fee Maria's bonus. "Oh, but I can't allow you to pay for mother's medicine too — please take it out of this." She offered the bonus back.

But Maria waved it aside. "No, Denise, it wasn't very much — part of your Christmas bonus."

"Oh, Mrs. Mason, Merry Christmas, indeed!" She put on her frayed coat, looked at her benefactress, then kissed her on the check.

"Oh, Denise, my goodness!" Maria ran to the package under the tree. "You simply must try this on — open it now."

Denise was already teary-eyed; when she saw the beautiful coat, she cried while Maria helped her into it. "It's so gorgeous! I won't know myself at Mass tomorrow—nor will anyone else!"

"No matter, Denise, you will always shine through — just as this will!" She couldn't resist opening the little felt box and placing the necklace round the girl's slender neck. "This is from Herb at work, a darling man."

"Oh, my, I'll feel like having been coronated at Mass!" Denise hugged her again; slipped behind the door, sobbing, "There is something so without words at a moment like this."

Before turning in, Maria brushed her teeth, a procedure she dreaded; for; when alive, her husband used to jest with her, because she brushed them so hard; the deafening sound of the brush vibrating on the ivory had been a source of comedy; now it was but a simple fight against decay—another day oozed down the basin drain. Her mouth felt refreshed eager to be kissed; that was not to be anymore. She slipped under the covers of the big bed; it was deathly cool and uninviting. She sobbed herself to sleep; the image of her late husband hung on her dreams until another layer of images slipped in:

The door bell stirred her from pleasant sleep;
Her eye lids parted from dawn's rosy sweep.
Snug in her spousal garb of solace enrobed
Airily through the quiet apartment she probed.
Like a dream in a dream she creaked open the door
There in the hall light was Santa's contour
Jellying merrily with billow air,
Bellying verily a rollicking blare:
"Merry Christmas, my Maria of Motherhood!"
Pointing proudly to where a familiar parcel stood
There by his boot was the heavy box she wrapped.
Curiously, to his wrist was loosely strapped
The tiny green box with a golden lock on the lid.
The opening of, he felt impelled to forbid:
"You must give me your word not to open this gift,
For there's nothing inside that's substantial to sift;
Yet emanates ambrosial ether of mythical charm,
Feeding the psyche powers in face of alarm.
Unsealed, truth within would fly in escape —
The world in mourning, covered in crepe.
"Enough, it's time for the sublime," he said;
"So lead me, a faithful friend, to Jimmy's bed;
For it's custom to wake to the merriment of me!"
With a grunt, and a laugh he flexed to one knee.
To Maria he presented Pandora's box
Noticing her tears teeming in paradox.
He tucked in the belly, to follow her in.
Then exhaled in Jim's room with a calm discipline:
"Wake up, Jimmy boy, it's Old Santa, your friend,
With a gift you've been wantin' since last Eve's end!"
The dawn spilled red in the room bewitching
With warm will wondrously the morn enriching.
Sleepily the boy eyed the inviting cheer;
A pillow he flung to a boyish sphere
And leaped from his bed toward the box to dig
His eye fell first on an engine so big

That he whirled with joy like a spinning top.
"Oh, Santa! Came this from the Northern Shop?
Truly I feared I wouldn't see you this year —
I'm so happy you knew where to steer the reindeer!
For the joy in his eyes his mother thus throbbed;
For the image in them she silently sobbed.
She saw in one train a manger of hay,
A Babe with a lamb and a camel lay,
Reminding her ever in modern times
Biblical heritage yet moves and rhymes.
She vowed this good grace would forever be
By keeping the chancy box under lock and key.

When she wakened early, she went to her son's room. He wasn't there; her heart flipped but then she heard muffled commotion. in the living room. She smiled. "Into the Christmas stocking already," she thought. She moved to the kitchen to put on a pot of coffee; it was already brewing. On the wall was Herb's clock and last year's calendar! She ran into the living room and tripped over an empty box — the same large box she had wrapped for Herb. Atop the tree glowed the angel!

At the tiny tree sat wide-eyed Jimmy as his father still in uniform was demonstrating the transformer as a magnificent train set circled the tree. Feeling faint she clung to the mantel, on which was the tiny silvery green box. Indeed, she dare not open it.

A Short Short: The Nazarene

Once again the children of Jehovah were under the yoke of yet another Empire near the turn of the fourth millennium. In the tiny town of Nazareth the son of a carpenter was born. As he nurtured it seemed he was a child of promise who quickly learned the Scriptures and was destined to fulfil the Mosaic thrust for freedom. As a young man his gentle manner and teachings captured the hearts of the villagers and he was soon known as simply the Nazarene who had come to teach the Commandments in a gentler kinder light through which one finds freedom within.

The priestly elders in Jerusalem heard of this and summoned the young man. They judged him an infidel, resulting in crucifixion. A handful of followers transcended the view of him as a simple Nazarene and made him a God.

Moral of The Story...

Once upon a time there was a king who ruled over a vast wasteland. His subjects naturally were very poor because of the lack of the kingdom's resources. Year after year they tilled the soil to feed the king's court, the army and themselves barely. During the winter months to stay alive the poor subjects had emigrated to a neighboring land called Goshen as it was a land of plenty to work its mills and handcraft shops.

The officials of Goshen welcomed the people of Wasteland because their own people had grown fat and content from their fortunate heritage. This expedient relationship went on for many years. Goshenians grew fatter and Wastelanders thinner. The more wealth the migrant workers returned with, the more the cruel king of Wasteland exacted. As a result the king became more prosperous and powerful and lavished festivities upon his court. The Army too was rewarded—if it exhibited excellence in war skills training.

Some of the bolder emigrants, disillusioned by the cruelty of their own country, remained in Goshen, slipping off to rich farm lands where the land gentry were eager to employ such dedicated workers. Eventually entire families deserted Wasteland to the chagrin of tax-collectors.

Goshen was delighted with these turn of events; for after a decade not one Goshen citizen was engaged in menial tasks. But its army too had become indolent and too well-fed.

The population of Wasteland dwindled drastically, the court pleaded with the king to take action. The king did nothing. Eminent nobles of the court sent dispatches to the commandant of Wasteland's army. Always they were returned with the seal unbroken. There was not one among the court who could face the crisis since all were strangers to ordeal. They roamed about the luxurious court and gardens sniveling to their ladies about the cowardice of the king and bemoaning the diminishing coffers that would inevitably lead to their impoverishment. Still, they continued their lavish ways.

In contrast, the king had turned to an ascetic life, never partaking the court festivities and remaining in his chambers in reclusion. The few times he did take the throne for matters of state, the court was astonished by his gaunt appearance. On occasion he would visit the army camp to assist the officers in keeping morale high during incessantly rigorous training with meager reward.

A decade had passed, and now even the nobility was fleeing the country for a better life at Goshen whose own nobility sympathized with them and readily accepted them because of their noble birth. One evening a special detachment of the palace guards on horseback thundered across the drawbridge after months of touring the kingdom. The officer in charge with scroll in hand dismounted in the inner ward and headed for the king's keep.

The officer was astonished upon entering the outer chambers by the bleak, Spartan ambience. All furnishings and art work had been removed; the king's magnificent desk table of marble and mahogany had been replaced by a peasant's table and the chopped remains of the throne were by the fireplace, which barely glowed. When he entered the king's sleeping quarters, he was even more taken a back: the great bed was gone and in its place was a thin layer of straw and an old horse-blanket upon which the king was kneeling in prayer. The officer waited until the king stood up and greeted him: "Welcome, captain, to my humble quarters … .Now, what have you to report after so long a journey?"

The captain cleared his throat and overcame his shock over the king's bowed, emaciated appearance. "Your majesty, the mission is accomplished." He handed the king the scroll.

The king waved it off. "My eyes are not what they used to be. Please, captain, read it to me."

The captain unrolled it and strained his eyes in the dim light. He shook his head and rolled up the scroll again. "I shall simply tell you about it, good king….All the villages and towns have been scoured and all the people but the sick and agéd have vanished."

The king mustered a smile and said, elatedly, "How marvelous!…Yet sad that the few have been abandoned. I trust you rewarded them for staying?"

"Oh, yea, your majesty, as you ordered."

"Good, they deserve it, poor souls. That is my one regret." The king tugged absently on his whiskers. "And the grain bins?"

"Thoroughly diminished, but for a few bushels here and there that I had to use as provisions for my men."

"Excellent! And the noblemen consigned to your charge? How fare they?"

"Out of the forty-five of your courtiers only six remain as true soldiers of the king."

"Oh?…And I take it the others deserted?"

"Nay, my liege, only a few made the attempt for which they were executed. The rest simply died from exhaustion or exposure. Three died nobly in the saddle."

"But six survived, eh?—miraculous!…Perhaps, in time they might warrant a commission of leadership."

"I shouldn't doubt it, my king; they are proven noblemen."

The king stroked his whiskers and asked, "And what of their ladies, what was their reaction to my dictum?"

"As you directed we left a contingency at each district of mercy, only a few protested, most seemed relieved that they were chosen to be useful."

"I'm happy to hear that—motivation is important. According to the Mother Superior's report they have taken admirably to nursing the sick and tilling the nunnery gardens." The king went to a dark corner and retrieved a suit of armor. "It appears, then, we are ready." He handed the captain sealed orders. "Take this to the commandant. This is one order he will open." The king laughed.

Thence in a few weeks, Goshen fell to the Spartan trained soldiers of Wasteland.

Nightmare of a Nerd

…A lean shadowy man, slumped over the mane of a black horse, was taken down by a burly stevedore and placed in a barge laden with other indefinable specters.

"Shove off, old man, that's the last of them," said the stevedore to a tall figure scarcely visible in the heavy mist at the bow of the barge. The old man thrust a pole into gloomy water and the craft edged away from a broken-down dock.

Moaning came from the ghostly bodies as the mist carried vapors of a strong stench. The last one aboard stirred among the strange fellow-passengers. He crawled over the bodies, edging his way to the bargeman. He tried desperately to get the bargeman's attention, but try as he may, no words could pass his lips. Reaching him, he touched the bargeman's cloak, which felt like the slime of albumen. Trying to rub it off his hand on his body, he gasped to find his body nude and covered in the same rubbery slime. The old bargeman turned. The horseman's eyes distended with horror, not at a face but an immense egg cracked all over and punctured grotesquely and jaggedly by some divine madness where the eyes and mouth would be.

The horseman shrunk back and instantly touched his own face. With his fingers he felt every inch of his face as a soldier under fire, thinking he had been wounded. He vented a shrill but only heavy vapors stirred as his fingertip found a hole where his eyes would be. With viscous palms he tried squeezing his head, hoping to mash it to eggshell shards. But the more pressure applied, the greater the frenzy from the deafening crunching from within and the clammy oozing from through the increasing fissures, produced more from turbulent implosion than the pressure from the hands. He swirled round and saw that the other bodies were futilely cracking their eggshell heads against the deck. Increasing cracks, notwithstanding, the ovals remained tormentedly intact.

Disdain for Kindness

There clanged and thumped the fury of sadistic gods at Troy laughing. Trojans by the hundreds, swarmed out of the gates to accept their gift. They hoisted bright Helene and smiling Paris in a nest filled with eggs and lashed them to the high saddle. They took Menelaus in effigy and hung it to the straw tail. Squads leaned into the huge wheels while dozens heaved on the rope to move the great gift inside the walls.

All that night they feasted and danced round the token of victory. Soldiers climbed the ladder to the saddle, interrupting Paris in his love-making to coo the lovely blonde bird who launched a ten year war while women below swayed under the sad-faced effigy while they chanted:

> Cuckold, thou hast yielded to her goddess ways
> Of loving all of man but thee.
> So why the doleful brays
> When we have found a happy, wagging tail for thee?

Among the women, however, one was not chanting merrily; her eyes filled up and her heart reached out for the man of straw. She grabbed a torch and climbed the haunch and mercifully set fire to the tortured figure. Before one of the women grabbed her hem to pull her down she tossed the torch up onto the nest-like saddle. The lovers half naked scrambled out of the burning nest and down the ladder. Enraged by the young woman's action, Helena immodestly flaunted her unclad body as she rushed toward the now frightened lass who ran under the horse. A trap door dropped open whereupon a powerful hand gripped her robe and pulled her up inside.

Collection ends

The following few pages give you a glimpse into the author's background.

Author's Afterword

My Mom, 1892—1980

Gone from the family twenty-six years my mom is still a verve of our daily lives. Whenever I call or see my sister and brother, we inevitably transcend the present to engage in conversation about our mom who, under one hundred pounds through most of her adult life, was an indomitable spirit in her demonstrative love and care on our behalf.

Oddly enough the very first memory of my early childhood was that of my father and my crying in seeing his big boots that he wore at the tuberculosis sanitarium. The first recollection of my mom was early in the morning packing treats and necessities into a suitcase for my father and then watching her walk down a long street in Throgs Neck to board a bus and subsequently a train destined to take her to where he was dying.

I was too young for the funeral, but I do remember being in my mom's arms as she wept for him at the wake in our home. Although I did not experience the same impact his death had on my mom and my older siblings — who had but five years before experienced the death of a baby brother who preceded me— I did have nightmares of the wake; apparently even at the young age of four I was skeptical when told, "Daddy was sleeping." I remember Mom consoling me when I would awake in the middle of the night screaming, "Daddy, Daddy!" from a recurrent nightmare of a black locomotive, my dead father shackled to it, speeding toward me.

After the death of Dad, my mom was a restless spirit and we moved constantly, from one apartment to another in the Bronx and then gradually emigrated to Queens, Brooklyn, and Long Island where she discovered renting a house with a small plot was just as inexpensive as city apartments while at the same time extending a sense of roots for her kids. Because my father's modest insurance had depleted early in support of us, Mom was one of the first to apply for the $16 a month support per child under sixteen from the new Social Security enactment, in behalf of widows, and took on innumerable temporary work as school custodian, Woolworth's clerk and often as nanny or housekeeper, despite her physical frailty continually plaguing her. There were moments in our growing up that Mom internalized a mournful soul, yet — and I suspect in spite of — she always portrayed a healthful spirit in our daily lives by never letting us forget what a saintly man was our father. This taught us that there was more to love than even intense affection, for without the depths of mutual worship it was not love at all.

To this day we marvel at her ability in having sustained the family pride by her positive spirit in deference to this remembrance of our father, notwithstanding the quandaries of the Great Depression. I can still recall vividly when I was about ten years old and asked her why I was labeled an "orphan" in school, she chastised me for such a thought; the next day Mom took the teacher to task by demonstrating that the mother was very much alive and the father still reigned in spirit! I, barely five, recall sitting up late, dozing intermittently, with my mom when my older sister [now deceased] was sixteen and out on a first date, Mom planted herself in front of the window when the midnight curfew neared. My sister overstepped the curfew by fifteen minutes. However young and half asleep, I could tell Mom was not happy by her softly pitched lecture for almost an hour. Apparently my sister was repentant — she joined the rest of us listening to the radio programs on Friday and Saturday evenings for quite a while.

When my siblings were still in Catholic grade schools, Mom somehow charmed the nuns to forgive the payments in arrears for their books. When I was to make my First Communion, Mom convinced the parish priest to commit heresy by permitting me to make Confirmation the following week; her reasoning was that it was entirely impractical to let a perfectly good suit go to waste as her son would have outgrown it by the time his Confirmation was scheduled two years hence. My sister closer to my age got the unenviable assignment of apprising me of the exercise and pounding the Apostles' Creed into my head.

As the lament of her son and husband slowly drifted away, Mom took on new energy as a wise money manager when her children became working adults and contributed to the support of the entire family. We never objected to giving as much as half our wages; in fact, we gave willingly, knowing that it was for the common good. I remember my first caddy assignment produced a buck and a quarter, and I couldn't wait to get home so I could contribute a hard earned dollar in the coffee canister marked "family needs." We were instructed to economize — light switches worked both ways; stingy with the coal-bin shovel; the heels of a loaf bread were not for bird-feeding nor discarded but toasted; furniture, clothing, shoes, linen, most foods were never purchased unless there was a super sale; tooth paste was a luxury; tooth powder was preferred and when out of either, salt or soap would have to do — I remember when my brother commuted to the city, he was conditioned to look for a daily newspaper or two left behind on the bus or subway. Brown bag lunches consisted of a nickel's worth of cheese among us, or simply apple butter or jam on A&P bread, together with a jar or thermos of milk or tea.

Prompted by three of her children's marriage before and during World War II, coupled with the worry of two sons and two sons-in-law in the armed services, Mom sought pragmatic comfort—not without ambivalence, owing allegiance to our Dad — in her own marriage to a hard working man considerably younger so as not to be a burden to the children as her health was increasingly in jeopardy. Always on her mind was that she had at the age of four lost her own mother.

Mom remarkably escaped the brunt of mother-in-law jokes: she was just too darn nice — she was the role model for "I have gained a son or daughter; the family has no losses" — for anyone to begrudge her. When they had children, Mom's loving spirit became the queen Nana to the chagrin of in-laws and the delight of grandchildren. She was the epitome of the loving, solicitous grandparent whose grandchildren could do no wrong and loved each and everyone of the fourteen children without favoritism. They could not have enough of their Nana whom they perceived as the life of the party whenever they were over to her house or Mom visited them or joined in family picnics. Even to this day, when my own children visit me, "Nana" is always in their lexicon of permanent memories.

Eulogy for Mom 1980 [from *Modest Impressions*]
Mom, you were our strength
orchestrating our personal concertos
into the texture of the family symphony;
Mom, you were our teacher:
That with love comes sorrow as well as joy
Blending integrity of giving, of sacrifice;

Mom, you brought us faith
in the sanctity of our father's memory
in the felicity of family identity;
Mom, you have consummated human existence
and now on your much deserved journey
toward divine existence;
Whence you still will be our strength,
still to teach us love
still to be our faith.

Other works by the author are

A Tale of Love & War [Saga of The Great Depression, WWII home front and action in the Pacific]

Modest Impressions [small book of poems]

Angel Queen [Medieval fantasy of epic proportions]

In Defense of Eve [Medieval clash of two immortals and knights]

Politics: Then & Now [Criticism of modern politics]

Drama Collection: One & Three Act Plays [Designed for high school classes and drama clubs]

New Fantasies [collection of new fables]

On Lulu: http://www.lulu.com/spotlight/rrksr [my ebooks as well]

All selections displayed on Internet bookstores, such as Amazon and Barnes & Noble

www.ingramcontent.com/pod-product-compliance
Lightning Source LLC
Chambersburg PA
CBHW031121030726
47496CB00002BA/635